OBJECT LESSONS

OBJECT LESSONS

the PARIS REVIEW

presents

THE ART OF THE SHORT STORY

⌗

Edited by

Lorin Stein and Sadie Stein

WILLIAM HEINEMANN: LONDON

Published by William Heinemann 2012

2 4 6 8 10 9 7 5 3 1

Object Lessons. Copyright © 2012 by *The Paris Review*. All rights reserved.

See also pages 355–358 for individual copyright information.

The short stories in this collection are works of fiction. All of the characters, organisations, and events portrayed in these stories are either products of the authors' imaginations or are used fictitiously.

First published in Great Britain in 2012 by
William Heinemann
Random House, 20 Vauxhall Bridge Road,
London SW1V 2SA

www.randomhouse.co.uk

Addresses for companies within The Random House Group Limited can be found at: www.randomhouse.co.uk/offices.htm

The Random House Group Limited Reg. No. 954009

A CIP catalogue record for this book
is available from the British Library

ISBN 9780434022250 (Hardback)
ISBN 9780434022267 (Trade Paperback)

The Random House Group Limited supports The Forest Stewardship Council (FSC®), the leading international forest certification organisation. Our books carrying the FSC label are printed on FSC® certified paper. FSC is the only forest certification scheme endorsed by the leading environmental organisations, including Greenpeace. Our paper procurement policy can be found at: www.randomhouse.co.uk/environment

MIX
Paper from
responsible sources
FSC
www.fsc.org   FSC® C014496

Printed and bound in Germany by GGP Media GmbH

Contents

✺

Editors' Note

Since its founding, in 1953, *The Paris Review* has been a laboratory for new fiction. The editors have never believed that there was one single way to write a story. We've never espoused a movement or school. We've never observed a word limit. We think every good story writes its own rules and solves problems of its own devising.

That's the idea behind this book. It is not a greatest hits anthology. Instead, we asked twenty masters of the genre to choose a story from *The Paris Review* archives—a personal favorite—and to describe the key to its success as a work of fiction. Some chose classics. Some chose stories that were new even to us.

Our hope is that this collection will be useful to young writers, and to others interested in literary technique. Most of all, it is intended for readers who are not (or are no longer) in the habit of reading short stories. We hope these object lessons will remind them how varied the form can be, how vital it remains, and how much pleasure it can give.

OBJECT LESSONS

Daniel Alarcón

on

Joy Williams's *Dimmer*

Joy Williams is one of those unique and instantly recognizable storytelling voices, capable of finding the mysterious and magical heart within even the most ordinary human acts. Her stories begin in unexpected places, and take surprising turns toward their eventual end. She doesn't describe life; she exposes it. She doesn't write scenes, she evokes them with a finely observed gesture, casually reinterpreted to provide maximum, often devastating, insight:

> He had straddled the baby as it crept across the ground as though little Mal were a gulch he had no intention of falling into.

The baby in this startling image is Mal Vester, the unlucky and unloved protagonist of "Dimmer." He is a survivor, but there is no romantic luster to his suffering. Mal is rough, untamed, stricken, desperate, and alone. His father, who never wanted him, dies in the first sentence; his mother, the only person who loved him without restraint, dies in the second. Her death haunts this beatiful, moving story, right up until the very last line; but what keeps us reading to the end is the prose, which constantly unpacks and explains Mal's unlikely world with inventive and striking images. Williams has done something special: she makes Mal's drifting, his lack of agency, narratively compelling. Life happens to Mal; it is inflicted upon him, a series of misfortunes that culminate in his exile. (A lonelier airport has never appeared in short fiction.) Mal never speaks, but somehow, I didn't realize it until the third time I'd read "Dimmer." I knew him so well, felt his tentative joy and fear so intimately, it was as if he'd been whispering in my ear all along.

Joy Williams

※

Dimmer

I

Mal Vester had a pa who died in the Australian desert after drinking all the water from the radiator of his Land Rover. His momma had died just like the coroner said she had, even though he had lost the newspaper clipping that would have proved it. Not lost exactly. He had folded up the story and put it in the pocket of his jeans for one year and one half straight because they were the only pants he had and the paper had turned from print into lint and then into the pocket itself and then the jeans had become as thin and as grey as the egg skins his momma had put over his boils when he was little.

He still had the jeans—spread out flat on the bottom of his suitcase but they were just a rag really, not even a rag but just a few threads insufficient even to cover up a cat hit in the street.

The coroner, in absolving anyone or everyone of guilt in Mal's mother's death, had stated to the press, represented by a lean young

man in a black suit with a nose blue and huge as a Doberman pin-
scher, that

> the murky water and distance from
> the shore precluded adequare wit-
> nessing of the terminal event. If
> the victim were in the process of
> having her upper extremity avulsed
> by a large fish she would have had
> little opportunity to wave or to
> render an intelligent vocal ap-
> praisal of her dealings at that par-
> ticular moment . . . Death being un-
> avoidable and by misadventure . . .

Mal thought the wording cold but swell.

Everyone had thought she was mucking about. It was dusk and
there were hundreds on the beach . . . cooking their meat, the children eating ice-cream pies, the old ones staring into the sun. There
was a man washing his greyhounds in a tidal pool. The water was
cold and pale, flecked with filthy foam, green like the scum of a
chicken stewing. Mal was in the cottage, fixing supper, pouring hot
water over the jello powder, browning the moki in the skillet oil, and
next door Freddie Gomkin was burning out another clutch as he
tried to coax his car up and over the hill to the flat races in Sydney.

It certainly did not seem at the time that anyone could be dying.
It was not the season. It was Durban's season.

And no one was really paying any attention. She was by herself
in water no deeper than her ribs, 100 feet down the beach from the
public conveniences. And she disappeared. Someone later said that
they thought they saw her disappearing. But they saw no fin. Blood

came shoreward in a little patch, bright and neat as a paper plate. The only thing that Mal Vester had to go on of course was that she never came back. A few days later, someone caught a tiger shark and when they cut it open, there was a bathing costume stamped with a laundry mark wrapped round its intestine. But the laundry mark was traced to a Mrs. Annie White of Toowoomba who was still alive and who worked in a doll hospital.

After it happened, he was unsure that it hadn't. He lay in the cottage and didn't know what to do. His mother always hated the water because she could not swim and because she was convinced that people pissed in it all the time. This had become a minor obsession with her. She went all white and shaky when she saw the women sitting on the sandbank, their legs stretched out into the waves, the water rattling in between their thighs. Mal was eleven and she held him close. The beach was no place to bring up a fatherless child by god she always said. Snorkels and men spitting. Women shuffling behind towels, dropping their clothes. Bleeding and coughing. Hair everywhere and rotting sandwiches. Unmentionables coming in with the tide.

He lay on a rolling cot and struck his hips with a loose fist. The moki was dumped charred into the sink. The clocks ran down. He moped about the cottage, practically starving to death while he thought of his mother and how she smelled. She had sung to him—all the American hits—

There ain't nothing in the world
But a boy and a girl
And love, love, love . . .

Accompanying herself with salad spoons. It had not been long ago that he had squirmed between her breasts, chewing on a smooth flat dug, smelling food, night spent somewhere by something in the branches. It was like sucking a penny.

Nothing ever came to him directly. Nothing occurred outright. The things that had changed him were blurred and discreet and this gave the life that yet remained for him to live a strange unwieldiness and improbability. Death was not thorough. It had no clean edges to it. And all that love and responsibility left behind—mewing and forever lost.

II

The spleen weighs 15 Gm. The capsule
is wrinkled, thin and red-purple. The
cut surface shows vascular congestion.
The lymph nodes and bone marrow are not
remarkable. The liver weighs 1500 Gm.
It is red-brown, smooth and glistening.

They had been farming in the desert for one year; the man tall and ropey-limbed with the studs of his blue jeans shining around his hips and the heels of his boots making broad coffin holes in the sand; the woman sulky, pulling spinifex spines out of her skinny legs, rubbing her soiled ankles. She nearly drove him mad, wanting him to press his ear against her belly to hear the heart beat. Sometimes hit was and sometimes hit weren't, he told her. Sometimes hit growled at him like any old mutt. She'd been eating wormy flour and was imagining things. She'd only gained three pounds.

But she was sure. The wolf, hating emptiness, fills his belly with mud and then disgorges it when he finds food. The woman hates emptiness. The woman is a glass waiting to be filled and her belly is heavy with hope before the seed. For a time, little Mal had been blood and air and sour dough, but then her breasts were swinging with yellow milk. She dreamt of things that her man had never told her. She dreamt of snow which she had never seen. She dreamt of eating books and knew that someone would die soon.

Mal himself, one noon, had dropped early from the womb with a full head of hair and a face white and soft as a candle dripping but what they believed to be his baby chortlings were only the mice clicking and ticking in the stove. For days he had no features at all. For weeks he still seemed unborn, his little eyes all pupil and of a peculiar green like something wedged in a privy crack, the bones growing beneath his face like weeds.

His eyes stayed funny. They were not strong and they were somehow ill-timed like a gesture of empty hands. His momma said that the heat and the weather had wrecked her honey's eyes just as the heat and the weather had wrecked her fine bone-handled hairbrush. She said that her honey's eyes were weak because his daddy had never quit doing with her.

His momma told him things were never what they seemed so it made no difference anyhow how much his eyes could see.

The man was never there in daylight and the child's only memory of him were his jeans, hanging on a hook, the leather boots not quite touching the floor, like the boots of a hanged man, extending up to the empty knee sockets, the jeans being plastered inside the boots by sweat and greasy creek clay, the cloth stringy in the hide. At night the child saw the pale torso quivering over his mother while the hips and legs dangled in shadow on the wall, and he saw it drop soundlessly like a white bird turning out of a storm.

In the morning he was not there. Only his mouth was on the taste of the fork stabbed into a pan of fatty mutton.

One night he was brought back dead on the haunch of a horse. The horse's legs were like the stems of tall flowers in the moonlight and the child could see that his throat had turned blue and that his brain had risen up and come out of a rent in his skull, hanging outside, white and lacy stiff like the coral sold in Sydney shops. Little Mal rubbed his eyes with ragged nails and the sight swung to the left and disappeared. He opened his mouth wide and stuffed the curtain in, kneeling on his mattress, frail scabby child with warm and gritty hair and he saw them truss his father up in canvas and bury him in the ground.

In daylight he dug on the other side of the house. For what if he should search and find nothing? What if there should be no grave full?

III

The heart weighs 350 Gm. There
is dilation of both chambers.
The superior and inferior venae
cavae, portal and hepatic veins
are patent. The valvular measure-
ments are within normal limits.
The myocardium is a homogeneous
red-brown.

He was an orphan with no distant kin and the house on the harbor began to smell like a kennel. He was eleven and a half and he began drinking gin, threatening motorists by falling in front of their cars. Being loved had taken up more time than he would have ever thought possible. His hair and legs grew long. His teeth became furry as stones in a brook. He ate his bread by the sea and cast the crusts upon the water. The world was Mal's grey graveyard and the rain ran into the sea from a sky pale as a winding sheet. The rain rang and sang off the prawners' slick jackets. It drummed upon the sand and upon his bony jaw.

For Mal had learned in his brief joyless life that nothing is faithful and that one needn't have a body to be able to mourn, for death is everywhere. Cyanide fills the peach pit. Meningitis in a napkin fold and polio on the wet shower boards. Eternity is in the evening air.

He read in a book that King Henry died from over-eating lampreys and that Princess Kristila succumbed from under-eating greens. There's no way to account for people's tastes. He read in the *Sun* that a farmer had a stroke in his pigpen and not a trace was found. Just his hat and a sack of untouched corn. There's no way to account for the taste of things.

At night he would have noisy odorous and colorful nightmares that would hurl him out of bed and into the wall. He would trot to and fro in the dark, tiny rhumba steps, his toes curled in the cold, his long yellow nails cracking against debris. At last his mind would clear and he would not be able to remember what had frightened him so.

For the most part, people were kind to him. They smiled at him and didn't smash his windows. Occasionally they left something in a covered dish or a sealed jar on the window ledge. But they were uneasy about him. He had a great absence of presence—a horrorful past, an uncertain future. He ran and the dust kicked up on the roadway, hissing like the rain on a searing day.

And it became spring and Mal was pubescent. He needed razor blades. He was very lean and the lack of love lay open on his face like a wound. Even though he smelled like a melon and was skittery as a bat, the girls found him attractive with his thick pretty hair and his way of chewing gum. His boy moanings were heard as he ran through the groves of kurajong trees. He was seen to have pollen in his hair.

It was spring and for days there was a black, large and silent dog sitting in front of his cottage. He had dug his paws deeply into the murky lawn, his tail fell in the direction of the sea, his haunches were hairy and dropping like ferns. The dog was very polite and very silent but he was regarded suspiciously by everyone and taken as a bad sign. No one had ever seen the dog before. He was a stranger and black as oblivion. Mal Vester never seemed to notice him which made them believe that the animal was his doom and gloomy future, visible because unavoidable. The dog was waiting for a bitch in heat. When the bitch didn't present herself, the dog went away. He was very polite and from another town, but by that time, everyone was convinced that he was not a normal dog.

Mal Vester was fourteen and he switched from gin to rye. Rice from weddings, confetti from the holidays were deep in his thick yellow hair. He went everywhere unasked in a soft sweater too small for him and trousers unraveling at the crotch. He sewed them up with red thread which was all he had. He wore a grey shirt buttoned at the throat and a string tie held by a steer raised from tin. He had bruises beneath his eyes. In the homes with young daughters, fathers lay sleepless and frantic, for when need is on the loose, running like a hungry hound, how does one protect the loved from love?

Freddie Gomkin's wife, who had a face like an ewe, gave birth to twins in January, when everyone knew that poor Fred had been gelded in the war . . . and gassed . . . and that he had a plate in his head and a glass eye and rubber bags hanging inside the clothes he wore. They knew that he was hardly a survivor at all. His only lusts were two—for dying and a winning pony—but he was happy with his heirs. He gave a party with brandy and beer, and although he didn't say a word, one could tell that he was pleased with the way his life was moving along, each day with its noon and now all those noons behind him, the days being maneuvered properly and with skill, his life moving along just like a real life, just like anybody's.

Mal was not invited but he came, with the water slapped onto his hair running into his ears, crouched with his elbows on the heating unit, gathering up the room with his slovenly eyes. The brandy rocked like mud in the paper cups. The wife smiled, the tip of her tongue curving shyly before her bad teeth. Mal wanted to see the twins but he was told by someone that they were in the pantry sleeping. The door was not hung properly but was pulled shut all the same with wadded newspapers sealing up the spaces. Otherwise the house was neat and bright and the sun shone in all the corners. The floor was white as a tub with sunlight. There were no bugs or rats. There were no hairs on the women's chins or dried nostril grime on the men. Everyone was there dressed soberly in brown and white— white shirts and dresses and faces and hands, brown trousers and beads and boots and hair—brown and white and moving like a bread pudding.

But there was no sign of the babies. No prints or droppings. No bark torn off the rough pine walls. Or cloth snagged on a splintered seat.

They all had brought gifts but none were being used right. Mal had brought an empty egg painted in bright colors with a string run through the pin holes. He imagined that the babies could bat it with their hands. But Freddie's wife had hung it on the Christmas tree, which was still up but dropping, falling but not over, pale as wheat now, incongruous, leaning like a person ill at ease, the berries strung there rotting. The egg rolled back and forth in the air. The needles clicked as they struck the floor.

The young girls bent over the twins' toy that lay by the sink on the breadboard. Something furry—a rabbit's foot. They drank hot sugared water, giggled at the spot where Mal was drinking his brandy down.

"A door is not a door until it's closed," Mal kindly thought, squinting at the colored funnies that hid his nest of young. The papers were old and crumbling. The news was history. The missing persons, listed in rows tiny and in code like the cricket scores, had all been found.

"Oh what is there about him that makes him so worthwhile . . ." the young girls thought, their legs twitching and joggling below their laps.

Everyone was ogling the spot where he was as though they wanted to sit there too but wouldn't. Mal swallowed his brandy, pushing his face deep inside the cup. He licked the bottom dry and put it down. He was sorry for the babies in the black pantry, rocking in their cribs like corn. Had they destroyed the babies he had made? Had she taken his sack of seed, tied it up and chucked it out as she would the gizzard bag in the pit of a grocery hen?

He walked away. No one said good-bye.

IV

> The kidneys are equal in size
> and shape. The capsules strip
> with ease. The esophageal mucosa
> is grey-white. No food is present
> other than a few intact, cooked
> beans.

The day had been very blue and the sea black but now the sea be-came blue and fearful like a shotgun's bore and the sky became black and scuddy with clouds. The water in the harbor began to pitch and foam as though it were about to give up its dead. Mal was pushed into town by the wind and he stood in a doorway and watched the storm. The doorway led to a mud-room and the mud-room to a cheap restaurant, filled with cowboys and wax flowers. The chaps of the cowboys smacked wetly as they walked. Little pieces of food flew in the air between them as they talked. The place was warm and steamy and stank of sheep. He sat at a tiny table for two in a corner by the window and a running toilet. No one bothered Mal Vester. No one asked for his order.

He was the only guest who was not a cowboy. Never had he wanted to be a cowboy. The cowboys were chewing and laughing and cutting the wire stems of the plastic flowers with their huge pocket knives. They threw the flowers at one another and entwined them in their lank and dripping hair. The knives turned and sawed white and watery like fish and the flowers fell clumsily into their hands and then onto the soaked and puddled floor. Wool had become embedded in the wounds of their fingers, spun out black and coarse like a paw's webbing. The blood of lambs lay caked beneath their nails.

On their dark arms they had tattoos. Legends of roses and tigers. Puce needle diggings. Stain of capillaries. The muscled petals that women love to touch.

But who knows what good might come from the least of us? From the bones of old horses is made the most beautiful Prussian blue.

It rained and rained. Mal wrung out his cuffs and watched the dim day through the steamy window. Someone had written a word on the glass. NICE, it said. The street was buckling. The rain was clattering like teeth in a cold mouth. Swings moved between poles in the park without children and the sea slammed against the pilings and carried off the crabs. Everything in the world was slick and trembling like a gland, like something gutted, roped and dangling from a tree.

Mal's eyes were fogging up like they always did. He touched them carefully, worked out a piece of grit. He bent his wide lashes back, propping them up with spit. One eye leaked something and it ran gooey down his cheek. He was too old to cry. He fingered the small paper cones of mustard and cream and salted his hand. The table was the best in the house for it offered a view of the street, but the toilet ran on and the wooden doors of the stalls banged in the draft. The menu was glued beneath the glass table-top. Moisture had soaked it with brown. Cuttlefish was unintelligible. As were the fried breads and the list of cola drinks. Actually, Mal couldn't make out any of the words at all. Life is a filthy bill of fare. Death by dyslexia. Still, everything is pretty much the same.

He tried thinking of things as though he could remember them. He could not recollect being born. He had depended upon the aberrant memories of others, upon their eccentric recall. His momma had told him that his little dick was a bright yummy bow like a piece of salt water taffy. His daddy had said nothing before he went away. He had straddled the baby as it crept across the ground as though little Mal were a gulch he had no intention of falling into.

The cowboys ate, wickering through their noses, the roses lurching at will on their hairy chests. The coach came in from the racing trials at Milk Creek. He wore a hooded jacket of purple silk and looked like a priest with a whistle hanging around his neck instead of a cross. His day had stopped three years ago although the school still kept him on. He ordered a pint and a meat pie.

"I went crook at them for running back along the bank instead of swimming," he said, "but how was I to know the kid had drowned."

He persisted in teaching the butterfly. His trunks sopped beneath his trousers leaving a stain like a map. He persisted. For the butterfly could not cease to exist simply because one of his charges had died, with his white membranous arms flailing in the current, with his young ribs swelling like hoops in the sunny water . . . The boy had been doing fine until he drowned. He had been making good time. When retrieved, he looked quite ordinary except for the tips of his fingers.

The coach ate quickly. The pie juices ran down his jowl. Mal, embarrassed, looked away, out into the street again, through the runny lines of NICE. A waitress went by, flicking her tail like a bird. On her lip there was a mole with two long hairs that drooped and crossed prettily upon her teeth when she smiled. But she did not smile at Mal Vester. She went about her work with a vengeful dish rag. She ran it across his folded hands, dug it into the knuckle cracks as though she were scouring a fork. His poor hands reeked and wobbled. They leapt across the table, almost falling off the edge like a pair of gloves.

He pretended he didn't notice.

The cowboys were mopping their plates with cake; the coach tapped his groin uncertainly and wriggled in his chair. From a hole in the wall, plates of food were shoved, the fingers lingering on the sandwiches, snipped off a dangling piece of lettuce with grace and love.

Outside in the rain, a hand waved feebly from the gutter. Mal was uncertain. He rubbed away the NICE. The street was empty. Everything was turning into a yellow dusk and the rain ran down with a tired sound over the small lame hand that flopped and sank. He ran out startled through the doors, falling in the mud-room, skidding along on his ear. He picked himself up gently as though he

were someone else and ran on to the gutter, his cheekbones stinging, string and ashes hanging from his light eyebrows. The air was
yellow. The tops of trees. The plastic protecting the druggist's window candy. The edge of town run off the hill. Did he have a liver
ailment? Had he slid by error down a commode? He yelled and
stumbled on.

The errant hand flopped like an empty sack. A bird's nest floated
by, trim and watertight, softly struck the fingers and was gone. There
were no grates on the city's sewer holes. Things fell down there and
lived beneath the town—dung black ponies and shit brindle cats.
Fish with white bones that shone through the gills. Eventually all
were tumbled away, moved by the moon and tidal heaves—horny
hoofs and claws and plushy meat out to the sharks banking like birds
off the seaweed ledges.

Mal knelt down in the rushing water, grabbing and tugging at
the hand soft as pork. The fingers, old-maidish and ringless, skinny
and worn down, did not grip him back and he felt sick, all that salt
he had licked in the restaurant rising in the back of his throat, his
eyes wet and ringing in his head. It was like pulling the glug from a
shower-drain. The arm came out stringy and then a little grey head,
rising peeved and fierce with lobeless ears. For a moment, he thought
it was his dear momma, for she had been lobeless too, all ear itself
and open mouth, hearing and saying and kissing him dry. He almost dropped her back in his joy, for one must not dwell on differences. The way to fidelity is through mistaken identity.

But of course it was not his momma, this slippery gloomy wretch
that he had hauled onto the street. Quite a crowd had assembled by
then to witness the rescue and the old lady lay drying in a muttering
circle of hobbled delight, her small feet lopped over the curbstone,
her skinned but bloodless knuckles up and rapping at the air.

The next day she was buried, for she had been found dead during the night with peroxide burns around her mouth.

V

> There is no evidence of
> trauma about the head. The
> central nervous system is
> not examined.

For nothing is faithful and nothing stays saved. The watery caul of our birth protects us from nothing and one can die by drowning beyond the sight of a sea.

The black jelly in the roadway was once off and running warm through the trees. And somewhere a place waits for us . . .

Mal was sixteen and a grateful town sent him to America, for although they all agreed that his intentions were good, there was no denying the traumatic concurrence of his adolescence with death and flood and pregnancy and now all the lambs in the pastures starving and dropping on their way to nurse. The men spat blood in their dinner soup for their daughters paid them no attention and were down at the laundromat, dancing to small radios, picking the lint from their soapy lacy things before the frightened boys, and their women lay immobilized in bed biting at the pillowcases and listening to the rabbits eat the flowers up.

The mayor had a high faint voice and cancer in a nasty place. The town hall was cold and listing, filled with poisoned saucers for the mice, a structure that had been built hurriedly with the threat of constant vows in mind. Mal stood timid and sweating before the extravagant praise, tipping with the pressure of the colored medal as they pressed it to his chest, his eyes opalescent beneath the low thick lids. They appeared that day to be grey in color.

The mayor moved on his rubber donut, his mouth pink and sagging at the corner from the weight of medicine spoons, his bowels bound up, all hope lost, the town's money gone and all his own, spent on shark nets and bubbler screens and keeping the public wards alive. And he was dying all the while. Dying, and his wife was not true, though she was taking in washing to pay for the stone, and each night for him, as he grew thinner, covering less and less space on the brass muggy bed, lisping words against the water glass, the sky turned into bright flame like wormwood falling, and now this troublesome licentious boy was out saving suicides.

There was only the mayor and Mal and the council sitting in an even row, their stomachs sick with a heavy breakfast waffle. They placed a plane ticket into Mal's seedy pocket, some folding money . . . for they did not wish him any harm. Gas blew up between their lips. The health inspector had butter on his sleeve.

The mayor tenderly licked his teeth for they were white and perfect, without cavities and strong as a dog's . . .

the rescue had taken place and should be suitably rewarded. It was unfortunate that the victim did not recover but beside the point. The old lady had resources that thwarted Mal's brave concern

. . . though one now seemed loose. He pushed his tongue against it and it lifted neatly out of its socket in the rotting gum and slid down his throat. He grew more pale than before and bolted from the room, his bony hips whirling against the desk, ripping open the drawer where hair ribbons lay tangled with a wet glue pot and discs of plaster painted like coins.

. . . And what is it that you protect and swaddle in your fashion? Your darling, your favorite, that part of you which you most fear for in the night?? Spine testes head breast lung eyeball?????? There's something for everyone. Some cyst or rupture, tumor or bacillus spore, fracture or fever for us all.

... And the place that you will last recall? Abandoned fridge? Train toilet? Electrocuted pony?

For death is everywhere and the zoo-keeper waits in his soul for the mauling, the coon dog for the master's meat, the maid for the bloody sheet . . .

Mal went meekly up the ramp with the nerveless calm of perfect fright and into the sky, his passport pinned above the medal to his chest, the photo punched across with green, his poor wet eyes closed but shining behind the lids like a kerchief Christ, and the plane lifted, leaving behind him all his dead, his momma in the foamy trickle, the black dog grinning on the slanting lawn, the rabbits drifting over his daddy's hollow . . .

VI

The attack occurred in a small
bay with a small watercourse at
its head. The victim was put into an ambulance but because of the
steep grade leading up from the
water's edge and the slippery surface the ambulance clutch burnt
out. There were several dogs taken
in the area last week.

He wore a tan suit, too tight at the armpits. The button at his neck was split in two and kept sliding through the eyelet, exposing his white throat. He refused dinner and a magazine. He felt as though he were dying. His ears were dully popping. There was a taste of garbage

at the very root of his tongue. The clouds gaped and he could see
the sea wallowing black and mean, the colors changing to yellow
and green over reefs and island shoals. A stewardess swished by,
smiling, he knew, like a lunatic. He crouched in his smelly seat. He
lifted his heels off the floor. Would they band him like a bird? Tat-
too his lip with a number as they did the polar bear? It wasn't a
question of affection or protection. They would just want to know
how far he had gone by the time he died. She stopped and dropped
her hands down to his hips. He looked at her beseechingly and
attempted to withdraw himself into his spine. His lap seemed as
vulnerable as a child's winter mitten . . . untidy soiled serge . . . as
the fingers advanced, long and blue near the nails, four like a fork,
with a thumb the spoon, her mouth full of Sen-Sen swinging by his
ear, ready to masticate, to subdue him forever. She scowled and
fumbled, mistakenly sticking her finger into his navel. It dropped in
a good inch like a score in a game. He was full of orifices. Like a
pinball machine. They could groove or notch or tag him anywhere.
They had ways. They could scoop out his brain, he figured, and no
one would ever know, because they were so clever, because they left
wounds with no scars.

She cinched him up and strolled away. The belt was buckled too
tightly, Mal knew, having bisected the cheese spread sandwich he
had brought aboard in his pocket. His discs were bunched like
poker chips. But he knew that he was safe, that his fate was not happening yet, and the blood began to course down again from his eyes
to the points of his stiff body.

The plane bucked. A baby across the aisle spit up into a National
Geographic. Mal's stomach rolled and rose, larding his ribs with
the fat of its wall. On the sea it was raining and blowing. He could
imagine the storm down there. He crossed his chest and closed his

eyes. He could see the tankers going down tonight; the tuna seiners with the nets sweeping over the dead men's eyes; women on yachts in diaphanous gowns, crying in their cabins, their earrings flying away in the howl, their sharp heels wedging in the decks . . .

A woman was holding the sick baby. "Do you think we'll crash?" she said to Mal. "Do you think this is the end for all of us? And me with my man in Hawaii?" Her voice rose, humming like a set of wings. The child spit all over her hands. "He's so young he don't smell yet. So I guess we can be thankful for that at least."

Mal didn't answer. He found his charm in looking grave. He had difficulty focusing on the child, whose nose was dripping, whose little face was the color of the seat. His hands were swelling. His eyes were silting up. When the woman realized that he wasn't going to answer, she shifted her eyes up and to the left, to pretend that she had never been addressing him at all, and wiped her hands on the baby's shirt.

"And me," she said, "only twenty and my sugar a soldier and far away."

The plane was being swatted around as though it were in the web of some enormous paw. A slice of jelly roll slid off a tray and flopped along the aisle, picking up in its cakey wet a bobby pin. Dust balls from the runner. Cigar ash. The stewardess had disappeared and the passengers began a slow liturgical wail. The lights blinked on and off, and the baby held his breath, the bridge of his nose turning blue.

The young woman pinched the child's cheeks. "I wish you was older so you could chew gum. That'd make you feel a whole lot better." She was a mother and serene, wearing a dress with a sweet round collar spotted with drool, her head full of bone and small thoughts breaking softly. She was not really alarmed about the storm, though her mouth was dry, one incisor snagging upon her lip. Sooner or later, Mal knew, the child would be left somewhere, in a movie theater or behind the matches and soap, abandoned without malice or intent, vaguely remaindered like potatoes on a plate. But he would survive, he would manage, because this was a smart-looking baby, thin and desperate. Temples beating on grimly. Long ears throbbing like antennae. Her man was in Hawaii in flowered bikini trunks, with the beach in his sheets, with her grey from poor nutrition too much rice and peanut butter Mal knew having never eaten properly himself, her skin grey and slick and cool as a trout, and the child would just crawl off someplace, into some orange moon of light and be taken in by natives, growing up to dynamite fish. For sharks, he'd learn to chum first, to bring them in, and then to lob grenades into their mouths. He would learn like Mal must, to rectify, and the meat would run like milk. But with a woman he'd be fine. He'd rinse off his hands in clear tap water.

Mal poked at his eye with a grievous thumb, then set to work weeding his eyelashes with his knuckles. Loosening, they made the very slightest pop a rough thicket with a pure white root. Through the plane's tiny window, past the oily prints of former heads, the discarded complexions of weary passengers, there was nothing but an echoing pallor. White and foaming. Mistaken for a glass of some-one else's seltzer water, Mal was being drowned. Had he been born with a caul they had to cut? He could not remember. But what would protect him from the air? His mother was ripping along on the tides beneath him, far below the surface where there is no wind or breakage. His mother was trying to keep up, he knew, but the Captain had a lisp, and his medal had unloosened and was stabbing at his heart.

In the hold, the pet dogs had given up howling and yapping at the engines. They had always lived unrealistically. Indignant with trust. They curled up tight with their noses deep beneath their tails.

But the storm had a range, an appointed round, a latitude and longitude responsible to charts, and the plane passed through. The day bobbed up—an invalid's morning, with the light like that after fever and chill, sharp and astonishing, white as a winding sheet. Everyone wiped up and retreated into bad habits. With the soul sinking back to a place between the armpit and the rib. No need to die when you've done it all up to it. A woman mouthed dreamily the hairs of her arm. The smell of death, that odor of sick animals, sweet like a nut and sulphurous, was taken up by comfy flatulence in rubber and wool. Everything proper. Steeping like tea.

Mal ate his cheese sandwhich. The bread was wet from his frightened hip. It had beaded up and the mess tasted warm and hybrid. With one determined wince it was gone and they were over Fiji with the music on and the woman with the baby, eying someone else, kissing him the French way in her silly head's eye.

His heart ached as though she had bitten it with her small bright teeth. Mal the father, fatherless, rubbed his chest and squinted at the man she favored—a gentleman with a part taken out of his chin and a cast to his hairline, scowling and untouched by her gaze, the suede patches on his elbows all slick from a puzzling use. She had always wanted someone with a fetish or a profession, not a boy like Mal who loved without method or distinction, who, in a country where everyone had to be spoken and accounted for in some manner, was neither a cowboy or a surfer or a hunter and no one's apprentice either, who had been banished from Australia, a land which refused almost nothing at all, rejected from Australia where even the poisoned rabbits are left lying on the land.

He certainly looked like a professional man. A man with a hobby or a cure for something. He had shiny eyes. Sun-cracked lips. An enormous blue and red tiepin upon which was engraved

MONZA AUTODROMO

Mal began to hiccough nervously, orange cheese smell scrabbling at the back of his throat. He gulped and tried to hold his breath but air dribbled out between symmetrical gaps between two hind teeth where his smile—when he smiled which was seldom—stopped. He gripped the sides of the seat, burping softly, the cheese rising stultifyingly in his nose bubbly like a bog. The professional man arose and lumbered to a rear compartment, tipping toward Mal as he hurried along, his right knee dipping just before he crashed against his shoulder, braiding Mal's torso like a rope while the part of him below the seat belt remained primly secure. The strange tiepin rapped sullenly against his eye, glowing like the eye of God. Mal lifted up his hand and snagged one finger in the wide buttonholes of the man's tweeds, tearing the nail below the quick. Wordless, the man bored on, while the girl applied fresh lipstick and the baby spit up once more and again into another magazine as though this was its life's sole occupation. Mal sucked his hand and the tears rose like an animal's, awash and gleaming in the sockets, unfallen.

He was frightened by the way people treated him. As though he were a table or a chair or a rock in the street, but worse than that, because at least those things they would use or avoid. Treating him instead as though they couldn't see him. As though he had already moved on and they were performing over the space he had vacated. And he was going to America where mice were found in bottled Coca-Cola straight from the machine. Where girls were scalped by wheels and engines that stacked celery threshed wheat picked cherries hulled pecans. Where there were circuses and rodeos and games of skill, and people knowing things he would never even think about.

Would he ever be able to escape? The dead boys ran away to sea misundertanding everything, for all they had wanted was the returning. Would he ever find a cute jelly to love him, to see him for what he was? Would he ever get the cure and set his momma's heart to rest?

He ordered a whiskey. It came in a tiny bottle with a tiny glass and napkin like a child's tea set. There was a little paper dish with six peanuts in it. He ordered three more whiskeys and between swallows, sucked on his hand, trying to settle the nail back in place with his tongue.

. . . his sweet momma who had danced with him, guiding him through the rooms of the settling house, into musty closets where moths drifted into his ears, dancing and rocking around and around, his nodding head clunking against her knobby pelvic bone. Riding on her wide fly-pocked feet when he tired. Around and around to the sounds of warped records. Huge birds resting one-legged on the lawn. Smell of low tide. Child bouncing a rubber ball against the privy wall.

His poor momma eaten alive as she worked the sand out of her suit. Who only the day before had trimmed his nails and swabbed his eyes. They were always hemorrhaging mildly from his digging at them. They itched and burned. Along with his teeth and something deep within his ears that he could not get at.

His sweet momma, her sharp bones bruising him every time she drew near, mending him every day, combing his thick hair with her fingers, combing and sweeping and patting it back until Mal thought he was dying, he felt so fine.

He ordered two more whiskeys and brought his hands in close to his chest as the man with the elbow patches shambled back up the aisle and didn't even hesitate before he lowered himself into the empty seat beside the girl. He smiled at her and his teeth were all gold. The tiepin rose and bound as he settled, a part of him that was not so much accessory as guide. Like those plastic balls that divers attach to their weight belts so that they will know in the black un-world in which direction the surface is.

Mal fell asleep while looking as the man turned his broad tweed back and hid the girl and baby from view.

VII

Injuries may be received from
camels either through the bites
from side kicks even when sitting down or from the animal
knocking a person over and falling upon him with the breast pad

He awoke in Los Angeles with the plane resting on its huge wheels. He was the only one on board. On the seat across the aisle was a powder puff and a rattle toy. Mal mopped up a bit of drool with his cuff, hoping he had not been sleeping with his mouth open. He was not able to disengage the buckle on his seat belt. It would have been useless to call the stewardess for the key. She was nowhere in sight and there wasn't any place on the belt where a key would go. He writhed and writhed, the buttons on his shirt tearing away with the strain. The collar came askew. He could see rust marks from the wire hanger. He could see the slick of corn meal still embedded in the fabric where someone at the Church Relief Fund had taken the iron scorch from the sleeve.

At last he slid out beneath the belt. He dropped the two unopened bottles into his pocket and buttoned his suit coat up to the neck to conceal the torn shirt. He walked out the door and into a black canvas tube which instead of sloping downward, remained level, throwing Mal off balance, causing him to bump against the soft walls. They were damp from the hot foggy night. It was as though he had collided with one of the sweating wrestlers he had watched so often in the free Sydney gyms. Loose soaking flesh with the scaffolding of bone beneath. Eyes blinded by the smother of hairless stomachs. Everything dark as concussion. Smooth as an egg.

Mal stayed in the terminal for days, for he had no other idea of what to do. It was vast and white and teeming and timeless. He had to walk for twenty minutes just in order to find a glass that was really a window to the outside, to the day or the night and the greasy sky and the planes rising drearily and incessantly with steam and clamor.

The toilets and movies were free. He saw *The War Lover* fourteen times. The aisles were terribly littered and Mal smashed a tonic bottle with his boot. No one turned about. They were all sleeping, grey in the backwash of the screen. Mal wished he had a leather flight jacket like the hero. If he had a jacket like that, lined with a sheep, fitting tight and casual, he'd be able to go anywhere.

He spent a day and a half in the theatre. When he re-entered the main terminal, he felt as though he had stepped into a refrigerator. Everything white and whirring and ticking with great florescent lights. It was colder than he ever remembered it being in Australia, and he pulled his suit coat tighter across his shattered shirt.

A boy Mal's age stood outside a luncheonette, holding out a tray of samples. Sections of wieners dipped in a yellow sauce. Pierced by toothpicks with cellophane bows. Mal sidled up and took one, jabbing his lip, in his haste, with the toothpick. He extended a grimy arm to accept another but the boy turned with the tray.

"Don't pull that stuff on me," he hissed. "I'll call the cops."

Mal turned quickly away, aiming for an orange sling chair against the opposite wall, but the boy pursued him, saying "lunk lunk lunk," as though he were choking, as though he were speaking through his lung. Mal slid into the chair, and the boy stood a few paces off, spitting by error onto the wieners.

"Lunk lunk lunk lunk lunk," he said. "Dope." He stamped angrily back to his post, the yellow sauce staining his fingers, his hairline high and ragged.

Mal stayed in one section of the terminal, in one acre, bounded on the north jog by a florist, on the south by a penny arcade, a steel pony at the entrance, the paint peeled from one eye, a quarter stuck in the box mounted on its mane. He sat quietly for the most part, his knees pressed together like a girl's, eating pressed meat on a stiff and oily bun. Along the walls there were cages of drugged cats. Tags ringing against the mesh. Like boom rings clinking against masts. Odor of piss and wood chips. Ladies took their pills at drinking fountains. Hardening lumps of Chiclets mounted all around.

He was beginning to get moles on his face. He tried to tidy himself up in the washroom, but the liquid soap, mounted in a glass bubble, screwed to the wall, irritated his skin, making his hands smell as though they had been packed in a paper trunk for the last decade. He had heard a great deal about moles. He didn't want to violate them in any way. He changed his clothes in the washroom, putting on a worn pair of khakis and a green tee shirt. He folded the suit and put it carefully in his suitcase, over the coroner's unreadable statement, between his momma's hairbrushes and the only thing he had ever found in his life, a fillet knife, discovered on the beach between burnt bricks. Thin bones lying everywhere. Jaw of small fierce teeth pointing out to sea.

He sat in the plastic sling chair, touching his eyes and the slick moles, trying to think.

On the sixth day, the boy with the tray of samples came over to Mal. He was carrying brownies, each piece no bigger than a thumbnail. "I'm gonna call the man on you," the boy snarled. "I've taken all I'm gonna take from you. You look so weird sittin' there and I've taken all that I'm ever gonna take from you."

He walked away, the brownies popping all over his tray and a few minutes later returned with a man in a grey uniform and a sweatband grid around his head where his cap had been. It looked as though a very tiny truck had been motoring around his skull. He looked slightly to the left of Mal and high, higher than Mal's head would be even if he were standing.

"Awright," he bawled. "Awright, whatarya trying to do, live your life in this place? Huh? Whatarya practicing here anyway?"

Mal looked wildly about and began to pant. Beneath his light shirt his shoulder blades felt like a wooden coat hanger had been sewn cleverly beneath the skin. He felt the bulk of all his bones keeping him down, weighing him to the chair and he hunched forward and panted harder.

"Since you don't seem to be doing anything at the present," the man said, "whyn't you come with me and you can mow the lawn around the county jail."

Mal shook his head. His sternum was heaving around beneath his tee shirt. He imagined it leaping through the cloth and scaring them all to death.

"Oh, then you must be waiting on somebody, huh," the man said.

"He ain't waiting on nobody. You'd best believe that. He's just weird is all. Sitting here for a week. Taking advantage. Like to drive me nuts." The boy, pale with indignation, had been clawing at the brownies. The tray was covered only with crumbs. The crumbs were blowing around and settling on everything.

"You waiting on somebody, boy?" the man asked Mal.

A girl walked out of the penny arcade. She wore a short faded dress and her hair was in a long yellow braid that hung down past her waist. The braid was tied with yarn and the loopy bow of it swayed below the hem of her dress. She wore dark glasses and yellow tennis shoes and carried a card. She walked over and stood between the man and Mal and said, "We're together and we're leaving. This here is my escort to Texas."

She patted Mal on the shoulder. She smelled clean and leafy as though she'd been swimming in a lake, and Mal got up and followed her away just as though he'd been free all the time to do just that.

VIII

> Walt Faulkner, sole survivor of the
> factory Lincoln team, was driving like
> a madman. Coming into Mexico City,
> peasants lined both sides of the road 50
> deep, touching the cars with their fin-
> gers as they thundered past. Faulkner
> never slowed his charge. He boomed thru
> the tunnel of humanity flat out. Later,
> when someone asked what he would have done
> had he plowed into the mob, he replied,
> "Turn on the windshield wipers."

It was a large white car. A very sensual car. Hot remote white and air-cooled, chilling his knees. An orange butterfly smashed delicately on the left headlight. Mal felt loving. His thick hair fell past his eyes, socked in the hollows of his cheeks. A balloon torso of a man tilted slightly toward the tinted glass on the passenger side. A plasticine mask on the bullet shaped head a real cloth coat and a clip-on tie. Wearing a cream ten-gallon hat. The girl turned a rubber petcock where the lap should have begun, flattened him out, folded him up and put him in her saddlebag handbag.

At a Texaco station they soaped off the butterfly and pumped 26 gallons into the machine while the girl talked incessantly and fed Mal Eskimo Pies and fried chicken and honey from a cardboard box. The cold of the ice cream sang in his teeth. The honey dripped down through his fingers and onto the cards that she showed him. One card was made of thick cardboard and on one side it said

A STRANGER IS THE WAY

and on the other side there was a drawing of a horseshoe and the words

KEEP ME SOMEWHERE IN YOUR HOME
AND YOUR LOVE WILL NEVER ROAM

"That's what slid out of the fortune-telling machine in the arcade," the girl said. "Same time I saw you sitting there this nickel card fell into my hand. The gypsy doll there in the corner between the hockey game and the bear shoot? You know?"

She gave him the other card. It said

DRIVERS WANTED
ANYWHERE
ALL GAS PAID 502-3061118

"This is how I get along. Drive anything though mostly tony cars. Cadillacs. Buicks. Lincolns. Because the people that like this service are rich and fly home and mostly old and feeble. I strip everything that's not needed for the thing to move forward, move back and stop. Air conditioners. Stereo tapes. I swap the batteries and the tires and the jacks with junks in yards 10 or 20 miles from my drop-off point. And no one notices. I wash it up properly before I arrive. Sweep it out. Everyone's happy as pie. Because they don't know a thing about cars. As long as it gets them to the druggist for their Preparation H. As long as it gets them to the grave site. They've all got brains wrapped in prophylactics. They don't allow *nothing* inside their heads. So this is how I manage. No way to make a killing but I see a lot of the country and I love to drive. Nothing I'd rather do than drive a big rocking ark like this for free. Driving a fast cool car going for places I don't know . . . You got a lot of moles honey. That's supposed to mean something, I read, though I can't recall what. Something about something."

Mal nodded, his cheek full of fowl wing.

"You know how to drive? No? Well, I'll teach you."

But she never did. She did all the driving, fast and smooth and aggressive, heavy on the horn and gas, her round elbow burning in the southwestern sun, her legs set wide apart on the floorboards, hoop earrings shaking and shining, long yellow braid hanging pure as a rope from a church belfry.

She never stopped talking. It was delicious. No one had talked to him like this since his momma with her fathomless loving prattle; her words after a few years no longer performing the function of speaking to him any more but of breathing for him. Providing his head with oxygen like an iron lung. Keeping him going. Tending him fit. The lids coming down and the nostrils pinching shut. The lips moving around the fingers she thrust at him to kiss.

"Them really your eyes, honey? You didn't get them out of one of those banks? Don't seem to lie in your head right."

Oh she was tough and constant, blonde lean and shiny. He touched her hair and it was soft and so yellow that he thought the color of it would come off on his fingers just as though he'd been rubbing up against a flower. She fed him for a thousand miles. He kept eating and felt weaker and weaker. Shrimp and candy bars. Peaches and grapes and whole pecan pies. Lasagne in a bucket. Loaves of salty rye. Washing it all down with vodka and orange crush as they drove. The huge car bucking and snaking through the traffic of the towns and then out onto the plains, the single note of birds leaping in his ears, traveling so fast that the bird was two miles back by the time it had finished its trill.

Oh she was hard and honest with the black glasses wrapped around her eyes even in the moonless night, handling the car as though it were an extension of herself. As though it were a steel claw attached to the wrist of a gone hand. Going through toll stations, she would pay for the strangers in the car behind, jetting off in their bafflement, leaving a coil of bluish smoke.

"It confuses them," she said. "It puts them in arrears."

Mal squeezed her arm tentatively. There was a hard hot determined little muscle there. She took two swallows of vodka for every one of crush from a bottle of chocolaty red. She had never even asked his name. He decided that if she did, he would say it was Monza. He wedged his head beneath her armpit.

"I never did much of that," she said and began kissing his neck, sucking up the skin beneath her teeth as though she were chewing on an artichoke, leaving round blue blossoms ringing his collarbone. She smelled so clean and distant—like something laundered in a brook and dried in the summer sun. He smelled like a wolf's pissing tree, he knew. His navel itched and reeked. His pretty hair was wadded to his head. But the girl kept feeding him and tweaking his side. Tacos and fritters. Chili dogs and sugar crullers. Shards of potato chips quivered in his stinging gums. His mouth was stained blue with berry tarts. In Lubbock, she bought a case of bourbon and a box of fortune cookies. Mal cracked his open, eager but exhausted. The moisture from the air-conditioner dripped and beaded on the hot asphalt. There had been carelessness at the factory. A typographical error in the confection seductively creased and joined. The lines of print were overlaid, the future foundered. She shook her head and looked distressed, a bit illicit and naïve in her short thin dress and canvas shoes. She turned the car out of the grocery store's lot, away from the sun-blackened bag boy, and onto the roadway toward salt water.

She settled him into a beach house while she delivered the car. Bones of cows holding up the window sashes. Cold sand clogged in corners. Insects by the rag-wrapped pipes. Rust on the undersides of everything. Mal had bathed by the time she returned by taxi, squatting in the truncated tub, scrubbing with a pillowcase. The water was sulphurous and had steadily turned a dark green as he soaped. Not unattractive. Not without its charm. Green like his eyes might have been when they were well. Clinging tenaciously without substance to the porcelain sides. Nothing he could put his finger on.

The sea air lapped his head. He felt on holiday. As though it were Boxing Day at home. He was Monza Dong from Wollongong. The sea birds flew by in a tight clutch and she said, "It flies to Chile and then to Greenland, that bird. Them sanderlings. And they aren't but a few inches long and tall."

She strung some twine from the shack to a sea grape and washed out their clothes and hung them out to dry. She curled up on the mildewed sheets all pale and frail and accessible except for the black glasses wrapped around her eyes, and with her hair yellow and warm as a buttered biscuit. In the night, Mal woke dizzy to the thick braid sliding from his cheek and the call of the whippoorwill and he saw her opening the refrigerator door, the light muffled somewhere from a bulb behind the hastily stocked shelves, exposing her as she pushed her throat back to drink milk from a carton, showing just to him her small breasts and curving ribs shining in the hum. Shining like wheat in a frost . . . and her chest was cool when she returned, her lips cold and sour. When she touched him, it was as though she were trying to get at something else, something in the damp mattress ticking, something in the punctured foam, as though she'd push her hand right through him to get it, cupping her hand through his chest and drawing out what she preferred. Mal rolled his eyes shut. He slept fitfully. Things rode across the shiny sand. The girl's dress rose and seized in the noiseless wind.

IX

It is stated that a lad in Victoria,
many years ago, climbed into the entrance of an occupied wombat's burrow.
The disturbed animal started to come
out and in passing the young man, feeling pressure on its back, immediately
raised its back to support the supposed
fall of its roof and pressed its victim
against the roof, killing him.

She cut off her braid and astonished him by not looking any different than she had before. Sawing it off with a blunt bread knife, tying it around his collapsed and peeling waist, going back to her bourbon in the flowered coffee cup.

"If I cut it off at just the right length," she said, "it'll grow right back in six or so months. Like a crab making up its biggest claw." She was great on hair and fingernails she told him. Like something in the grave.

Mal was shy. With not too much effort, he could see a withered face within it. Caulked nostrils. Little glass eyes. He hung it in the shade, poured sand in the last of the whiskey bottles and looked back at the shore where he had been watching a school of fish rising white and predisposed through a wave. The girl went back to sleeping on the beach, slung in a small depression, her cleavered hair curling around her ear lobes, her stomach pulsing like her heart, her square toenails pointing out to the fog coming off the water.

She'd later wrap the braid around him and they'd walk along the heat-heaved road, holding hands and sweating in the dark. The hair chaffed him though she washed it in shampoo and braided it fresh each day. It was gold. The tub was now a decided green. Very modern looking. His own hair was the color of walnuts and hid the painful knobs of his spine. He was frightened that it would set to smolder in the sun. At night it would seem to steam.

The road had been made cheaply with large quantities of sand and it was pocky and dangerous. Cars bottomed out. In the rains some floated and some didn't. Everything in the area was made with sand. Houses and bridges and benches. The statue of a cow in town. Toys were filled with it. They cheated and beat at you with sand, the girl said. They treated and tempered the things you used. The sand was disappearing from the beach. All that was left were gravelly pockets and people writing ORAMIT in the smooth tidal wash, which she had seen, in letters so big they could only be for an airplane or a chopper or the Chile flying bird. She was waiting for them to make a car from sand that ran on salt water, she said, and she'd be happy as a princess then, she'd be smug and set forever. They had already made cars with frames of wood, of glass. In a wreck it would slide up under your skin like a sliver, punching into your heart as though you were a fiend. In a smash it would slice you up like a 2000 pound beer bottle. Caroming icicles. All crackling like snow on the heat of the overhead cams.

In a sand car, she said, they'd go to Florida and eat coconut ice cream. They'd see a reptile show. They'd have to carry straws to be prepared, to push up through the weight if it collapsed, to use for breathing until the rescue party dug them out, in the meantime, however, using them to draw on the frozen daiquiris that she would pack in the thermos. Mal giggled slowly and adjusted the hair cocoon. He stopped and kissed her. Her tongue rooted out his chewing gum.

At noon, she would often run ice cubes across his wrists. She noted that he had no lines on the palms of his hands.

One morning as they were playing boule on the beach, they saw several trucks and cranes traveling up the road. They parked in the ditch not far away. The men swung down from the cabs and walked back toward the town. Mal and the girl tried to ignore them but they were huge and brightly painted. No one ever attended them or moved them any further up the road. They just canted in the sand and shone in the sun, the chrome so clear that cardinals hopped over them all day long, admiring their own scarlet, dashing selves.

Mal went back to playing the pretty game. The sight of the balls as they arched heavily through the air and the sound of them as they struck one another was very pleasant to him. The sun was a sockeye salmon weaving in the mist. The clouds were foaming gin. Sometimes Mal would fall asleep while standing.

The girl left in the morning for limes. The tide was out, a bar exposed. He could still see the moon in the sky. He thought the shark was a rubber tire until he had reached its snout. Someone had carved out the jaws. It was deflated, the stomach covered its side, all black and orange like a bad squash. He sat down to watch it and discovered that he couldn't think about it any more. He walked down the beach to see what else he could find. When he turned back, he could see dimly that the house had been leveled. The machines were further down the road and all that remained was a stack of boards and insects fleeing across the sand, and the boule balls in a ragged nest.

Mal ran around in a tight little circle like a dog trying to bite himself. He didn't know if he would see the braid waving from the aerial, whipping like a squirrel's tail on the right, on the side of her protective jockey which was blown up by her own damp and narrow and nervous lips. He didn't know what, in that which he saw passing on the road, he should regard as his own.

No one was immune. The wilderness snapped and glided like a varmint. He could hear it at dusk, whirring and wheeling, hooting in his ear. The oceanic desert. The jungled marsh. Didn't she know? There were rabid foxes and loose tie rods. Current rattled up through the bidet. Sails luffed. Brain pans bent and burnt.

Mal started to run. Snapping from car aerials were flags and flowers and underwear. Inside the people were smiling and shifting around and drinking from paper cups. And over it all was the smell of rubber and oil and salt in the light and the bright sunshine. The beach was endless and Mal ran and ran.

Ann Beattie

on

Craig Nova's *Another Drunk Gambler*

The narrator could not tell this story unless the levels of complexity, duplicity, and suspense were understood by him when he begins. If he has the complete picture from the get-go, isn't it unfair to be withholding, isn't it disingenuous to tell a story that seems to unfold, when the ending is already known?

Answer: Good storytellers, in life as in fiction, reveal information in a way that mimics life's seeming importance and conclusiveness in the moment—moments so often undone, undercut, or somehow changed by the different perspective the future will provide. From moment to moment, though, how we weigh the story's small scenes will figure in our ultimate opinion about how heavy the story seems to us when it concludes, since serious stories don't tend to end with a punch line.

Of course, Nova could have selected an omniscient narrator's point of view, though he chose, instead, to make this a story within a story. Therefore, whatever we read is bracketed or contextualized by the presence of a particular internal perceiver. We don't have a

faddish unreliable narrator. He pretty much retreats into the background. This narrator passes no moral judgment. We do not know
enough about him to conflate his life with the story about other
people that he narrates, except for the obvious fact that he thinks it's
important to tell this particular story. We do know that things more
or less take off when an American named Harlow notices horse shit.
And remembering the story's first line, we know that that time has
passed, and Harlow has become a congressman. Politics figures
hugely, but subtly, in this story.

As the story evolves, we think we have enough information to assume something about the characters' secrets and desires. There is a
horse race, which of course happens publically, but only then do we
realize that another more subtle race to the finish has been going on,
and that things other than one horse's winning are at stake. I can't in
good conscience ruin the moment, but when Xannie—complicitous,
and therefore also with an ability to blackmail Harlow—makes his
personal wishes known, it is for the reader a second surprising,
ghastly aspect of this "horse race." The end of the story lays everything out as simply as someone showing his fanned-out winning
cards. The foreigner, Xannie, has lured in the American, Harlow—no
different from any other wild animal who would be curious to explore
some source of light. Animals, men—they just want to see what's going on. Xannie, it turns out, has been the consummate gambler, playing a game of his own devising, warping his desires to whatever the
web of destiny allows for.

The language, as always with Craig Nova, is a wonder: the internal injury that figures prominently in the story is echoed though not
conflated with the bruised sky; the Malaysian pediatrician—the doctor we never meet; the Godot of doctors—has her doctorly actions of
scrubbing imitated by men whose dirty arms tell their dirty secret;
and the rain, so desired in Eliot's *The Waste Land,* here turns into

punishing monsoons, those times it does not tease in the "sea-like" movements of the almost perfect horse. When this rain falls, it saves nothing, but rather exposes hypocrisy. There is also much to say about blindness: the jockey who trusts his instincts to decide on something based on touch, though he strokes the deceptive surface of an untouchable flaw; the suffering people, sometimes afflicted in body, sometimes unsighted: virtual vs. moral blindness. Americans might find themselves in Ipoh, but if not that place, then as well another. "[Harlow] hated to be a bystander. He tried to explain gambling by saying that it was the difference between walking through an abandoned orchard with a gun and a dog, looking for grouse, and just walking."

Right. Americans hate to be bystanders, so we aren't.

Craig Nova

※

Another Drunk Gambler

I know more secrets than any man I have ever met. My neighbor, Harlow Pearson, was a gambler, although this was never a secret and many people knew about it, even when he was in Congress. He came from New England, was tall, and thin, broad in the chest. I am an old man now. I sit in my house, hearing the shutters banging in the winter wind, and I think of things from a long time ago, like the time when Harlow was a young man in Ipoh. His gambling before Ipoh had been done in European casinos, especially those with chandeliers and chamber music played by musicians in evening clothes, and where there were men who stood around the roulette tables with small notebooks taking down the number on each turn of the wheel. Gambling made Harlow feel as though he were participating in the world. He hated to be a bystander. He tried to explain gambling by saying that it was the difference between walking through an abandoned orchard with a gun and a dog, looking for grouse, and just walking.

Harlow had a houseboy, and his name was Xan Thu. In America he was called Xannie. Xannie's parents had been Asian tribesmen, and in 1950 Xannie was working as a groom at the race track at Ipoh, in Malaysia. He spent his nights there at the race track, too, sleeping at the back of a barn, his bed made on bales of hay, on which he stretched out, hearing the rustle of it and feeling the itch through a thin blanket he spread there and smelling the dusty, grassy odor. He took his meals alone, eating while he squatted and leaned against a stall door, or back where he slept. There were other grooms, too, and they found their places to sleep in the barn, each one having a small bag in which there were a few personal things, a book, a photograph, a comb, an extra white shirt, a pair of dark pants.

The man Xannie worked for most often was half French and half Burmese; he was heavy, bald, and had greenish eyes. His skin was smooth, an olive brown color. His suits were made in London, and he wore a large, gold watch that gave the time for any place on the earth. The man's name was Pierre Bouteille. There were times when he couldn't sleep and came to wake Xannie up.

"Are you sleeping?" said Pierre.

"No," said Xannie.

"Have you seen any thieves?" said Pierre.

"No," said Xannie.

Then Pierre said, "Come outside." Xannie went with him, and Pierre gave him an American cigarette, a Camel, and they both smoked, feeling the wet, Malaysian sky, and seeing the clouds floating along, made visible by the sickly light of the city.

Pierre told Xannie about the places he'd been. He said Parisian women and Dutch women, too, would do anything for money, that New York was filled with madmen, that there was a desert in Yugoslavia. America had more food than anyone thought imaginable. There were Malaysians and Burmese who had made money gambling and in restaurants in America, and some had become doctors and university professors. There was a Malaysian pediatrician in

Chicago. . . . Xannie smoked a cigarette and thought about piles of food: he saw a cone, high as a volcano, that was made of rice. He smoked the cigarette down to the butt, burning his fingers.

Pierre had a horse he'd bought in the Philippines. It was a good horse with fine breeding and had originally come from Lexington, Kentucky. Pierre was concerned about the horse, afraid that it would be stolen, and he spent nights looking into its stall, saying that there were dishonest people around, and that you had to be on guard against them. Pierre had once gotten drunk in town and fallen asleep in an alley, and when he had woken up, he saw that someone had stolen his shoes. They had been white shoes. When Pierre stood and stared into the stall, Xannie was with him, wanting to hear about the Parisian and Dutch women and the food in America, but he only stared into the dark stall, hearing the restless movement of the horse. When Pierre felt reassured he said, "Let's go for a cigarette."

The horse was worked regularly. One night after the horse had been pushed a little harder than usual by the trainer, Pierre came into the room where Xannie slept and woke him by shaking his leg, and then told Xannie to go into town in a taxi and to bring a veterinarian. It was after one o'clock in the morning and Xannie was to tell the vet that he had a sick dog. Pierre gave Xannie a pack of Camels, and Xannie rode in the taxi, with the windows rolled up in a thunderstorm, smoking a cigarette. He brought the veterinarian back, a Frenchman who looked carefully into the taxi and who waited for it to air out before he got into it. When they got back to the track, Xannie left alone in front of the barn to watch while the veterinarian went back to take a look.

In the morning the horse was gone, but the next night, about one, it was brought back. The veterinarian had taken the animal to his clinic, where he had an X-ray machine and a table for the horse, and soon the doctor was back again to talk to Pierre and to show him the strange black and white photographs of a bone in one of the horse's feet. There was a long, definite crack in it, and the veterinarian told Pierre that one, good hard run, and the bone would break. The veterinarian said the foot would "explode." It was best to sell the animal right away, he said, and then he left.

For a few days Xannie heard nothing, but in the middle of the night Pierre came into his room and asked if he was sleeping and if Xannie had seen any thieves. Xannie noticed that Pierre didn't say "thieves" with the same horror as ususal: there was a softness in his tone that verged on the affectionate. Xannie said he hadn't seen any thieves, and then he and Pierre went outside to smoke. Pierre had been drinking, and he weaved from side to side as he said, "You know that goddamned vet blabbed? Everyone knows about the horse. How the hell can I sell him now?"

Pierre hadn't offered a cigarette and Xannie looked at the lights of the city. When Pierre spoke, he gestured with the hand that held the cigarette, and the orange tip of it streaked through the night, making lines that looked like neon tubing, and Xannie watched the bright, curved shapes and listened to Pierre's deep breathing.

"Is the horse insured?" said Xannie.

"Yes," said Pierre.

They both looked at the lights of the city and the grey and yellow clouds above it.

"Is it insured for theft?" said Xannie.

"Yes," said Pierre.

"It would take a stupid thief to steal a lame horse," said Xannie.

"Not everyone knows," said Pierre, "and is it my business to worry about the brains of thieves? They've been known to make a mistake or two. Look."

He pointed to the horizon, at a light there, which was in the direction of the jail at Ipoh. Behind them there was the large, wooden barn, the sense of the animals in it, uneasy in the stalls filled with sawdust.

"It can be arranged," said Xannie.

"I want to know nothing about it," said Pierre.

They stood side by side. After a while Xannie said, "Six hundred dollars. Tens and twenties."

"Three hundred," said Pierre. "I am not a rich man."

"All right," said Xannie. "Three hundred and fifty and a set of papers for a horse with different breeding. Bad breeding, a different color, but the same age and sex."

Pierre sighed and said, "All right. Would you like a cigarette? A Camel?"

Xannie took one and lighted it, pulling the smoke into his mouth and standing there, watching the lights of the city, the large, lumpy clouds, and thinking, while he heard the horses moving in the stalls behind him, of the Parisian and Dutch women and of the piles of rice in America as big as mountains.

The next day the horse and Xannie were gone.

In 1950, Harlow was in the navy, and he spent some time in Malaysia, at Ipoh. Ipoh is a crowded city, and during the monsoon it rained so hard it made you feel as though you were standing in a shower with your clothes on. The sky turned purple during the monsoon, dark as an ugly bruise. Anyway, one day Harlow was walking down a street that was lined with closed-up shops and warehouses. The shops were shut up with metal doors that rolled down from above the windows, and the warehouses had large padlocks, some of which were as large as a book. At the back and front of each building's roof there were rolls of barbed wire. The warehouses were used on a short-term basis, and could be rented for as little as twenty-four hours

at a time. Harlow walked down the street and stopped in front of
one that held bicycles. The city was filled with pedestrians, cars,
motorcycles, and bicycles, but Harlow had never seen a horse in it.
There wasn't enough room in the city for horses. He stopped in front
of the bicycle warehouse because he had almost stepped in a pile of
horse manure.

The door of the warehouse wasn't locked, and when Harlow
pushed it open he saw by the dusky light in the street that bicycles
were stacked on the floor and hung from the walls and rafters. When
the light from the street hit the wheels of the bicycles they looked
delicate, almost fragile, like the spokes of an umbrella without the
cloth. After a while, Harlow heard someone say, "Close the door."

Harlow pushed the door shut, and the hinges made a slow, insect-
like screech. He didn't close the door completely. When he turned
around, an electric light came on, and the bicycles were clearly
visible, hanging in the air overhead. At the back of the room, which
was narrow and not very long, there was an Asian man, dressed in
a pair of dark pants and a white shirt, who was holding the halter
of a horse. The horse, even in the dim, yellowish light, was clearly
a thoroughbred.

Harlow came a little closer, stepping over the bicycles and looking around the warehouse, but he saw no one else. There was only
the uncomfortable, confined horse, the Asian man, the grey walls of
the place, the shiny spokes of the bicycles and the piles of black rubber tires and inner tubes, many of which had been patched so many
times as to look exotic, like the coils of some enormous pink and
black snake. Harlow and the Asian man didn't stand close together,
but they each took a long, frank look into the other's face, and while
they stood there, it became clear that what had begun as an intru-
sion or perhaps even a burglary had ended, for a while anyway, as a
limited partnership.

Harlow introduced himself. The man said his name was Xan Thu. Harlow ran his hand over the horse's cheek, along the muscled, arched neck, and down its chest.

"Where did you get the horse?" said Harlow.

Xannie blinked at him.

"Is it stolen?" said Harlow.

"No," said Xannie, "it's not hot. But, in all honesty, I'd have to say that it's a little warm."

"Hmmm," said Harlow, "how warm?"

Xannie blinked again.

"Let's put it this way," said Harlow, "do you think anyone at the track here would recognize it?"

"Anything is possible," said Xannie.

Harlow looked over the horse a little more. When he faced Xannie again he found on a crate next to Xannie's elbow a piece of newsprint. It hadn't been there before, and when Harlow picked it up he saw it was a past performance sheet, two months old, that had come from a track in Manila. It had been neatly folded, but it was still water marked and yellowed. In the center, circled with a lead pencil, there was a chart for a three year old horse that in fifteen starts had showed in three, placed in three, and won nine. Harlow recognized the breeding.

"What do you say," said Harlow, "why don't we run him at the track here?"

"There's the problem of being recognized," said Xannie.

"We can fix that," said Harlow. "Let's change the color."

"Yes," said Xannie, looking at the horse. "Let's change the color."

"What's the penalty for stealing a horse here?" said Harlow.

Xannie said it depended on the owner. Some had been known to take the law into their own hands. Both Harlow and Xannie had seen the tattooed gangsters in the city, some of whom had a stump instead of a finger, the digit given to a hoodlum as a gesture of loyalty. Harlow looked over the horse again, read the performance chart, took another frank look at Xannie's face.

"I wouldn't want to have any trouble," said Harlow.

"No," said Xannie, "isn't that why dyeing the horse is a good idea?"

Harlow sighed and said he guessed it was. Then he went out of the warehouse and down the street to the avenue, where he took a taxi to a grocery. The taxi waited while Harlow bought ten packages of black Rit dye, two natural sponges, and a stack of towels. Then he got back into the taxi. When they were close to the warehouse, Harlow told the driver to let him off on the corner, and, as he walked along the street, he looked over his shoulder.

Xannie and Harlow found a galvanized tub and they filled it with water. They mixed in the dye, a little at a time, and while they stirred it around, they looked into one another's face, each thinking about the odds on the day they'd race the horse. Then they went to work, neither one of them saying a word about the color, since both of them had already decided on grey.

Harlow dipped a sponge into the tub and tried it against the horse's withers, and Xannie used one of the towels to rub the place dry. They stood back and admired the sickly, grey-black color. Then Xannie took the other sponge and they went to work, rubbing the dye into the horse's coat, drying it, and standing back to judge the change. When they were done the horse was covered with the doubt-inspiring color, which was suggestive of bad breeding and lousy nerves. More than anything else, it was the color of a weathered headstone in a New England cemetery.

Both Xannie and Harlow looked as though they were wearing

skin tight gloves that went up to the middle of the forearm. They held their hands out, away from their clothes and felt the dye as it dried on their skin and left it feeling dusty.

"That," Xannie said, pointing one of his stained hands at the horse, "is my ticket out of here. Thank God. I've heard there are piles of rice in America and that there is a Malaysian pediatrician in Chicago. Is this true?"

"I guess so," said Harlow. "I don't know much about doctors, though. It could be true. Is there some place to wash?"

Xannie pointed to the back of the warehouse, and when Harlow walked up to the cold water tap there and turned it on, Xannie said, "And what about Dutch and Parisian women? What will they do for money?" but Harlow had already turned the tap on, and didn't hear. He washed his hands and arms, seeing the white, cold lather turn grey and then swirl down the stone sink.

When Harlow came back, he found another piece of paper on the upturned box. This paper was heavier, and the printing was better, and there was a fine scroll around the edges of it. It looked a little like a certificate of stock, and at the top there was a description of a grey, three year old thoroughbred. The breeding was given, too, and it didn't look very distinguished.

"Where did you get the papers?" said Harlow.

Xannie blinked.

"They came from a long way away," said Xannie. "It's safe for us to use them here."

They put the empty packages of dye into the sack Harlow had used to bring them from the store. Xannie said he'd burn them in the alley. It was still early in the day, and Harlow said he'd get to the track and look around for a jockey. Then he went back to the corner and found a taxi.

In the evening, two hours after the last race, Harlow returned with Harry Laue. He was dark, overweight for a jockey, and a little drunk. Harlow opened the door of the warehouse, and Laue stepped in. Xannie was feeding the horse from a bucket. There were some carrots, too, and Xannie held them up, one at a time, and pushed them between the opened lips, and the regular, moving, and faintly curved teeth. Laue stepped up to the animal, went over it, and said to himself, as he touched the muscles, the neck, the legs of the thing, "Well, well, well. . . ."

"What do you think?" said Harlow.

"I got two thousand in the bank," said Laue. "I'm getting it out." Then Laue went back to the horse, his small, calloused hands going over it again, and from the dim place where he bent down, Harlow and Xannie heard his half-sober chuckling. "That two thousand was for leaving town. Can you imagine what it would be like to be trapped here?" He went back to chuckling again, his hands now carefully going over the horse's legs.

Two days later the horse was entered in the eighth race at Ipoh. Harlow and Xannie walked around the track, feeling the excitement in the air. They drank scotch and soda in tall glasses. Xannie had a pair of dark glasses, and he took them from his pocket and put them on and looked around, and then took them off, fiddling with them while he drank long swallows. Xannie had three hundred dollars and Harlow had nine hundred. They found two chairs and sat in front of the tote board, their faces blank and bored. When the first prices went up the horse was listed at fifty to one, and when, before the race, the price went to ninety-nine to one, Harlow and Xannie bought two more drinks and went to the windows, where there were long lines of people, Malaysian, Chinese, even English and Americans, not to mention a lot of French, all figuring on forms with a bit of pencil and

looking over their shoulders through the smoky air, seemingly expecting that someone or at least some news was coming up behind
them.

Harlow and Xannie waited in separate lines. Harlow stood in
his dress whites, looking clean and young among the other bettors.
At the side of the windows there were people lying on the ground or
leaning against the wooden planks of a fence there. Many of them
had only one leg, and they sat with their crutches (the top covered
with a rag) leaning behind them, and there was a woman who had a
leg so large that it must have weighed as much as the rest of her.
There were children there, too, and two of them were blind. They
sat together touching each other's face and smiling. There were men
who had no teeth, and one who had a long, white scar that ran from
his hairline to the top of his shirt. It looked as though someone had
taken a brush axe and had tried to cut him in half with it. He sat
with the others at the fence and watched those who collected on a
winning ticket.

Xannie came to the window, and stood opposite the clerk. He
took the three hundred dollars from his pocket, and then stood
there for a moment. The clerk told him to hurry up. Xannie first put
only ten dollars onto the counter, but then he hesitated, wondering
if there was any possibility that the horse's leg would hold up for the
entire race. It was problematical: the vet was good with horses and
was usually right about things like this, but then there was the possibility that the leg might hold up until the horse had crossed the
finish line. And what then? Xannie stood at the counter for a moment. Then he split the three hundred dollars in half, betting a hundred and fifty on the horse and putting the rest in his pocket, patting
it there as he did so and keeping his eyes on the men and women
who leaned against the fence.

Before the race, as the horses were led to the gate, the grey being put into the first position, Xannie said, "What if the horse wins? How are we going to get the cash out of here?"

Harlow opened the jacket of his dress whites and inside there was a service .45 automatic in a holster, which was worn high and to one side. Harlow left his jacket unbuttoned, not because he cared so much about the pistol showing, but because he wanted to be able to get to it easily.

It seemed as though the grey horse came out of the gate a length ahead. And at a distance, as the horses ran from the gate along the long backstretch of the six furlong race, Harlow and Xannie saw the odd, sea-like and gentle movement of the horse as it seemed to stretch out and lift off the track a little, moving faster than even they had hoped. Before the turn it was five lengths ahead and still gaining, its tail out and flying, its mane out like a flag, too, as Laue tried to rein the grey horse back a little, since even at Ipoh there were some standards to worry about.

In the turn it looked as though the horse was going too fast to make it. More than anything else, there seemed to be a momentary straightness in its path, a tangent that, if followed, would take it to the fence. The people in the stands were already standing and screaming, but, in the moment the horse seemed to step out from the path it should take, the screams changed to a long, deep groan. The horse continued to go straight, though not for long. It dipped a shoulder and then turned a quick, high cartwheel, in which Laue and his tack and the horse's mane and tail blended together. The circular motion of the animal and the color of it appeared for the briefest instance, like a puff of smoke from an explosion, a light, streaming collection of grey on grey, with a boot, a stirrup, a hand, or a bit of silk, a sharp hoof flashing into the clear air and then disappearing again into the confusion. The horse hit the ground, rolled over, and tried to get up, but didn't.

Harlow walked through the crowd, and Xannie hung onto his jacket, which pulled him along until they came to the rail. Harlow jumped over and began running across the soft, loamy soil of the track, which was deep and made the long run seem dream-like and difficult. Harlow crossed the infield grass, and as he went, the people from the stands came behind him, the crowd of them spreading into a large V.

Laue was standing and looking at the horse when Harlow arrived, and for a moment, while the horse pawed the ground and tried to get up, falling each time it put weight on the broken leg, its head rising and sinking with the effort and the pain, Harlow and Laue looked at each other until Laue said, "It'll have to be killed." And as Xannie came running ahead of the crowd which streamed across the infield, as the stewards drove in a Chevrolet pick-up truck from the side of the track where the grandstand was, Harlow took the .45 pistol from under his coat and stood before the horse and shot it between the eyes, once, and then again, and the horse gently and slowly put its nose onto the soft loam of the track. As the horse lay still, the crowd arrived, Xannie at its head.

Xannie stood on the side of the horse opposite Harlow and wailed, throwing his arms into the air, crying openly. Harlow stood with blood on his dress whites, still holding the pistol. People crowded around him, looked at the horse and then were pushed aside by others, who were talking quickly and screeching, gesticulating, showing with their hands how the horse had gone straight and then turned end over end. Xannie screamed at Harlow, now speaking not English but a Chinese or Malaysian dialect Harlow understood not at all. A young man in a blue work shirt with a tie said to Harlow, "He wants the gun."

"Why?" said Harlow.

The young man spoke so quickly that his cheeks seemed to flutter.

"He wants to shoot himself," said the man in the work shirt.

Xannie stood on the other side of the horse, one hand out, the other making gestures toward his open palm. The crowd around the horse made a sea-like muttering, a slight, endless babble. Harlow put the pistol into the holster and said, "No. Tell him to come along."

Xannie stood on the other side of the horse, palm still out, his cheeks marked with tears.

"All right," said Harlow. "Tell him I'll take him to America."

The man in the work shirt shouted, opening his mouth so wide as to make a web of his cheek when he spoke. Xannie stared at Harlow. Then he spoke in the language Harlow didn't understand.

"What's that?" said Harlow.

"He wants to know if it will be by boat or airplane," said the man in the work shirt.

Xannie and Harlow stared at one another, and as they did so, with the crowd around them, it began to rain. The sky was purplish, dark. The clouds had no texture. Instead they came in one piece, only marked by the perfect, silver lines of rain. Harlow and Xannie both stared at the horse, and in the heavy rain they saw that the water running from it was getting a little dark, and that when it streamed into the red soil of the track, it left black marks that reminded Harlow of a woman's cheeks when her mascara began to run. The stewards began to look at it, too. Then Xannie climbed over the horse and said, in his crisp, accented English, "It's all right. I'll take the boat."

They turned and pushed through the crowd and walked through the heavy mud of the track, their feet becoming large and misshapen with it, their fingers and knees still trembling as they went toward the greyish grandstand with its web-like supports, and as they went by the rail there was a man standing against it. He was bald, heavy, wore a dark suit made in England, and his skin was an olive-brown. His eyes were green. He was a little drunk and he had been crying, but now he said, his voice watery and sibilant, while looking at Xannie, "Carrés d'agneau, Truites de rivière de grillées, Homard à la crème. L'argent pour les femmes."

Roast young lamb, grilled trout, lobsters in cream. Money for the women.

They continued walking, and the crowd closed in around them, obscuring the track, the grass of it, the white rail, and making a sound like running water, but as they went, there still came over the noise of the crowd the steady, half drunk voice of Pierre, as he shouted, "Salmon glacé à la Parisienne!"

Glazed salmon!

"Wait a minute," said Xannie, and then he went to the rail where Pierre stood. Xannie said, "I'll tell you if there is a Malaysian pediatrician in Chicago."

Pierre nodded, and put his arms around Xannie, hugged him, and then gave Xannie a polite, Gallic kiss on each cheek.

"Who's he?" said Harlow.

"Another drunk gambler," said Xannie.

Then they walked along the track, passing the high, dark stands, the supports of them, the umbrella-like gussets at the top of each post, the almost gloomy space under the roof, where people sat, wearing dark glasses and waiting for the next race to begin, and they passed, too, the blind children who played with the features of one another's face.

I first heard this story years ago, when I was having dinner at Harlow's house. Xannie hadn't been in the country long, and Harlow had moved into his father's house and brought Xannie to live there.

Harlow was already inviting to dinner some local political . . . allies, and one of them asked Xannie what he would have done if Harlow had passed over the pistol, but Xannie only blinked at the man and then said, "Don't you think it's nice here in America?"

After a while I was able to find a time to be alone with Xannie and then I asked him in a mild, friendly, and sympathetic tone, how long he had waited in the warehouse for Harlow to come along.

Xannie stared at me full in the face and said, "Have you ever been to Malaysia?"

It came out slowly. Every now and then, when I saw Xannie, he'd mention Pierre Bouteille, the stables, the X-rays of the horse, the papers. He knew that once he had the horse, all he had to do was sit tight: the right American would come along. There were a lot of us in Ipoh at the time. I don't know why. And, of course, no American can resist fixing a horse race. We're fascinated by these things. In Asia, Xannie said, things are more ordinary. He once had a ticket for a horse winning a race in Malaysia, and when he went to cash it the clerk slammed the window shut, saying that although Xannie had the winning ticket, the horse wasn't supposed to win. Xannie had almost formed a partnership with an enlisted man from Mt. Sterling, Kentucky, but at the last moment he backed out, since the enlisted man didn't look like he had the money for a trip to America. Xannie waited for Harlow to put his head in the door.

Xannie had been certain, too, that no American in the world would let him use the pistol on himself. He had been waiting for the moment when an American would stop him. Xannie had banked on it. If you figured this out, he became your friend.

David Bezmozgis

on

Leonard Michaels's *City Boy*

F or God's sake, Morris, don't be banal," snaps the shrewish Mrs.
Cohen at her husband moments before he makes the discovery
that sets Leonard Michaels's "City Boy" into its headlong, synco-
pated motion. In the context of the story, the line has a specific
meaning, but it also served as a guiding principle for Leonard Michaels over the course of his career. "City Boy," one of the first stories he published, already involves the subject that most fascinated
him, and that he once described as "the way men and women seem
unable to live with and without each other." But because this subject is so common, so familiar, to write about it one perpetually risks
falling into the trap of the banal. After all, what hasn't been written
about erotic love? What transpires between lovers that doesn't con-
form to some archetype? "City Boy" is no exception. At root, it's a
stock tale about young lovers who get caught in flagrante by the
girl's father. In Michaels's account, the story is essentially comic,
but convincingly strange and sinister too.

With that in mind, what is the form of "City Boy?" How does
Michaels create a story that manages to be both comic and sinister—

like a smile with sharp teeth? He does so by moving the story from realism to absurdity and back again. "City Boy" begins in a realistic mode with Veronica's line: "Phillip, this is crazy." The lines that follow are essentially objective. "I bit her neck. She kissed my ear. It was nearly three in the morning. We had just returned. The apartment was dark and quiet." Soon, however, the sentences grow more subjective. As Phillip and Veronica have sex in the dark room, Phillip observes: "The chairs smirked and spit between their feet. The chandelier clicked giddy teeth. The clock ticked as if to split its glass." Once Phillip, now a naked fugitive, decides to walk on his hands, we undeniably depart from reality until Phillip reaches the street and drops to his feet. From here Michaels gradually brings the story back to its origins in something like objective reality. This movement from realism to absurdity and back gives the story a substantial and provocative power.

Leonard Michaels

✠

City Boy

P hillip," she said, "this is crazy."

I didn't agree or disagree. She wanted some answer. I bit her
neck. She kissed my ear. It was almost three in the morning. We had
just returned. The apartment was dark and quiet. We were on the
living room floor and she repeated, "Phillip, this is crazy." Her
crinoline broke under us like cinders. Furniture loomed all around
in the darkness—settee, chairs, a table with a lamp. Pictures were
cloudy blotches drifting above. But no lights, no things to look at,
no eyes in her head. She was underneath me and warm. The rug
was warm, soft as mud, deep. Her crinoline cracked like sticks. Our
naked bellies clapped together. Air fired out like farts. I took it as
applause. The chairs smirked and spit between their feet. The
chandelier clicked giddy teeth. The clock ticked as if to split its
glass. "Phillip," she said, "this is crazy." A little voice against the
grain and power. Not enough to stop me. Yet once I had been a man
of feeling. We went to concerts, walked in the park, trembled in the
maid's room. Now in the foyer, a flash of hair and claws. We stum-

bled to the living room floor. She said, "Phillip, this is crazy." Then silence, except in my head where a conference table was set up, ashtrays scattered about. Priests, ministers and rabbis were rushing to take seats. I wanted their opinion, but came. They vanished. A voice lingered, faintly crying, "You could mess up the rug, Phillip, break something . . ." Her fingers pinched my back like ants. I expected a remark to kill good death. She said nothing. The breath in her nostrils whipped mucus. It cracked in my ear like flags. I dreamed we were in her mother's Cadillac, trailing flags. I heard her voice before I heard the words. "Phillip, this is crazy. My parents are in the next room." Her cheek jerked against mine, her breasts were knuckles in my nipples. I burned. Good death was killed. I burned with hate. A rabbi shook his finger, "You shouldn't hate." I lifted on my elbows, sneering in pain. She wrenched her hips, tightened muscles in belly and neck. She said, "Move." It was imperative to move. Her parents were thirty feet away. Down the hall between Utrillos and Vlamincks, through the door, flick the light and I'd see them. Maybe like us, Mr. Cohen adrift on the missus. Hair sifted down my cheek. "Let's go to the maid's room," she whispered. I was reassured. She tried to move. I kissed her mouth. Her crinoline smashed like sugar. Pig that I was, I couldn't move. The clock ticked hysterically. Ticks piled up like insects. Muscled lapsed in her thighs. Her fingers scratched on my neck as if looking for buttons. She slept. I sprawled like a bludgeoned pig, eyes open, loose lips. I flopped into sleep, in her, in the rug, in our scattered clothes.

Dawn hadn't showed between the slats and the blinds. Her breathing sissed in my ear. I wanted to sleep more, but needed a cigarette. I thought of the cold avenue, the lonely subway ride. Where could I buy a newspaper, a cup of coffee? This was crazy, dangerous, a waste of time. The maid might arrive, her parents might wake.

I had to get started. My hand pushed along the rug to find my shirt, touched a brass lion's paw, then a lamp cord.

A naked heel bumped wood.

She woke, her nails in my neck. "Phillip, did you hear?" I whispered, "Quiet." My eyes rolled like Milton's. Furniture loomed, whirled. "Dear God," I prayed, "save my ass." The steps ceased. Neither of us breathed. The clock ticked. She trembled. I pressed my cheek against her mouth to keep her from talking. We heard pajamas rustle, phlegmy breathing, fingernails scratching hair. A voice, "Veronica, don't you think it's time you sent Phillip home?"

A murmur of assent started in her throat, swept to my cheek, fell back like a drowned child in a well. Mr. Cohen had spoken. He stood ten inches from our legs. Maybe less. It was impossible to tell. His fingernails grated through hair. His voice hung in the dark with the quintessential question. Mr. Cohen, scratching his crotch, stood now as never in the light. Considerable. No tool of his wife, whose energy in business kept him eating, sleeping, overlooking the park. Pinochle change in his pockets four nights a week. But were they his words? Or was he the oracle of Mrs. Cohen, lying sleepless, irritated, waiting for him to get me out? I didn't breathe. I didn't move. If he had come on his own he would leave without an answer. His eyes weren't adjusted to the dark. He couldn't see. We lay at his feet like worms. He scratched, made smacking noises with his mouth.

The question of authority is always with us. Who is responsible for the triggers pulled, buttons pressed, the gas, the fire? Doubt banged my brain. My heart lay in the fist of intellect, which squeezed out feeling like piss out of kidneys. Mrs. Cohen's voice demolished doubt, feeling, intellect. It ripped from the bedroom.

"For God's sake, Morris, don't be banal. Tell the schmuck to go home and keep his own parents awake all night, if he has any."

Veronica's tears slipped down my cheeks. Mr. Cohen sighed,

shuffled, made a strong voice. "Veronica, tell Phillip . . ." His foot came down on my ass. He drove me into his daughter. I drove her into his rug.

"I don't believe it," he said.

He walked like an antelope, lifting hoof from knee, but stepped down hard. Sensitive to the danger of movement, yet finally impulsive, flinging his pot at the earth in order to cross it. His foot brought me his weight and character, a hundred fifty-five pounds of stomping *schlemiel,* in a mode of apprehension so primal we must share it with bugs. Let armies stomp me to insensate pulp—I'll yell "Cohen" when he arrives.

Veronica squealed, had a contraction, fluttered, gagged a shriek, squeezed, and up like a frog out of the hand of a child I stood spreadlegged, bolt naked, great with eyes. Mr. Cohen's face was eyes in my eyes. A secret sharer. We faced each other like men accidentally met in hell. He retreated flapping, moaning, "I will not believe it one bit."

Veronica said, "Daddy?"

"Who else you no good bum?"

The rug raced. I smacked against blinds, glass broke and I whirled. Veronica said, "Phillip," and I went off in streaks, a sparrow in the room, here, there, early American, baroque and rococo. Veronica wailed, "Phillip." Mr. Cohen screamed, "I'll kill him." I stopped at the door, seized the knob. Mrs. Cohen yelled from the bedroom, "Morris, did something break? Answer me."

"I'll kill that bastid."

"Morris, if something broke you'll rot for a month."

"Mother, stop it," said Veronica. "Phillip, come back."

The door slammed. I was outside, naked as a wolf.

I needed poise. Without poise the street was impossible. Blood shot to my brain, thought blossomed. I'd walk on my hands. Beards were fashionable. I kicked up my feet, kicked the elevator button, faced the door and waited. I bent one elbow like a knee. The posture of a clothes model, easy, poised. Blood coiled down to my brain, weeds bourgeoned. I had made a bad impression. There was no other way to see it. But all right. We needed a new beginning. Everyone does. Yet how few of us know when it arrives. Mr. Cohen had never spoken to me before; this was a breakthrough. There had been a false element in our relationship. It was wiped out. I wouldn't kid myself with the idea that he had nothing to say. I'd had enough of his silent treatment. It was worth being naked to see how mercilessly I could think. I had his number. Mrs. Cohen's, too. I was learning every second. I was a city boy. No innocent shitkicker from Jersey. I was the A train, the Fifth Avenue bus. I could be a cop. My name was Phillip, my style New York City. I poked the elevator button with my toe. It rang in the lobby, waking Ludwig. He'd come for me, rotten with sleep. Not the first time. He always took me down, walked me through the lobby and let me out on the avenue. Wires began tugging him up the shaft. I moved back, conscious of my genitals hanging upside down. Absurd consideration; we were both men one way or another. There were social distinctions enforced by his uniform, but they would vanish at the sight of me. "The unaccommodated thing itself." "Off ye lendings!" The greatest play is about a naked man. A picture of Lear came to me, naked, racing through the wheat. I could be cool. I thought of Ludwig's uniform, hat, whip-cord collar. It signified his authority. Perhaps he would be annoyed, in his authority, at the sight of me naked. Few people woke him at such hours. Worse, I never tipped him. Could I have been so indifferent month after month? In a crisis you discover everything. Then it's too late. Know yourself, indeed. You need a crisis every day. I refused to think about it. I sent my mind after objects. It returned with the chairs, settee, table and chandelier. Where were my clothes?

I sent it along the rug. It found buttons, eagles stamped in brass. I recognized them as the buttons on Ludwig's coat. Eagles, beaks like knives, shrieking for tips. Fuck'm, I thought. Who's Ludwig? A big coat, a whistle, white gloves and a General MacArthur hat. I could understand him completely. He couldn't begin to understand me. A naked man is mysterious. But aside from that, what did he know? I dated Veronica Cohen and went home late. Did he know I was out of work? That I lived in a slum downtown? Of course not.

Possibly under his hat was a filthy mind. He imagined Veronica and I might be having sexual intercourse. He resented it. Not that he hoped for the privilege himself, in his coat and soldier hat, but he had a proprietary interest in the building and its residents. I came from another world. *The* other world against which Ludwig defended the residents. Wasn't I like a burglar sneaking out late, making him my accomplice? I undermined his authority, his dedication. He despised me. It was obvious. But no one thinks such thoughts. It made me laugh to think them. My genitals jumped. The elevator door slid open. He didn't say a word. I padded in like a seal. The door slid shut. Instantly, I was ashamed of myself, thinking as I had about him. I had no right. A better man than I. His profile was an etching by Dürer. Good peasant stock. How had he fallen to such work? Existence precedes essence. At the controls, silent, enduring, he gave me strength for the street. Perhaps the sun would be up, birds in the air. The door slid open. Ludwig walked ahead of me through the lobby. He needed new heels. The door of the lobby was half a ton of glass, encased in iron vines and leaves. Not too much for Ludwig. He turned, looked down into my eyes. I watched his lips move.

"I vun say sumding. Yur bisniss vot you do. Bud vy you mek her miserable? Nod led her slip. She has beks unter her eyes."

Ludwig had feelings. They spoke to mine. Beneath the uniform, a man. Essence precedes existence. Even rotten with sleep, thick, dry bags under his eyes, he saw, he sympathized. The discretion demanded by his job forbade anything tangible, a sweater, a hat. "Ludwig," I whispered, "you're all right." It didn't matter if he heard me. He knew I said something. He knew it was something nice. He grinned, tugged the door open with both hands. I slapped out onto the avenue. I saw no one, dropped to my feet and glanced back through the door. Perhaps for the last time. I lingered, indulged a little melancholy. Ludwig walked to a couch in the rear of the lobby. He took off his coat, rolled it into a pillow and lay down. I had never stayed to see him do that before, but always rushed off to the subway. As if I were indifferent to the life of the building. Indeed, like a burglar. I seized the valuables and fled to the subway. I stayed another moment. Watching good Ludwig, so I could hate myself. He assumed the modest, saintly posture of sleep. One leg here, the other there. His good head on his coat. A big arm across his stomach, the hand between his hips. He made a fist and punched up and down.

I went down the avenue, staying close to the buildings. Later I would work up a philosophy. Now I wanted to sleep, forget. I hadn't the energy for moral complexities: Ludwig cross-eyed, thumping his pelvis in such a nice lobby. Mirrors, glazed pots, rubber plants ten feet high. As if he were generating all of it. As if it were part of his job. I hurried. The buildings were on my left, the park on my right. There were doormen in the buildings; God knows what was in the park. No cars were moving. No people in sight. Streetlights glowed in a receding sweep down to Fifty-ninth Street and beyond. A wind pressed my face like Mr. Cohen's breath. Such hatred. Imponderable under any circumstances, a father cursing his daughter. Why? A fright in the dark? Freud said things about fathers and daughters. It was too obvious, too hideous. I shuddered and went more quickly. I began to run. In a few minutes I was at the spit-mottled steps of the subway. I had hoped for vomit. Spit is no challenge for bare feet. Still, I wouldn't complain. It was sufficiently disgusting to make me live in spirit. I went down the steps flatfooted, stamping, elevated by each declension. I was a city boy, no mincing creep from the sticks.

A Negro man sat in the change booth. He wore glasses, a white shirt, black knit tie and a silver tie clip. I saw a mole on his right cheek. His hair had spots of grey, as if strewn with ashes. He was reading a newspaper. He didn't hear me approach, didn't see my eyes take him in, figure him out. Shirt, glasses, tie—I knew how to address him. I coughed. He looked up.

"Sir, I don't have any money. Please let me through the turnstile. I come this way every week and will certainly pay you the next time."

He merely looked at me. Then his eyes flashed like fangs. Instincitvely, I guessed what he felt. He didn't owe favors to a white man. He didn't have to bring his allegiance to the transit authority into question for my sake.

"Hey, man, you naked?"

"Yes."

"Step back a little."

I stepped back.

"You're naked."

I nodded.

"Get your naked ass the hell out of here."

"Sir," I said, "I know these are difficult times, but can't we be reasonable? I know that . . ."

"Scat, mother, go home."

I crouched as if to dash through the turnstile. He crouched, too. It proved he would come after me. I shrugged, turned back toward the steps. The city was infinite. There were many other subways.

But why had he become so angry? Did he think I was a bigot? Maybe I was running around naked to get him upset. His anger was incomprehensible otherwise. It made me feel like a bigot. First a burglar, then a bigot. I needed a cigarette. I could hardly breathe. Air was too good for me. At the top of the steps, staring down, stood Veronica. She had my clothes.

"Poor, poor," she said.

I said nothing. I snatched my underpants and put them on. She had my cigarettes ready. I tried to light one, but the match failed. I threw down the cigarette and matchbook. She retrieved them as I dressed. She lit the cigarette for me and held my elbow to help me keep my balance. I finished dressing, took the cigarette. We walked back toward her building. The words "thank you" sat in my brain like driven spikes. She nibbled her lip.

"How are things at home?" My voice was casual and morose, as if no answer could matter.

"All right," she said, her voice the same as mine. She took her tone from me. I liked that sometimes, sometimes not. Now I didn't like it. I discovered I was angry. Until she said that I had no idea I was angry. I flicked the cigarette into the gutter and suddenly I knew why. I didn't love her. The cigarette sizzled in the gutter. Like truth. I didn't love her. Black hair, green eyes, I didn't love her. Slender legs. I didn't. Last night I had looked at her and said to myself, "I hate communism." Now I wanted to step on her head. Nothing less than that would do. If it was a perverted thought, then it was a perverted thought. I wasn't afraid to admit it to myself.

"All right? Really? Is that true?"

Blah, blah, blah. Who asked those questions? A zombie: not Phillip of the foyer and rug. He died in flight. I was sorry, sincerely sorry, but with clothes on my back I knew certain feelings would not survive humiliation. It was so clear it was thrilling. Perhaps she felt it, too. In any case she would have to accept it. The nature of the times. We are historical creatures. Veronica and I were finished. Before we reached her door I would say deadly words. They'd come in a natural way, kill her a little. Veronica, let me step on your head or we're through. Maybe we're through, anyway. It would deepen her looks, give philosophy to what was only charming in her face. The dawn was here. A new day. Cruel, but change is cruel. I could bear it. Love is infinite and one. Women are not. Neither are men. The human condition. Nearly unbearable.

"No, it's not true," she said.

"What's not?"

"Things aren't all right at home."

I nodded intelligently, sighed. "Of course not. Tell me the truth, please, I don't want to hear anything else."

"Daddy had a heart attack."

"Oh God," I yelled. "Oh God, no."

I seized her hand, dropped it. She let it fall. I seized it again. No use. I let it fall. She let it drift between us. We stared at one another. She said, "What were you going to say? I can tell you were going to say something."

I stared, said nothing.

"Don't feel guilty, Phillip. Let's just go back to the apartment and have some coffee."

"What can I say?"

"Don't say anything. He's in the hospital and my mother is there. Let's just go upstairs and not say anything."

"Not say anything. Like moral imbeciles go slurp coffee and not say anything? What are we, nihilists or something? Assassins? Monsters?"

"Phillip, there's no one in the apartment. I'll make us coffee and eggs . . ."

"How about a roast beef? Got a roast beef in the freezer?"

"Phillip, he's *my* father."

We were at the door. I rattled. I was in a trance. This was life. Death!

"Indeed, your father. I'll accept that. I can do no less."

"Phillip, shut up. Ludwig."

The door opened. I nodded to Ludwig. What did he know about life and death? Give him a uniform and a quiet lobby—that's life and death. In the elevator he took the controls. "Always got a hand on the controls, eh Ludwig?"

Veronica smiled in a feeble, grateful way. She liked to see me get along with the help. Ludwig said, "Dots right."

"Ludwig has been our doorman for years, Phillip. Ever since I was a little girl."

"Wow," I said.

"Dots right."

The door slid open. Veronica said, "Thank you, Ludwig." I said, "Thank you, Ludwig."

"Vulcum."

"Vulcum? You mean 'welcome'? Hey, Ludwig, how long you been in this country?"

Veronica was driving her key into the door.

"How come you never learned to talk American, baby?"

"Phillip, come here."

"I'm saying something to Ludwig."

"Come here right now."

"I have to go, Ludwig."

"Vulcum."

She went directly to the bathroom. I waited in the hallway between the Vlamincks and Utrillos. The Utrillos were pale and flat.

The Vlamincks were thick, twisted and red. Raw meat on one wall, dry stone on the other. Mrs. Cohen had an eye for contrasts. I heard Veronica sob. She ran water in the sink, sobbed, sat down, peed. She saw me looking and kicked the door shut.

"At a time like this . . ."

"I don't like you looking."

"Then why did you leave the door open? You obviously don't know your own mind."

"Go away, Phillip. Wait in the living room."

"Just tell me why you left the door open."

"Phillip, you're going to drive me nuts. Go away. I can't do a damn thing if I know you're standing there."

The living room made me feel better. The settee, the chandelier full of teeth and the rug were company. Mr. Cohen was everywhere, a simple, diffuse presence. He jingled change in his pocket, looked out the window and was happy he could see the park. He took a little antelope step and tears came into my eyes. I sat among his mourners. A rabbi droned platitudes: Mr. Cohen was generous, kind, beloved by his wife and daughter. "How much did he weigh?" I shouted. The phone rang.

Veronica came running down the hall. I went and stood at her side when she picked up the phone. I stood dumb, stiff as a hatrack. She was whimpering, "Yes, yes . . ." I nodded my head yes, yes, thinking it was better than no, no. She put the phone down.

"It was my mother. Daddy's all right. Mother is staying with him in his room at the hospital and they'll come home together tomorrow."

Her eyes looked at mine. At them as if they were as flat and opaque as hers. I said in a slow, stupid voice, "You're allowed to do that? Stay overnight in a hospital with a patient? Sleep in his room?"

She continued looking at my eyes. I shrugged, looked down. She took my shirt front in a fist like a bite. She whispered. I said, "What?" She whispered again, "Fuck me." The clock ticked like crickets. The Vlamincks spilled blood. We sank into the rug as if it were quicksand.

Lydia Davis

on

Jane Bowles's *Emmy Moore's Journal*

Many of Jane Bowles's typical superb narrative characteristics are evident in just the first two pages of this small story: the clear and forceful narrating voice; the odd female protagonist; the humor arising from this eccentric protagonist's worldview; her obviously tenuous hold on "reality"; the inevitable distinct and funny secondary characters (here, the "society salesman" whom the narrator has "accosted" in the Blue Bonnet Room); the pathos of the main character's valiance, disorientation, and ultimate defeat.

A closer look, tracing the progress of the story over just these two pages, sentence by sentence, shows the following shifts: The story opens without prologue or preamble, with a clear and plain declaration in simple, forceful language, by a strong first-person voice: "On certain days I forget why I'm here." Already, we experience this narrator as emphatic but not quite in this life or not quite competent. In the second sentence, we sense a certain insecurity: "Today once again I wrote my husband all my reasons for coming." The fact of her introducing him as "my husband," instead of by his name, suggests an emphasis on his role in relation to her rather than on his unique individual identity in a larger public world. In the third sentence, her reliance on him ("He encouraged me to come") as well as her insecurity ("each time I was in doubt") is emphasized further. She hesitates, he urges. In these first three sentences, we haven't yet seen any sign of the humor that is almost omnipresent in Bowles's writing. In the fourth sentence, it appears: first, along with a reiteration of her husband's authority, there is the oddity of the faux-clinical phrase "state of vagueness": "He said that the worst danger for me was a state of vagueness . . ." Then comes the name of the hotel, so prosaic, so deliberately flat or unromantic (for a hotel): ". . . so I wrote telling him why I had come to the Hotel Henry." (Compare her naming of Camp Cataract, in her short story of the same name.) Still in the same sentence, there is then a third moment of humor: "—my eighth letter on this subject—"

But with that statement, something else has crept in. The narrator is declaring that she is writing to her husband for no less than the eighth time about why she has come to the Hotel Henry. Since this is unarguably many more times than would seem necessary to anyone else, it suggests that the narrator is someone obsessed, or highly anxious, perhaps neurotic, perhaps even seriously disturbed. The fourth sentence is not yet over, though, and now the tone changes: "but with each new letter I strengthen my position." With this change in tone comes another moment of humor, arising from the disproportion between the language used by the narrator, which might be that of diplomacy or international relations—"strengthen my position"—and the subject: why she has come to the Hotel Henry. The new tone is one of sudden self-confidence.

Now the long paragraph continues in the same confident tone, which evolves, even, to sound a note of defiance: "Let there be no mistake. My journal is intended for publication." And develops, further, into the heroic, now colored by delusions of grandeur: "I want to publish for glory, but also in order to aid other women"—the choice of the lofty "aid" over the more common "help" enhancing, with a single word, the suggestion that the protagonist has unrealistically high ambitions. (Compare, in "Camp Cataract," this wonderful bit of dialogue: "'Not a night fit for man or beast,' [Harriet] shouted across to Sadie, using a voice that she thought sounded hearty and yet fashionable at the same time.")

The paragraph then relaxes a bit, rambling on with some disjointed information about her husband, his knowledge of mushrooms, herself, her physical attributes, her Anglo stock ("Born in Boston"), and some incoherent generalizations about "the women of my country." Eventually the narrator trails off altogether, lapsing into uncertain, repetitive speculations about Turkish women and their veils.

Typically, given the skewed hierarchies of Bowles's characters, the event with the best possibilities for some drama is tossed away within a parenthesis at the end of the second paragraph: "(written yesterday, the morrow of my drunken evening in the Blue Bonnet Room when I accosted the society salesman.)" The subject of drink will reappear in a deadpan, touchingly simple statement later in the story: "When I'm not drunk I like to have a cup of cocoa before going to sleep. My husband likes it too." As for the unfamiliar term "society salesman," it will be defined through the unfolding of the story—although the incident will not be fully narrated—and the man himself, an exceptionally wealthy department-store clerk, will soon be described with Bowles's typical vivid precision and ear for the percussive possibilities of English as "a man with a lean red face and reddish hair selling materials by the bolt."

Jane Bowles's odd, half-unworldly, off-kilter heroines are of course versions of aspects of herself, in her troubled course through an often flamboyant or exotic bohemian life to her end in a clinic in

Spain, where, weakened by alcoholism and a previous stroke, she died in May 1973, at the age of fifty-six, soon after, in fact, writing "Emmy Moore's Journal." It may be too easy to say with hindsight, but the bleak return to the bottle at the end of the story—really, the story's bleakness throughout—seems to announce Bowles's imminent capitulation in her decades-long struggle with the challenges of her life, which included many episodes of manic-depressive psychosis, and of her writing, which was hard won from regularly recurring severe writer's block. Nearly fifty years ago, in 1967, John Ashbery called her "one of the finest modern writers of fiction in any language." Although she is still considered one of the best by many contemporary writers and readers, she remains stubbornly underrecognized.

Jane Bowles

⌖

Emmy Moore's Journal

On certain days I forget why I'm here. Today once again I wrote my husband all my reasons for coming. He encouraged me to come each time I was in doubt. He said that the worst danger for me was a state of vagueness, so I wrote telling him why I had come to the Hotel Henry—my eighth letter on this subject—but with each new letter I strengthen my position. I am reproducing the letter here. Let there be no mistake. My journal is intended for publication. I want to publish for glory, but also in order to aid other women. This is the letter to my husband, Paul Moore, to whom I have been married sixteen years. (I am childless.) He is of North Irish descent, and a very serious lawyer. Also a solitary and lover of the country. He knows all mushrooms, bushes and trees, and he is interested in geology. But these interests do not exclude me. He is sympathetic towards me, and kindly. He wants very much for me to be happy, and worries because I am not. He knows everything about me, including how much I deplore being the feminine kind of woman that I am. In fact, I am unusually feminine for an American of Anglo stock. (Born in Boston.) I am almost a "Turkish" type. Not physically, at least not entirely, because though fat I have ruddy Scotch cheeks and my eyes are round and not slanted or almond-shaped. But sometimes I feel certain that I exude an atmosphere very similar to theirs (the Turkish women's) and then I despise myself. I find the women in my country so extraordinarily manly and independent, capable of leading regiments, or of fending for themselves on desert islands if necessary. (These are poor examples, but I am getting my point across.) For me it is an experience simply to have come here alone to the Hotel Henry and to eat my dinner and lunch by myself. If possible before I die, I should like to become a little more independent, and a little less Turkish than I am now. Before I go any further, I had better say immediately that I mean no offense to Turkish women. They are probably busy combating the very same Turkish quality in themselves that I am controlling in me. I understand, too (though this is irrelevant) that many Turkish women are beautiful, and I think that they have discarded their veils. Any other American woman would be sure of this. She would know one way or the other whether the veils had been discarded, whereas I am afraid to come out with a definite statement. I have a feeling that they really have got rid of their veils, but I won't swear to it. Also, if they have done so, I have no idea when they did. Was it many years ago or recently?

Here is my letter to Paul Moore, my husband, in which there is more about Turkish women. Since I am writing this journal with a view to publication, I do not want to ramble on as though I had all the space in the world. No publisher will attempt printing an *enormous* journal written by an unknown woman. It would be too much of a financial risk. Even I, with my ignorance of all matters pertaining to business, know this much. But they may print a small one.

My letter: (written yesterday, the morrow of my drunken eve-

ning in the Blue Bonnet Room when I accosted the society salesman.)

Dearest Paul:

*I cannot simply live out my experiment here at the Hotel Henry
without trying to justify or at least explain in letters my reasons for
being here, and with fair regularity. You encouraged me to write whenever I felt I needed to clarify my thoughts. But you did tell me that I
must not feel the need to* justify *my actions. However, I* do *feel the
need to justify my actions, and I am certain that until the prayed-for
metamorphosis has occurred I shall go on feeling just this need. Oh,
how well I know that you would interrupt me at this point and warn
me against expecting too much. So I shall say in lieu of metamorphosis, the prayed-for* improvement. *But until then I must justify myself
every day. Perhaps you will get a letter every day. On some days the
need to write lodges itself in my throat like a cry that must be uttered.*

*As for the Turkish problem, I am coming to it. You must under-
stand that I am an admirer of Western civilization; that is, of the
women who are members of this group. I feel myself that I fall short
of being a member, that by some curious accident I was not born in
Turkey but should have been. Because of my usual imprecision I cannot even tell how many countries belong to what we call Western
Civilization, but I believe Turkey is the place where East meets West,
isn't it? I can just about imagine the women there, from what I have
heard about the country and the pictures I have seen of it. As for being troubled or obsessed by real Oriental women, I am not. (I refer to
the Chinese, Japanese, Hindus, and so on.) Naturally I am less concerned with the Far Eastern women because there is no danger of
my being like them. (The Turkish women are just near enough.) The
Far Eastern ones are so very far away, at the opposite end of the
earth, that they could easily be just as independent and masculine as*

the women of the Western world. The ones living in-between the two masculine areas would be soft and feminine. Naturally I don't believe this for a minute, but still, the real Orientals are so far away and such a mystery to me that it might as well be true. Whatever they were, it couldn't affect me. They look too different from the way I look. Whereas Turkish women don't. (Their figures are exactly like mine, alas!)

Now I shall come to the point. I know full well that you will consider the above discourse a kind of joke. Or if you don't, you will be irritated with me for making statements of such a sweeping and inaccurate nature. For surely you will consider the picture of the world that I present as inaccurate. I myself know that this concept of the women (all three sets—Western, Middle and Eastern) is a puerile one. It could even be called downright idiotic. Yet I assure you that I see things this way, if I relax even a little and look through my own eyes into what is really inside my head. (Though because of my talent for mimicry I am able to simulate looking through the eyes of an educated person when I wish to.) Since I am giving you such a frank picture of myself, I may as well go the whole hog and admit to you that my secret picture of the world is grossly inaccurate. I have completely forgotten to include in it any of the Latin countries. (France, Italy, Spain.) For instance, I have jumped from the Anglo world to the semi-Oriental as if there were no countries in between at all. I know that these exist. (I have even lived in two of them.) But they do not fit into my scheme. I just don't think about the Latins very much, and this is less understandable than my not thinking about the Chinese or Javanese or Japanese women. You can see why without my having to explain it to you. I do know that the French women are more interested in sports than they used to be, and for all I know they may be indistinguishable from Anglo women by now. I haven't been to France recently so I can't be sure. But in any case the women of those countries don't enter into my picture of the world. Or shall I say that the fact of having forgotten utterly to consider them has not altered the way I visualize the division of the world's women? Incredible though it may seem to you, it hasn't altered anything. (My having forgotten all Latin countries, South America included.) I want you to know the whole truth about me. But don't imagine that I wouldn't be capable of concealing my ignorance from you if I wanted to. I am so wily and feminine that I could live by your side for a lifetime and deceive you afresh each day. But I will have no truck with feminine wiles. I know how they can absorb the hours of the day. Many women are delighted to sit around spinning their webs. It is an absorbing occupation and the women feel they are getting somewhere. And so they are, but only for as long as the man is there to be deceived. And a wily woman alone is a pitiful sight to behold. Naturally.

I shall try to be honest with you so that I can live with you and yet won't be pitiful. Even if tossing my feminine tricks out the window means being left no better than an illiterate backwoodsman, or the bottom fish scraping along the ocean bed, I prefer to have it this way. Now I am too tired to write more. Though I don't feel that I have clarified enough or justified enough

I shall write you soon about the effect the war has had upon me. I have spoken to you about it, but you have never seemed to take it very seriously. Perhaps seeing in black and white what I feel will affect your opinion of me. Perhaps you will leave me. I accept the challenge. My Hotel Henry experience includes this risk. I got drunk two nights ago. It's hard to believe that I am forty-seven, isn't it?

My love,

Emmy

Now that I have copied this letter into my journal (I had forgotten to make a carbon), I shall take my walk. My scheme included a

few weeks of solitude at the Hotel Henry before attempting anything. I did not even intend to write in my journal as soon as I started
to, but simply to sit about collecting my thoughts, waiting for the
knots of habit to undo themselves. But after only a week here—two
nights ago—I felt amazingly alone and disconnected from my past
life, so I began my journal.

My first interesting contact was the salesman in the Blue Bonnet
Room. I had heard about this eccentric through my in-laws, the
Moores, before I ever came up here. My husband's cousin Laurence Moore told me about him when he heard I was coming. He
said: "Take a walk through Grey and Bottle's Department Store,
and you'll see a man with a lean red face and reddish hair selling
materials by the bolt. That man has an income and is related to Hewitt
Molain. He doesn't need to work. He was in my fraternity. Then he
disappeared. The next I heard of him he was working there at Grey
and Bottle's. I stopped by and said hello to him. For a nut he seemed
like a very decent chap. You might even have a drink with him. I think
he's quite up to general conversation."

I did not mention Laurence Moore to the society salesman because I thought it might irritate him. I lied and pretended to have
been here for months, when actually this is still only my second
week at the Hotel Henry. I want everyone to think I have been here
a long time. Surely it is not to impress them. Is there anything impressive about a lengthy stay at the Hotel Henry? Any sane person
would be alarmed that I should even ask such a question. I ask it
because deep in my heart I *do* think a lengthy stay at the Hotel Henry
is impressive. Very easy to see that I would, and even sane of me to
think it impressive, but not sane of me to expect anyone else to think
so, particularly a stranger. Perhaps I simply like to hear myself telling it. I hope so. I shall write some more tomorrow, but now I must
go out. I am going to buy a supply of cocoa. When I'm not drunk I

like to have a cup of cocoa before going to sleep. My husband likes it too.

* * *

She could not stand the overheated room a second longer. With some difficulty she raised the window, and the cold wind blew in. Some loose sheets of paper went skimming off the top of the desk and flattened themselves against the bookcase. She shut the window and they fell to the floor. The cold air had changed her mood. She looked down at the sheets of paper. They were part of the letter she had just copied. She picked them up: *"I don't feel that I have clarified enough or justified enough,"* she read. She closed her eyes and shook her head. She had been so happy copying this letter into her journal, but now her heart was faint as she scanned its scattered pages. "I have said nothing," she muttered to herself in alarm. "I have said nothing at all. I have not clarified my reasons for being at the Hotel Henry. I have not justified myself."

Automatically she looked around the room. A bottle of whiskey stood on the floor beside one of the legs of the bureau. She stepped forward, picked it up by the neck, and settled with it into her favorite wicker chair.

Issue 56, 1973

Dave Eggers

on

James Salter's *Bangkok*

B angkok" is a nine-page master class in dialogue from James
Salter, whose command of the form is well established and rarely
matched. There are many lessons in this very short story; here are
just a few of them:

—Some of the best dialogue occurs when at least one of the
two people talking doesn't want to be there. In this story, Hollis
wants nothing to do with an ex-lover, Carol, who visits his book-
shop unexpectedly. He tells her to leave, repeatedly, but before
she does, we get an explosive conversation that's made all the
more tense because Hollis is—or seems to be—an unwilling par-
ticipant.

—Carol says a handful of nasty, sexually charged things to Hollis,
and though Hollis gets his dander up, he doesn't end the conversation. What Carol says about Hollis's daughter and wife should be
more than enough to provoke him to get up, usher Carol out of the
shop, and lock the door behind her. But he doesn't. This tells us a

lot about their history, which must have been perverse, twisted, and full of similar provocations. He's inured to her games, and maybe a little bit intrigued, too.

—Deep into the story, Carol calls Hollis by another name, Chris. It's slipped into a soliloquy, and we barely notice it, but it matters. Until then, Hollis is the name we know him by, and Hollis is the name of a man who would have had relations with a tough and unsentimental predator like Carol. So for most of the story we're in a universe bordering on noir. The two characters are well traveled, have lived romantic lives—in the midcentury ideal of romanticism, at least, lives of travel and drinking and porous sexual boundaries. But then there is this mention of the name Chris, a name that implies fragility and decency—it's common, almost pedestrian. If we start the story thinking it's about Chris and Carol, it alters our whole perception of their dynamic. But start the story with Hollis, and we picture a strong and confident guy not to be trifled with—a match for Carol (another strong name). But then, at the moments when Carol shows some vulnerability, when she wants to know whether he ever loved her, she uses this name, Chris. This is no coincidence.

—We don't know where the story takes place, and we assume, for most of the story, that it's Bangkok. That Hollis operates some kind of expat antiquarian shop. But when the word "Bangkok" finally appears, we know why Salter's named the story thus. He doesn't make a big show of it, but Bangkok represents all that Hollis has given up in favor of his wife and daughter, a life of routine and (to Carol's mind) pedestrian pleasures. And here we find out that Hollis, though sure of his choices, is not without some lingering, or at least occasional, doubts. Thus Bangkok is like the gun at the beginning of the movie. You know it'll go off, but you don't know when.

—Finally, and maybe most importantly, Salter doesn't tell us much about Hollis's state of mind throughout the conversation. Here and there he indicates how he feels about something Carol's said. We know he wants her gone, but then again, not so much. We get his state of mind only through what he says himself, and we assume Carol's jabs and taunts are having little to no effect on him. But then, when she walks out, Salter lets us know that Hollis has been putting on an act. Suddenly the "room was swimming" and he realizes he should have kicked her out, that "He should not have listened." Her words will be with him for a long time. She has great power over him, and she's put into question the life he's chosen. This method, of having the reader hold their breath just as Hollis does, waiting till she leaves to exhale, gives the story magnificent power. At the end, we're spent, and are reeling just as Hollis is reeling.

James Salter

⌗

Bangkok

Hollis was in the back at a table piled with books and a space among them where he was writing when Carol came in.

Hello, she said.

Well, look who's here, he said coolly. Hello.

She was wearing a gray jersey sweater and a narrow skirt—as always, dressed well.

Didn't you get my message? she asked.

Yes.

You didn't call back.

No.

Weren't you going to?

Of course not, he said.

He looked wider than the last time and his hair, halfway to the shoulder, needed to be cut.

I went by your apartment but you'd gone. I talked to Pam, that's her name, isn't it? Pam.

Yes.

We talked. Not that long. She didn't seem interested in talking. Is she shy?

No, she's not shy.

I asked her a question. Want to know what it was?

Not especially, he said.

He leaned back. His jacket was draped over the back of the chair and his sleeves rolled partway up. She noticed a round wristwatch with a brown leather strap.

I asked her if you still like to have your cock sucked.

Get out of here, he ordered. Go on, get out.

She didn't answer, Carol said.

He had a moment of fear, of guilt almost, about consequences. On the other hand, he didn't believe her.

So, do you? she said.

Leave, will you? Please, he said in a civilized tone. He made a dispersing motion with his hand. I mean it.

I'm not going to stay long, just a few minutes. I wanted to see you, that's all. Why didn't you call back?

She was tall with a long, elegant nose like a thoroughbred. What people look like isn't the same as what you remember. She had been coming out of a restaurant one time, down some steps long after lunch in a silk dress that clung around the hips and the wind pulled against her legs. The afternoons, he thought for a moment.

She sat down in the leather chair opposite and gave a slight, uncertain smile.

You have a nice place.

It had the makings of one, two rooms on the garden floor with a little grass and the backs of discreet houses behind, though there was just one window and the floorboards were worn. He sold fine books and manuscripts, letters for the most part, and had too big an inventory for a dealer his size. After ten years in retail clothing he had found his true life. The rooms had high ceilings, the bookcases were filled and against them, on the floor, a few framed photographs leaned.

Chris, she said, tell me something. Whatever happened to that picture of us taken at the lunch Diana Wald gave at her mother's house that day? Up there on that fake hill made from all the old cars? Do you still have that?

It must have gotten lost.

I'd really like to have it. It was a wonderful picture. Those were the days, she said. Do you remember the boathouse we had?

Of course.

I wonder if you remember it the way I remember it.

That would be hard to say. He had a low, persuasive voice. There was confidence in it, perhaps a little too much.

The pool table, do you remember that? And the bed by the windows.

He didn't answer. She picked up one of the books from the table and was looking through it; *e.e. cummings.* The Enormous Room, *dust jacket with some small chips at bottom, minor soil on title page, otherwise very good. First edition.* The price was marked in pencil on the corner of the flyleaf at the top. She turned the pages idly.

This has that part in it you like so much. What is it, again?

Jean Le Nègre.

That's it.

Still unrivaled, he said.

Makes me think of Alan Baron for some reason. Are you still in touch with him? Did he ever publish anything? Always telling me about Tantric yoga and how I should try it. He wanted to show it to me.

So, did he?

You're kidding.

She was leafing through the pages with her long thumbs.

They're always talking about Tantric yoga, she said, or telling you about their big dicks. Not you, though. So, how is Pam, incidentally? I couldn't really tell. Is she happy?

She's very happy.

That's nice. And you have a little girl now, how old is she again?

Her name is Chloe. She's six.

Oh, she's big. They know a lot at that age, don't they? They know and they don't know, she said. She closed the book and put it down. Their bodies are so pure. Does Chloe have a nice body?

You'd kill for it, he said casually.

A perfect little body. I can picture it. Do you give her baths? I bet you do. You're a model father, the father every little girl ought to have. How will you be when she's bigger, I wonder? When the boys start coming around.

There're not going to be a lot of boys coming around.

Oh, for God's sake. Of course there will. They'll be coming around just quivering. You know that. She'll have breasts and that first, soft pubic hair.

You know, Carol, you're disgusting.

You don't like to think of it, that's all. But she's going to be a woman, you know, a young woman. You remember how you felt about young women at that age. Well, it didn't all stop with you. It continues, and she'll be part of it, perfect body and all. How is Pam's, by the way?

How's yours?

Can't you tell?

I wasn't paying attention.

Do you still have sex? she asked unconcernedly.

There are times.

I don't. Rarely.

That's a little hard to believe.

It never measures up, that's the trouble. It's never what it should be or used to be. How old are you now? You look a little heavier. Do you exercise? Do you go to the steam room and look down at yourself?

I don't have the time.

Well, if you *had* more time. If you were free you'd be able to steam, shower, put on fresh clothes and, let's see, not too early to go down to, what, the Odeon and have a drink, see if anyone's there, any girls. You could have the bartender offer them a drink or simply talk to them yourself, ask if they were doing anything for dinner, if they had any plans. As easy as that. You always liked good teeth. You liked slim arms and, how to put it, great tits, not necessarily big—good-sized, that's all. And long legs. Do you still like to tie their hands? You used to like to, it's always exciting to find out if they'll let you do it or not. Tell me, Chris, did you love me?

Love you? He was leaning back in the chair. For the first time she had the impression he might have been drinking a little more than usual these days. Just the look of his face. I thought about you every minute of the day, he said. I loved everything you did. What I liked was that you were absolutely new and everything you said and did was. You were incomparable. With you I felt I had everything in life, everything anyone ever dreamed of. I adored you.

Like no other woman?

There was no one even close. I could have feasted on you forever. You were the intended.

And Pam? You didn't feast on her?

A little. Pam is something different.

In what way?

Pam doesn't take all that and offer it to someone else. I don't come back from a trip unexpectedly and find an unmade bed where you and some guy have been having a lovely time.

It wasn't that lovely.

That's too bad.

It was far from lovely.

So, why did you do it, then?

I don't know. I just had the foolish impulse to try something different. I didn't know that real happiness lies in having the same thing all the time.

She looked at her hands. He noticed again her long, flexible thumbs.

Isn't that right? she asked coolly.

Don't be nasty. Anyway, what do you know about true happiness?

Oh, I've had it.

Really?

Yes, she said. With you.

He looked at her. She did not return his look, nor was she smiling.

I'm going to Bangkok, she said, well, Hong Kong first. Have you ever stayed at the Peninsula Hotel?

I've never been to Hong Kong.

They say it's the greatest hotel anywhere, Berlin, Paris, Tokyo.

Well, I wouldn't know.

You've been to hotels. Remember Venice and that little hotel by the theater? The water in the street up to your knees?

I have a lot of work to do, Carol.

Oh, come on.

I have a business.

Then how much is this e.e. cummings? she said. I'll buy it and you can take a few minutes off.

It's already sold, he said.

Still has the price in it.

He shrugged a little.

Answer me about Venice, she said.

I remember the hotel. Now let's say good-bye.

I'm going to Bangkok with a friend.

He felt a phantom skip of the heart, however slight.

Good, he said.

Molly. You'd like her.

Molly.

We're traveling together. You know Daddy died.

I didn't know that.

Yes, a year ago. He died. So my worries are over. It's a nice feeling.

I suppose. I liked your father.

He'd been a man in the oil business, sociable, with certain freely admitted prejudices. He wore expensive suits and had been divorced twice but managed to avoid loneliness.

We're going to stay in Bangkok for a couple of months, perhaps come back through Europe, Carol said. Molly has a lot of style. She was a dancer. What was Pam, wasn't she a teacher or something? Well, you love Pam, you'd love Molly. You don't know her, but you would. She paused. Why don't you come with us? she said.

Hollis smiled slightly.

Shareable, is she? he said.

You wouldn't have to share.

It was meant to torment him, he knew.

Leave my family and business, just like that?

Gauguin did it.

I'm a little more responsible than that. Maybe it's something you would do.

If it were a choice, she said. Between life and . . .

What?

Life and a kind of pretend life. Don't act as if you didn't understand. There's nobody that understands better than you.

He felt an unwanted resentment. That the hunt be over, he thought. That it be ended. He heard her continue.

Travel. The Orient. The air of a different world. Bathe, drink, read . . .

You and me.

And Molly. As a gift.

Well, I don't know. What does she look like?

She's good-looking, what would you expect? I'll undress her for you.

I'll tell you something funny, Hollis said, something I heard. They say that everything in the universe, the planets, all the galaxies, everything—the entire universe—came originally from something the size of a grain of rice that exploded and formed what we have now, the sun, stars, earth, seas, everything there is, including what I felt for you. That morning on Hudson Street, sitting there in the sunlight, feet up, fulfilled and knowing it, talking, in love with one another—I knew I had everything life would ever offer.

You felt that?

Of course. Anyone would. I remember it all, but I can't feel it now. It's passed.

That's sad.

I have something more than that now. I have a wife I love and a kid.

It's such a cliché, isn't it? A wife I love.

It's just the truth.

And you're looking forward to the years together, the ecstasy.

It's not ecstasy.

You're right.

You can't have ecstasy daily.

No, but you can have something as good, she said. You can have the anticipation of it.

Good. Go ahead and have it. You and Molly.

I'll think of you, Chris, in the house we'll have on the river in Bangkok.

Oh, don't bother.

I'll think of you lying in bed at night, bored to death with it all.

Quit it, for God's sake. Leave it alone. Let me like you a little bit.

I don't want you to like me. In a half whisper she said, I want you to curse me.

Keep it up.

It's so sweet, she said. The little family, the lovely books. All right, then. You missed your chance. Bye, bye. Go back and give her a bath, your little girl. While you still can, anyway.

She looked at him a last time from the doorway. He could hear the sound of her heels as she went through the front room. He could hear them go past the display cases and towards the door where they seemed to hesitate, then the door closing.

The room was swimming, he could not hold on to his thoughts. The past, like a sudden tide, had swept back over him, not as it had been but as he could not help remembering it. The best thing was to resume work. He knew what her skin felt like, it was silky. He should not have listened.

On the soft, silent keys he began to write: *Jack Kerouac, typed letter signed ("Jack"), 1 page, to his girlfriend, the poet Lois Sorrells, single-spaced, signed in pencil, slight crease from folding.* It was not a pretend life.

Jeffrey Eugenides

on

Denis Johnson's *Car Crash While Hitchhiking*

A short story must be, by definition, short. That's the trouble with short stories. That's why they're so difficult to write. How do you keep a narrative brief and still have it function as a story? Compared to writing novels, writing short fiction is mainly a question of knowing what to leave out. What you leave in must imply everything that's missing.

If you'd like to learn how to do this, you'd be well advised to study Denis Johnson's blisteringly acute "Car Crash While Hitchhiking." In this story—and indeed, in all of the stories in Johnson's brilliant collection, *Jesus' Son*—Johnson found a way to leave out the maximum in terms of plot, setting, characterization, and authorial explanation while finding a voice that suggested all these things, a voice whose brokenness is the reason behind the narrative deprivation, and therefore a kind of explanation itself.

The first two paragraphs of the story divulge the entirety of its action: "A salesman who shared his liquor and steered while sleeping . . . A Cherokee filled with bourbon . . . A VW no more than a bubble of hashish fumes, captained by a college student . . .

And a family from Marshalltown who headonned and killed forever a man driving west out of Bethany, Missouri . . ." This appears to be a straightforward recounting of events except for that one word: *forever*. What "killed forever" means isn't entirely clear. It's a strange thing to say, as if it were possible for a person to be killed temporarily. Soon, other unusual statements appear. "The travelling salesman had fed me pills that made the linings of my veins feel scraped out. My jaw ached. I knew every raindrop by its name. I sensed everything before it happened. I knew a certain Oldsmobile would stop for me even before it slowed, and by the sweet voices of the family inside of it I knew we'd have an accident in the storm."

And then comes the kicker: "I didn't care."

We are, at this point, about twenty lines into the story, and the ground has fallen away beneath us. Who is this guy (identified, elsewhere in the collection, only as "Fuckhead")? What has happened to get him in this altered state? Why is he capable of making vatic utterances about the weather and of registering the sweetness of human voices while not caring about their impending demise? No explanation is given. The story rolls on, rubber-necking its way through the car crash, the individual sentences veering from poetic reverie ("Under Midwestern clouds like great gray brains") to detached commentary ("The interstate through western Missouri was, in that era, nothing more than a two-way road.") The description of the accident is frightening in the extreme, and leads to a scene in a hospital, when the wife of the injured man learns of his death: "The doctor took her into a room with a desk at the end of the hall, and from under the closed door a slab of brilliance radiated as if, by some stupendous process, diamonds were being incinerated there. What a pair of lungs! She shrieked as I imagined an eagle would shriek. It felt wonderful to be alive to hear it! I've gone looking for that feeling everywhere."

It's impossible for the reader to know how to interpret this. Customary narrative procedure has disappeared and you realize that you've entered, or better, been sucked into, Fuckhead's world. By removing any rational linkage from the story, by refusing to provide any form of accepted behavior on the part of the narrator, Johnson brings the reader to a place where these things are no longer operative, as they are, after all, in an addict's twisted mind. The story hasn't told you about an experience so much as made that experience your own. Which is as good a definition of fiction writing as I can think of.

Up to this point, however, as chilling as "Car Crash While Hitchhiking" is, it still isn't a story. It doesn't become a story until the last paragraph, where Johnson makes an amazing move. Mirroring the chronological liberties of the opening paragraph, he leaps forward: "Some years later, one time when I was admitted to the Detox at Seattle General Hospital, I took the same tack." Fuckhead goes on to describe the voices that are speaking to him in the room, and the lush hallucinations that appear before his eyes, as a "beautiful nurse" gives him an injection.

By the end of the story, then, we glimpse the narrator's eventual descent into drug-fueled insanity, and we get a clue to the reason he's been able to write about these events with such clarity. The story is a description of "the pity of a person's life on this earth" as well as a testimonial of redemption, without any sentimentality or even the prospect of permanence. (That "one time when I was admitted to the Detox" suggests that it happened more than once.) The narrator's recovery, which allows him to relate these events, doesn't absolve him of his heartlessness during them or bring the dead people back to life. That's the meaning of "killed forever." Sobriety and sanity, precious as they are, do not compensate for the tragic senselessness of life. Redemption is glorious, and it isn't nearly enough. It saves only one person at a time, and the world is full of people.

As if to emphasize this hard truth, the story concludes with a furious last line: "And you, you ridiculous people, you expect me to help you." Fuckhead isn't Jesus. He's Jesus' Son, which is a different thing entirely. He's a person graced with an intuition of heaven who still lives in hell on earth.

All this Denis Johnson does in a little over a thousand words. By conflating registers of time and tone, he delivers a narrative where the personal brushes up against the eternal, all from a single incident, or accident, on a rainy night.

Denis Johnson

Car Crash While Hitchhiking

A salesman who shared his liquor and steered while sleeping . . . A Cherokee filled with bourbon . . . A VW no more than a bubble of hashish fumes, captained by a college student . . .

And a family man from Marshalltown who headonned and killed forever a man driving west out of Bethany, Missouri . . .

. . . I rose up sopping wet from sleeping under the pouring rain, and something less than conscious, thanks to the first three of the people I've already named—the salesman and the Indian and the student—all of whom had given me drugs. At the head of the entrance ramp I waited without hope of a ride. What was the point, even, of rolling up my sleeping bag when I was too wet to be let into anybody's car? I draped it around me like a cape. The downpour raked the asphalt and gurgled in the ruts. My thoughts zoomed pitifully. The travelling salesman had fed me pills that made the linings of my veins feel scraped out. My jaw ached. I knew every raindrop by its name. I sensed everything before it happened. I knew a certain Oldsmobile would stop for me even before it slowed, and by the sweet voices of the family inside of it I knew we'd have an accident in the storm.

I didn't care. They said they'd take me all the way.

The man and the wife put the little girl up front with them and left the baby in the back with me and my dripping bedroll. "I'm not taking you anywhere very fast," the man said. "I've got my wife and babies here, that's why."

You are the ones, I thought. And I piled my sleeping bag against the left-hand door and slept across it, not caring whether I lived or died. The baby slept free on the seat beside me. He was about nine months old.

. . . But before any of this, that afternoon, the salesman and I had swept down into Kansas City in his luxury car. We'd developed a dangerous cynical camaraderie beginning in Texas, where he'd taken me on. We ate up his bottle of amphetamines, and every so often we pulled off the Interstate and bought another pint of Canadian Club and a sack of ice. His car had cylindrical glass holders attached to either door and a white, leathery interior. He said he'd take me home to stay overnight with his family, but first he wanted to stop and see a woman he knew.

Under Midwestern clouds like great gray brains we left the superhighway with a drifting sensation and entered Kansas City's rush hour with a sensation of running aground. As soon as we slowed down, all the magic of travelling together burned away. He went on and on about his girlfriend. "I like this girl, I think I love this girl—but I've got two kids and a wife, and there's certain obligations there. And on top of everything else, I love my wife. I'm gifted with love. I love my kids. I love all my relatives." As he kept on, I felt jilted and sad: "I have a boat, a little sixteen-footer. I have two cars. There's room in the back yard for a swimming pool." He found his girlfriend at work. She ran a furniture store, and I lost him there.

The clouds stayed the same until night. Then, in the car, I didn't see the storm gathering. The driver of the Volkswagen, a college

man, the one who stoked my head with all the hashish, let me out
beyond the city limits just as it began to rain. Never mind the speed
I'd been taking, I was too overcome to stand up. I lay out in the
grass off the exit ramp and woke up in the middle of a puddle that
had filled up around me.

And later, as I've said, I slept in the back seat while the
Oldsmobile—the family from Marshalltown—splashed along through
the rain. And yet I dreamed I was looking right through my eyelids,
and my pulse marked off the seconds of time. The Interstate through
western Missouri was, in that era, nothing more than a two-way road,
most of it. When a semi truck came toward us and passed going the
other way, we were lost in a blinding spray and a warfare of noises
such as you get being towed through an automatic car wash. The wip-
ers stood up and lay down across the windshield without much effect.
I was exhausted, and after an hour I slept more deeply.

I'd known all along exactly what was going to happen. But the
man and his wife woke me up later, denying it viciously.

"Oh—*no!*"

"NO!"

I was thrown against the back of their seat so hard that it broke.
I commenced bouncing back and forth. A liquid which I knew right
away was human blood flew around the car and rained down on my
head. When it was over I was in the back seat again, just as I had
been. I rose up and looked around. Our headlights had gone out.
The radiator was hissing steadily. Beyond that, I didn't hear a thing.
As far as I could tell, I was the only one conscious. As my eyes adjusted I saw that the baby was lying on its back beside me as if nothing had happened. Its eyes were open and it was feeling its cheeks
with its little hands.

In a minute the driver, who'd been slumped over the wheel sat up and peered at us. His face was smashed and dark with blood. It made my teeth hurt to look at him—but when he spoke, it didn't sound as if any of his teeth were broken.

"What happened?"

"We had a wreck," he said.

"The baby's okay," I said, although I had no idea how the baby was.

He turned to his wife.

"Janice," he said. "Janice, Janice!"

"Is she okay?"

"She's dead!" he said, shaking her angrily.

"No she's not." I was ready to deny everything myself now.

Their little girl was alive, but knocked out. She whimpered in her sleep. But the man went on shaking his wife.

"Janice!" he hollered.

His wife moaned.

"She's not dead," I said, clambering from the car and running away.

"She won't wake up," I heard him say.

I was standing out here in the night, with the baby, for some reason, in my arms. It must have still been raining, but I remember nothing about the weather. We'd collided with another car on what I now perceived was a two-lane bridge. The water beneath us was invisible in the dark.

Moving toward the other car I began to hear rasping, metallic snores. Somebody was flung halfway out the passenger door, which was open, in the posture of one hanging from a trapeze by his ankles. The car had been broadsided, smashed so flat that no room was left inside of it even for this person's legs, to say nothing of a driver or any other passengers. I just walked right on past.

Headlights were coming from far off. I made for the head of the bridge, waving them to a stop with one arm and clutching the baby to my shoulder with the other.

It was a big semi, grinding its gears as it decelerated. The driver rolled down his window and I shouted up at him. "There's a wreck. Go for help."

"I can't turn around here," he said.

He let me and the baby up on the passenger side, and we just sat there in the cab, looking at the wreckage in his headlights.

"Is everybody dead?" he asked.

"I can't tell who is and who isn't," I admitted.

He poured himself a cup of coffee from a thermos and switched off all but his parking lights.

"What time is it?"

"Oh, it's around quarter after three," he said.

By his manner he seemed to endorse the idea of not doing anything about this. I was relieved and tearful. I'd thought something was required of me, but I hadn't wanted to find out what it was.

When another car showed, coming in the opposite direction, I thought I should talk to them. "Can you keep the baby?" I asked the truck driver.

"You'd better hang on to him," the driver said. "It's a boy, isn't it?"

"Well, I think so," I said.

The man hanging out of the wrecked car was still alive as I passed, and I stopped, grown a little more used to the idea now of how really badly broken he was, and made sure there was nothing I could do. He was snoring loudly and rudely. His blood bubbled out of his mouth with every breath. He wouldn't be taking many more I knew that, but he didn't, and therefore I looked down into the great pity of a person's life on this earth. I don't mean that we all end up dead, that's not the great pity. I mean that he couldn't tell me what he was dreaming, and I couldn't tell him what was real.

Before too long there were cars backed up for a ways at either end of the bridge, and headlights giving a night-game atmosphere to the steaming rubble, and ambulances and cop cars nudging through so that the air pulsed with color. I didn't talk to anyone. My secret was that in this short while I had gone from being the president of this tragedy to being a faceless onlooker at a gory wreck. At some point an officer learned that I was one of the passengers, and took my statement. I don't remember any of this, except that he told me, "Put out your cigarette." We paused in our conversation to watch the dying man being loaded into the ambulance. He was still alive, still dreaming obscenely. The blood ran off him in strings. His knees jerked and his head rattled.

There was nothing wrong with me, and I hadn't seen anything, but the policeman had to question me and take me to the hospital anyway. The word came over his car radio that the man was now dead, just as we came under the awning of the emergency-room entrance.

I stood in a tiled corridor with my wet sleeping bag bunched against the wall beside me, talking to a man from the local funeral home.

The doctor stopped to tell me I'd better have an X-ray.

"No."

"Now would be the time. If something turns up later . . ."

"There's nothing wrong with me."

Down the hall came the wife. She was glorious, burning. She didn't know yet that her husband was dead. We knew. That's what gave her such power over us. The doctor took her into a room with a desk at the end of the hall, and from under the closed door a slab of brilliance radiated as if, by some stupendous process, diamonds were being incinerated in there. What a pair of lungs! She shrieked as I imagined an eagle would shriek. It felt wonderful to be alive to hear it! I've gone looking for that feeling everywhere.

"There's nothing wrong with me"—I'm surprised I let those words out. But it's always been my tendency to lie to doctors, as if good health consisted only of the ability to fool them.

Some years later, one time when I was admitted to the Detox at Seattle General Hospital, I took the same tack.

"Are you hearing unusual sounds or voices?" the doctor asked.

"Help us, oh God, it hurts," the boxes of cotton screamed.

"Not exactly," I said.

"Not exactly," he said. "Now, what does that mean?"

"I'm not ready to go into all that," I said. A yellow bird fluttered close to my face, and my muscles grabbed. Now I was flopping like a fish. When I squeezed shut my eyes, hot tears exploded from the sockets. When I opened them, I was on my stomach.

"How did the room get so white?" I asked.

A beautiful nurse was touching my skin. "These are vitamins," she said, and drove the needle in.

It was raining. Gigantic ferns leaned over us. The forest drifted down a hill. I could hear a creek rushing down among rocks. And you, you ridiculous people, you expect me to help you.

Issue 110, 1989

Mary Gaitskill

on

Mary-Beth Hughes's *Pelican Song*

P elican Song" is horrendously sad. Its sadness is accentuated by the ridiculousness suggested in the title; a malevolent ridiculousness that has been put over the story's heroine like a suffocating bag that, in the name of familial duty, she must wear as if it is an elegant gown. And so, as a naturally dutiful person, wear it she does, politely, uncomplainingly, and blindly, crashing into the feverishly appointed marble-tabled, pinwheel wall-papered, green glassed tiki-torched obstacle course that has been created for her by her near-mad family.

It does not help that she happens to live in a cultural moment that allows people in their thirties to believe that they are artists even if they produce no actual art. It does not help that her parents are able to send a giant check to the person choreographing their daughter's final dance performance before her transition into writing—the Pelican Song of the title, as it is sarcastically dubbed by her step-grandfather— in lieu of attending said performance.

Step-grandfather may or may not be aware of the pelican's Christ-like iconography, according to which mother pelicans will cut open their own breasts to nourish their young; certainly a great deal of cutting and rending goes on in this story, and some of it purports to be nurturing. But in this story all nurture is limned with poison, and the elegant abundance of the character's world is more than equaled by its emotional perversity. "Pelican Song" is one of the most convincing depictions of the horrors that only the wealthy can inflict upon their own that I have ever read. That the heroine wants to believe in love and goodness even as she walks through these horrors is more than convincing. It is heartbreaking.

Mary-Beth Hughes

✠

Pelican Song

I was the kind of thirty year old who had only recently left adolescence behind. I was mostly a modern dancer. I rehearsed, I went to class. I worked the concession stand in an art-movie theater where actors and filmmakers ushered. A novelist with strong powers of concentration manned the ticket booth. I had a studio apartment in Gramercy Park that looked out on an ivied brick wall. When I wanted to get out of the city I would take the bus to visit my mother in central Jersey. My mother was far along into her second marriage. She and her husband had built a house in an abandoned peach orchard with the proceeds from the sale of my childhood home and his antique-car-supply boutique. They acted as their own general contractors and saved a lot of money. Now that the house was finished they had their collective eye open for an investment scheme.

Like the ticket taker, the man my mother married was really a novelist. My mother created an author's den for him in the upper portion of their beautiful new house. She decorated it with my lost father's old desk, very attractive and manly with brass inlays, and his leather chair. Everything faced out over the in-ground swimming pool and the putting green, and beyond that to the old orchard and then the woods. Couldn't be more inspiring, everyone said.

My mother, always interested in words, took seriously, in a way lost to the world of my generation, the role of helpmate. She typed her husband's manuscripts, judiciously editing them as she went along. She served lunch on a tray, left atop a small marble pedestal outside of the den door. And she checked the mailbox at the end of the long drive for the latest news from his literary agent. If there was another rejection waiting, she prepared the gentlest delivery.

At the art-movie theater in the West Village we took failure for granted. In the house in the orchard the stakes were much higher. Each time a rejection letter came, though often flattering, even encouraging, it represented an enormous blow to the whole enterprise. Even so, I decided to try my own hand at writing fiction. I joined a group. I wrote one-paragraph stories that I liked to read out loud to my mother over her kitchen speakerphone while she was preparing the meals that went upstairs. For Christmas that year, my mother's husband gave me a lovely, quite serious pen, with a kind note folded inside the box. But at the movie theater no one allowed my mini-stories any more importance than my modern dance performances. My biggest obstacle to respect, however, had to do with men.

I had an odd figure for a modern dancer. Rubenesque, my composer boyfriend called my body when pressed for compliments. This was long before I found the tiny crimson panties tucked beneath his buckwheat pillow. I also heard him say Rembrandt. My mother, it's worth noting, took figures very seriously. I often felt this was another feature of her generation, like the typing and the meals on trays. In my time, I believed, a body could be different and still be okay. But when the composer mentioned Botero, I lost confidence.

After the panty disclosure, I started seeing a painting student. He ushered part-time and still lived with his parents on the Upper

East Side. His beard had developed only under his mouth and nose so far, and though born at New York Hospital he spoke with an English accent. Some days I'd meet him after class at Cooper Union. He was a freshman. I felt like his nanny waiting at the curb. But he was understanding, in a way I think was more intense because he was still living at home, when I began getting the late-night phone calls from my mother.

The calls started some time after the Christmas I received the pen. I'd come by myself for the holiday; the painter had his own plans with his mother and father. I stayed Christmas night in the guest suite next to the writing den. My presents made a nice pile at the foot of the bed, and I must have slept late, because the sun was high over the snow-covered putting green and I could smell coffee long past its first perc wafting from the room next door. My mother's husband tended to stay all day in the writing den so I didn't change out of my pajamas, just went downstairs to find my mother and scare up some breakfast.

At the foot of the stair I heard a loud bang. My mother was a big redecorator, so I assumed she was moving a sofa, and then I heard a louder bang, more like a chest of drawers against a wall. Voices like growls could only be the television tuned to a low volume, so as not to disturb the writing process.

I took a quick look at the manger display my mother set out in the foyer—sweet, a big part of my childhood. Even the hay was arranged nicely and all the ceramic farm animals had pleasant shapes. I heard the word *cunt* quite distinctly from the kitchen and turned my head. The chest of drawers banged against a wall one more time. My mother had painted an old heavy cabinet with white enamel, and I thought—without really thinking—she might be wrestling it into place.

But then I felt a strange fear that buckled my legs as I rounded the corner into the kitchen and found my mother backed against the wall, her husband pressed up hard against her, face purple. I wasn't sure what I was seeing, and when they both turned to look at me, my mother laughed but with an odd kind of disdain. She pushed her husband off of her. He said something about coffee and left the room through the dining room door.

I didn't know what to ask, and my head hurt as if it were my skull that had been bounced. My mother attended to her hair. She coughed and smiled. Lifted a hand and her eyebrows as if to curtail the next obvious thing I might say, and walked past me through the door I'd entered to meet her husband at the manger. But he'd beaten her to the foyer and was already walking slowly—I could hear him above me—down the long book-lined hallway to the writing den.

My mother's husband didn't just want to write novels, he wanted to write best-sellers. At the art-movie theater we understood what he would never believe, which was that no one—we liked to talk in terms of multiple lightning strikes; we weren't entirely original in this—got the recognition they deserved. We tended to read, perform, and scrutinize, often with devastating candor, the work of each other. We were envious, backbiting, and deeply critical, even scathing and destructive during lag-time discussions in our polyester smocks. We were lucky though. We had a context, and we had an audience, and there were more than two of us. When things got too painful we switched our shifts. My mother and her husband only had each other in a house that they'd built to be so graceful and accommodating they'd never have to leave it.

When my mother called me on Valentine's eve from the local Hilton, which she said was perfectly charming, two towns away from their home, I was surprised, but not entirely. She just wanted me to know where she was in case I needed her. She was fine. Her husband was working very hard and wanted a little privacy. Did I think cranberry velvet seat cushions would be pretty in the bay window of the dining room? I had no opinion on this, and wrote down her room number at the Hilton. The next afternoon she called to say she was home and sending me something special. A beautiful dictionary arrived in a day or so inscribed with love from the two of them.

I was a little worried about my mother, but I had romantic problems of my own. I may have underestimated the maturity level of the painting student because he was such a fine kisser, and his drawings were intricate and intelligent. For Valentine's Day he wrote my name in pink rose petals on the covered stoop of my apartment building, and then lay down naked there, in the cold, but not snowy, night, and waited for me to come home from the art-movie theater. He was very slender, and the chill he caught kept him out of classes for two full months. His parents didn't appreciate my sick-room visits. The housekeeper looked genuinely alarmed to see a robust thirty year old teetering at the end of his trundle bed, so we communicated by late-night phone calls, which his mother listened to, breathing with complete audibility, on the extension. He couldn't wait until he'd gotten through art school so that he could just make his own money and leave. It was oppressive and he had the courage to say so.

My painter friend was still malingering when my mother's husband's father died. An old bear, someone who felt cruelty was power. And in a way it was. No holiday was ever complete until old Sven had dialed in to ridicule the hopes of his aging son. Novelist-smovelist, his voice boomed through the kitchen over the speakerphone like he was actually making sense.

Just unplug the bastard, I suggested. And though my mother cast me a weary eye when I said such things, her husband ignored me. He did this in a noble way that suggested strong men listen to the ravings of their fathers.

But it turned out I was a prophet. Old Sven's brain blew a gasket early in the new year. My mother's husband, who had power-of-attorney, pulled the plug in record time. And so during the first big holiday gathering without Sven, the Easter egg hunt, there was a peculiar silence. And everyone, I could sense, believed this was somehow my fault.

My mother called me after that to change our Mother's Day plans. Why didn't I come to the Hilton? she said. There was a great indoor pool, and a sauna. I could share her suite and we could have a really good time. Because it was an unusually mild spring in the West Village, I was able to get the weekend off. Who wanted to go to the movies when cherry blossoms were sprinkling the café tables?

I took the bus to Freehold. My mother was waiting in her little blue sports Caddy, wearing wraparound sunglasses from the seventies. Traditionally she liked to leap out of the car and hug me like I'd just finished my first full day at pre-school, but today, and maybe she was anxious to show me the pool, she just started the engine and waved her left hand. I dipped down into the passenger bucket and took a good look before speaking. It wasn't just the sling, it was the way she didn't seem able to turn her head. And when she lifted her free hand to the wheel it was swollen like a mitt, her knuckles strafed with red slashes.

Even facing straight ahead she could still issue the look not to say anything. You want to wait until we're at the Hilton? I said. She laughed. We weren't going to the Hilton, it turned out. We were staying with a friend, Faye, who had lent my mother, for the purpose of this holiday visit, the guest cottage on her waterfront property. You'll love this, she said, you've always loved the water. I couldn't remember loving water, but was sure my mother was right.

Faye had problems of her own. Her thieving ex-husband had run off with a golf club locker-room attendant she'd over-tipped for years. It was disgusting! Even so, Faye had taken time to fill the lar-

der and the bar at the guest cottage, and let it be known, before going off to the lawyer to skewer her lousy ex, that if my mother's husband
put one foot on her property he'd regret it. My mother sighed and
smiled her gratitude. But when the sound of Faye's MG died out, my
mother explained that Faye was consumed by rage. It was a terrible,
wasteful shame.

Faye's guest cottage had twin chaises that looked out from the
verandah to the bay. In the early evening light, sailboats bumped
and tilted around delicate crescent waves. The sun went down,
turning everything pink for a while, and my mother's face behind
her sunglasses looked a little less distorted. She told me there'd been
a particularly harsh rejection letter that week, and now the novel
was dead. Which novel? I asked. I knew there had been several. My
mother was quiet. A small boat tacked back straight into the last
sliver of sun. Mom?

Maybe all of them. It's possible.

I was quiet, out of respect, but then said, Sometimes people just
feel that way. I told her a story of despair and renewal at the movie
theater. An actor-usher who'd met Francis Ford Coppola at the
McDonald's on Sixth Avenue was now a night intern at his literary
magazine. Who knows what will happen next? And he'd just about
given up! And what about my own friend whose oppressive home
environment and fevers cut his art down to bare scratches for a while?
Second runner-up in the Cooper Union Gesture Drawing Competition last Monday! And what about me?

Sweetheart, you're a dreamer. She gave me a one-cornered close-
mouthed smile that was a dead ringer for her husband's. I'd seen
this smile before, trotted out for this very subject. Her husband was
a professional. It was different. They weren't children.

Well, I'm not exactly a child either, I said. But I was, her non-
reply said. And this all came down to the checks she sent me, and

the cash gifts, and the winter coats and boots I got for nearly every birthday, and the microwave and the matched living room set. And the arrangement she'd made years ago with my co-op board and with ConEd. I paid my own transportation and food from the pay-check from the art-movie theater, but the rest, as everyone knew who came to my mother's house, and about which old Sven had been particularly vocal, basically came from my allowance. Meanwhile my mother's smug friends' children were busy working out plans for third babies and second homes. Even Faye had a daughter with a time-share in Aspen.

The financial side of pursuing our art wasn't subject to deep truth-telling we otherwise advocated at the movie theater. I liked to quote Virginia Woolf to myself, now that I was leaning toward fic-tion, about the five hundred pounds and the lonely room. Was there some caveat about not getting that from your mother?

My mother gently pressed her vodka collins up against her face and squinted at the dark water. The reflection of the tiki torches looked like jellyfish wriggling on the black surface.

Maybe you'd like to hear my new story?

Darling, you'll wreck your eyes reading in the dark.

It's short, I'll recite it!

Oh, bunny. Well.

But then gunshot revs of Faye's MG sounded in gravel beside the guest cottage. Did I imagine my mother's relief? There suddenly was Faye, hopping mad, sucker punching the hydrangea. The scum had married the locker-room floozy. Could we believe it? My mother was lovely and magnanimous. Something like this, she knew, could never happen to her. She said sweet, smart things that made Faye laugh.

I was still thinking about my story, maybe Faye would like to hear it? My mother offered to mix some healing martinis. But Faye said she'd do it herself. With that hand—she tipped her perky head at my mother's sling—they'd be slugging down pure vermouth. At this, Faye and my mother made little mews with their mouths at the same time, and I was startled that my mother could be so friendly, so intimate, with a female who wasn't me. This seemed new.

But the biggest news, along with the disastrous rejection letter, was that old Sven had done something naughty with his will. Faye and my mother hunkered down, stem glasses balanced in the air, to talk it over. It turned out he'd left an enormous chunk to the Authors Guild! And on a cruel Post-it note, in a scrawly hand, he'd written to my mother's husband: For your colleagues, thought you'd be pleased.

He wasn't, my mother said, and Faye slid her an appreciative glance. Both drained their glasses, and I offered again to recite my story. Sweetness, they drawled out in tandem, then collapsed into giggles. Unstoppable giggles, they bent their sculptural coifs over slim, extended legs and roared. Oh god. Darling, my mother tried, and then waved her swollen hand quickly as if shooing a mosquito, and Faye laughed harder still. Finally Faye stood and coughed to say she'd handle this. Though her eyes were still weeping with laughter, her mouth looked somber. My angel, she addressed me, and my mother kept her face tilted down. Don't you think your mother has had just about enough literature for today? I'd say, really, enough for a lifetime. Yes?

Oh, Faye, stop, my mother said. Sweetie, I'll hear your story in the car tomorrow, um? Faye, stop it. Then I can really concentrate. Okay?

That's okay.

Good girl, said Faye.

Sweetheart, my mother sighed.

Don't worry about it.

Well, maybe when it's a little longer than a paragraph, you'll send it to me and I can take a good hard look.

It's supposed to be a paragraph.

Faye smirked, and now that it was really dark outside, my mother took off her sunglasses and gave her a serious look. But that communication was lost because my mother's eyes were so swollen, so deeply purpled and bruised even in the dim light of the tiki torches, that Faye stopped laughing and put down her stem glass.

I'm calling Lou, Faye said. Lou was her scum of an ex-husband. But he was also an orthopedic surgeon. My mother said, Absolutely not. But Faye pulled her ears with soft-looking fingers and marched straight into the guest house. Lou arrived within fifteen minutes. He and Faye were surprisingly cordial for two people who hated each other's guts. Lou remembered me fondly from golf-club brunches when I was a child and then forgot me completely while he dressed my mother's wounds in the surgical light of Faye's guest dressing room. He gave my mother a sedative. In the morning she was very tired, so Faye drove me to the bus.

I had to work that afternoon at the movie theater, and my mother had urged me to go. Don't worry, my mother said. She was incredibly sleepy. Don't worry, Faye said. Don't worry, said the painter when I told him on the phone.

Soon after that, my legs began to give out spontaneously, I didn't even have to think about my mother. My legs would wobble out of the blue and then hip, knee, ankle would collapse into a ripple. It made it tricky to walk. The steps down to the subway, which I was obliged to take from Gramercy Park to the movie theater, became a special challenge. This wouldn't have been that big a deal, since I was already making the transition from modern dance to fiction writing, but I had one last performance scheduled at the famous White Columns. My Pelican Song, old Sven had called it over the speakerphone at Christmas. His last pronouncement, as it turned out. My mother and her husband had always planned to attend. They'd sent a giant check to the choreographer during his holiday fund-raiser. And he'd tacked on a three-minute solo at the end of the piece, "Wings of Love," for me! Now the performance was minutes away. And my sudden leg-melts were trying the patience of even this well-funded choreographer.

I decided to address my condition by writing about it. Master the problem by making it conscious. So I began work on a full-scale paragraph to describe what I understood about my mother and her husband. This was more difficult than I'd guessed. In my mother's husband's novels, the women, I knew from several brief glances over the years, had fabulous, surprisingly active nipples and insatiable appetites for very straight-ahead penis-worshipping sex acts. In my paragraph, there was sex, certainly, but of a different order.

The two weeks between my Mother's Day visit and the performance were terrible. The worry, the rehearsals, the distress of composition (I began, oddly, to sympathize about this with my mother's husband). And the rain. Every single day. I was forced to work double shifts pouring bagged popcorn into the pretend popper unit. Everyone in the West Village was coming to the movies, it seemed. By the time I got home each night, it was late, and the phone at Faye's guest cottage rang and rang.

My painter finally recovered enough to spend a night of love on my air mattress. We jiggled and drooled and painted our chests with Nutella. When the phone blared after midnight we assumed it was his mother, who'd insisted on taking my number. But the answering machine speaker played out an echoing voice in the little room which even without words, only crying, I knew was my own mother instead. I scrambled to pluck up the receiver. Wait, wait, I said, hello?

She was still there, breathing hard, whimpering, Darling? And now I felt my sternum shudder and give. Where are you? I asked.

At home. She was locked in her bathroom, the one with the

pinwheel wallpaper, and the Jacuzzi tub, and the pocket door she had long debated: solid core or green glass? I could hear, even behind her harsh breathing, the bang of a fist against the swirly maple she'd finally picked and a muffled growl just like old Sven warming up for his holiday message. It's locked, she said. I listened. The window, she said. And I thought hard. The window opened onto a trellis down to a patio which bounded the putting green. If she pushed her pelvis—she didn't like that word—hips then, I said, keep your hips close to the wall of the house. She could probably shimmy down.

That's crazy, said the painter, and laughed. (That laugh ended our relationship.) Flush the toilet I said in a whisper, as if her husband could hear me, flush before you open the latch. I would get the next bus to Freehold. Just walk into town, can you do that?

Of course, she said, putting me in my place. If she could get out the window, she'd see my there. He called me a sick, rotting cunt? she said, as a question, as if reviewing whether she was making the right move.

Well, you're not, I said. Be careful of your feet. There might be broken glass.

Sweetheart, she whispered, for goodness sake.

My mother was a woman who dressed for bed. When the bus pulled in at the all-night diner in Freehold I scanned beyond the parking lot for where her cream satin peignoir might be flitting through the holly bushes. The exhaust-smelling heat of the bus had made the Nutella gluey. My sleep T-shirt stuck to my chest. I backed down the exit steps, uncertain. The bus driver stared at me. Eyes on the road, you pervert, I barked, then felt ashamed. My mother would be ashamed, too, if she'd heard me.

I had a coat for her and some shoes. Sneakers are for athletes, she always maintained. So I carried my only pair of black slingbacks and a lovely silk overcoat she'd given me, but no money. I'd borrowed the fare from the painter. Now I realized, as the bus chugged away, and the quiet settled in, that my mother probably didn't have much cash on her either. Didn't matter. First I'd find her, and then, once she was appropriately dressed, we'd hitchhike our way to Faye's guest cottage.

Was it an hour? It's hard to know in the dark. But eventually, when she didn't show up, I began the long walk past the cornfields to her house. I was shivering though the weather was balmy, and I was hungry. Each lumpy-looking shadow made me afraid I might find her lying by the side of the road like some fallen animal. But I didn't find her. When I came to the end of her drive the house was lit as if for a holiday party. The button lights glowed to trace the curve of the drive through the fragrant peach trees. The deep porch, its long planters thick with ivy and juniper aglow. It seemed every room was lit, the writer's den, the guest suite, all the reception rooms, the master bedroom. Around back the garage doors were flung open as if the party might flood into its bays. The blue Caddy my mother liked to drive was parked close to the mudroom door, but the Mercedes, her husband's staid sedan, was missing. I didn't need to go inside the house to know she wasn't there.

My dearest heart, my mother wrote to me. *You'll find it strange I know, but we've flown away to try again. It's difficult for a writer, maybe for any true artist, to make a good life here. Old Sven was kinder to you than to his own son, as you will see from the enclosed. I love you more than anything, always have, always will.*

My birth date was penciled on the envelope. A bonded courier slid it beneath my door. The letter was typed and unsigned. The bank check was for a hundred thousand dollars.

The house in the orchard was sold by old Sven's personal lawyer in a private auction. He phoned me about furniture, and of course, the manger, but I didn't want anything. This lawyer tells me from time to time, when I press, that they are both fine, they are in a quiet place now, they just need a little peace. He tells me that my mother sends her best love, as though she's right there waiting on another extension. Sometimes I think my mother is still looking for me. She just doesn't recognize me in my suit and leather shoes. Sometimes I scan the back pages of books. I pay close attention to long murder mysteries with women as dispensable, secondary characters. I read the acknowledgments, especially of the authors with phony-sounding names, hoping he will have the courage someday to say how amazing she was, how beautiful, and how she made everything, absolutely everything, possible.

Issue 170, 2004

Aleksandar Hemon

on

Jorge Luis Borges's *Funes,*
the Memorious

The work of Jorge Luis Borges belongs to the tradition of literature with cosmic ambition: the Bible, the *Iliad,* the *Divine
Comedy, Paradise Lost, Ulysses,* etc.—the works that strive to convey
complete universes, containing *everything.* They're contingent upon
(and thus imply the belief in) the totality of language: all of history,
all of memory, all of current cosmology and/or theology, all the un-
breakable continuity of human experience can be deposited and
narrated in language. Indeed, in such works language seems to be
able to cover the perpetual entirety of the past, present, and future
and involve the real, the imagined, and all that is in between. They
offer crucial evidence that it is utterly impossible to conceptualize
humanity without literature. Their philosophical/ethical/aesthetical
ambition demands total commitment from the reader—an ideal reader
would devote his/her entire life to the exegesis of, say, Joyce's *Ulysses,*
thereby erasing all the nonreaderly aspects of his/her existence.

Such a reader, of course, would be a perfect Borgesian character,
for whom the experience of life is unavailable outside literature.
Funes, the Memorious is as Borgesian a character as they come, a

man tormented by his hyperencylopedic mind, tragically unable to forget anything. "I alone have more memories than all mankind has probably had since the world has been the world," Funes laments. Seemingly fulfilling the most hubristic of human ambitions—to remember/know *everything*—he is incapacitated by the compulsive absoluteness of his knowledge, unable to think and communicate with the rest of the humanity. Casting himself as the imperfect, inferior countercharacter to Funes, Borges suggests that forgetting— that is, forgetting *ceaselessly*—is essential and necessary for thought and language and literature, for simply being a human being.

What makes human beings amazing is that we do not abandon our striving in the face of our constant failure to transcend our mortal, biological limits. The great works of cosmic ambition—including Funes's projects: "an infinite vocabulary for the natural series of numbers, a useless mental catalogue of all the images of his memory"— never achieve the totality they seek, because there is no way they ever could. The essential necessity of forgetting blocks the very possibility of containing *everything*, but without forgetting such ambition would not be possible at all. We think there is *everything*, because we forget everything. We want it, because we forget we can't have it. The magnificent ambition is fundamentally reliant upon the indelible impossibility of its fulfillment. Visionaries and geniuses die drooling, just like everybody else.

Of course, if there were God, *everything* would be available. "The truth is that we live out our lives putting off all that can be put off," Borges writes, "perhaps we all know deep down that we are immortal and that sooner or later all men will do and know all things." If Funes and his absolute knowledge could live on, God would be in evidence, and we would all be immortal, beginning with Borges: "I thought that each of my words (that each of my movements) would persist in his implacable memory." Within a sentence, Funes and his implacable memory are dead, as is God. Death and forgetting triumph, and with them triumphs, in all its glory and tragedy, the humanity, forever enduring the "multiform, instantaneous and almost intolerably precise world."

Jorge Luis Borges

✠

Funes, the Memorious

I remember him (I have no right to utter this sacred verb, only one man on earth had that right and he is dead) with a dark passion flower in his hand, seeing it as no one has ever seen it, though he might look at it from the twilight of dawn till that of evening, a whole lifetime. I remember him, with his face taciturn and Indian-like and singularly *remote,* behind the cigarette. I remember (I think) his angular, leather-braiding hands. I remember near those hands a maté gourd bearing the Uruguayan coat of arms; I remember a yellow screen with a vague lake landscape in the window of his house. I clearly remember his voice: the slow, resentful, nasal voice of the old-time dweller of the suburbs, without the Italian sibilants we have today. I never saw him more than three times; the last was in 1887 . . . I find it very satisfactory that all those who knew him should write about him; my testimony will perhaps be the shortest and no doubt the poorest, but not the most impartial in the volume you will edit. My deplorable status as an Argentine will prevent me from indulging in a dithyramb, an obligatory genre in Uruguay whenever the subject is an Uruguayan. *Highbrow, city slicker, dude:* Funes never

spoke these injurious words, but I am sufficiently certain I represented for him those misfortunes. Pedro Leandro Ipuche has written that Funes was a precursor of the supermen, "a vernacular and
rustic Zarathustra"; I shall not debate the point, but one should not
forget that he was also a kid from Fray Bentos, with certain incurable limitations.

My first memory of Funes is very perspicuous. I can see him on
an afternoon in March or February of the year 1884. My father, that
year, had taken me to spend the summer in Fray Bentos. I was returning from the San Francisco ranch with my cousin Bernardo
Haedo. We were singing as we rode along and being on horseback
was not the only circumstance determining my happiness. After a
sultry day, an enormous slate-colored storm had hidden the sky. It
was urged on by southern wind, the trees were already going wild; I
was afraid (I was hopeful) that the elemental rain would take us by
surprise in the open. We were running a kind of race with the storm.
We entered an alleyway that sank down between two very high brick
sidewalks. It had suddenly got dark; I heard some rapid and almost
secret footsteps up above; I raised my eyes and saw a boy running
along the narrow and broken path as if it were a narrow and broken
wall. I remember his baggy gaucho trousers, his rope-soled shoes. I
remember the cigarette in his hard face, against the now limitless
storm cloud. Bernardo cried to him unexpectedly: "What time is it,
Ireneo?" Without consulting the sky, without stopping, he replied:
"It's four minutes to eight, young Bernardo Juan Francisco." His
voice was shrill, mocking.

I am so unperceptive that the dialogue I have just related would
not have attracted my attention had it not been stressed by my cousin,
who (I believe) was prompted by a certain local pride and the desire
to show that he was indifferent to the other's tripartite reply.

He told me the fellow in the alleyway was one Ireneo Funes,

known for certain peculiarities such as avoiding contact with people
and always knowing what time it was, like a clock. He added that he
was the son of the ironing woman in town, María Clementina
Funes, and that some people said his father was a doctor at the meat
packers, an Englishman by the name of O'Connor, and others that
he was a horse tamer or scout from the Salto district. He lived with
his mother, around the corner from the Laureles house.

During the years eighty-five and eight-six we spent the summer
in Montevideo. In eighty-seven I returned to Fray Bentos. I asked,
as was natural, about all my acquaintances and, finally, about the
"chronometrical" Funes. I was told he had been thrown by a half-
tamed horse on the San Francisco ranch and was left hopelessly
paralyzed. I remember the sensation of uneasy magic the news produced in me: the only time I had seen him, we were returning from
San Francisco on horseback and he was running along a high place;
this fact, told me by my cousin Bernardo, had much of the quality of
a dream made up of previous elements. I was told he never moved
from his cot, with his eyes fixed on the fig tree in the back or on a
spider web. In the afternoons, he would let himself be brought out
to the window. He carried his pride to the point of acting as if the
blow that had felled him were beneficial . . . Twice I saw him behind the iron grating of the window, which harshly emphasized his
condition as a perpetual prisoner: once, motionless, with his eyes
closed; another time, again motionless, absorbed in the contempla-
tion of a fragrant sprig of santonica.

Not without a certain vaingloriousness, I had begun at that time
my methodical study of Latin. My valise contained the *De viris il-
lustribus* of Lhomond, Quicherat's *Thesaurus,* the commentaries
of Julius Caesar and an odd volume of Pliny's *Naturalis historia,*
which then exceeded (and still exceeds) my moderate virtues as a

Latinist. Everything becomes public in a small town; Ireneo, in his house on the outskirts, did not take long to learn of the arrival of these anomalous books. He sent me a flowery and ceremonious letter in which he recalled our encounter, unfortunately brief, "on the seventh day of February of the year 1884," praised the glorious services my uncle Gregorio Haedo, deceased the same year, "had rendered to our two nations in the valiant battle of Ituzaingó" and requested the loan of any one of my volumes, accompanied by a dictionary "for the proper intelligence of the original text, for I am as yet ignorant of Latin." He promised to return them to me in good condition, almost immediately. His handwriting was perfect, very sharply outlined; his orthography, of the type favored by Andrés Bello: *i* for *y, j* for *g.* At first I naturally feared a joke. My cousins assured me that was not the case, that these were peculiarities of Ireneo. I did not know whether to attribute to insolence, ignorance or stupidity the idea that the arduous Latin tongue should require no other instrument than a dictionary; to disillusion him fully, I sent him the *Gradus ad Parnassum* of Quicherat and the work by Pliny.

On the fourteenth of February, I received a telegram from Buenos Aires saying I should return immediately, because my father was "not at all well." May God forgive me; the prestige of being the recipient of an urgent telegram, the desire to communicate to all Fray Bentos the contradiction between the negative form of the message and the peremptory adverb, the temptation to dramatize my suffering, affecting a virile stoicism, perhaps distracted me from all possibility of real sorrow. When I packed my valise, I noticed the *Gradus* and the first volume of the *Naturalis historia* were missing. The *Saturn* was sailing the next day, in the morning; that night, after supper, I headed towards Funes' house. I was astonished to find the evening no less oppressive than the day had been.

At the respectable little house, Funes' mother opened the door for me.

She told me Ireneo was in the back room and I should not be surprised to find him in the dark, because he knew how to pass the idle hours without lighting the candle. I crossed the tile patio, the little passageway; I reached the second patio. There was a grape arbor; the darkness seemed complete to me. I suddenly heard Ireneo's high-pitched, mocking voice. His voice was speaking in Latin; his voice (which came from the darkness) was articulating with morose delight a speech or prayer or incantation. The Roman syllables resounded in the earthen patio; my fear took them to be indecipherable, interminable; afterwards, in the enormous dialogue of that night, I learned they formed the first paragraph of the twenty-fourth chapter of the seventh book of the *Naturalis historia*. The subject of that chapter is memory; the last words were *ut nihil non iisdem verbis redderetur auditum.*

Without the slightest change of voice, Ireneo told me to come in. He was on his cot, smoking. It seems to me I did not see his face until dawn; I believe I recall the intermittent glow of his cigarette. The room smelled vaguely of dampness. I sat down; I repeated the story about the telegram and my father's illness.

I now arrive at the most difficult point in my story. This story (it is well the reader know it by now) has no other plot than that dialogue which took place half a century ago. I shall not try to reproduce the words, which are now irrecoverable. I prefer to summarize with veracity the many things Ireneo told me. The indirect style is remote and weak; I know I am sacrificing the efficacy of my narrative; my readers should imagine for themselves the hesitant periods which overwhelmed me that night.

Ireneo began by enumerating, in Latin and in Spanish, the cases of prodigious memory recorded in the *Naturalis historia:* Cyrus, king of the Persians, who could call every solider in his armies by name; Mithridates Eupator, who administered the law in twenty-two languages of his empire; Simonides, inventor of the science of mnemonics; Metrodorus, who practiced the art of faithfully repeating what he had heard only once. In obvious good faith, Ireneo was amazed that such cases be considered amazing. He told me that before that rainy afternoon when the blue-gray horse threw him, he had been what all humans are: blind, deaf, addlebrained, absent-minded. (I tried to remind him of his exact perception of time, his memory for proper names; he paid no attention to me.) For nineteen years he had lived as one in a dream: he looked without seeing, listened without hearing, forgetting everything, almost everything. When he fell, he became unconscious; when he came out, the present was almost intolerable in its richness and sharpness, as were his most distant and trivial memories. Somewhat later he learned that he was paralyzed. The fact scarcely interested him. He reasoned (he felt) that his immobility was a minimum price to pay. Now his perception and his memory were infallible.

We, at one glance, can perceive three glasses on a table; Funes, all the leaves and tendrils and fruit that make up a grape vine. He knew by heart the forms of the southern clouds at dawn on the 30th of April, 1882, and could compare them in his memory with the mottled streaks on a book in Spanish binding he had only seen once and with the outlines of the foam raised by an oar in the Río Negro the night before the Quebracho uprising. These memories were not simple ones; each visual image was linked to muscular sensations, thermal sensations, etc. He could reconstruct all his dreams, all his half-dreams. Two or three times he had reconstructed a whole day; he never hesitated, but each reconstruction had required a whole day. He told me: "I alone have more memories than all mankind has probably had since the world has been the world." And again: "My dreams are like you people's waking hours." And again, towards dawn: "My memory, sir, is like a garbage heap." A circle drawn on a blackboard, a right triangle, a lozenge—all these are forms we can fully and intuitively grasp; Ireneo could do the same with the stormy mane of a pony, with a herd of cattle on a hill, with the changing fire and its innumerable ashes, with the many faces of a dead man throughout a long wake. I don't know how many stars he could see in the sky.

These things he told me; neither then nor later have I ever placed them in doubt. In those days there were no cinemas or phonographs; nevertheless, it is odd and even incredible that no one ever performed an experiment with Funes. The truth is that we live out our lives putting off all that can be put off; perhaps we all know deep down that we are immortal and that sooner or later all men will do and know all things.

Out of the darkness, Funes' voice went on talking to me.

He told me that in 1886 he had invented an original system of numbering and that in a very few days he had gone beyond the twenty-four-thousand mark. He had not written it down, since anything he thought of once would never be lost to him. His first stimulus was, I think, his discomfort at the fact that the famous thirty-three gauchos of Uruguayan history should require two signs and two words, in place of a single word and a single sign. He then applied this absurd principle to the other numbers. In place of seven thousand thirteen, he would say (for example) *Máximo Pérez;* in place of seven thousand fourteen, *The Railroad;* other numbers were *Luis Melián Lafinur, Olimar, Sulphur, the reins, the whale, the gas, the caldron, Napoleon, Augustín de Vedia.* In place of five hundred, he would say *nine.* Each word had a particular sign, a kind of mark; the last in the series were very complicated . . . I tried to explain to

him that this rhapsody of incoherent terms was precisely the opposite of a system of numbers. I told him that saying 365 meant saying
three hundreds, six tens, five ones, an analysis which is not found in
the "numbers" *The Negro Timoteo* or *meat blanket*. Funes did not
understand me or refused to understand me.

Locke, in the seventeenth century, postulated (and rejected) an
impossible language in which each individual thing, each stone,
each bird and each branch, would have its own name; Funes once
projected an analogous language, but discarded it because it seemed
too general to him, too ambiguous. In fact, Funes once remembered
not only every leaf of every tree of every wood, but also every one
of the times he had perceived or imagined it. He decided to reduce
each of his past days to some seventy thousand memories, which
would then be defined by means of ciphers. He was dissuaded from
this by two considerations: his awareness that the task was interminable, his awareness that it was useless. He thought that by the hour
of his death he would not even have finished classifying all the
memories of his childhood.

The two projects I have indicated (an infinite vocabulary for the
natural series of numbers, a useless mental catalogue of all the images of his memory) are senseless, but they betray a certain stammering grandeur. They permit us to glimpse or infer the nature of
Funes' vertiginous world. He was, let us not forget, almost incapable
of ideas of a general, Platonic sort. Not only was it difficult for him
to comprehend that the generic symbol *dog* embraces so many un-
like individuals of diverse size and form; it bothered him that the dog
at three fourteen (seen from the side) should have the same name as
the dog at three fifteen (seen from the front). His own face in the
mirror, his own hands, surprised him every time he saw them. Swift
relates that the emperor of Lilliput could discern the movement of

the minute hand; Funes could continuously discern the tranquil advances of corruption, of decay, of fatigue. He could note the progress of death, of dampness. He was the solitary and lucid spectator of a multiform, instantaneous and almost intolerably precise world. Babylon, London and New York have overwhelmed with their ferocious splendor the imaginations of men; no one, in their populous towers or their urgent avenues, has felt the heat and pressure of a reality as indefatigable as that which day and night converged upon the hapless Ireneo, in his poor South American suburb. It was very difficult for him to sleep. To sleep is to turn one's mind from the world; Funes, lying on his back on his cot in the shadows, could imagine every crevice and every molding in the sharply defined houses surrounding him. (I repeat that the least important of his memories was more minute and more vivid than our perception of physical pleasure or physical torment.) Towards the east, along a stretch not yet divided into blocks, there were new houses, unknown to Funes. He imagined them to be black, compact, made of homogeneous darkness; in that direction he would turn his face in order to sleep. He would also imagine himself at the bottom of the river, rocked and annihilated by the current.

With no effort, he had learned English, French, Portuguese and Latin. I suspect, however, that he was not very capable of thought. To think is to forget differences, generalize, make abstractions. In the teeming world of Funes, there were only details, almost immediate in their presence.

The wary light of dawn entered the earthen patio.

Then I saw the face belonging to the voice that had spoken all night long. Ireneo was nineteen years old; he had been born in 1868; he seemed to me as monumental as bronze, more ancient than Egypt, older than the prophecies and the pyramids. I thought that each of my words (that each of my movements) would persist in his implacable memory; I was benumbed by the fear of multiplying useless gestures.

Ireneo Funes died in 1889, of congestion of the lungs.

Translated by James E. Irby

Issue 28, 1962

Amy Hempel

on

Bernard Cooper's *Old Birds*

"My father wanders. And I don't just mean in conversation." The speaker is an architect who receives a phone call from his elderly father who is on a Los Angeles city street on foot, asking strangers in cars for help opening a jar of peanut butter. The son is at work, designing a retirement home that will, by the end of the story, feature an aviary. With information insufficient to locate his father, the urgent search begins over the phone. Exasperation and tenderness, longing and fear—this is Bernard Cooper's territory: love and loss, rendered in the language of illumination, conjuring people for whom grief and desire are often conjoined.

A similar father, younger and not yet unhoused by Alzheimer's, appears in sad comedies in several of the stellar essays in Cooper's *Truth Serum*, and later in his memoir, *The Bill from My Father* (the bill is the one Cooper's father presented to him for the cost of raising the author). Donald Rumsfeld may be an odd one to come to mind while reading Bernard Cooper, but think of Rumsfeld's infamous remark: "You go to war with the army you have, not the army you might want or wish to have at a later time." Substitute "father" for

"army" and you have this domestic front. Until definitive loss—
death—supplants ambiguous loss—the father is, in effect, missing in
action—this narrator will battle it out in the shouting match that is
their lifelong conversation, two men trying to have the last word.

Bernard Cooper

Old Birds

My father calls one afternoon to ask if I've made funeral arrangements. "For you," I ask, "or for me?"

"I know this is a morbid subject," he says, "but your number's gonna be up someday just like everybody else's. You could be walking down the street, minding your own business and—Wham! Heart attack or truck, you'll never know what hit you. It wouldn't hurt to be prepared."

"I've already made plans," I tell him.

"So you couldn't use a casket?"

"I'm going to be cremated."

His hearing aid whines. "You're what?"

"I'm going to be cremated!" I shout. The phone is in the spare room I use as an office. Sketches are taped to my drafting board, blueprints spread across the floor.

"Your mother's sister, Estelle was cremated," my father informs me. "You probably don't remember her because she died before you were born, but let me tell you her ashes were heavy, all those little bits of bone. Of course, Estelle was a big gal. *Zaftig,* we called it.

Jake, her husband, invented the windshield wiper, but the idiot didn't apply for a patent and that's how he ruined their lives."

"I see," I say. The ringing phone had awakened me from an afternoon nap, but I was too embarrassed to tell my father. He likes to point out that, even though he's the senior citizen, I'm the sedentary man in the family, a family that consists of him and me. I often crawl into bed toward the end of the day and contemplate a project, and not even my inexhaustible father can convince me that lying there isn't work. Of course, to the naked eye it looks like I'm loafing, when buildings are actually taking shape—elevations, complex floor plans, isometric drawings instead of dreams. I once read that Albert Einstein spent hours lying in bed, his arm suspended over the edge of the mattress, a stone clasped in his hand; if he drifted off, his palm would open and the stone woke him when it hit the floor. It was here, in the ether of half-sleep, that he claimed to discover his finest ideas. Anyway, no matter how proud my father is of famous Jews, he'd be quick to remind me that I'm no Einstein, and that lying down in daylight is a waste of time.

At the age of eighty-nine, my father's hands shake and his thoughts are often muddled, but his energy never seems to wane. When she was alive, my mother used to say that my father plugged himself into a wall socket at night in order to recharge his battery—"a battery," she liked to joke, "that I haven't seen since our honeymoon." Despite a slew of infirmities and the medications keeping them in check, my father could be the subject of a longevity experiment, though he's been obsessed with his imminent death for the last ten years.

"I put a down payment on a casket today," he says. "Waterproof. Rosewood. Pretty as a piano. The funeral director—the son of a guy who hired me to carpet the place I don't know how many years ago—was having a two-for-one sale. That's why I'm asking; they're going cheap."

"Thanks," I say. "That's awfully . . . thoughtful."

"You should see how that shag held up. Still as white and fluffy as a cloud. The perfect pile for Haven of Rest."

Only then do I hear the whoosh of passing traffic. I brace myself. "Dad," I ask, "where are you?" Silence, as my father no doubt peers around for a familiar landmark, squinting at street signs, cocking his head.

"You'd think someone would have the common decency to help me open a jar of peanut butter," he says. I'm certain he's holding the jar up to show me—it's Jif or Skippy, one of the brands my mother used to buy—as though I could see it, reach through the phone and twist off the lid. "I'm hungry!" he says.

My father wanders. And I don't just mean in conversation. The whole mess began after I'd moved him into an apartment complex in my neighborhood, one of the countless stucco boxes that line the streets of Hollywood, remnants from the building boom of the six-ties. My father's apartment is on the second story, at the end of a narrow balcony whose wrought-iron railing vibrates with footfalls, like the string of some giant violin. Though modest by most stan-dards, our old house had become too big for him in the decade since my mother's death, and only after he'd moved out did it occur to me that, instead of feeling lost in those rooms, my father might lose his way in the streets.

The first time it happened, I was driving home from a lecture called *Utopia: A Myth of Modernism?* when I stopped at a red light close to home and noticed an old man tottering up to the cars ahead of mine. He motioned people to roll down their windows, hoisting toward them what appeared to be a jar of pickles. Not until the man approached the car of the woman in front of me did I realize he was my father. I saw the woman quickly lock her doors and look away, as if my father was a derelict or specter. My first impulse was to punish her with a blast of my horn, but before I knew it, my father was standing beside my door. "Hey Jimmy," he said with eerie nonchalance, handing me a jar of kosher dills. I stared at him, incredulous. "Arthritis," he remarked, as if that explained why he was standing in the middle of Franklin Avenue. It was a warm night. My windows were rolled down, the radio tuned to a local college station playing Japanese koto music, its warped chords, in the unexpected presence of my father, suddenly too lugubrious and loud. "Are they killing a cat?" he asked, nodding toward the radio. I clamped the jar between my knees and struggled with the lid, imagining an argument with the manager of the pickle factory, in which I gave him a tongue-lashing on behalf of all the arthritic people who'd had to do battle with his vacuum seals. Returning the open jar to my father, I inhaled a whiff of vinegar. I was about to insist that my father either get in the car or out of the road, when the drivers behind me began to honk—I hadn't seen the light turn green—and my father shooed me off with a flap of his hand. In the rear view mirror, I saw him brave the glaring headlights and screeching brakes. Once he'd made it safely to the sidewalk, he sauntered toward the street where he lived, passing the windows of Daily Donuts, Dress-for-Less, and Insta-Tan, those obstinate weeds of commerce sprouting all over town.

Only after I arrived home did I realize that pickle juice had sloshed onto my fly, and while dabbing my crotch with tap water, I tried to remember when I first became aware of having a father. I would have settled for any recollection, no matter how fleeting or incomplete: a vision of his hair, black and lacquered, or the cooing moon of his face floating above my crib. I had just turned fifty, and standing in the bathroom of a house I almost owned, the distance between me and my history seemed immense, unbridgeable. It was as if I'd never been an infant, or as if my father had always been old, aimless in his quest for favors, irate when the world refused to help.

"Listen to me, Dad," I say, gripping the receiver. "Ask the next person who walks by where you are." He could have been anywhere. Just last month he'd ended up in Norwalk, nearly twenty miles and two bus transfers away from the mailbox at his corner where, several hours before he phoned, he'd gone to mail a gas bill, sans the stamp.

"Where am I?" I hear him ask a passerby.

"What city?"

"No," barks my father. "What galaxy. Jimmy," he says in the general vicinity of the mouthpiece, "Is it me, or are people plain stupid these days?"

"Screw you, old man."

"Dad . . ."

"Don't 'Dad' me. Here comes someone else."

"Hello?" It's the voice of a girl, maybe twelve, to whom my father must have handed the phone.

"Could you please tell me what street you're on and then give the telephone back to my father?"

"Is this a trick?" she asks. I can tell from her voice that she's smiling.

"My father's lost and you'd be doing me a big favor if you could look around for a street sign and let me know where he's calling from."

"Can't he see for himself?"

"Not very well."

"Is that why his glasses are so thick? They make his eyes look really creepy."

"What are you?" I hear my father ask her, "a goddamn optometrist?" Suddenly there's an airy swishing, and I picture the receiver swinging back and forth at the end of its cord, the booth abandoned.

"Hello?" I shout. "Hello?"

"You know," says my father, barely able to contain his rage. "You don't have to treat me like an invalid. I'm not some invalid!"

"I know," I say. "You're the opposite, whatever that is." I start to worry that I couldn't find him even if I organized a dragnet or called out the hounds. "Did that girl tell you where you are?"

"I'm on Central."

"Avenue?"

"She didn't say."

There are at least a dozen streets in Los Angeles named Central. From an urban-planning standpoint, this defeats the very idea of the plaza, the city square, the convergence of far-flung neighborhoods into a single place. Naming more than one street Central is like calling all of your children Fred.

"Does it look like downtown, Dad? Are there tall buildings around you?"

"Whaddya call tall?'

His question seems as cryptic as a riddle. "Ten stories or more."

"I suppose you could call them . . . I see . . . oy," he sighs. "I'm too hungry to concentrate."

"Dad, if you're on Central Avenue downtown, I can be there in ten minutes, so don't worry."

"Who's worried?" he says, irritably. "I've got food, don't I?"

When deprived of protein, his blood sugar plummets, and confusion spins him like a wobbly top. Recently, I bought him Chinese takeout, and he was so hungry by the time he opened the door that he momentarily mistook me for his own reflection in a full-length mirror. A doctor would probably see this as proof of his mental deterioration. It also proved to me, however, that the older I get, the more alike we look: receding hairline, cleft chin, a tendency to freckle— hurtling toward the common end with which my father is so obsessed. "Maybe if you bang the lid of the jar against something, you can loosen it enough to open it by yourself. A little food might tide you over till I can get there."

After the impact, a deafening clatter. "Dad?"

"Incredible," he says. "The table for the phone book must have been stuck on with Scotch tape!"

"Are you okay?"

"How can you ask me that when I can't open the peanut butter! I paid good money for it! I'm ridiculous, Jimmy. What will I have to say for myself when I meet my maker?"

"You built a terrific business."

"Carpets?"

"How about me?" I say. "I must be a wonderful consolation for the indignities of old age." I laugh, alone.

"Were you sleeping when I called?"

"No, Dad. I was working."

"In bed, I bet."

"I'm working on a project for Mid-Wilshire, near where your store used to be. It'll be low-income housing for the people who used to live in the neighborhood but can't afford to retire there."

"Bunch of old birds," he grumbles. "Half my friends are dead."

"Mine too," I tell him.

He clears his throat. "You don't have the AIDS though, do you, Jim?"

"No, but . . ."

"But what?" he says, alarmed.

But there was Greg, I want to tell him, *and Douglas and Jesse and Hank and Luis.* I try to remember each of my friends, and more precisely, the parts of themselves they fought to keep: their balance and vision and appetite, sensation in their fingers, control of their bowels. Yet some days all I recall of each man is how he let go of his body at last. No wonder cenotaphs and tombs make up the bulk of visionary architecture, with domes like eyes gazing toward heaven and endless flights of memorial steps; the dead have always outnumbered the living.

"I'm as healthy as a horse," I assure him.

"You and me both. But who knows for how long. When can you get me?"

"I've got an idea. Look on the telephone and tell me the number and area code."

"Someone must've scratched it out"

"What about the phone next to yours? Are you at a row of booths?"

"I wouldn't call them booths, exactly. They're like hoods on poles, with telephones inside."

A woman's prerecorded voice breaks in. "Please deposit fifty cents." Her inflections are all wrong, like a kitchen appliance trying to sound feminine.

My father says, "Fifty cents!"

"Take it easy," I tell him.

The woman repeats her request.

"I don't have any more change," shouts my father. "Can't you wait till I get home and find my wallet?" It's hard to tell whether the plea is directed at me or the disembodied voice. "I thought I'd only be gone a minute. I'm in my slippers!"

"Dad," I say, trying to sound calm, "look in the booth next to yours and tell me the number; I'll call you back on *that* phone."

I wait. I pace. Phone pressed against my ear, I listen to muffled, rush-hour horns. Eager as I am to find my father, I'm ready to crawl into bed again. I love the surrender, the stillness of repose, gravity like a stone I hold and won't let fall. It's almost dusk, but the light is warm for a California winter, when the sun shines obliquely and shadows are long. The house creaks as it does every evening, wind rustling the trees in my yard. *Old birds,* I keep thinking. And then it hits me: a retirement home that's an aviary! It's a weird idea, but workable. I can see the spacious atrium that houses flocks of exotic birds. Beneath a great skylight grow tropical palms and stands of banyan. The residents will gaze from their windows at airborne canaries, parrots engaged in extravagant disputes, finches preening and singing to their kind.

Then the telephone goes dead. Not dead, but that vast, desolate hiss of static, and I call out for my father a final time.

Issue 153, 1999

Jonathan Lethem

on

Thomas Glynn's *Except for the Sickness I'm Quite Healthy Now. You Can Believe That.*

The Paris Review, sure, but a New York story all the way, in a mode let's call Crumbling Tenement Grotesque, familiar from Sol Yurick, Paula Fox, Malamud's "The Tenants," and dozens of other instances. There's also a measure of Joyce Cary's Gulley Jimson from "The Horse's Mouth," and a bit of Henry Miller (who gazes at starving Parisian bohemians through Brooklyn Tenement Grotesque eyes), but Glynn's distinction is to tip this mode into ecstatic irrational cataclysm. His sentences are glottally clotted, scraped onto the page's canvas by paintbrushes used without cleaning them first. His paragraphs sculptural, furniture heaped up to burn for heat but then, having caught the angled winter light from the window, too alluring to ignite. So he paints the heap as a still life instead. This story is the equivalent of Kenneth Koch's "The Artist" or Frank O'Hara's "Why I Am Not a Painter," a New York School story. It wants to be a painting even as it tests the absurd limits of that impulse. It wants to be a painting that's too big to be a painting, because it wants to gobble up character and voice, too, to wonder at the old men wandering in the street, to cast them as artists and critics, to tell you what they do when they wander off the edge of the canvas (and one of these days it's going to get around to telling you about Golub, it swears!). The voice demands the gestural freedom of the painter but wants to uncork its irascible, lustful glance in a hundred directions the paint can't go. In that way it resembles the paintings of a painter frustrated with the narrative limits of his art, like Philip Guston when he exploded his sublime abstractions in favor of grubby self-portraits of stubbly painters with cigars and hob-nail boots. Guston had to paint dozens of them to tell his story, one wouldn't do. For Glynn, language may be the color blue that's used in the place of all other colors: the paint that won't actually let you see the painting, but can do absolutely anything you need it to do anyway.

Thomas Glynn

※

Except for the Sickness I'm Quite Healthy Now. You Can Believe That.

This morning a man came to my door and asked if I had taken a bath. I told him I was an artist and he left. I called Sinkowiz and asked him what that meant but he didn't know. I like to know what things mean, their deeper significance. So then I asked my slum landlord, Solomon Golub, but he only lied and said it was the man from the water department. Someday I'll tell you about Golub, king of the slum landlords, but not now. Not with the pain I've got.

Funny how a room can turn around. I mean you can stand in one place, with your feet on solid floor, and the room can spin around like a top. Ever watch colors then? Red, green, violet, they all turn into blue. The pain helps and then sometimes when I'm not on my feet the paints will change colors and tubes and those goddam rats are partial to navy blue, they eat right through the tubes, metal, plastic and all and then gorge on the paint.

Stark came over last night and I showed him my new picture. He said it was all right except for the red. He says that just to gall me, Stark does. I say what red and he says there and points to a place which is blue and I say that's blue and he says red. Stark! What does he know. He can't even walk on the ground. If you watch him closely you see that he walks on air. Two inches of air. How can anybody who walks on air know anything about painting? Still, I ask him, sucker that I am. Lately I am asking more people like that. Even Golub, who likes art if it can cover up a bad hole in the wall. Next time you see Stark, look at his pants. They come down over his heels, brushing the ground. How can anyone tell he's walking on air if his pants are too long and touch the ground? He tries to hide it. He's embarrassed about walking on air.

Stark sews. He has a showing at the Stampfli of old sheets. They're all stained, his sheets. Also, a showing of laundry tickets at the Almalfi.

Did you ever see Stark and Golub argue? Stark is five feet four and Golub is five feet six. But with Stark two inches off the ground he comes up level to Golub. They stand and shout, mouth to mouth, and Golub puts his hands on Stark's shoulders and pushes him the remaining two inches down to the ground, but unless he keeps his hands there Stark just pops up again, crew cut to crew cut with Golub. Being artists, they both argue economics. Stark lives below me, a tenant of madman Golub. Golub is trying to put hot water in our lofts so he can raise the rent. Each day the plumbers come, and each night Stark and I are busy with pipe wrenches undoing their work. Once the hot water is in and running the rent goes up. So far we are even with the plumbers, but Golub is thinking of adding more to keep ahead. That's Golub. Always thinking.

Another thing about blue. My model has varicose veins which fascinate me. Did you ever see a really good showing? I don't mean the beginnings, those immature spiderwebs with their picky little microscopic traces. I'm talking about your great over-hanging ropes, your great knotted, clotted masses of bulging misshapen inoperative veins that are congealed like wet cotton. What shades of blue! From dark to light, sea to sky, fire to ice. The picture I'm working on now, with my model bent over so that from the rear I can see her patch, is all varicose vein. Title: Varicose Veins at Sunrise. I keep her standing all day in a tub of cold water. It brings texture, adds depth to the blue tubes. She's fifty-three, afraid I'll fire her and get a younger girl. I talk about breasts that stay up and flesh that holds together and she breaks down, blubbering. But I wouldn't have a younger model. Give me the flesh that shifts, the breasts that sag!

Snow is blue, and when you walk on snow that's blue on blue, but of course Stark doesn't make any tracks when he walks so he can't know what I'm talking about. But snow is pale blue really, the color of chipped china or faded blotters. I thought of that yesterday during the heat wave. If I feel up to it, and the pain isn't so bad, I put snow in my pictures, lots of fat flakes with a footprint or two. If Jenny can shiver when I paint so much the better. She has rheumatism and shivering comes easy to her. I make it simple by keeping her in a bucket of water, her large blistered feet rubbing the sides of the rusty iron tub. Sometimes if I leave a window open in the dead of winter, which I'm liable to do, it looks like a colony of mice is running beneath her skin. Then when I see her shake I get inspired and often do six or seven completed nudes in one day. Titles: Jenny Shivering in a Bucket of Water, Jenny Under Delusions of Cold, Jenny's Veins, Jenny Without Food For Three Days (and its corollary, Jenny Fainting From Lack of Food and Falling Head First into the Iron Bucket), Blue Jenny, Jenny In Between, and my big one, Jenny Jumps. The last one is the size of my wall. I wanted to do a big picture and nailed canvas to one of the walls, propping chairs and tables and ladders against it so I could hop around on my one good leg and fill the canvas with lines. I had Jenny jumping from one of the ceiling beams in the loft. I wanted to get that look people have on their face when they go through the air. Have you seen that look? It's like modeling a face in damp seersucker shorts. The mouth has this absent-minded look about it, the eyes seem to be hurricane centers. Jenny jumped, her blubber trailing behind, adding buoyancy, floating like potato angels. Jenny is all fluff and old chocolate, and when she jumps, she expands. This is art, that expansion. I'm doing a sequel to Jenny Jumps. Jenny Lands. Setting: Old broken cement, blistered sidewalk all cracks and acne, dry bones for plants and rust-red blood scattered like pandemonium seeds. In the middle, in parts, lies Jenny, full of hope, her mouth bleeding belief and the shock of the real blended miraculously into her limbs. Great stores of curious onlookers and large cities burning in the background, crucifixions and pilgrims walking, bombs exploding and lovers opening letters. The surroundings of Jenny. It will be the greatest thing I, or anybody, has done yet. It's what I've been trying to say for years.

Golub says he'll buy it to cover a hole in the wall.

I'll take praise wherever I can find it.

Stark, who should know, says Jenny Lands can hang side by side with Giambo.

I'll tell you more about Golub as soon as the pain goes away. Golub sleeps during the day on a small canvas cot upstairs. If Stark or I feel like waking him we pound on the pipes with a monkey wrench until he stirs. With that noise he'll run out into the street thinking his building is falling down, and just to convince him we sometimes throw things out the window. Packing crates and type fonts and baby carriages with little nephews. Then he'll run to the phone booth and call the Health Department, complaining that the "Roooskeeies are coming," and he's getting the first bomb.

I don't think I told you about the pain. There are two kinds. Professional and amateur. In between is Golub. I'll talk about that later.

Half the numbers under ten are prime, so there must be a connection there somewhere. But try to tell that to Stark! I asked him about emotion in painting. I told him I thought it was a net full of feelings, some of which poked fingers and toes into the picture. All he said was that I had too much blue. Here here here and here he said, too much blue. Change this to vermilion, this to ochre, that to beige, and this to sienna. I leave him alone he kicks my paintings. I have to put ropes around him when he comes into the studio. He doesn't understand blue. Paint by the stars he says. He pulls out his astrology handbook, a Carrol Richter special, mumbles some Latin names and comes up with exact dates and times when I should paint. Stark, floating two inches off the ground, says I should paint on the twenty-third of March at two-thirty in the afternoon, again on the twenty-fifth at seven, and then wait until the sixteenth of April when I can paint the whole day.

One day I showed him a new picture which he said was out of my horoscope and kicked a hole in it before I could hit him with my iron easel. I painted around the hole. But what can you do with a critic?

When Stark gets excited he rises, and if he's really enthusiastic about something he floats up to the ceiling. Jumping after him doesn't do any good, he'll just bob along the ceiling like a moth after cotton candy.

Remember that faggot farmboy in Nebraska who killed eleven people? I'm doing a series on him. Three-quarter profile set in plaster of Paris surrounded by a movie marquee, rerun of an old George Brent picture. Halloween death mask and magic lantern eyes under dime store plastic rims and larger than life proboscis. Munger leveling his gun and out pops a flag, *love*. I like things surrounding other things in my pictures, and I like people hiding, using masks and stepping out of dark alleys wearing capes and frightening drunks. But try to get *that* into a painting. And that's just the beginning. When you add up the trading stamps and the formica counters and the bedwetters and the high school Spanish teachers, where does that leave you? In Toledo with El Greco. The canvas isn't big enough. I'll have to block off the intersections and lay my linen in the streets, paint with dripping buckets from tenement roofs.

Stark is taking lessons to fly, so he can't understand. When you look down, what can you see? Only birdshit and slugs, if you happen to be a bird. I tell Stark, what do you want to fly for? He thinks it will help his art. When I try to explain about art he's bumping his head against the ceiling. So who can you talk to about art?

Much more on Golub later.

Sinkowiz is calling now. I think I'll tell him about the pain. Did you know the monarch butterfly will go thousands of miles just to get a good piece of ass?

Talking to Golub after I've taken down his pipes. I take him up to my studio and show him my paintings. I flip though canvas after canvas, put slivers in my fingers, and smile. Golub is not one of your wishy-washy art owners. He buckles his shoes every morning. Buttons on his pants. Who can beat lead pipe enlightenment like that?

When Stark floats, he fills himself up like a blowfish. Huff and puff, taking in great balloons of air, inflating his cheeks. His skin distends, his face changes from purple to red to pink. He floats above our heads, a network of veins. Golub looking up.

Golub would be a hunchback if he had the choice, but lacking the will to deform he stares popeyed. I have a thing in yellow. Title: Golub Staring. I have a hole in my floor where I build most of my fires and I put him in this. There were three stages. Golub in the hole, me painting over him on the floor, and Jenny above both of us on a swing. I fixed it so Golub could look up her dress and when he did, then I had the look I wanted. I could have titled it Golub Staring Under Jenny's Dress or Golub in Discomfort, but I liked the neutral tones of Golub Staring better. His forehead is freckled, and what occupies the center of the picture is this forehead, this sandy, speckled forehead. The more I looked at his forehead the more it reminded me of a beach, so I painted it as a beach. Sand, with grey wood and broken shells and faded glass. I didn't use a brush but scraped large clumps of crusty oil on the canvas. I used paint that had dried, sticking it on in sections, like a statue. I mixed some sand in with the paint, and far off, in a wrinkle of the left brow, I had a beach city burning, concrete bunkers exploding and dog legs falling through storm clouds and old newspapers with faded ocean print spelling forgotten tragedies buried under the sand. All that was on Golub's forehead, staring up. And much more. Golub has acne, pits of flesh that insult the eyes, his adolescent blitzkrieg. These became pop bottles with lost notes inserted by myopic teenage girls who worked from dawn to dusk in glass factories dreaming of orgasms. Old bones (naturally), insect bodies blowing like dry bamboo in the Philippine wind, spittle damp and bubbly drawing together hundreds of grains into a small spitball. Women's liquids, deposited in secret places, harsh droppings, folded under thin straw-colored leaves and spent in quick spurts. All that was on Golub's forehead. I worked fast, in a rage, throwing paint, building this forehead up like a plaster wall. And underneath, dim but not lost, two faint firefly eyes shining through the wind, looking hopefully up at Jenny.

Sinkowiz gave me a good price for it, almost enough to pay off my lawsuit.

If Stark takes to flying too much I can't have him in my studio, I made that resolution yesterday.

The pain starts in the left leg and runs up through the right testicle like a silver wire, where it shorts over to the left ball, down the right leg where it gathers in little hair balls, which is what happens if you're not careful and swallow hair. Then the surface of the leg goes bad, and no matter how you slap it, from thigh to knee, nothing is felt, you might as well have plastic for skin. I told the doctors about it and they told me it was sciatica compounded by a pinched vein. I thanked them and paid my bill, slapping my leg, which still felt like plastic. When the pain comes I can't talk much and that's not because it hurts. Pain is squeezed out of me and coats my walls. I have an aching knee over by the window that must take up a good four square feet. It's almost an inch thick, and on bad nights it vibrates, crumbling the plaster in its tendon fingers. I sit smoking, watching it. How can I paint then, watching that wall shake, my knee ache, with such pain? Pain jumps too, and one flew out my window and landed on a bum below, crippling his other leg. Sometimes when the pain comes I try to paint my big picture, but often the walls shake so that nothing is steady.

Jenny talks with Golub and that's when I'm sure they're plotting something even though all Golub can talk about is lead pipes. And his driving tests. Golub is a great conversationalist. He fascinates. He is beyond the bore. With him it is a matter of reality, like dropping a plumb line to the center of the earth. What you find there you talk about. Golub dropped and found. Lead pipes and driving tests. Take your number three lead pipe, he'd say, and indeed I had already taken it the night before and dropped it out the window, letting it fall in the cellar doorway where he and I have our agreement. Did I tell you about the agreement? Take your number three lead pipe, he says, talking as if he had a cigar in his mouth. Conforms to your ASA specifications as cited in code number thirty-seven of the plumbing and heating contractors. Golub tells me all about lead pipes, about shear strengths and thread pitch, about decay factors and incessant vibration strain. I like that last one, the one about incessant vibration strain. I thought it applied somehow. To something. I let it roll around on my tongue, coating the consonants with saliva and tickling the s's on the roof of my mouth. Golub has a winner there, in that incessant vibration strain.

Goddam that Stark!

He's getting to act more like a bird every day. Soon as he comes in the first thing he wants to do is fly up to a rafter and drop bird shit on the forks. No manners at all and he's constantly shedding. What good is he up there, on the rafters? I brought him down one evening with my Crossman, lead pellet in the wing, because he was making tracks over my canvas.

Golub tells me about his driving lessons. What he does with the clutch and how he turns the wheel with one hand and signals with the other. Golub's feet on the pedals: small, tiny little hooves gloved in leather and reaching a delicate point at the front. Golub has weak legs and can't press the pedals hard enough, too cheap for power brakes and automatic transmission. Last Tuesday during one of his road tests he smashed into a bread truck. I got a call on the phone and rushed down, paints in hand. Used a lot of yellow and red. Noticed that when metal bends it turns yellow. Used the flat of the spatula, quick strokes like cutting turkey. Golub leaning his head through the cracked window, thoughtfully bleeding and I had a tube of vermilion that did the job nicely. I like the warm shine of vermilion, and the rich sheen before it dries. I have since tried to rework it in blue, but a certain power is missing.

Golub fails driver's tests with alarming regularity. Stark came down from the ceiling long enough to make a suggestion. He told me to look for connections. Before I could ask him what with what, he flew back up again, and since he's out of range of the Crossman I'll have to be content with that enigmatic phrase. Typical of Stark.

I didn't tell you about my big picture yet. Invited Steinmetz up to talk about it. He's the only one left. He's a cigar store clerk downstairs and I suspect also a friend of Golub's, but what can you do when you're trapped? Steinmetz listens to me, sucking his teeth. He's good at lit matches, and just this week almost burnt down my studio. That would have gotten Stark out, but I'll have to watch Steinmetz because I think he talks to Golub. Did I ever tell you why Golub is always taking driving tests? Clutch chatter and low octane knock are second nature to him. He wishes he could get his hands greasy. Stark just dropped another egg. Two since this morning.

Steinmetz brought his mother over, and that's something even Sinkowiz won't do. His mother is Danish and smokes cigars and that's how he got his start in the business, but of course he's German. She wears long black gabardine dresses that come down to her ankles and has a small charcoal mustache at the corner of her mouth. I wanted to do a picture of her and Steinmetz, title: Steinmetz's Mother, but with him in the picture since I thought he was a part of her. All blacks and shoe-polish browns, like the one I did of Golub's feet, title: Golub's Feet on the Pedals, size eight pumps in soft calfskin, hand stitched and shivering, dancing in the air. I painted Golub's feet from underneath, to get the character, and I wanted to do the same with Steinmetz's Mother, showing old smoke and forgotten tobacco and falling folds of garbadine, locked rooms and stained books with bitter scenes, *Who is to remember this?* Hanging over the drawing room like a long Danish winter night. But try to get that in. All black and brown and colors they don't have yet. Try to mix them!

Anyway I couldn't do it, working in blue now and I don't see those lips in anything but long brown rolled cadavers of tobacco wrappers.

Golub tells me that Stark refuses to pay rent since he's a bird. I can see he thinks Stark is setting a dangerous precedent.

My big picture, the one with *everything* in, is going to be in blue. I told Sinkowiz about it and he says he's got a buyer lined up but the only one I can talk to about it now is Steinmetz's mother. I've given up on Steinmetz. He spends all his time sucking his teeth. Yesterday he swallowed two fillings, gold, and his bowel movements are watched with great eagerness.

The big picture. Everything has to be in it. I've decided to do a falling picture. Things falling. I think blue will put that across best. How big should the canvas be? Don't know. Might have to knock out a wall. What falls? Jenny, Golub's Feet, Steinmetz's Mother. But that's just a start.

I used to get invitations from Sinkowiz to go to openings, but now he feels I work best through a front. I still haven't met his mother. She wears chrome-rimmed glasses, and her face, like my leg, is plastic. I'd love to see that face, but Sinkowiz is adamant. No mother, no plastic face.

People will fall two ways in my painting. Head first or feet first. Eisenhower will fall head first, but Jenny and the Virgin Mary will fall feet first. Steinmetz's mother wanted to know if she could fall in my picture and I said yes. Not that I consider this a compromise since I'd planned to have her falling anyway. I gave her a choice of head or feet first, and she took head first. She's afraid that if she falls feet first her dress will billow up over her head. Everybody is in blue, the Duke of Windsor is in navy-blue plus fours while his wife is in sky blue tennis shorts and an off-blue polo shirt. Naturally they fall holding hands. Steinmetz came up and he wants to fall too, though he'll settle for whatever way I put him, feet or head first. He'd like to fall with his cigars. Golub wants to fall too, but he wants to fall with his driving lessons, and I told him that just people will be falling in this picture. He wants to know if he could fall with a gearshift lever in his hand, maybe a brake pedal or two. I'll have to

think about that. I think I'll put Golub falling in between Mao Tse-
tung and De Gaulle. He asked if he could fall in his blue serge, and
I told him yes. Sinkowiz came up and wanted to know how the big
one was coming and I told him, but he wanted to see. Funny about
Sinkowiz, he never listens to words. He has ears, but I think they're
sealed over on the inside. He must read lips. I think I'll have Sinkowiz
falling in my picture, upside down next to Eisenhower, reading his
lips. Sinkowiz would fall good. He has that look about his face, the
look of someone used to falling, eyeballs detached, cheeks inflated
like a parachute, hair grabbing for air. Some people are good at falling, and some not. I'll show this in my picture. My picture takes
place in an elevator shaft. Everybody crowding in at the top, falling
in the middle. There is no landing. Nobody ever lands. There will be
arms and legs and dog heads twirling past elevator cables, some
people will slide, holding onto the greased cables with bloody hands
and a look of automated horror. Others will ignore the cables and
fall like Buddhists burning in Saigon, arrow sure. The grabbers will
reach out, twirl, shiver, and fall like animated cartwheels in a fire-
cracker carnival. Everyone will fall in my picture. Heads of state,
models, safecrackers, highway patrolmen. I'm considering other
things falling. Alarm clocks and forks and crutches.

Stark came down and wants to know if he can fall, but I told him no.
Then he told me I could fly if I wanted to. He told me to fill my
cheeks with air and breathe fast. I tried but only my heels came off
the ground. We talked about blue and Stark said that black was
blue, that everything was black and that was why he was flying. He
laid an egg and flew back up to the ceiling.

The painting is turning out to be larger than I thought. It already
covers two walls, and everyone who sees it wants to fall in it. Jenny
wants to fall in her furs and I asked if she meant that old muskrat
coat she wears. Like all old people when they get upset, Jenny's

nostrils flutter and go pale, the tissue drained of blood. Blue again. I told her she could fall in her furs. She's happy.

If you look towards the center of your nose and press the corner of your eye, you can see a small cornea of the visible spectrum. Newton in the Optics.

Steinmetz's mother wanted to know why people fell and I asked her if she knew Sinkowiz's mother but she said she never associated with anyone who had a plastic face. I can see why. Her's is leather. Cracked and peeling, like a blue Michelangelo ceiling, with faint flakes that fall like flesh showers on her teacup. She takes no notice. Still, we can talk.

She speaks in blue syllables, like old river icicles. She takes one bony peeling hand and reaches inside her dress, the black gabardine crinkling like a forest fire. Fingers fumble, feeling old linen and immigrant undergarments. When she finds the word she wants, she has no hesitancy in bringing it out, holding it between her dead fish fingers like a cracked amethyst. We spent one evening talking of Japan. She attributed her old age to cigar smoking.

Did I tell you the Pope, His Holiness, is falling in my picture? To be sure. Along with the entire College of Cardinals and selected artifacts of Vatican City. They fall feet first, their robes billowing up like mushrooms. His Holiness holds a miter in one hand and a fork in the other. It is Friday and he is eating cod.

Sinkowiz came and said the picture was too big. It now covers three walls, and I have half the upper chamber of the New York State Legislature falling along with two dozen rock-and-roll stars, five respected surgeons, and ten policemen, arm in arm, who are ceremoniously trampling on a select group of Ban the Bomb demonstrators. Sinkowiz saw the last vignette and wanted to know if I was going political and I told him I would if I could. Did you ever notice the look on someone's face when they get testy? All wound up, like a rusty screw that's been worked on backwards? That's Sinkowiz. I'm having reservations about him. He talks with Golub too much, and lately is getting very commercial. Stark thinks commerce is good for art but after my last arrest I don't agree.

Jenny's teeth hurt. I told her they would. At her age what can you expect. She took them out and showed them to me. They were hurting. She has arguments with her teeth several times a day. She says they make her say things she doesn't want to say.

I told her I'd put her teeth in the picture, falling.

Golub tried to hit me with a lead pipe.

With Sinkowiz, it's the mouth. I tried to explain that to him the other day. I told him, look Sinkowiz, your mouth is shaped like a saucer and that's why you say what you do. It may be the last we'll see of Sinkowiz. O.K. with me. Have been trusting him less since he started brushing his teeth.

Yesterday we celebrated the King of Denmark's birthday and everybody came. Steinmetz and Steinmetz's mother, Jenny, and even Golub, who brought his own control panel with him. Golub is very intent on passing his driving test. Wherever he goes he takes his steering wheel, pedals, windshield, gear shift lever, and bench seat. We had ice cream and cake and Jenny passed out party hats, shiny little elastic domes with a rubber that fit around the neck. Golub sat shifting gears and making Plymouth noises. He takes his test on a Plymouth, six cylinder, though at the present he's having clutch trouble. Stark flew down and read a poem though he's no poet. Jenny gave him a hat and he complained about the elastic. Someday I'll have to have a good talk with Stark.

Why do old men walk in the streets in winter?

Last night Sinkowiz came and knocked on my door, late at night. I had trouble with some of the chains, and at least one padlock had rusted shut, but I finally got the door open. Sinkowiz asked me if I

believed in art for art's sake, and I told him I might. Who knows?
He said if I did I should cut up my big picture and sell the pieces. I
let him into the main studio because I liked a vein that was throbbing on the side of his temple. It wasn't a big vein, actually about the
size of a fingernail, but it jumped up and down like a snail stran-
gling. Someday I'll tell you more about Sinkowiz. That he's a prick,
in the aforementioned sense, you know, but did you know that he
wears white hair silvered and has a camel's hair coat which he's
thrown up on three times already? His face is the color of shiny pig-
skin, and that always fascinates me. I'm a sucker for Sinkowiz's face,
I must admit. It's like new money rubbed into old leather. There's a
sheen about it, soft, as if he spent his entire life crying in expensive
sand. So I let him in and sat him on a kitchen chair over which hung
an electric light bulb, swaying on the end of a frayed line. Sinkowiz's head danced on the floor like a sea horse in a storm as the bulb
swung first one way and then the other. When the bulb was at one
end of its arc I could see that vein, throbbing like salmon sperm,
dark blue, the color of the Baltic. At the other end of the arc the vein
was hidden in the shadow of his head, beating, but beating unseen.
I wanted to reach over and touch his vein. All I could think of was
electricity and telephone lines. Sinkowiz blubbered on about how
he had to have that picture to sell, that he was committed to sell it,
that he needed the money, that it was too big to sell in its present
size. It now covers all four walls and the end is not in sight. It's heading for the roof, my canvas, my resurrected linen, unfolding its scroll
like equator up to the heavens. But with his vein and my unfinished
canvas and Sinkowiz's blubbering, I had to set up a new canvas. I
worked fast, sketching him in charcoal. Titanium blue, zinc red,
and some old yellow that has been drying up in a forgotten tube. I
started with a brush but couldn't get the paint on fast enough to
match the frenzy of that throbbing so I moved on to a spatula and

then fingers, trying to keep up with the mad army of blood that raced through that temple. Let me tell you what I put in. First of all electricity running through frayed lines, sputtering, and then shadows crossing soft faces, old olives, the sun in Sicily, expensive conversations, and of course Sinkowiz's face in triplicate, pleading, smiling, crying, being soothed by costly salves and rubbed with blushing liquids from near-nude virgins. Hair like hoarfrost, looked at in mirrors, often combed. If you look closely at Sinkowiz's face you'll find it's hideously smoothed by small scars, brushed shining like tight leather over upholstery. And the vein, beating its own metronome, reckoning the cost of cocktails and canvas, calligraphy and Corot.

I finished at five a.m., and Sinkowiz was asleep, so I wrapped his lank, slack body in the dirty camel's hair coat and carried him over to my couch. I pulled the coat around his shoulders with the feeling I was wrapping a piece of fish.

No more room in the studio.

I'm painting on the roof. Set up curtain stretchers weighted down with bricks. Stark flies up now and then to see how I'm coming. I show him the new fallers. The mayor and the city council, five rabbis making liberal pronouncements, a dozen candy store owners, innumerable mothers with babies in arms, two thousand Gideon Bibles placed here for your convenience and enlightenment, and seven irreproachable Miss America contestants.

Word has gotten out about my picture, and everybody wants to fall in it. Stark sells tickets and Jenny seats them in a chair, or tells them to stand. There is no longer room on the roof, so I let the painting drape down the side of the building. Last night it rained, altering the composition of one section. Stark is against touching it up. He feels that whatever happens *is*, and should be left. I can see now that this painting will have no end. I hate to disappoint Sinkowiz and the mortgage on his Long Island home.

An accident.

Better explain about it from the ending. We had a fire. Golub keeps insisting that I had a fire, but he says that for the benefit of the insurance agent who stands perpetually at his elbow. The insurance agent says he can't understand how the fire got started, but it's perfectly simple. Stark did it. Of course he really didn't do it, but since we're going backwards to explain (which is really the only way to explain), he did it. How did he start it the agent asks. With the ash from his cigar I say. The agent tells me that birds don't smoke but I try to explain to him that Stark is no bird. Temporarily, a phase. Behind all those feathers stands Stark, the real commercial menace. Now why is Stark smoking a cigar? Easy. He is upset. And where did he get the cigar? Another easy one. Steinmetz and his mother, Steinmetz's mother, went in halvsies on a box of slim Panatellas, Stark's favorites. Stark goes for your riverboat-gambler cigar, and likes to fiddle with a gold watchchain when he smokes. For the benefit of the insurance agent, I explained why Stark was upset. This was because of the argument I was having with Golub. Now why was I having an argument with Golub? Simple. Because I was having an argument with Sinkowiz. Golub and I were arguing over what Sinkowiz had said. I told Golub he couldn't hear because he keeps his driving gloves in his ears. He doesn't have pockets on his pants. So the only place he can keep his gloves are in his ears. They hang down to his shoulders, easily the world's longest, with deep folds in which he keeps all the things he normally would keep in his pockets. But as a result of this he has trouble hearing. Maybe that's why he fails his driving tests. Try to take something out of his ears and he says his ears get cold. His earmuffs look like knee-length socks. What were Sinkowiz and I arguing about? About Golub's ears. Sinkowiz claims they're normal ears, like everyone else's. He says they don't hang down, but I claim they do. When ears hang, they hang. No one can tell you different. I tell Golub he should face his long ears. Then he could accept disappointment.

Golub wants to set up a driving school in my studio. He has a plan to buy old junks and haul them up here for beginners. Golub loves driving. He figures with his own driving school he'll be able to pass his driving tests. How can you argue with a man who carries gear-shift knobs in his ears?

Steinmetz's mother wants to know if this is all real, and she has a point there. Jenny argues yes, but then she always was an incurable romantic. Steinmetz doesn't say much. Did I tell you his eyebrows and hair were completely burned off? Steinmetz's mother thinks the whole idea of people falling is unreal. She suggested I do old ladies with lap dogs, or something classic like Man Brushing his Wig, or Portia Surprised. She's a great one for people being surprised. She says that real people are always being surprised. But this she says, waving a bony peeling hand in front of my people falling picture, this is not real. I tried to tell her that people are always falling. They even fall surprised.

New fallings: five generals in full battle dress, seven postmen delivering dead letters, twenty precocious epileptics.

Golub is upset.

I tried to hit him over the head with a lead pipe. He also claims I tried to tie his ears in knots. He is currently pushing a Studebaker into my studio. It's wedged rather tightly in the elevator door.

At eight a.m. Golub is out in the rear of the elevator, feet wedged against the elevator wall, polished little landlord hands on the rear bumper of the Studebaker trying to push it into the studio. And me? I stand on the floor trying to push it back into the elevator. Golub gives a grunt, pushes, and a small drop of businessman's sweat drops from his oily brow. At ten we break for coffee, at twelve for lunch, and by special agreement we knock off at four. He is persistent, this Golub, and shows amazing strength for a landlord. The Studebaker is three inches in his favor. I calculated this amount to a bumper so I cut it off with my acetylene torch and threw it in the back yard. Golub claims he'll sue. He comes back with a lawyer, who helps him push.

Sinkowiz came over and helped me push, but he's like a lawyer, no back or shoulder muscles to speak of. Again he's crying for the big picture.

Fat men keep coming into the ground floor, but never leaving. I can see them now, wedged bulging hip to portly shoulder, Golub's Dachau. If the pain wasn't so bad I'd go downstairs and let them out. Golub's probably hoarding them, for the time when there'll be a shortage of fat men.

When fat men fall, they flutter. I've shown that. Sizzling little pork butterflies.

Steinmetz finally gave me the idea!

He sucks his teeth, but he sucks a new set each day. He has seven sets of false teeth. A Monday set, a Tuesday set, and so on. That means he returns to his sucked teeth. I call them Steinmetz's Revolving Sucked False Teeth.

The same thing with my picture. Mount it on a gigantic revolving drum, spectators at the apex. My Revolving Falling People.

And soon I'll start on the drum too, when the fire in the elevator shaft dies down and the claws on my hand turn back into fingers.

Issue 42, 1968

Sam Lipsyte

on

Mary Robison's *Likely Lake*

In the famous Mary Robison story "Yours," an elderly man and his young wife carve pumpkins on their porch for Halloween. Hers are messy and mediocre, while the husband, a retired doctor and "Sunday watercolorist," creates inventive, expressive faces. Later, after a startling turn in this very short story, the old man wishes he could tell his wife his truth, "that to own only a little talent, like his, was an awful, plaguing thing; that being only a little special meant you expected too much, most of the time, and liked yourself too little."

It's a fascinating idea to consider in relation to Robison, one of the enormous talents (and great practitioners) of the short story in America. Maybe it speaks to her deep knowledge of the various ways life tears at us, that there are the monstrous crushings—death, abandonment—and then there are constant abrasions. Most people learn to live with both. Most people, Robison's people, also, while maybe waiting around for the pain to subside, or at least turn briefly amusing, laugh, console each other, make dinner, sit on a bench, and try new tricks for better candlelight.

Many of them also secretly revel in language, in keeping an ear out for the bounties and desolations of speech. Robison not so secretly revels in language, in the odd surprises of everyday utterance, the potentially stirring rhythms. Her prose, often called minimalist during the 1980s, isn't. She suggested *subtractionist,* but another word is *exacting.* When you are exacting, you are a master of the notes and the space between the notes, as Robison has always been. In "Likely Lake," when Buddy decides he will "*dissuade*" Connie, it is as though the strategy could not exist if Buddy had not struck upon the right word. Robison's stories often depend on the rightness of the word, or the right wrongness.

That wrongness, or awkwardness, is layered into her work. She might not have known that "awkward" would be a national catchphrase someday, but Robison has always understood the emotional power of discomfort, self-consciousness, and the manner in which people, eager for real connection (or sometimes not), slide past each other, shrugging, remonstrating, cracking wise. Robison's stories and novels illuminate day-to-day confusion, as well as the great hurts that sweep down upon us. They are urgent and elegiac, funny and beautiful. If you begin to read them, they will dissuade you from doing anything else for a long time.

Mary Robison

✠

Likely Lake

His doorbell rang and Buddy peered through the viewer at a woman in the courtyard. She had green eyes and straight black hair, cut sharply like a fifties Keely Smith. He knew her. She did bookkeeping or something for the law partners next door, especially at tax times. He also remembered her from his wife's yard sale, although that was a couple years ago and the wife was now his ex. She'd bought a jewelry case and a halogen lamp. He could picture her standing on the walk there—her nice legs and the spectator pumps she wore. She'd driven a white VW Bug in those days. But it must have died because later he had noticed her arriving for work in cabs.

He had lent her twenty bucks, in fact. Connie was her name. Last June, maybe, when his garden was at its peak. He'd been out there positioning the sprinkler, first thing in the morning, when a cab swerved up and she was in back. She had rolled down her window and started explaining to him. She was coming in to work early but had ridden the whole way without realizing she'd brought an empty handbag. She *showed* it to him—a beige clutch. She even undid the clasp and held the bag out the window.

Now she waved a twenty as Buddy opened the door.

"That isn't necessary, Connie," he said.

She thanked him with a nod for remembering her name. She said, "Don't give me any argument." She came close and tucked the bill into his shirt pocket. "You see here?" she said. "This is already done."

"Well, I thank you," Buddy said. He stroked the pocket, smoothing the folded money flat. It was a blue cotton shirt he'd put on an hour earlier when he got home from having his hair cut.

She was still close and wearing wonderful perfume, but he didn't think he should remark on that. He kept his eyes level and waited as if she were a customer and he a clerk. He said, "So, are you still in the neighborhood? I rarely see you."

"They haven't needed me." She pretended a pout. "Nobody's needed me." She stepped back. It was the first week of September, still mild. She wore a fitted navy dress with a white collar and had a red cardigan sweater over her arms. Her large shapely legs were in sheer stockings.

"We have one last problem," she said. She held up a finger.

He looked at her, his eyebrows lifted.

Her hand fell and she gazed off and spoke as if reading, as if her words were printed over in the sky there to the right. "I have a crush on you," she said. "Such a crush on you, Buddy. The worst, most ungodly crush."

"No, you don't. You couldn't."

"The, worst, crush."

"Well," Buddy said. "Well dee well-dell-dell."

He owned the house—a two-story, Lowcountry cottage. It was set on a lane that led into Indian Town and beyond that were the roads and highways into north Pennsylvania. He sat on a divan near a window in the living room now and, in the noon light, looked through some magazines and at a book about birds.

He had a view from this window. Behind the house stood a tall ravine and Buddy could see through its vines and trees to the banks of Likely Lake.

His son had died after an accident there. Three years ago, August. Matthew. When he was two days short of turning twenty-one. His Jet Ski had hit a fishing boat that slid out of an inlet. The August after that, Buddy's wife left him.

He had stopped going out—what his therapist referred to as "isolating." He knocked the walls off his son's bedroom suite and off the room where Ruthie used to sew and he converted the whole upper floor into a studio. He began bringing all his assignments home. He was a draftsman, the senior draftsman at Qualitec, a firm of electromechanical engineers he had worked with for years.

"Beware of getting out of touch," his therapist had warned. "It happens gradually. It creeps over you by degrees. When you're not interacting with people, you start losing the beat. Then blammo. Suddenly, you're that guy in the yard."

"I'm who?" asked Buddy.

"The guy with the too-short pants," said the therapist.

He would *dissuade* the Connie woman, Buddy told himself now as he poked around in the kitchen. He yanked open a drawer and considered its contents, extracted a vegetable peeler, put it back in its place. He would dissuade her nicely. He didn't want to make her feel like a bug. "Let her down easy," he said aloud and both the cats spurted in to study him. Buddy had never learned to tell the cats apart. They were everyday cats, middle sized and yellow. Matt's girl-friend, Shay, had presented them as kittens, for a birthday present, the same week he died. The cats stayed indoors now and kept close to Buddy. He called one of them Bruce and the other Bruce's Brother.

He went into a utility closet off the kitchen now and rolled out a canister vacuum. He liked vacuuming. He liked jobs he could quickly complete. And he wanted things just-so when Elise came over to-night. She had changed things for him in the months since they had met. Everything was different because of her.

One way to go with the Connie woman, he was thinking, would be to parenthetically mention Elise. That might have its effect. Or a stronger method would be to say, "My girlfriend is the jealous type," or some such.

The cats padded along into the dining area and watched as Buddy positioned the vacuum and unwound its mile of electric cord. "Don't ever touch a plug like this," he told them. "It is hot, hot, hot."

Elise phoned from work around two. She was a group counselor at Cherry Trees, a psychiatric hospital over in the medical park. Buddy saw his therapist in another building on the grounds and he had met Elise there, in fact, in the parking area. It was on a snowy day last February when he'd forgotten and left his fog lights burning. She had used yellow jumper cables to rescue him. Buddy had invited her to go for coffee and the two of them drove off in his black Mercury, zooming along the Old Post Highway to get the car battery juiced.

They ended up having lunch at a French place, where Elise put on horn-rimmed glasses and read from the menu aloud. Without the glasses, she reminded him of Jean Arthur—her figure, the freckles and bouncy, curly hair. Elise's French was awful and full of oinky sounds but Buddy liked her for trying it anyway. He liked her laugh, which went up and came down.

"Vincent escaped," she said now on the phone. "He broke out somehow. From right in the middle of a Life Challenges Meeting."

"I'm fortunate I don't know what that is," Buddy said.

"The problem for *me* is, with Vincent loose and Security looking for him, I can't take my people outside. Which means no Smoke Walk."

"Right, because you're the only one with a lighter. So that they have to trail along behind you."

"Well they're not dogs. But they're getting mighty grumpy. And being critical of Vincent. They think he should be shot."

"Hard to know whose side to take," said Buddy.

"That it is," Elise said, and told him she had to go.

This flower garden was Buddy's first, but *gorgeous*. He no longer understood people who spoiled and killed plants. The therapist had suggested gardening, so one Saturday when Elise was free, she and Buddy went to Tristie's Arboretum and bought starter materials. She also helped shape the garden. They put in a design like a collar around the court and walk.

Buddy had watered, fed, and misted his flowers. With each day they bloomed, grew large, stood tall. "What more could I ask of you?" he asked them. "Nuts and fruit?"

He thought he might recruit Elise to help lay in winter pansies around the side porch if that didn't seem boring. She was good at a hundred things. She could play bridge and poker and shuffle cards. She could play the piano. She liked listening to jazz and she *knew* most of it. They'd dress up and go dancing at Sky Mountain or at

the Allegheny Club where there was an orchestra. Elise had beautiful evening clothes. She'd take him to all kinds of things—to midnight movies or a raunchy comedy club. Last spring they'd even
taken a train trip to New Orleans for Jazz Fest.

From close by, Buddy heard a woman's voice and froze. It might
be Connie's. He didn't feel up to another encounter with her, just
yet. She seemed interesting and he liked her. She certainly was a
handsome woman. She had mentioned peeking out her office window, how she always found herself watching for him. That was flattering, but still. He'd felt jarred by it. What if he were just out on
some stupid errand, grabbing the paper or the mail out of the box, if
he hadn't shaved or his shirt was on sideways?

The voice came a second time. It was *not* Connie's. However,
the next one might be, he warned himself. He shook off his gloves
and poked his tools back in their wire caddy. It was four something.
She probably got off work pretty soon.

As he scrubbed his hands, he rehearsed telling Elise the Connie
story. Elise was coming over for dinner after she finished her shift.

He started organizing the food he had bought earlier at the farmer's market. He got out a lemon and some lettuce in cello wrap, a net
bag of radishes, a plum tomato. He heaped what he wanted of that
into a wooden bowl; returned to the refrigerator and ripped a few
sprigs of parsley. "Less like a picnic," he said to himself. He arranged
a serving plate with slices of honey-baked ham; another with deviled
egg halves and used the parsley for garnish. He knew he was not a
great cook. With the exception of the jumbo shrimp he had grilled
for Elise and her mom on July 4th. Those were delicious.

He carried the serving dishes into the dining room. It was too
soon but he wanted to try the food to see how it looked set on the

table. He got out a big linen tablecloth, gripped it by the ends, and flapped it hugely in the air to wave out the folds.

The cats somersaulted in. They leapt onto the sideboard. They stood poised and still and gazed at the platter of ham.

"Scary monster," Buddy told them, but sighed and dropped the tablecloth. He marched the ham back to the kitchen and hid it deep inside the refrigerator.

Elise knew a lot, in his opinion. She'd earned a degree in social psych and she was popular with the patients at Cherry Trees. Maybe he would skip complaining to her about Connie. That could only cause worry. He should be more circumspect. Why bother Elise?

He did call, but merely to ask how she was doing and to confirm their dinner plans. "I don't want anything," he said when she came to the phone.

"They sent Martha to the Time Out Room," Elise said. "The woman admitted last Saturday? You should see her now, though. Calm and quiet. Like she's had some realizations. Or been given back her doll."

"Who else is in your group?" Buddy asked. "I know you've told me."

"Well, it's evil and immoral that I did and I'll probably roast in hell for it. Donna, with the mysterious migraines. She's been here the longest. Next is Lorraine, the obsessive one who bought a hundred clear plastic tote bags. Barry, the ER nurse. He's tired, is all that's wrong with that man. And there's Doug, the Pilot Error guy. Martha. Vincent. Oh, and the new girl. I love her! She reminds me of somebody. Kim Novak maybe."

"Then I love her too," Buddy said.

"Or she's one of the Gabors. With her collar turned up? Always dancing and singing with a scarf tied on her wrist, like this is a musical. I have to go, Buddy."

"I know you do," he said. "How'd they make out with Vincent? They captured him yet?""

"No, unfortunately. But he has been seen." She said, "Well, of course, he's been seen! At practically every patient's window. And in their closets. Or he's standing right beside them in the mirror."

"Don't make jokes," Buddy said.

"No, I have to," said Elise, and she clicked off.

Buddy had the dinner table all prepared and he wanted to start the candles. He had read on the carton that the wicks would flame more evenly if lighted once in advance. He went hunting for stick matches, which weren't where they were supposed to be, in the cabinet over the stove. The sun was going down, and he glanced through the sliding glass doors to the side porch. Connie was here, sitting in the swing, mechanically rocking an end of it. She held a cigarette and was staring ardently at the floor.

Buddy forgot himself for a second. He wasn't sure what to do. He crept out of the room, turned around and came back.

"Nine one one," he said to the cats before he slid the door and took himself outside.

"So, what's shaking?" he asked. He made an unconcerned walk across the porch and to the railing. Half the sky had grown purple. There were red clouds twisted like a rope above the lake.

Connie went on gazing at the floorboards but stopped the swing with the heels of her shoes. They were snakeskin or lizard, very dark maroon. "Don't be mad," she said.

"I'm not," said Buddy.

"I like to sit in strange places, don't you? Especially if it's someone else's place. I play a little game of seeing what effect it has on them."

The curve of her throat when she looked up now was lovely. That surprised Buddy out of making a comment on the game.

"I wonder if it's ever occurred to you," she said. "These past two summers. The drought, right? You've heard about it on the news. You probably aren't aware that I live in Langley. My father and I. You always hear it called 'Scrap Pile' but it's Langley. It is poor and it's all wrecked. Of course, my father didn't guess that would *happen* when he inherited our house. This is only about eight miles—"

"Isn't that . . . Crabapple?" Buddy asked.

"No, it isn't. Crabapple's about twelve miles. Or was, it hardly exists anymore. But you wouldn't go there, so that's part of my point."

Buddy shuffled over and lowered next to her in the swing.

"When I'm coming to work?" She spoke straight into his face. "It gets greener. And greener. Until it's this lush—I don't know what. There's no drought here. You folks don't have a drought."

Buddy was nodding slowly. "I'm ashamed to admit it . . ."

Connie exhaled smoke and now rearranged something in herself, as if she were closing one folder and opening the next. "I feel very embarrassed. About the confession I made to you earlier," she said.

"Oh," he said and laughed once. "It's not like I could mind."

"Horseshit." She rose in her seat and flicked her cigarette expertly across the porch into a huddle of savanna shrubs.

"Connie, my girlfriend is a counselor over at Cherry Trees."

"What about it?" she asked and Buddy winced.

"Sorry," he said, as they both nodded and shrugged.

"You people." Her hand worked in the air. She clutched at nothing, let it go.

She said, "I am happy about this much. I've finally been at my job long enough that I've earned some time off for the things I enjoy. Such as travel."

"Where to?" Buddy asked.

"I'm thinking Belize," Connie said, and after a moment, "I've heard you don't really go anywhere. Mr. Secrest or someone said. No, it was he. He knew your wife. He said you hardly ever go out since your son died."

"That's mostly correct."

She said, "I didn't mean it as a criticism."

The phone began ringing and—certain the caller was Elise—Buddy apologized, scooted off the swing and hurried inside.

"I'll never get out of here," Elise said. "I know it ruins our plans. There's no alternative."

"It doesn't matter. We'll do it tomorrow."

"Everyone's so spooked. I wouldn't dare leave. And the nurses have them so doped up on sedatives. You should see this, Buddy. They could *hurt* themselves. It's like they're walking on shipboard."

He was smiling.

"It's because we're now told that Vincent is inside the hospital. So there's an all-out search," she said. "Anyway, I did one thing. I raced over to Blockbuster and rented them a movie—*The Matrix* is what they voted for. That is helping. It's got them focused. All in their pajamas, all in the Tomorrow Room with their bed pillows, doubled up on the couches and lying over chairs."

"*I* want to do that. That sounds great!"

"No, you're not invited," said Elise.

She giggled at something on her end and said to Buddy, "You remember how I said they're always nicknaming the psychiatrists? I just heard, 'Here comes Dr. Post-It Note accompanying Drs. Liar and Deaf.'"

"My therapist looks like Al Haig."

"See, that's what I mean. That's why you don't belong here," Elise said.

"I'll call you later on," she told him.

From where he stood, he'd been viewing his dining-room setup. His table had crystal, candlesticks, and thirty red chrysanthemums in a vase. He hadn't realized, until the line went dead, how very sharp was his disappointment.

He had stepped down off the porch to inspect the walkway where a couple slate tiles had strayed out of line. He was stooped over, prompting a piece back into place with his shoe. Here were weeds. Here were ants, too, crawling in a long contorted file.

Connie watched him, smoking hard and unhappily, still in the swing. "I need to say a few things. About my feelings," she said.

He stuffed his hands in his pockets and rejoined her on the porch. He leaned on the far railing, facing her. They were quiet a moment. "I'm sorry. I'm an oaf," he said.

She answered that silently and with a brief, sarcastic smile.

He said, "I do want to hear."

She looked at the ceiling.

"Okay, I probably just don't understand then, Connie." He brought his hands from his pockets, bunched his fingers, and consulted them. "Is it that you have a kind of *fantasy* about me?"

"God, no!" she said and clicked her tongue. "It's actually a little more adult than that." She pronounced the word "*aah*-dult."

Her smile grew reproachful. "So you know all about my feelings."

"Oh, I don't think that."

She said, "Since you're Mister Perfect." She began fussing with the cultured pearl in her ear. "Bet you wish I'd kept my feelings to my own fuckin' self."

It was one of the unhappiest conversations Buddy could recall. "I really don't think any of that," he said.

Connie's long legs were folded now with her feet tucked to the side. She had the grace of someone who had been an athlete or a dancer. And she used her hands prettily, holding one in the other or touching the prim white collar on her dress. Her hair was fascinating—a gleaming black. But there was sorrow in her eyes, or so Buddy thought. They moved slowly, when they did move. Her gaze seldom shifted. Her eyes were heavy, and gave an impression of defeat.

He was thinking, patting his fingertips. He said, "I'll tell you a few things about myself. The morning Matt died, by the time I arrived at the ICU and could locate Ruthie, my wife, she was standing with her face to a wall, clenching her diaphragm like she'd run a marathon and couldn't breathe. So I tiptoed over and tapped her on the shoulder to show I was there. Only she didn't feel it or was too distressed. At any rate, she didn't acknowledge. I wasn't sure. I just stayed there waiting. Until, when she finally did turn, she looked straight through me. So, what I did? I gave her this huge *tick-tock* wave. Like, hidee-ho."

He smoothed his hair a few times. "How much have I thought about that! It was just a bad moment probably, a slipup, but it might've paved the way for this second thing, a situation I found myself in."

He said, "My son was riding his Jet Ski, I don't know what you heard about it."

Connie's head moved, no.

Buddy's head nodded. "On the lake. He crashed into a fishing boat that had a couple of high-school boys. No one else was killed but damn near. I found it hard. Hard to stop picturing. Then this urge came that if I could talk to someone I didn't know very well. Have a plain conversation with no mention of my son. So, for some reason I chose a woman who's the floor rep at Zack's Print Shop. We'd exchanged a few words. I doubt if she remembered my name. I gave her some information, the first call. I told her their sign—for the rear parking whatchumajiggy—had fallen down. Then I started calling with everything you could name—a TV contest, or foreseeing a weather problem. Or call and make some joke about Zack. Ten, fifteen times a day. Sitting in a spindly chair there with the phone, not even comfortable. And my poor wife, having to overhear all of this, was just beside herself. As to why I kept harassing this woman. Who, finally, when it got too much, went downtown and filed a restraining order."

"Man!" Connie said.

"She did indeed," said Buddy.

He got up. The cats were yowling and hopping at the glass door. "I have to stop for a second and give them dinner. I'll be right back."

"Go," Connie said, "go," and signaled with a flick of her hand that she understood.

While he was filling the dish with Science Diet, he had caught her figure in the shadows, descending the porch stairs.

Buddy rocked on his shoes. A light switched on at the lawyers' place next door.

He watched as the cats chowed. He refreshed their water.

He stood in the center of the kitchen and waited, without going to a window, for the effect of a taxicab's headlights out on the lane.

It was quiet where Elise was. She almost had to whisper. "This is eerie. All the patients' colored faces in the TV light? It's despicable that I'm always canceling on you. It's the worst thing I do. It's what destroyed every relationship I've had."

"Oh God, let that be true," Buddy said.

He was flicking a stub of paper around on the countertop, to no end. "Are you ever nervous around me?" he asked Elise.

"What?"

"Nervous *about* me, I mean. Because of the way I bothered that woman."

"Don't insult me," Elise said.

"Excuse me?"

"I'm a smart person. One of the smart ones. They insisted on textbooks where I went to school."

"Oh," he said.

There was a pause between them. Buddy paced up and back a step, holding the phone. The room was overly warm and the cats had taken to the cool of the floor tiles.

"I should go," Elise said. "I really have to pee. Plus they're right now carrying Vincent in on a stretcher. Directed towards the Time Out Room is my guess. Will you be okay? Do you feel okay?"

"Maybe I'll just keep that to my own fucking *self*," he said and grinned. "It's a joke you don't know. I'm sorry. I'll explain it to you some other time."

"They don't need me that bad. I'm free to talk," Elise said.

"No, I feel fine. The joke isn't even about me." His index finger traced around and around one of the blue tiles set in the countertop.

"Listen to me a second," she said. "Are you there? This is the last thing I want to say before I have to hang up. Grief is very mysterious, Buddy. It's very personal.

"Bye for now," she said, and Buddy stayed a moment after he'd closed the phone, his hand on the receiver, his arm outstretched.

He stood on the side porch. The night was warm and a full white moon dawdled over Likely Lake.

Across the lane at the Tishman's a car was adjusting behind a line of cars—latecomers for the bridge party Carl and Suzanne hosted every other week. One of them or somebody appeared in the entryway, there to welcome in the tardy guest.

Buddy was thinking about other nights, when he and Elise had sat out here until late, telling each other stories and drinking rum. On his birthday, she had worn a sequined red dress. There were nights with his wife, their last sad year.

How silly, he thought, that Connie's confession had bothered him. He should have absorbed it. He should have taken her hand and held her hand, as a friend, or even clenched it, and said what a very long life it can seem.

Ben Marcus

on

Donald Barthelme's
Several Garlic Tales

Donald Barthelme was a magician of language, and it would be most respectful, perhaps even ethical, not to look too closely into the workings of his magic. But it's to the brilliant Barthelme's credit that analysis of his methods does nothing to erode the joy of his stories. Like all good magic, Barthelme's just cannot be explained away. And thank God for that. His first sentence here, like many of his sentences throughout his hundreds of delirious stories, could be yanked out of context and pressed into service as the perfect *Barthelmean* emblem: "Amelia and Paul moved dreaming through the color photographs of human lives. . . ." This gets at the funny feeling his characters have, a feeling of the uncanny, of queasy, unstable familiarity, of dreaming while waking. The falsity of the real, and the fascination and beauty of the unreal. But Barthelme didn't just create characters who feel absurd—even though this was 1966—he fitted his stories with some kind of release mechanism that catapults this absurd feeling deep into the heart of the reader. His strangeness is visceral, chemical. It's delicious to read him, but scary, too, because through the antics and whimsy of his characters Barthelme always had his eye out for how sorrow could be smuggled into his sentences. If he is among our funniest short story writers, he is also among the most gifted at making real sorrow on the page.

In "Several Garlic Tales," Paul and Amelia travel the world. I think. Or maybe Ezra fumes at Paul. Or Elspeth inspects an army, and discovers that Paul, the climber, has joined up. "Anything for a stripe, is that it, Paul?" Which leaves us in Greece, to collect ourselves, not at all unhappily confused. If anything, Barthelme proves that, in reading a story, it's not the facts—what we know—that matters, but what we feel, and sometimes the business of making feeling from language necessitates a disloyalty to quotidian sense and stability. Barthelme cares about his characters, sure, but he also would seem to understand that his characters don't really exist. They are a means to get at something emotional. He needs them, but he is also prepared to spin them in circles if the rush of resulting color will look beautiful. He writes, "I think what ought to obtain is a measure of *audacity*, an audacity component, such as turning your amplifier up a little higher than anyone else's . . . I insist only that it be *relevant*, in a strange way, to the scene that has chosen to spread itself out before us, the theatre of our lives."

Donald Barthelme

֍

Several Garlic Tales

I

A melia and Paul moved dreaming through the color photographs of human lives *in articulo mortis,* in Europe, in the album. "First," Paul said, regarding the first photograph closely, "we visit Denmark's unique Tivoli Gardens with their bursting green, red and blue and silver fireworks at a quarter to twelve. Bawdy pantomime it says here." They looked in every direction but all they could see was a few hundred chaps from the U.S. Department of Commerce. "Those chaps from Commerce turn up everywhere," Amelia noted. "That must be a really fascinating Department to have so many decent-looking young men, chaps I mean, in it, at the point of death." Paul looked at Amelia as if he would like to strangle her. What a thing to say! Especially now, on Thermidor the thirteenth! (It's too bad Amelia is Japanese. Not in itself, for I like Japanese people and their warm buttered legs, but this pachinko parlor is driving me . . .)

II

Ezra looked carefully around the French room. Yes, it was empty. If one excluded Paul. Excluding Paul was the reason Ezra was looking around the room. Ezra pretended not to see Paul. Yet Paul was palpably present. There he is, sitting on a cask, mending his pike. (Well, I can't ignore him forever, Ezra concluded.) That damned Paul is always busy. Never an idle moment to imbue with the raincoat colors of fancy under the ax. Would that I could say of you, Paul that you left things alone once in a while. But in fact you are always tampering. Those strong brown fingers forever shuttling back and forth like some insane loom weaving beautiful Czasy tapestries in brilliant hues.

Paul is not serious. It is what everybody says of him. How to give him a degree of seriousness that would lift his works to importance?

"Did you bring the twine?"

"Yes, here's your damned twine!"

III

I took her to the picture show. The pictures "moved." We saw "pictures." A certain number of apologies were offered. I have divided the "moving" pictures into forty-eight squares, eight across, six down. Each square contains a part of either Greta Garbo, C. Aubrey Smith, John Gilbert, or pseudo-medieval décor. The "picture" is of course *Queen Christina*. The length of the film is, I don't know, an hour or so. If each "frame" is divided into forty-eight squares and each square described meticulously, in the Turkish manner, there is a danger of tedium. Especially if we also "fold in" (Rombauer) the emotions and responses excited in the brains and breasts of those hired to "watch" the "picture."

"All this literary criticism," Elspeth said to Paul. "I don't know. I don't know if I like it. I don't know if it pleases me." They regarded the Ankara critic on the shelf.

IV

Paul stood before a fence in Luxembourg. The fence was covered with birds. Their problem, in many ways a paradigm of their own, was to "fly." "The engaging and wholly charming way I stand in front of this fence here," Paul said to himself, "will soon persuade someone to discover me." Lanky, generous-hearted Paul! "If I had been born well prior to 1920 I could have ridden with Pershing against Pancho Villa. Alternately, I could have ridden with Villa against the landowners and corrupt government officials of the time. In either case, I would have had a horse. How little opportunity there is for young men to have personally-owned horses in the bottom half of the twentieth century! A wonder that we U.S. youth can still fork a saddle at all . . . Of course there are those 'horses' under the hoods of Buicks and Pontiacs, the kind so many of my countrymen favor. But those 'horses' are not for me. They take the tan out of my cheeks and the lank out of my arms and legs. Tom Lea or Pete Hurd will never paint me standing by this fence if I am sitting inside an Eldorado, Starfire, Riviera or Mustang, no matter how attractively the metal has been bent."

Howard was extremely irritated. What about the "match" scheduled for tonight? Would it be called off, as so many other scheduled activities had been?

V

Ezra's father put down his instrument case.

"I love acting in this Czechoslovakian People's Theatre," he said. "But the director is a fool. Trying to cover up our American accents with these trombones."

VI

The trawler made a smooth landing in the fjord country of Norway. "Sightseeing" would be a cheap word for what they were experiencing.

Yum Yum wrinkled behind her fan. Paul resolved to "have it out" with her. "Have a cigar," he said. "All the Scandinavian girls smoke them."

Amelia, or "Yum Yum," stamped her tiny imperious foot in its "geta," or wooden sandal, on the square "paving stone," or big flat piece of rock. "All the Scandinavian girls smoke them! All the Scandinavian girls smoke them! All the Scandinavian girls smoke them! All the Scandinavian girls smoke them! All the Scandinavian girls smoke them! Paul you are trying to make me something I'm not. Just like when you wanted me to wear those white rubber pajamas! I don't care if they were in all the newspapers! And just like when you wanted me to be like that girl in the film! I don't care if it did win the Golden Fig at Cannes! And just like when you wanted me to be like the beautiful horse in that book! I don't care if you did own the first North American serial rights! I can't stand it any longer! Do you hear me!"

(Quell. To quell. Quelling the outburst.) "There is nothing to get excited about," Paul said.

VII

The bishop in his red mantelpiece strode forward. "Yes, we are
in a terrible hurricane here," he acknowledged to the wrecked
cries of the survivors. "If we can just cross that spit of land there,"
(gesture with fingers, glitter of episcopal rings) "and get to that har-
lot over there," (sweep of arm in white lacy alb) "pardon, I meant
hamlet, we can perhaps find shelter against this particular vicissi-
tude sent by God to break our backs for our sins." The "flock"
moaned aloud. They had been eight days without . . . The sudden
pall on the fourth day had been the worst. There was a silence. Silence. Everything silent. Not a sound for six hours. Nothing. "This is
the worst," they murmured to one another in sign language not wanting to . . . break the . . . A few young men of good family crawled
away into the night to find help (tingle of mace against bone). The
Marchesa de G. had fainted again. Blockflutes were heard.

"So this is Spain!"

VIII

Elspeth inspected the new German army. Well, I'll say one
thing, the Germans certainly know how to "put on" an army!
From the mortar pit where she was standing she could see all the
way back to O.K.H. headquarters. So many soldiers "ranked up" in
lines! And such good-looking lines! No wonder General de Gaulle
was thoughtful. "Are you going to behave, this time?" She asked a
common soldier. "Da," he said.

But who is that? in the rearmost rank? Isn't that *Paul?*

"Paul what are you doing in that foreign army? Don't you know
that's a good way to get your passport blown out?"

They drank "rosinwasser." A sadness drifted over them. Then came "lunch."

Anything for a stripe, is that it, Paul?

IX

G reece. "When we turn our amplifiers on," said Eliot, strumming his suit, "already cant is forming over some people's minds, like the brown crust on bread, or the silence that 'crusts over' inappropriate remarks. I think there ought to be, and remember I'm talking normatively here, I think what ought to obtain is a measure of *audacity,* an audacity component, such as turning your amplifier up a little higher than anybody else's, or using a fork to pick and strum, rather than a plectrum or the carefully calloused fingertips, or doing something with your elbow, I don't care what, I insist only that it be *relevant,* in a strange way, to the scene that has chosen to spread itself out before us, the theatre of our lives. And if you other gentlemen will come with me down to the quai, carrying your amplifiers in boxes, and not forgetting the trailing cords, which have to be 'plugged in' so that we can 'turn on' . . ."

X

P aul handed over the green and gold armband. What a defeat for one who had hoped to make the Italian Postal Service his entire life and breath! "I hope you don't mind that I have left my shirt in that damned Otis elevator." "No. I don't mind. I like chests. Especially with strong American brains behind them." Elspeth wondered what attitude she should adopt. If only she were not pledged to Howard. Howard with his preoccupation with "boxing." Even now, she suspected, Howard was out somewhere, on the streets, in the midst of this . . . *noise,* with his friend Pete. Pete, who always remembered something. Those interminable remembered fragments!

Amelia pulled her brilliant silver, green and black kimono more tightly around her slight but incredibly beautiful Japanese "figure." Paul was welding flanges to everything in sight. He looked very athletic and workmanlike in his great mask. His sparks contributed to the . . . In the sky black clouds appeared, like fine-line seventeenth-century steel engravings showing Raleigh being stripped of his honors. "Half-life," the radium salesman said, "in the case of radium for instance is estimated at—" Now everything has been clarified. A half-life! That is what I wanted all the time! That is what I have been searching ceaselessly, for.

Will we ever fly without the aid of mechanical contrivances? Without seat-belts? Without roar?

David Means

on

Raymond Carver's
Why Don't You Dance

A great story is like an itch that has to be scratched eternally. It opens up a singular feeling forever in the reader that arises out of what seems to be a paradigmatic stance. We're left with more questions than answers, and more answers than questions; therefore, the paradoxical quality of a good story is that it seems to give us everything we need and yet not quite enough to fulfill a sense of having been shown a full life. All we're given is a sliver of some wider existence, a collection of minutiae, a shift of viewpoint, a statement made weeks later. The poetics of the modern story are both anachronistic (tapping old modes of myth and folklore) and contemporary (the pop song, the thirty-second commercial spot). One must—as a writer and a reader—crystallize deep meaning from a few, slight gestures: a man puts all of his household furnishings on his front lawn. A young man and a young woman arrive to find a yard full of abandoned furnishings. The older man arrives back at the house with a sack of food and drink and begins a brief verbal give-and-take in which the irredeemably sad distance between lonely souls is expressed. The older man and the younger woman dance. Weeks later, the young woman tells the story of the man and his furniture on the lawn. Her voice is distinctly bright, lively, and sharp with judgment. She has passed on to the green pastures and, presumably, what she feels is an enlightened grip on reality. Her comments pass retroactively through the previous slice of narrative, casting light on the scene in the yard while, again paradoxically, throwing everything forward into the infinite silence and open just ahead, at the end of the story. "There was more to it, but she couldn't get it all talked out. After a time, she quit trying." (Note: She quits trying, but we, as readers, can never quit.)

Raymond Carver brought an art form back around into relation with itself. He moved the short story forward but seemed to be rehashing and digging up his style from some buried aboriginal source. James Joyce did the same thing in *Dubliners*. He reengineered the short story, solidifying it with a new type of lyric firmness. It might seem, because Carver's style is so pristine, so simple-sounding, that the lesson of his work is that one should keep the writing clear and simple. It might seem that the lesson of his work is that one must revert to the Hemingway technique of cinematic reportage, zeroing in on the peak of the meaningful action and image while leaving everything else submerged. Maybe, maybe not. Carver's style teaches us that the bare bones of a story—no matter how ornate or twisty a style might get—are always simple, rudimentary, and arriving from a deeply humane source. Heart and style and story must be united, somehow. In other words, you have to care, and care a lot. Fancy prose—wildly interesting mannerisms, snarky jokes, weird cartoonish futures—are all fine and dandy, as long as the bare bones of the story come from a pure, honest, humane concern.

In the end, it doesn't take much to instruct the reader on what to see in a fictive world. There's a complex mimetic and aesthetic formula at work, of course, and one wrong move and a story can implode, or explode, but at the same time the truth is that it only takes a few words to put characters in motion through a fictive landscape, to give the reader everything that is necessary in order to see. Carver opens in the kitchen, moves to action—pouring a drink— and then *we* follow as the narrator gazes out the window to see the bedroom suite in the front yard. In less than a beat, we're pulled into a deep, internal thought: his side, her side. All this in a little more than sixty words. After a space break, a girl and a boy appear in the yard, poke around. She stretches on the bed, and they kiss. Lights go on, up and down the street. Another space break, the man arrives with a sack of sandwiches, beer, and whiskey, and then from that point everything leads to the older man and the younger woman— woozy and drunk—dancing together.

The critic Hugh Kenner once made the point that the short story—starting perhaps with Hemingway, or perhaps Joyce—went from being mainly an entertainment convention to a form of high art. (I shudder at the phrase *high art* as much as anyone, but there's no other way to put it.) At that point, the short story began to lean on poetics, to demand as much of the reader as the writer. The old adage—everything matters!—became deeply true when it came to reading a story. For example, Carver understands the poetic power of space breaks if used properly. Suddenly, at the very end, the story hinges, folds itself opens, spreads out over time. Weeks have passed and the girl is recalling the night from a vast distance. The vast distance is indicated by a few blank lines on the page. For me, personally, that final space break is the secret of this particular story. The final space break folds it over. It's that simple. As a reader you're left both reading the end and remembering the beginning in a simultaneous, crystalline, twist of the gut and heart. At the risk of redundancy, let me say: A good short story—any good story—is like one of the cave paintings in Herzog's movie, *Cave of Forgotten Dreams*. The essential mysteries of the human condition, of the fact that we can make art at all, are reduced to a few strokes, a primal essence, bare-boned, stark, pulled out of the dimness with the flickering light of a flaming torch, which in contemporary times takes the form of a highly sensitive, poetically minded reader flickering his/her soul—across the text. Carver, who has been mistakenly pegged as some kind of simpleton, self-taught, uneducated, a working-stiff writer was, in fact, well-read, educated, and deeply sophisticated. He worked with great care and intellectual intensity. But he was also smart enough—in an age totally hung up on authenticity of authorial sources—to carefully nurture his back story, to strike a public stance that kept early readers from seeing that he was as radical and experimental—with some early help from Gordon Lish's blue pencil—as Picasso. In other words, he knew exactly what he was doing. He understood the power of those space breaks.

Raymond Carver

※

Why Don't You Dance

In the kitchen, he poured another drink and looked at the bed-room suite in his front yard. The mattress was stripped and the candy-striped sheets lay beside two pillows on the chiffonier. Except for that, things looked much the way they had in the bedroom—nightstand and reading lamp on his side of the bed, nightstand and reading lamp on her side.

His side, her side.

He considered this as he sipped the whiskey.

The chiffonier stood a few feet from the foot of the bed. He had emptied the drawers into cartons that morning, and the cartons were in the living room. A portable heater was next to the chiffonier. A rattan chair with a decorator pillow stood at the foot of the bed. The buffed aluminum kitchen-set took up a part of the driveway. A yellow muslin cloth, much too large, a gift, covered the table and hung down over the sides. A potted fern was on the table, along with a box of silverware and a record-player, also gifts. A big console-model television set rested on a coffee table, and a few feet away from this, stood a sofa and chair and a floor lamp. The desk was pushed against the garage door. A few utensils were on the desk, along with a wall clock and two framed prints. There was also in the driveway a carton with cups, glasses, and plates, each object wrapped in newspaper. That morning he had cleared out the closets and, except for the three cartons in the living room, all the stuff was out of the house. He had run an extension cord on out there and everything was connected. Things worked, no different from how it was when they were inside.

Now and then a car slowed and people stared. But no one stopped. It occurred to him that he wouldn't either.

"It must be a yard sale," the girl said to the boy.

This girl and boy were furnishing a little apartment.

"Let's see what they want for the bed," the girl said.

"And the TV," the boy said.

The boy pulled into the driveway and stopped in front of the kitchen table.

They got out of the car and began to examine things, the girl touching the muslin cloth, the boy plugging in the blender and turning the dial to MINCE, the girl picking up a chafing dish, the boy turning on the television set and making adjustments. He sat down on the sofa to watch. He lit a cigarette, looked around, and flipped the match into the grass. The girl sat on the bed. She pushed off her shoes and lay back. She thought she could see the evening star.

"Come here, Jack. Try this bed. Bring one of those pillows," she said.

"How is it?" he said.

"Try it," she said.

He looked around. The house was dark.

"I feel funny," he said. "Better see if anybody's home."

She bounced on the bed.

"Try it first," she said.

He lay down on the bed and put the pillow under his head.

"How does it feel?" the girl said.

"Feels firm," he said.

She turned on her side and put her hand to his face.

"Kiss me," she said.

"Let's get up," he said.

"Kiss me," she said.

She closed her eyes. She held him.

He said, "I'll see if anybody's home."

But he just sat up and stayed where he was, making believe he was watching the television.

Lights came on in houses up and down the street.

"Wouldn't it be funny if," the girl said and grinned and didn't finish.

The boy laughed, but for no good reason. For no good reason, he switched on the reading lamp.

The girl brushed away a mosquito, whereupon the boy stood up and tucked in his shirt.

"I'll see if anybody's home," he said. "I don't think anybody's home. But if anybody is, I'll see what things are going for."

"Whatever they ask, offer ten dollars less. It's always a good idea," she said. "And, besides, they must be desperate or something."

"It's a pretty good TV," the boy said.

"Ask them how much," the girl said.

The man came down the sidewalk with a sack from the market. He had sandwiches, beer, and whiskey. He saw the car in the driveway and the girl on the bed. He saw the television set going and the boy on the porch.

"Hello," the man said to the girl. "You found the bed. That's good."

"Hello," the girl said, and got up. "I was just trying it out." She patted the bed. "It's a pretty good bed."

"It's a good bed," the man said, and put down the sack and took out the beer and the whiskey.

"We thought nobody was here," the boy said. "We're interested in the bed and maybe the TV. Maybe the desk. How much do you want for the bed?"

"I was thinking fifty dollars for the bed," the man said.

"Would you take forty?" the girl asked.

"Okay, I'll take forty," the man said.

He took a glass out of the carton. He took the newspaper off it. He broke the seal on the whiskey.

"How about the TV?" the boy said.

"Twenty-five."

"Would you take fifteen?" the girl said.

"Fifteen's okay. I could take fifteen," the man said.

The girl looked at the boy.

"You kids, you'll want a drink," the man said. "Glasses in the box. I'm going to sit down. I'm going to sit down on the sofa."

The man sat on the sofa, leaned back, and stared at the boy and the girl.

The boy found two glasses and poured whiskey.

"That's enough," the girl said. "I think I want water in mine."

She pulled out a chair and sat at the kitchen table.

"There's water in the spigot over there," the man said. "Turn on that spigot."

The boy came back with the watered whiskey. He cleared his throat and sat down at the kitchen table. He grinned. But he didn't drink anything.

Birds darted overhead for insects, small birds that moved very fast.

The man gazed at the television. He finished his drink and started another, and when he reached to turn on the floor lamp, his cigarette dropped from his fingers and fell between the cushions.

The girl got up to help him find it.

"So what do you want?" the boy said to the girl.

The boy took out the checkbook and held it to his lips as if thinking.

"I want the desk," the girl said. "How much money is the desk?"

The man waved his hand at this preposterous question.

"Name a figure," he said.

He looked at them as they sat at the table. In the lamplight, there was something about their faces. It was nice or it was nasty. There was no telling which.

"I'm going to turn off this TV and put on a record," the man said. "This record-player is going, too. Cheap. Make me an offer."

He poured more whiskey and opened a beer.

"Everything goes."

The girl held out her glass and the man poured.

"Thank you," she said. "You're very nice."

"It goes to your head," the boy said. "I'm getting it in the head." He held up his glass and jiggled it.

The man finished his drink and poured another, and then he found the box with the records.

"Pick something," the man said to the girl, and he held the records out to her.

The boy was writing the check.

"Here," the girl said, picking something, picking—anything— for she did not know the names on these records. She got up from the table and sat down again. She did not want to sit still.

"I'm making it out to cash," the boy said.

"Sure," the man said.

They drank. They listened to the record. And then the man put on another.

Why don't you kids dance? he decided to say, and then he said it. "Why don't you dance?"

"I don't think so," the boy said.

"Go ahead," the man said. "It's my yard. You can dance if you want to."

Arms about each other, their bodies pressed together, the boy and girl moved up and down the driveway. They were dancing. And when the record was over, they did it again, and when that one ended, the boy said, "I'm drunk."

The girl said, "You're not drunk."

"Well, I'm drunk," the boy said.

The man turned the record over and the boy said, "I am."

"Dance with me," the girl said to the boy and then to the man, and when the man stood up, she came to him with her arms open.

"Those people over there, they're watching," she said.

"It's okay," the man said. "It's my place," he said. "We can dance."

"Let them watch," the girl said.

"That's right," the man said. "They thought they'd seen everything over here. But they haven't see this, have they?" he said.

He felt her breath on his neck. "I hope you like your bed," he said.

The girl closed and then opened her eyes. She pushed her face into the man's shoulder. She pulled the man closer.

"You must be desperate or something," she said.

Weeks later she said: "The guy was about middle-aged. All his things right there in his yard. No lie. We got real pissed and danced. In the driveway. Oh, my God. Don't laugh. He played us these records. Look at this record-player. The old guy gave it to us. These crappy records, too. Will you look at this shit?"

She kept talking. She told everyone. There was more to it, but she couldn't get it all talked out. After a time, she quit trying.

Lorrie Moore

on

Ethan Canin's *The Palace Thief*

There is a kind of long, fate-obsessed story of which Ethan Canin has become an American master. His accomplished handling of time—sometimes seeming to take a life in its entirety, exploding then knitting it together slightly out of sequence to better reveal the true meaning of an experience—results in fictions of tremendous depth, wisdom, and architectural complexity.

In "The Palace Thief" narrative time is woven whole by the mournful voice of a man looking back at the debilitating confines of his life. He is like a monk in a moral hair shirt, sitting on the edge of an extremely narrow (Procrustean?) bed. Images of cells, prisons, slavery show up in the story to underscore the service to the rich and powerful that has constituted not just this man's livelihood but his entire spiritual existence. His lack of self-pity is a kind of blind spot—and the sly coincidence of his expertise in ancient Rome is not lost on the reader. Canin does not sentimentalize his protagonist and make him more respected, admired, or powerful than he is. The story keeps the ruling class in their golden palaces and will not allow into the story the reassuring sop that the rich do not always win—or anything that would let us imagine that. (One sometimes forgets that in the tale of David and Goliath, David quickly becomes a figure of power and might: not here where the smallness of one man remains so no matter what authorial fondness is draped upon him.) It is Melville of whom we may be reminded: *Bartleby the Scrivener* or *Billy Budd* or *Benito Cereno* are perhaps the models. Canin lets his narrator look behind the images and events that may prompt our awe, especially those attached to power and social class but also those attached to service, devotion, the enforcement of justice—not to leave them smashed and demolished but to reassemble them with a tempered and diminished faith. By the end the story allows us to see even more than its protagonist and narrator can.

The unworldliness of schoolteachers, from Miss Jean Brodie to Mr. Chips, is hardly without literary precedent—but it is a trickier task in shorter form. And what it means to be an American teacher of the privileged in the twentieth century has its own angles and puzzles. The compression of this long story summing up not just one life but several is an ingenious accomplishment. Moreover, it contains Canin's special skill at mixing public and private events—part of the national experience too often ignored by our writers. Canin's fiction is always a construction of vital surprise, what the literary critic James Wood has called "livingness," and is set forth in perfectly textured prose. He is interested in the moment when a person's life turns, or his destiny is defied, or his character is revealed or anatomized for the inexplicable thing it is. He makes time rush forward like Gatsby's car or Ahab's ship, while his men remain children in the bodies of the old. It is heartbreaking business, and, here, expertly done.

Ethan Canin

✠

The Palace Thief

I tell this story not for my own honor, for there is little of that here, and not as a warning, for a man of my calling learns quickly that all warnings are in vain. Nor do I tell it in apology for St. Benedict's School, for St. Benedict's School needs no apologies. I tell it only to record certain foretellable incidents in the life of a well-known man, in the event that the brief candle of his days may sometime come under the scrutiny of another student of history. That is all. This is a story without surprises.

There are those, in fact, who say I should have known what would happen between St. Benedict's and me, and I suppose that they are right; but I loved that school. I gave service there to the minds of three generations of boys and always left upon them, if I was successful, the delicate imprint of their culture. I battled their indolence with discipline, their boorishness with philosophy and the arrogance of their stations with the history of great men before them. I taught the sons of nineteen senators. I taught a boy who, if not for the vengeful recriminations of the tabloids, would today have been the President of the United States. That school was my life.

This is why, I suppose, I accepted the invitation sent to me by
Mr. Sedgewick Bell at the end of last year, although I should have
known better. I suppose I should have recalled what kind of boy he
had been at St. Benedict's forty-two years before instead of posting
my response so promptly in the mail and beginning that evening to
prepare my test. He, of course, was the son of Senator Sedgewick
Hyram Bell, the West Virginia demagogue who kept horses at his
residence in Washington, D.C., and had swung southern states for
Wendell Wilkie. The younger Sedgewick was a dull boy.

I first met him when I had been teaching history at St. Benedict's
for only five years, in the autumn after his father had been delivered
to office on the shoulders of southern patricians frightened by the
unionization of steel and mines. Sedgewick appeared in my classroom in November of 1945, in a short-pants suit. It was midway
through the fall term, that term in which I brought the boys forth
from the philosophical idealism of the Greeks, into the realm of
commerce, military might and the law, which had given Julius
Caesar his prerogative from Macedonia to Seville. My students, of
course, were agitated. It is a sad distinction of that age group, the
exuberance with which the boys abandon the moral endeavor of
Plato and embrace the powerful, pragmatic hand of Augustus. The
more sensitive ones had grown silent, and for several weeks our
class discussions had been dominated by the martial instincts of the
coarser boys. Of course I was sorry for this, but I was well aware of
the import of what I taught at St. Benedict's. Our headmaster, Mr.
Woodbridge, made us continually aware of the role our students
would eventually play in the affairs of our country.

My classroom was in fact a tribute to the lofty ideals of man,
which I hoped would inspire my boys, and at the same time to the
fleeting nature of human accomplishment, which I hoped would
temper their ambition with humility. It was a dual tactic, with which

Mr. Woodbridge heartily agreed. Above the doorframe hung a tablet, made as a term project by Henry L. Stimson when he was a boy here, that I hoped would teach my students of the irony that history bestows upon ambition. In clay relief, it said:

> I am Shutruk-Nahhunte, King of Anshan and Susa,
> sovereign of the land of Elam.
> By the command of Inshushinak,
> I destroyed Sippar, took the stele of Naram-Sin,
> and brought it back to Elam,
> where I erected it as an offering to my god,
> Inshushinak.

> —Shutruk-Nahhunte, 1158 B.C.

I always noted this tablet to the boys on their first day in my classroom, partly to inform them of their predecessors at St. Benedict's, and partly to remind them of the great ambition and conquest that had been utterly forgotten centuries before they were born. Afterward I had one of them recite, from the wall where it hung above my desk, Shelley's "Ozymandias." It is critical for any man of import to understand his own insignificance before the sands of time, and this is what my classroom always showed my boys.

As young Sedgewick Bell stood in the doorway of that classroom his first day at St. Benedict's, however, it was apparent that such efforts would be lost on him. I could see that not only was he a dullard but a roustabout. The boys happened to be wearing the togas they had made from sheets and safety pins the day before, spreading their knees like magistrates in the wooden desk chairs and I was taking them through the recitation of the emperors when Mr. Woodbridge entered alongside the stout, red-faced Sedgewick and introduced him to the class. I had taught for five years, as I have said, and I knew the frightened, desperate bravura of a new boy. Sedgewick Bell did not wear this look.

Rather, he wore one of disdain. The boys, fifteen in all, were instantly intimidated into sensing the foolishness of their improvised cloaks, and one of them, Clay Walter, the leader of the dullards—though far from a dullard himself—said, to mild laughter, "Where's your toga, kid?"

Sedgewick Bell answered, "Your mother must be wearing your pants today."

It took me a moment to regain the attention of the class, and when Sedgewick was seated I had him go to the board and copy out the Emperors. Of course, he did not know the names of any of them, and my boys had to call them out, repeatedly correcting his spelling as he wrote out in a sloppy hand:

Augustus
Tiberius
Caligula
Claudius
Nero
Galba
Otho

all the while lifting and resettling the legs of his short pants in mockery of what his new classmates were wearing. "Young man," I said, "this is a serious class, and I expect that you will take it seriously."

"If it's such a serious class, then why're they all wearing dresses?" he responded, again to laughter, although by now Clay Walter had loosened the rope belt at his waist, and the boys around him were shifting uncomfortably in their togas.

From that first day, Sedgewick Bell became a boor and a bully, a damper to the illumination of the eager minds of my boys and a purveyor of the mean-spirited humor that is like kerosene in a school such as ours. What I asked of my boys that semester was simple, that they learn the facts I presented to them in an "Outline of Ancient Roman History," which I had whittled, through my years of teaching, to exactly four closely typed pages; yet Sedgewick Bell was unwilling to do so. He was a poor student, and on his first exam could not even tell me who it was that Mark Antony and Octavian had routed at Philippi, nor who Octavian later became, although an average wood beetle in the floor of my classroom could have done so with ease.

Furthermore, as soon as he arrived he began a stream of capers using spitballs, wads of gum and thumbtacks. Of course it was common for a new boy to engage his comrades thusly, but Sedgewick Bell then began to add the dangerous element of natural leadership—which was based on the physical strength of his features—to his otherwise puerile antics. He organized the boys. At exactly fifteen minutes to the hour, they would all drop their pencils at once or cough or slap closed their books so that writing at the blackboard my hands would jump in the air.

At a boys' school, of course, punishment is a cultivated art. Whenever one of these antics occurred I simply made a point of calling on Sedgewick Bell to answer a question. General laughter usually followed his stabs at answers, and although Sedgewick himself usually laughed along with everyone else, it did not require a great deal of insight to know that the tactic would work. The organized events began to occur less frequently.

In retrospect, however, perhaps my strategy was a mistake, for to convince a boy of his own stupidity is to shoot a poisonous arrow indeed. Perhaps Sedgewick Bell's life would have turned out more nobly if I had understood his motivations right away and treated him differently at the start. But such are the pointless speculations of a teacher. What was irrefutably true was that he was performing poorly on his quizzes, even if his behavior had improved somewhat, and therefore I called him to my office.

In those days, I lived in small quarters off the rear of the main hall, in what had been a slave's room when the grounds of St. Benedict's had been the estate of the philanthropist and horse breeder, Cyrus Beck. Having been at school as long as I had, I no longer lived in the first-form dormitory that stood behind my room, but supervised it, so that I saw most of the boys only in matters of urgency. They came sheepishly before me.

With my bed folded into the wall, the room became my office, and shortly after supper one day that winter of his first-form year, Sedgewick Bell knocked and entered. Immediately he began to inspect the premises, casting his eyes, which had the patrician set of his father's, from the desk, to the shelves, to the bed folded into the wall.

"Sit down, boy."

"You're not married, are you, sir?"

"No, Sedgewick, I am not. However, we are here to talk about *you*."

"That's why you like puttin' us in togas, right?"

I had, frankly, never encountered a boy like him before, who at the age of thirteen would affront his schoolmaster without other boys in audience. He gazed at me flatly, his chin in hand.

"Young man," I said, sensing his motivations with sudden clarity, "we are concerned about your performance here, and I have made an appointment to see your father."

In fact, I had made no appointments with Senator Bell, but at that moment I understood that I would have to. "What would you like me to tell the senator?" I said.

His gaze faltered. "I'm to try harder, Sir, from now on."

"Good, Sedgewick. Good."

Indeed, that week the boys reenacted the pivotal scenes from *Julius Caesar,* and Sedgewick read his lines quite passably and contributed little that I could see to the occasional fits of giggles that circulated among the slower boys. The next week, I gave a quiz on the Triumvirate of Crassus, Pompey and Caesar, and he passed for the first time yet, with a C+.

Nonetheless, I had told him that I was going to speak with his father, and this is what I was determined to do. At the time, Senator Sedgewick Hyram Bell was appearing regularly in the newspapers and on the radio in his stand against Truman's plan for national health insurance, and I was loathe to call upon such a well-known man concerning the behavior of his son. On the radio his voice was a tobacco drawl that had won him populist appeal throughout West Virginia, although his policies alone would certainly not have done so. I was at the time in my late twenties, and although I was armed with scruples and an education, my hands trembled as I dialed his office. To my surprise, I was put through, and the senator, in the drawl I recognized instantly, agreed to meet me one afternoon the following week. The man already enjoyed national stature, of course, and although any other father would no doubt have made the journey to St. Benedict's himself, I admit that the prospect of seeing the man in his own office intrigued me. Thus I journeyed to the capital.

St. Benedict's lies in the bucolic, equine expanse of rural Virginia, nearer in spirit to the Carolinas than to Maryland, although the drive to Washington requires little more than an hour. The bus followed the misty, serpentine course of the Passamic, then entered the marshlands that are now the false-brick suburbs of Washington and at last left me downtown in the capital, where I proceeded the rest of the way on foot. I arrived at the Senate office building as the sun moved low against the bare-limbed cherries among the grounds. I was frightened but determined, and I reminded myself that Sedgewick Hyram Bell was a senator but also a father, and I was here on business that concerned his son. The office was as grand as a duke's.

I had not waited long in the anteroom when the man himself appeared, feisty as a game hen, bursting through a side door and clapping me on the shoulder as he urged me before him into his office. Of course I was a novice then in the world of politics and had not yet realized that such men are, above all, likable. He put me in a leather seat, offered a cigar, which I refused, and then with real or contrived wonder—perhaps he did something like this with all his visitors—he proceeded to show me an antique sidearm that had been sent to him that morning by a constituent and that had once belonged, he said, to the coachman of Robert E. Lee. "You're a history buff," he said, "right?"

"Yes, sir."

"Then take it. It's yours."

"No, sir. I couldn't."

"Take the damn thing."

"All right, I will."

"Now, what brings you to this dreary little office?"

"Your son, sir."

"What the devil has he done now?"

"Very little, sir. We're concerned that he isn't learning the material."

"What material is that?"

"We're studying the Romans now, sir. We've left the Republic and entered the Empire."

"Ah," he said. "Be careful with that, by the way. It still fires."

"Your son seems not to be paying attention, sir."

He again offered me the box of cigars across the desk and then bit off the end of his own. "Tell me," he said, puffing the thing until it flamed suddenly, "what's the good of what you're teaching them boys?"

This was a question for which I was well prepared, fortunately, having recently written a short piece in *The St. Benedict's Crier* answering the same challenge put forth there by an anonymous boy. "When they read of the reign of Augustus Caesar," I said without hesitation, "when they learn that his rule was bolstered by commerce, a postal system and the arts, by the reformation of the senate and by the righting of an inequitable system of taxation, when they see the effect of scientific progress through the census and the enviable network of Roman roads, how these advances led mankind away from the brutish rivalries of potentates into the two centuries of *pax romana,* then they understand the importance of character and high ideals."

He puffed at his cigar. "Now, that's a horse who can talk," he said. "And you're telling me my son Sedgewick has his head in the clouds."

"It's my job, sir, to mold your son's character."

He thought for a moment, idly fingering a match. Then his look turned stern. "I'm sorry, young man," he said slowly, "but you will not mold him. I will mold him. You will merely teach him."

That was the end of my interview, and I was politely shown the door. I was bewildered, naturally, and found myself in the elevator before I could even take account of what had happened. Senator Bell was quite likable, as I have noted, but he had without doubt cut me, and as I made my way back to the bus station, the gun stowed deep in my briefcase, I considered what it must have been like to have been raised under such a tyrant. My heart warmed somewhat toward young Sedgewick.

Back at St. Benedict's, furthermore, I saw that my words had evidently had some effect on the boy, for in the weeks that followed he continued on his struggling, uphill course. He passed two more quizzes, receiving an A– on one of them. For his midterm project he produced an adequate papier-mâché rendering of Hadrian's gate, and in class he was less disruptive to the group of do-nothings among whom he sat, if indeed he was not in fact attentive.

Such, of course, are the honeyed morsels of a teacher's existence, those students who come, under one's own direction, from darkness into the light, and I admit that I might have taken a special interest that term in Sedgewick Bell. If I gave him the benefit of the doubt on his quizzes when he straddled two grades, if I began to call on him in class only for those questions I had reason to believe he could answer, then I was merely trying to encourage the nascent curiosity of a boy who, to all appearances, was struggling gamely from beneath the formidable umbra of his father.

The fall term was by then drawing to a close, and the boys had begun the frenzy of preliminary quizzes for the annual Mister Julius Caesar competition. Here again, I suppose I was in my own way rooting for Sedgewick. Mister Julius Caesar is a St. Benedict's tradition, held in reverence among the boys, the kind of mythic ritual that is the currency of a school like ours. It is a contest, held in two phases. The first is a narrowing maneuver, by means of a dozen written quizzes, from which three boys from the first form emerge victorious. The second is a public tournament, in which these three take the stage before the assembled student body and answer questions about ancient Rome until one alone emerges triumphant, as had Caesar himself from among Crassus and Pompey. Parents and graduates fill out the audience. Out front of Mr. Woodbridge's office, a plaque attests to the Misters Julius Caesar of the previous half-century—a list that begins with John F. Dulles in 1901—and although the ritual might seem quaint to those who have not attended St. Benedict's, I can only say that, in a school just like ours, one cannot overstate the importance of a public joust.

That year I had three obvious contenders: Clay Walter, who, as I intimated, was a somewhat gifted boy; Martin Blythe, a studious type; and Deepak Mehta, the son of a Bombay mathematician, who was dreadfully quiet but clearly my best student. It was Deepak, in fact, who on his own and entirely separate from the class had studied the disparate peoples, from the Carthaginians to the Egyptians, whom the Romans had conquered.

By the end of the narrowing quizzes, however, a surprising configuration had emerged: Sedgewick Bell had pulled himself to within a few points of third place in my class. This was when I made my first mistake. Although I should certainly have known better, I was impressed enough by his efforts that I broke one of the cardinal rules of teaching: I gave him an A on a quiz on which he had earned only a B, and in so doing, I leap-frogged him over Martin Blythe. On March 15th, when the three finalists took their seats on stage in front of the assembled population of the school, Sedgewick Bell was among them, and his father was among the audience.

The three boys had donned their togas for the event and were arranged around the dais on which a pewter platter held the green, silk garland that, at the end of the morning, I would place upon the brow of the winner. As the interrogator, I stood front row, center, next to Mr. Woodbridge.

"Which language was spoken by the Sabines?"

"Oscan," answered Clay Walter without hesitation.

"Who composed the Second Triumvirate?"

"Mark Antony, Octavian and Marcus Aemilius Lepidus, Sir," answered Deepak Mehta.

"Who was routed at Philippi?"

Sedgewick Bell's eyes showed no recognition. He lowered his head in his hands as though pushing himself to the limit of his intellect, and in the front row my heart dropped. Several boys in the audience began to twitter. Sedgewick's own leg began to shake inside his toga. When I looked up again I felt that it was I who had put him in this untenable position, I who brought a tender bud too soon into the heat, and I wondered if he would ever forgive me; but then, without warning, he smiled slightly, folded his hands and said, "Brutus and Cassius."

"Good," I said, instinctively. Then I gathered my poise. "Who deposed Romulus Augustulus, the last Emperor of the Western Empire?"

"Odoacer," Clay Walter answered, then added, "in A.D. 476."

"Who introduced the professional army to Rome?"

"Gaius Marius, Sir," answered Deepak Mehta, then himself added, "in 104 B.C."

When I asked Sedgewick his next question—Who was the leading Carthaginian General of the Second Punic War?—I felt some unease because the boys in the audience seemed to sense that I was favoring him with an easier examination. Nonetheless, his head sank into his hands, and he appeared once again to be straining the limits of his memory before he looked up and produced the obvious answer, "Hannibal."

I was delighted. Not only was he proving my gamble worthwhile but he was showing the twittering boys in the audience that, under fire, discipline produces accurate thought. By now they had quieted, and I had the sudden, heartening premonition that Sedgewick

Bell was going to surprise us after all, that his tortoiselike deliberation would win him, by morning's end, the garland of laurel.

The next several rounds of questions proceeded much in the
same manner as had the previous two. Deepak Mehta and Clay Walter answered without hesitation, and Sedgewick Bell did so only
after a tedious and deliberate period of thought. What I realized, in
fact, was that his style made for excellent theater. The parents, I could
see, were impressed, and Mr. Woodbridge next to me, no doubt
thinking about the next annual drive, was smiling broadly.

After a second-form boy had brought a glass of water to each of
the contestants, I moved on to the next level of questions. These had
been chosen for their difficulty, and on the first round Clay Walter
fell out, not knowing the names of Augustus's children. He left the
stage and moved back among his dim-witted pals in the audience.
By the rule of clockwise progression the same question then went to
Deepak Mehta, who answered it correctly, followed by the next one,
which concerned King Jugurtha of Numidia. Then, because I had
no choice, I had to ask Sedgewick Bell something difficult: "Which
General had the support of the aristocrats in the civil war of 88 B.C.?"

To the side, I could see several parents pursing their lips and
furrowing their brows, but Sedgewick Bell appeared to not even
notice the greater difficulty of the query. Again he dropped his head
into his hands. By now the audience expected his period of deliberation, and they sat quietly. One could hear the hum of the ventila-
tion system and the dripping of the icicles outside. Sedgewick Bell
cast his eyes downward, and it was at this moment that I realized he
was cheating.

I had come to this job straight from my degree at Carleton College, at the age of twenty-one, having missed enlistment due to myo-
pia, and carrying with me the hope that I could give to my boys the
more important vision that my classical studies had given to me. I

knew that they responded best to challenge. I knew that a teacher who coddled them at that age would only hold them back, would keep them in the bosoms of their mothers so long that they would remain weak-minded through preparatory school and inevitably then through college. The best of my own teachers had been tyrants. I well remembered this. Yet at that moment I felt an inexplicable pity for the boy. Was it simply the humiliation we had both suffered at the hands of his father? I peered through my glasses at the stage and knew at once that he had attached the "Outline of Ancient Roman History" to the inside of his toga.

I don't know how long I stood there, between the school assembled behind me and the two boys seated in front, but after a period of internal deliberation, during which time I could hear the rising murmurs of the audience, I decided that in the long run it was best for Sedgewick Bell to be caught. Oh, how the battle is lost for want of a horse! I leaned to Mr. Woodbridge next to me and whispered, "I believe Sedgewick Bell is cheating."

"Ignore it," he whispered back.

"What?"

Of course, I have great respect for what Mr. Woodbridge did for St. Benedict's in the years he was among us. A headmaster's world is far more complex than a teacher's, and it is historically inopportune to blame a life gone afoul on a single incident in childhood. However, I myself would have stood up for our principles had Mr. Woodbridge not at that point said, "Ignore it, Hundert, or look for another job."

Naturally, my headmaster's words startled me for a moment; but being familiar with the necessities of a boy's school, and having recently entertained my first thoughts about one day becoming a headmaster myself, I simply nodded when Sedgewick Bell produced the correct answer, Lucius Cornelius Sulla. Then I went on to the next question, which concerned Scipio Africanus Major. Deepak Mehta answered it correctly, and I turned once again to Sedgewick Bell.

In a position of moral leadership, of course, compromise begets only more compromise, and although I know this now from my own experience, at the time I did so only from my study of history. Perhaps that is why I again found an untenable compassion muddying my thoughts. What kind of desperation would lead a boy to cheat on a public stage? His father and mother were well back in the crowded theater, but when I glanced behind me my eye went instantly to them, as though they were indeed my own parents, out from Kansas City. "Who were the first emperors to reign over the divided Empire?" I asked Sedgewick Bell.

When one knows the magician's trick, the only wonder is in its obviousness, and as Sedgewick Bell lowered his head this time I clearly saw the nervous flutter of his gaze directed into the toga. Indeed I imagined him scanning the entire "Outline," from Augustus to Jovian, pasted inside the twill, before coming to the answer, which, pretending to ponder, he then spoke aloud: "Valentinian the First, and Valens."

Suddenly Senator Bell called out, "That's my boy!"

The crowd thundered, and I had the sudden, indefensible urge to steer the contest in young Sedgewick Bell's direction. In a few moments, however, from within the subsiding din, I heard the thin, accented voice of a woman speaking Deepak Mehta's name; and it was the presence of his mother, I suppose, that finally brought me to my senses. Deepak answered the next question correctly, about Diocletian, and then I turned to Sedgewick Bell and asked him, "Who was Hamilcar Barca?"

Of course, it was only Deepak who knew that this answer was not on the "Outline," because Hamilcar Barca was a Phoenician general eventually routed by the Romans; it was only Deepak, as I have noted, who had bothered to study the conquered peoples. He briefly widened his eyes at me—in recognition? in gratitude? in disapproval?—while, beside him, Sedgewick Bell again lowered his head into his hands. After a long pause, Sedgewick asked me to repeat the question.

I did so, and after another, long pause, he scratched his head. Finally, he said, "Jeez."

The boys in the audience laughed, but I turned and silenced them. Then I put the same question to Deepak Mehta, who answered it correctly, of course, and then received a round of applause that was polite but not sustained.

It was only as I mounted the stage to present Deepak with the garland of laurel, however, that I glanced at Mr. Woodbridge and realized that he too had wanted me to steer the contest toward Sedgewick Bell. At the same moment, I saw Senator Bell making his way to the rear door of the hall. Young Sedgewick stood limply to the side of me, and I believe I had my first inkling then of the mighty forces that would twist the life of that boy. I could only imagine his thoughts as he stood there on stage while his mother, struggling to catch up with the senator, vanished through the fire door at the back. The next morning, our calligraphers would add Deepak Mehta's name to the plaque outside Mr. Woodbridge's office, and young Sedgewick Bell would begin his lifelong pursuit of missed glory.

Yet perhaps because of the disappointment I could see in Mr. Woodbridge's eyes, it somehow seemed that I was the one who had failed the boy, and as soon as the auditorium was empty I left for his room. There I found him seated on the bed, still in his toga, gazing out the small window to the lacrosse fields. I could see the sheets of my "Outline" pressed against the inside of his garment.

"Well, young man," I said, knocking on the doorframe, "that certainly was an interesting performance."

He turned around from the window and looked at me coldly.

What he did next I have thought about many times over the years, the labyrinthine wiliness of it, and I can only attribute the precociousness of his maneuvering to the bitter education he must have received at home. As I stood before him in the doorway, Sedgewick Bell reached inside his cloak and one at a time lifted out the pages of my "Outline."

I stepped inside and closed the door. Every teacher knows a score of boys who do their best to be expelled; this is a cliché in a school like ours, but as soon as I closed the door to his room and he acknowledged the act with a feline smile, I knew that this was not Sedgewick Bell's intention at all.

"I knew you saw," he said.

"Yes, you are correct."

"How come you didn't say anything, eh, Mr. Hundert?"

"It's a complicated matter, Sedgewick."

"It's because my pop was there."

"It had nothing to do with your father."

"Sure, Mr. Hundert."

Frankly, I was at my wit's end, first from what Mr. Woodbridge had said to me in the theater and now from the audacity of the boy's accusation. I myself went to the window then and let my eyes wander over the campus so that they would not have to engage the dark, accusatory gaze of Sedgewick Bell. What transpires in an act of omission like the one I had committed? I do not blame Mr. Woodbridge, of course, any more than a soldier can blame his captain. What had happened was that instead of enforcing my own code of morals, I had allowed Sedgewick Bell to sweep me summarily into his. I did not know at the time what an act of corruption I had committed, although what is especially chilling to me is that I believe that Sedgewick Bell, even at the age of thirteen, did.

He knew also, of course, that I would not pursue the matter,

although I spent the ensuing several days contemplating a disciplin-
ary action. Each time I summoned my resolve to submit the boy's
name to the honor committee, however, my conviction waned, for at
these times I seemed to myself to be nothing more than one criminal
turning in another. I fought this battle constantly, in my simple
rooms, at the long, chipped table I governed in the dining hall and
at the dusty chalkboard before my classes. I felt like an exhausted
swimmer trying to climb a slippery wall out of the sea.

Furthermore, I was alone in my predicament, for among a board-
ing school faculty, which is as perilous as a medieval court, one does
not publicly discuss a boy's misdeeds. This is even true if the boy is
not the son of a senator. In fact, the only teacher I decided to trust
with my situation was Charles Ellerby, our new Latin instructor and
a kindred lover of antiquity. I had likes Charles Ellerby as soon as
we had met because he was a moralist of no uncertain terms, and
indeed when I confided in him about Sedgewick Bell's behavior and
Mr. Woodbridge's response, he suggested that it was my duty to
circumvent our headmaster and speak to Senator Bell again.

Less than a week after I had begun to marshall my resolve, however, the senator himself called *me*. He proffered a few moments of
small talk, asked after the gun he had given me, and then said gruffly,
"Young man, my son tells me the Hannibal Barca question was not
on the list he had to know."

Now, indeed, I was shocked. Even from young Sedgewick Bell I
had not expected this audacity. "How deeply the viper is a viper," I
said, before I could help myself.

"Excuse me?"

"The Phoenician General was *Hamilcar* Barca, Sir, not
Hannibal."

The senator paused. "My son tells me you asked him a question that was not on the list, which the Oriental fellow knew the answer to in advance. He feels you've been unfair, is all."

"It's a complex situation, sir," I said. I marshalled my will again by imagining what Charles Ellerby would do in the situation. However, no sooner had I resolved to confront the senator than it became perfectly clear to me that I lacked the character to do so. I believe this had long been clear to Sedgewick Bell.

"I'm sure it is complex," Senator Bell said. "But I assure you, there are situations more complex. Now, I'm not asking you to correct anything this time, you understand. My son has told me a great deal about you, Mr. Hundert. If I were you, I'd remember that."

"Yes, sir," I said, although by then I realized he had hung up.

And thus young Sedgewick Bell and I began an uneasy compact that lasted out his days at St. Benedict's. He was a dismal student from that day forward, scratching at the very bottom of a class that was itself a far cry from the glorious, yesteryear classes of John Dulles and Henry Stimson. His quizzes were abominations and his essays were pathetic digestions of those of the boys sitting next to him. He chatted amiably in study hall, smoked cigarettes in the third-form linen room, and when called upon in class could be counted on to blink and stutter as if called upon from sleep.

But perhaps the glory days of St. Benedict's had already begun their wane, for even then, well before the large problems that beset us, no action was taken against the boy. He became a symbol for Charles Ellerby and me, evidence of the first tendrils of moral rot that seemed to be twining among the posts and timbers of our school. Although we told nobody else of his secret, the boy's dim-witted recalcitrance soon succeeded in alienating all but the other students. His second- and third-form years passed as ingloriously as his first, and by the outset of his last with us he had grown to mythic infamy among the faculty members who had known the school in its days of glory.

He had grown physically larger as well, and now when I chanced upon him on the campus he held his ground against my disapproving stare with a dark one of his own. To complicate matters, he had cultivated, despite his boorish character, an impressive popularity among his schoolmates, and it was only through the subtle intervention of several of his teachers that he had failed on two occasions to win the presidency of the student body. His stride had become a strut. His favor among the other boys, of course, had its origin in the strength of his physical features, in the precocious evil of his manner, and in the bellowing timbre of his voice, but unfortunately such crudities are all the more impressive to a group of boys living out of sight of their parents.

That is not to say that the faculty of St. Benedict's had given up hope for Sedgewick Bell. Indeed, a teacher's career is punctuated with difficult students like him, and despite the odds one could not help but hope for his eventual rehabilitation. As did all the other teachers, I held out promise for Sedgewick Bell. In his fits of depravity and intellectual feebleness I continued to look for glimpses of discipline and progress.

By his fourth-form year, however, when I had become dean of seniors, it was clear that Sedgewick Bell would not change, at least not while he was at St. Benedict's. Even with his powerful station, he had not even managed to gain admission to the state university, and it was with a sense of failure then, finally, that I handed him his diploma in the spring of 1949, on an erected stage at the north end of the great field, on which he came forward, met my disapproving gaze with his own flat one and trundled off to sit among his friends.

It was with some surprise then that I learned in *The Richmond Gazette,* thirty-seven years later, of Sedgewick Bell's ascension to the chairmanship of EastAmerica Steel, at that time the second largest corporation in America. I chanced upon the news one morning in the winter of 1987, the year of my great problems with St. Benedict's, while reading the newspaper in the east-lighted breakfast room of the Assistant Headmaster's House. St. Benedict's, as everyone knows, had fallen upon difficult times by then, and an unseemly aspect of my job was that I had to maintain a lookout for possible donors to the school. Forthwith, I sent a letter to Sedgewick Bell.

Apart from the five or six years in which a classmate had written to *The Benedictine* of his whereabouts, I had heard almost nothing about the boy since the year of his graduation. This was unusual, of course, as St. Benedict's makes a point of keeping abreast of its graduates, and I can only assume that his absence in the yearly alumni notes was due to an act of will on his own part. One wonders how much of the boy remained in the man. It is indeed a rare vantage that a St. Benedict's teacher holds, to have known our statesmen, our policy-makers, and our captains of industry in their days of short pants and classroom pranks, and I admit that it was with some nostalgia that I composed the letter.

Since his graduation, of course, my career had proceeded with the steady ascension that the great schools have always afforded their dedicated teachers. Ten years after Sedgewick Bell's departure, I had moved from dean of seniors to dean of the upper school, and after a decade there to dean of academics, a post that some would consider a demotion but that I seized with reverence because it afforded me the chance to make inroads on the minds of a generation. At the time, of course, the country was in the throes of a violent, peristaltic rejection of tradition, and I felt a particular urgency to my

mission of staying a course that had led a century of boys through
the rise and fall of ancient civilizations.

In those days, our meetings of the faculty and trustees were ran-
corous affairs in which great pressure was exerted in attempts to alter
the time-tested curriculum of the school. Planning a course was like
going into battle, and hiring a new teacher was like crowning a king.
Whenever one of our ranks retired or left for another school, the different factions fought tooth-and-nail to influence the appointment. I
was the dean of academics, as I have noted, and these skirmishes
naturally waged around my foxhole. For the lesser appointments I
often feinted to gather leverage for the greater ones, whose campaigns
I fought with abandon.

At one point especially, midway through that decade in which
our country had lost its way, St. Benedict's arrived at a crossroads.
The chair of humanities had retired, and a pitched battle over his
replacement developed between Charles Ellerby and a candidate
from outside. A meeting ensued in which my friend and this other
man spoke to the assembled faculty and trustees, and though I will
not go into detail, I will say that the outside candidate felt that, because of the advances in our society, history had become little more
than a relic.

Oh, what dim-sighted times those were! The two camps sat on
opposite sides of the chapel as speakers took the podium one after
another to wage war. The controversy quickly became a forum concerning the relevance of the past. Teacher after teacher debated the
import of what we in history had taught for generations, and assertion after assertion was met with boos and applause. Tempers blazed.
One powerful member of the board had come to the meeting in blue
jeans and a tie-dyed shirt, and after we had been arguing for several
hours and all of us were exhausted he took the podium and chal-

lenged me personally, right then and there, to debate with him the merits of Roman history.

He was not an ineloquent man, and he chose to speak his plea first, so that by the time he had finished his attack against antiquity I sensed that my battle on behalf of Charles Ellerby, and of history itself, was near to lost. My heart was gravely burdened, for if we could not win our point here among teachers, then among whom indeed could we win it? The room was silent, and on the other side of the chapel our opponents were gathering nearer to one another in the pews.

When I rose to defend my calling, however, I also sensed that victory was not beyond my reach. I am not a particularly eloquent orator, but as I took my place at the chancel rail in the amber glow of the small rose window above us, I was braced by the sudden conviction that the great men of history had sent me forward to preserve their deeds. Charles Ellerby looked up at me biting his lip, and suddenly I remembered the answer I had written long ago in *The Crier*. Its words flowed as though unbidden from my tongue, and when I had finished I knew that we had won. It was my proudest moment at St. Benedict's.

Although the resultant split among the faculty was an egregious one, Charles Ellerby secured the appointment, and together we were able to do what I had always dreamed of doing: we redoubled our commitment to classical education. In times of upheaval, of course, adherence to tradition is all the more important, and perhaps this was why St. Benedict's was brought intact through that decade and the one that followed. Our fortunes lifted and dipped with the gentle rhythm to which I had long ago grown accustomed. Our boys won sporting events and prizes, endured minor scandals and occasional tragedies and then passed on to good colleges. Our endowment rose

when the government was in the hands of Republicans, as did the
caliber of our boys when it was in the hands of Democrats. Senator
Bell declined from prominence, and within a few years I read that he
had passed away. In time, I was made assistant headmaster. Indeed it
was not until a few years ago that anything out of the ordinary happened at all, for it was then, in the late 1980s, that some ill-advised
investments were made and our endowment suffered a decline.

Mr. Woodbridge had by this time reached the age of seventy-
four, and although he was a vigorous man, one Sunday morning in
May while the school waited for him in Chapel he died open-eyed in
his bed. Immediately there occurred a Byzantine struggle for suc-
cession. There is nothing wrong with admitting that by then I myself coveted the job of headmaster, for one does not remain four
decades at a school without becoming deeply attached to its fate; but
Mr. Woodbridge's death had come suddenly and I had not yet begun the preparations for my bid. I was, of course, no longer a young
man. I suppose, in fact, that I lost my advantage here by underesti-
mating my opponents who indeed were younger, as Caesar had done
with Brutus and Cassius.

I should not have been surprised, then, when after several days
of maneuvering, my principal rival turned out to be Charles Ellerby.
For several years, I discovered, he had been conducting his own,
internecine campaign for the position, and although I had always
counted him as my ally and my friend, in the first meeting of the
board he rose and spoke accusations against me. He said that I was
too old, that I had failed to change with the times, that my method
of pedagogy might have been relevant forty years ago but that it was
not today. He stood and said that a headmaster needed vigor and
that I did not have it. Although I watched him the entire time he
spoke, he did not once look back at me.

I was wounded, of course, both professionally and in the hidden part of my heart in which I had always counted Charles Ellerby as a companion in my lifelong search for the magnificence of the past. When several of the older teachers booed him, I felt cheered. At this point I saw that I was not alone in my bid, merely behind, and so I left the meeting without coming to my own defense. Evening had come, and I walked to the dining commons in the company of allies.

How it is, when fighting for one's life, to eat among children! As the boys in their school blazers passed around the platters of fish-sticks and the bowls of sliced bread, my heart was pierced with their guileless grace. How soon, I wondered, would they see the truth of the world? How long before they would understand that it was not dates and names that I had always meant to teach them? Not one of them seemed to notice what had descended like thunderheads above their faculty. Not one of them seemed unable to eat.

After dinner, I returned to the Assistant Headmaster's House in order to plot my course and confer with those I still considered al-lies, but before I could begin my preparations there was a knock at the door. Charles Ellerby stood there, red in the cheeks. "May I ask you some questions?" he said breathlessly.

"It is I who ought to ask them of you," was my answer.

He came in without being asked and took a seat at my table. "You've never been married, am I correct, Hundert?"

"Look, Ellerby, I've been at St. Benedict's since you were in prep school yourself."

"Yes, yes," he said, in an exaggeration of boredom. Of course, he knew as well as I that I had never married, nor started a family, be-cause history itself had always been enough for me. He rubbed his head and appeared to be thinking. To this day, I wonder how he knew about what he said next, unless Sedgewick Bell had somehow told him the story of my visit to the senator. "Look," he said. "There's a rumor you keep a pistol in your desk drawer."

"Hogwash."

"Will you open it for me," he said, pointing there.

"No, I will not. I have been a dean here for twenty years."

"Are you telling me there is no pistol in this house?"

He then attempted to stare me down. He was a man with little character, however, and the bid withered. At that point, in fact, as his eyes fell in submission to my determined gaze, I believe the headmastership became mine. It is a largely unexplored element of history, of course, and one that has long fascinated me, that a great deal of political power and thus a great deal of the arc of nations arises not from intellectual advancements nor social imperatives but from the simple battle of wills among men at tables, such as had just occurred between Charles Ellerby and me.

Instead of opening the desk and brandishing the weapon, however, which of course meant nothing to me but no doubt would have seized the initiative from Ellerby, I denied to him its existence. Why, I do not know; for I was a teacher of history, and was not the firearm its greatest engine? Ellerby, on the other hand, was simply a gadfly to the passing morals of the time. He gathered his things and left my house.

That evening I took the pistol from my drawer. A margin of rust had appeared along the filigreed handle, and despite the ornate workmanship I saw clearly now that in its essence the weapon was ill-proportioned and blunt, the crude instrument of a violent, historically meager man. I had not even wanted it when the irascible demagogue Bell had foisted it upon me, and I had only taken it out of some vague sentiment that a pistol might eventually prove decisive. I suppose I had always imagined firing it someday in a moment of drama. Yet now, here it stood before me in a moment of torpor. I turned it over and cursed it.

That night I took it from the drawer again, hid it in the pocket of

my overcoat and walked to the far end of the campus, where I crossed
the marsh a good mile from my house, removed my shoes and stepped
into the babbling shadows of the Passamic. *The die is cast,* I said and
I threw it twenty yards out into the water. The last impediment to
my headmastership had been hurdled, and by the time I came ashore,
walked back whistling to my front door, and changed for bed, I was
ecstatic.

Yet that night I slept poorly, and in the morning when I rose and
went to our faculty meeting, I felt that the mantle of my fortitude had
slipped somehow from my shoulders. How hushed is demise! In the
hall outside the faculty room, most of the teachers filed by without
speaking to me, and once inside I became obsessed with the idea
that I had missed the most basic lesson of the past, that conviction
is the alpha and the omega of authority. Now I see that I was doomed
the moment I threw that pistol in the water, for that is when I lost my
conviction. It was as though Sedgewick Bell had risen, all these years
later, to drag me down again. Indeed, once the meeting had begun,
the older faculty members shrunk back from their previous support
of my bid, and the younger ones encircled me as though I were a
limping animal. There might as well have been a dagger among the
cloaks. By four o'clock that afternoon, Charles Ellerby, a fellow antiquarian whose job I had once helped secure, had been named headmaster, and by the end of that month he had asked me to retire.

And so I was preparing to end my days at St. Benedict's when I received Sedgewick Bell's response to my letter. It was well-written,
which I noted with pleasure, and contained no trace of rancor, which
is what every teacher hopes to see in the maturation of his disagree-
able students. In closing he asked me to call him at EastAmerica
Steel, and I did so that afternoon. When I gave my name first to one

secretary and then to a second, and after that, moments later, heard Sedgewick's artfully guileless greeting, I instantly recalled speaking to his father forty years before.

After small talk, including my condolences about his father, he told me that the reason he had returned my letter was that he had often dreamed of holding a rematch of Mister Julius Caesar, and that he was now willing to donate a large sum of money to St. Benedict's if I would agree to administer the event. Naturally, I assumed he was joking and passed off the idea with a comment about how funny it was, but Sedgewick Bell repeated the invitation. He wanted very much to be on stage again with Deepak Mehta and Clay Walter. I suppose I should not have been surprised, for it is precisely this sort of childhood slight that will drive a great figure. I told him that I was about to retire. He expressed sympathy but then suggested that the arrangement could be ideal, as now I would no doubt have time to prepare. Then he said that at this station in his life he could afford whatever he wanted materially—with all that this implied, of course, concerning his donation to the Annual Fund—but that more than anything else, he desired the chance to reclaim his intellectual honor. I suppose I was flattered.

Of course, he also offered a good sum of money to me personally. Although I had until then led a life in which finances were never more than a distant concern, I was keenly aware that my time in the school's houses and dining halls was coming to an end. On the one hand, it was not my burning aspiration to secure an endowment for the reign of Charles Ellerby; on the other hand, I needed the money, and I felt a deep loyalty to the school regarding the Annual Fund. That evening, I began to prepare my test.

As assistant headmaster, I had not taught my beloved Roman history in many years, so that poring through my reams of notes was like returning at last to my childhood home. I stopped here and there among the files. I reread the term paper of young Derek Bok on "The Search of Diogenes," and the scrawled one of James Watson on "Archimedes's Method." Among the art projects, I found John Updike's reproduction of the Obelisk of Cleopatra, and a charcoal drawing of the baths of Caracalla by the abstract expressionist, Robert Motherwell, unfortunately torn in two and no longer worth anything.

I had always been a diligent notetaker, furthermore, and I believe that what I came up with was a surprisingly accurate reproduction of the subjects on which I had once quizzed Clay Walter, Deepak Mehta and Sedgewick Bell, nearly half a century before. It took me only two evenings to gather enough material for the task, although in order not to appear eager I waited several days before sending off another letter to Sedgewick Bell. He called me soon after.

It is indeed a surprise to one who toils for his own keep to see the formidable strokes with which our captains of industry demolish the tasks before them. The morning after talking to Sedgewick Bell I received calls from two of his secretaries, a social assistant and a woman at a New York travel agency, who confirmed the arrangements for late July, two months hence. The event was to take place on an island off the Outer Banks of Carolina that belonged to EastAmerica Steel, and I sent along a list from the St. Benedict's archives so that everyone in Sedgewick Bell's class would be invited.

I was not prepared, however, for the days of retirement that intervened. What little remained of that school year passed speedily in my preoccupation, and before I knew it the boys were taking their final exams. I tried not to think about my future. At the commencement exercises in June, a small section of the ceremony was spent in my honor, but it was presided over by Charles Ellerby and gave rise to a taste of copper in my throat. "And thus we bid adieu," he began, "to our beloved Mr. Hundert." He gazed out over the lectern, extended his arm in my direction, and proceeded to give a nostalgic rendering of my years at the school to the audience of jacketed businessmen, parasoled ladies, students in St. Benedict's blazers and children in church suits, who, like me, were squirming at the meretriciousness of the man.

Yet how quickly it was over! Awards were presented, "Hail Fair Benedict's" was sung, and as the birches began to lean their narrow shadows against the distant edge of the marsh, the seniors came forward to receive their diplomas. The mothers wept, the alumni stood misty-eyed, and the graduates threw their hats into the air. Afterward, everyone dispersed for the headmaster's reception.

I wish now that I had made an appearance there, for to have missed it, the very last one of my career, was a far more grievous blow to me than to Charles Ellerby. Furthermore, the handful of senior boys who over their tenure had been pierced by the bee-sting of history no doubt missed my presence or at least wondered at its lack. I spent the remnants of the afternoon in my house, and the evening walking out along the marsh, where the smell of woodsmoke from a farmer's bonfire and the distant sounds of the gathered celebrants filled me with the great, sad pride of teaching. My boys were passing once again into the world without me.

The next day, of course, parents began arriving to claim their children; jitney buses ferried students to airports and train stations; the groundsman went around pulling up lacrosse goals and baseball bleachers, hauling the long black sprinkler hoses behind his tractor into the fields. I spent most of that day and the next one sitting at the desk in my study, watching through the window as the school wound down like a clockspring toward the strange, bird-filled calm of that second afternoon of my retirement, when all the boys had left and I was alone, once again, in the eerie quiet of summer. I own few things besides my files and books; I packed them, and the next day the groundsman drove me into Woodmere.

There I found lodging in a splendid Victorian rooming house run by a descendant of Nat Turner who joked, when I told her that I was a newly retired teacher, about how the house had always welcomed escaped slaves. I was surprised at how heartily I laughed at this, which had the benefit of putting me instantly on good terms with the landlady. We negotiated a monthly rent, and I went upstairs to set about charting a new life for myself. I was seventy-one years old—yes, perhaps, too old to be headmaster—but I could still walk three miles before dinner and did so the first afternoon of my freedom. However, by evening my spirits had taken a beating.

Fortunately, there was the event to prepare for, as I fear that without it, those first days and nights would have been unbearable. I pored again and again over my old notes, extracting devilish questions from the material. But this only occupied a few hours of the day, and by late morning my eyes would grow weary. Objectively speaking, the start of that summer should have been no different from the start of any other; yet it was. Passing my reflection in the hallway mirror at the head of the stairs on my way down to dinner I would think to myself, *is that you?* and on the way back up to my room, *what now?* I wrote letters to my brothers and sister, and to several of my former boys. The days crawled by. I introduced myself to the town librarian. I made the acquaintance of a retired railroad man who liked as much as I did to sit on the grand, screened porch of that house. I took the bus into Washington a few times to spend the day in museums.

But as the summer progressed, a certain dread began to form in my mind, which I tried through the diligence of walking, museum-going and reading, to ignore; that is, I began to fear that Sedgewick

Bell had forgotten about the event. The thought would occur to me in the midst of the long path along the outskirts of town; and as I reached the Passamic, took my break and then started back again toward home, I would battle with my urge to contact the man. Several times I went to the telephone downstairs in the rooming house and twice I wrote out letters that I did not send. *Why would he go through all the trouble just to mock me?* I thought; but then I would recall the circumstances of his tenure at St. Benedict's and a darker gloom would descend upon me. I began to have second thoughts about events that occurred half a century before: should I have confronted him in the midst of the original contest? Should I never have leap-frogged another boy to get him there? Should I have spoken up to the senator?

In early July, however, Sedgewick Bell's secretary finally did call, and I felt that I had been given a reprieve. She apologized for her tardiness, asked me more questions about my taste in food and lodging, and then informed me of the date, three weeks later, when a car would call to take me to the airport in Williamsburg. An East-America jet would fly me up from there to Charlotte, from whence I was to be picked up by helicopter.

Helicopter! Less than a month later I stood before the craft, which was painted head to tail in EastAmerica's green and gold insignia, polished to a shine, with a six-man passenger bay and red, white and blue sponsons over the wheels. One does not remain at St. Benedict's for five decades without gaining a certain familiarity with privilege, yet as it lifted me off the pad in Charlotte, hovered for a moment, then lowered its nose and turned eastward over the gentle hills and then the chopping slate of the sea channel, I felt a headiness that I had never known before; it was what Augustus Caesar must have felt millennia ago, carried head-high on a litter past the Tiber. I clutched my notes to my chest. Indeed I wondered what my life might have been like if I had felt this just once in my youth. The rotors buzzed like a beehive. On the island I was shown to a suite of rooms in a high corner of the lodge, with windows and balconies overlooking the sea.

For a conference on the future of childhood education or the plight of America's elderly, of course, you could not get one tenth of these men to attend, but for a privileged romp on a private island it had merely been a matter of making the arrangements. I stood at the window of my room and watched the helicopter ferry back and forth across the channel, disgorging on the island a *Who's Who* of America's largest corporations, universities and organs of policy.

Oh, but what it was to see the boys! After a time, I made my way back out to the airstrip, and whenever the craft touched down on the landing platform and one or another of my old students ducked out, clutching his suit lapel as he ran clear of the snapping rotors, I was struck anew with how great a privilege my profession had been.

That evening all of us ate together in the lodge, and the boys toasted me and took turns coming to my table, where several times one or another of them had to remind me to continue eating my food. Sedgewick Bell ambled over and with a charming air of modesty showed me the flashcards of Roman history that he'd been keeping in his desk at EastAmerica. Then, shedding his modesty, he went to the podium and produced a long and raucous toast referring to any number of pranks and misdeeds at St. Benedict's that I had never even heard of but that the chorus of boys greeted with stamps and whistles. At a quarter to nine, they all dropped their forks onto the floor, and I fear that tears came to my eyes.

The most poignant part of all, however, was how plainly the faces of the men still showed the eager expressiveness of the first-form boys of forty years ago. Martin Blythe had lost half his leg as an officer in Korea, and now, among his classmates, he tried to hide his lurching stride, but he wore the same knitted brow that he used to wear in my classroom; Deepak Mehta, who had become a professor of Asian history, walked with a slight stoop, yet he still turned his eyes downward when spoken to; Clay Walter seemed to have fared physically better than his mates, bouncing about in the Italian suit and alligator shoes of the advertising industry, yet he was still drawn immediately to the other do-nothings from his class.

But of course it was Sedgewick Bell who commanded everyone's attention. He had grown stout across the middle and bald over the crown of his head, and I saw in his ear, although it was artfully concealed, the flesh-colored bulb of a hearing aid; yet he walked among the men like a prophet. Their faces grew animated when he approached, and at the tables I could see them competing for his attention. He patted one on the back, whispered in the ear of another, gripped hands and grasped shoulders and kissed the wives on the lips. His walk was firm and imbued not with the seriousness of his post, it seemed to me, but with the ease of it, so that his stride among the tables was jocular. He was the host and clearly in his element. His laugh was voluble.

I went to sleep early that evening so that the boys could enjoy themselves downstairs in the saloon, and as I lay in bed I listened to their songs and revelry. It had not escaped my attention, of course, that they no doubt spent some time mocking me, but this is what one grows to expect in my post, and indeed it was part of the reason I left them alone. Although I was tempted to walk down and listen from outside the theater, I did not.

The next day was spent walking the island's serpentine spread of coves and beaches, playing tennis on the grass court, and paddling in wooden boats on the small, inland lake behind the lodge. How quickly one grows accustomed to luxury! Men and women lounged on the decks and beaches and patios, sunning like seals, gorging themselves on the largess of their host.

As for me, I barely had a moment to myself, for the boys took turns at my entertainment. I walked with Deepak Mehta along the beach and succeeded in getting him to tell me the tale of his rise through academia to a post at Columbia University. Evidently his rise had taken a toll, for although he looked healthy enough to me he told me that he had recently had a small heart attack. It was not the type of thing one talked about with a student, however, so I let this revelation pass without comment. Later, Clay Walter brought me onto the tennis court and tried to teach me to hit a ball, an activity that drew a crowd of boisterous guests to the stands. They roared at Clay's theatrical antics and cheered and stomped their feet whenever I sent one back across the net. In the afternoon, Martin Blythe took me out in a rowboat.

St. Benedict's, of course, has always had a more profound effect than most schools on the lives of its students, yet nonetheless it was strange that once in the center of the pond, where he had rowed us with his lurching stroke, Martin Blythe set down the oars in their locks and told me he had something he'd always meant to ask me.

"Yes," I said.

He brushed back his hair with his hand. "*I* was supposed to be the one up there with Deepak and Clay, wasn't I, sir?"

"Don't tell me you're still thinking about that."

"It's just that I've sometimes wondered what happened."

"Yes, you should have been," I said.

Oh, how little we understand of men if we think that their childhood slights are forgotten! He smiled. He did not press the subject further, and while I myself debated the merits of explaining why I had passed him over for Sedgewick Bell four decades before, he pivoted the boat around and brought us back to shore. The confirmation of his suspicions was enough to satisfy him, it seemed, so I said nothing more. He had been an Air Force major in our country's endeavors on the Korean peninsula, yet as he pulled the boat onto the beach I had the clear feeling of having saved him from some torment.

Indeed, that evening when the guests had gathered in the lodge's small theater, and Deepak Mehta, Clay Walter and Sedgewick Bell had taken their seats for the reenactment of Mister Julius Caesar, I noticed an ease in Martin Blythe's face that I believe I had never seen in it before. His brow was not knit, and he had crossed his legs so that above one sock we could clearly see the painted wooden calf.

It was then that I noticed that the boys who had paid the most attention to me that day were in fact the ones sitting before me on the stage. How dreadful a thought this was—that they had indulged me to gain advantage—but I put it from my mind and stepped to the microphone. I had spent the late afternoon reviewing my notes, and the first rounds of questions were called from memory.

The crowd did not fail to notice the feat. There were whistles and stomps when I named fifteen of the first sixteen emperors in order and asked Clay Walter to produce the one I had left out. There was applause when I spoke Caesar's words, *"Iacta alea est,"* and then, continuing in carefully pronounced Latin, asked Sedgewick Bell to recall the circumstance of their utterance. He had told me that afternoon of the months he had spent preparing, and as I was asking the question, he smiled. The boys had not worn togas, of course—although I personally feel they might have—yet the situation was familiar enough that I felt a rush of unease as Sedgewick Bell's smile then waned and he hesitated several moments before answering. But this time, all these years later, he looked straight out into the audience and spoke his answers with the air of a scholar.

It was not long before Clay Walter had dropped out, of course, but then, as it had before, the contest proceeded neck and neck between Sedgewick Bell and Deepak Mehta. I asked Sedgewick Bell about Caesar's battles at Pharsalus and Thapsus, about the shift of power to Constantinople and about the war between the patricians and the plebeians; I asked Deepak Mehta about the Punic Wars, the conquest of Italy and the fall of the republic. Deepak, of course, had an advantage, for certainly he had studied this material at university, but I must say that the straightforward determination of Sedgewick Bell had begun to win my heart. I recalled the bashful manner in which he had shown me his flashcards at dinner the night before, and as I stood now before the microphone I seemed to be in the throes of an affection for him that had long been under wraps.

"What year were the Romans routed at Lake Trasimene?" I asked him.

He paused. "217 B.C., I believe."

"Which general later became Scipio Africanus Major?"

"Publius Cornelius Scipio, sir." Deepak Mehta answered softly.

It does not happen as often as one might think that an unintelligent boy becomes an intelligent man, for in my own experience the love of thought is rooted in an age long before adolescence; yet Sedgewick Bell now seemed to have done just that. His answers were spoken with the composed demeanor of a scholar. There is no one I like more, of course, than the man who is moved by the mere fact of history, and as I contemplated the next question to him I wondered if I had indeed exaggerated the indolence of his boyhood. Was it true, perhaps, that he had simply not come into his element yet while at St. Benedict's? He peered intently at me from the stage, his elbows on his knees. I decided to ask him a difficult question. "Chairman Bell," I said, "which tribes invaded Rome in 102 B.C.?"

His eyes went blank and he curled his shoulders in his suit. Although he was by then one of the most powerful men in America, and although moments before that I had been rejoicing in his discipline, suddenly I saw him on that stage once again as a frightened boy. How powerful is memory! And once again, I feared that it was I who had betrayed him. He brought his hand to his head to think.

"Take your time, sir," I offered.

There were murmurs in the audience. He distractedly touched the side of his head. A man's character is his fate, says Heraclitus, and at that moment, as he brushed his hand down over his temple, I realized that the flesh-colored device in his ear was not a hearing aid but a transmitter through which he was receiving the answers to my questions. Nausea rose in me. Of course I had no proof, but was it not exactly what I should have expected? He touched his head once again and appeared to be deep in thought, and I knew it as certainly as if he had shown me. "The Teutons," he said, haltingly, "and—I'll take a stab here—the Cimbri?"

I looked for a long time at him. Did he know at that point what I was thinking? I cannot say, but after I had paused as long as I could bear to in front of that crowd, I cleared my throat and granted that he was right. Applause erupted. He shook it off with a wave of his hand. I knew that it was my duty to speak up. I knew it was my duty as a teacher to bring him clear of the moral dereliction in which I myself had been his partner, yet at the same time I felt myself adrift in the tide of my own vacillation and failure. The boy had somehow got hold of me again. He tried to quiet the applause with a wave of his hand, but this gesture only caused the clapping to increase, and I am afraid to say that it was merely the sound of a throng of boister-ous men that finally prevented me from making my stand. Quite suddenly I was aware that this was not the situation I had known at St. Benedict's School. We were guests now of a significant man on his splendid estate, and to expose him would be a serious act indeed. I turned and quieted the crowd.

From the chair next to Sedgewick Bell, Deepak Mehta merely looked at me, his eyes dark and resigned. Perhaps he too had just realized, or perhaps in fact he had long known, but in any case I simply asked him the next question; after he answered it, I could do nothing but put another before Sedgewick Bell. Then Deepak again, then Sedgewick, and again to Deepak, and it was only then, on the third round after I had discovered the ploy, that an idea came to me. When I returned to Sedgewick Bell I asked him, "Who was Shutruk-Nahhunte?"

A few boys in the crowd began to laugh, and when Sedgewick Bell took his time thinking about the answer, more in the audience joined in. Whoever was the mercenary professor talking in his ear, it was clear to me that he would not know the answer to this one, for if he had not gone to St. Benedict's School he would never have heard of Shutruk-Nahhunte; and in a few moments, sure enough, I saw Sedgewick Bell begin to grow uncomfortable. He lifted his pant leg and scratched at his sock. The laughter increased, and then I heard the wives, who had obviously never lived in a predatory pack, trying to stifle their husbands. "Come on, Bell!" someone shouted, "Look at the damn door!" Laughter erupted again.

How can it be that for a moment my heart bled for him? He, too, tried to laugh, but only half-heartedly. He shifted in his seat, shook his arms loose in his suit, looked uncomprehendingly out at the snickering crowd, then braced his chin and said, "Well, I guess if Deepak knows the answer to this one, then it's *his* ballgame."

Deepak's response was nearly lost in the boisterous stamps and whistles that followed, for I am sure that every boy but Sedgewick recalled Henry Stimson's tablet above the door of my classroom. Yet what was strange was that I felt disappointment. As Deepak Mehta smiled, spoke the answer, and stood from his chair, I watched confusion and then a flicker of panic cross the face of Sedgewick Bell.

He stood haltingly. How clear it was to me then that the corruption in his character had always arisen from fear, and I could not help remembering that as his teacher I had once tried to convince him of his stupidity. I cursed that day. But then in a moment he summoned a smile, called me up to the stage, and crossed theatrically to congratulate the victor.

How can I describe the scene that took place next? I suppose I was naïve to think that this was the end of the evening—or even the point of it—for after Sedgewick Bell had brought forth a trophy for Deepak Mehta, and then one for me as well, an entirely different cast came across his features. He strode once again to the podium and asked for the attention of the guests. He tapped sharply on the microphone. Then he leaned his head forward, and in a voice that I recognized from long ago on the radio, a voice in whose deft leaps from boom to whisper I heard the willow-tree drawl of his father, he launched into an address about the problems of our country. He had an orator's gift of dropping his volume at the moment when a less gifted man would have raised it. *We have opened our doors to all the world,* he said, his voice thundering, then pausing, then plunging nearly to a murmur, *and now the world has stripped us bare.* He gestured with his hands. The men in the audience, first laughing, now turned serious. *We have given away too much for too long,* he said. *We have handed our fiscal leadership to men who don't care about the taxpayers of our country, and our moral course to those who no longer understand our role in history.* Although he gestured to me there, I could not return his gaze. *We have abandoned the moral education of our families.* Scattered applause drifted up from his classmates, and here, of course, I almost spoke. *We have left our country adrift on dangerous seas.* Now the applause was more hearty. Then he quieted his voice again, dropped his head as though in supplication and announced that he was running for the United States Senate.

Why was I surprised? I should not have been, for since child-hood the boy had stood so near to the mantle of power that its shadow must have been as familiar to him as his boyhood home. Virtue had no place in the palaces he had known. I was ashamed when I realized he had contrived the entire rematch of Mister Julius Caesar for no reason other than to gather his classmates for dona-tions, yet still I chastened myself for not realizing his ambition be-fore. In his oratory, in his physical presence, in his conviction, he had always possessed the gifts of a leader, and now he was using them. I should have expected this from the first day he stood in his short-pants suit in the doorway of my classroom and silenced my students. He already wielded a potent role in the affairs of our coun-try; he enjoyed the presumption of his family name; he was blindly ignorant of history and therefore did not fear his role in it. Of course it was exactly the culmination I should long ago have seen. The crowd stood cheering.

As soon as the clapping abated a curtain was lifted behind him, and a band struck up "Dixie." Waiters appeared at the side doors, a dance platform was unfolded in the orchestra pit, and Sedgewick Bell jumped down from the stage into the crowd of his friends. They clamored around him. He patted shoulders, kissed wives, whispered and laughed and nodded his head. I saw checkbooks come out. The waiters carried champagne on trays at their shoulders, and at the edge of the dance floor the women set down their purses and stepped into the arms of their husbands. When I saw this I ducked out a side door and returned to the lodge, for the abandon with which the guests were dancing was an unbearable counterpart to the truth I knew. One can imagine my feelings. I heard the din late into the night.

Needless to say, I resolved to avoid Sedgewick Bell for the re-mainder of my stay. How my mind raced that night through human-ity's endless history of injustice, depravity and betrayal! I could not

sleep, and several times I rose and went to the window to listen to
the revelry. Standing at the glass I felt like the spurned sovereign in
the castle tower, looking down from his balcony onto the procession
of the false potentate.

Yet, sure enough, my conviction soon began to wane. No
sooner had I resolved to avoid my host than I began to doubt the
veracity of my secret knowledge about him. Other thoughts came
to me. How, in fact, had I been so sure of what he'd done? What
proof had I at all? Amid the distant celebrations of the night, my
conclusion began to seem far-fetched, and by the quiet of the morning I was muddled. I did not go to breakfast. As boy after boy
stopped by my rooms to wish me well, I assiduously avoided com-
menting on either Sedgewick Bell's performance or on his announce-
ment for the Senate. On the beach that day I endeavored to walk
by myself, for by then I trusted neither my judgment of the incident nor my discretion with the boys. I spent the afternoon alone in
a cove across the island.

I did not speak to Sedgewick Bell that entire day. I managed to
avoid him, in fact, until the next evening, by which time all but a few
of the guests had left, when he came to bid farewell as I stood on the
tarmac awaiting the helicopter for the mainland. He walked out and
motioned for me to stand back from the platform, but I pretended
not to hear him and kept my eyes up to the sky. Suddenly, the shining craft swooped in from beyond the wave break, churning the
channel into a boil, pulled up in a hover and then touched down on
its flag-colored sponsons before us. The wind and noise could have
thrown a man to the ground, and Sedgewick Bell seemed to pull at
me like a magnet, but I did not retreat. It was he, finally, who ran out
to me. He gripped his lapels, ducked his head and offered me his
hand. I took it tentatively, the rotors whipping our jacket-sleeves. I

had been expecting this moment and had decided the night before what I was going to say. I leaned toward him. "How long have you been hard of hearing?" I asked.

His smile dropped. I cannot imagine what I had become in the mind of that boy. "Very good, Hundert," he said. "Very good. I thought you might have known."

My vindication was sweet, although now I see that it meant little. By then I was on the ladder of the helicopter, but he pulled me toward him again and looked darkly into my eyes. "And I can see that *you* have not changed either," he said.

Well, had I? As the craft lifted off and turned westward toward the bank of clouds that hid the distant shoreline, I analyzed the situation with some care. The wooden turrets of the lodge grew smaller and then were lost in the trees, and I found it easier to think then, for everything on that island had been imbued with the sheer power of the man. I relaxed a bit in my seat. One could say that in this case I indeed had acted properly, for is it not the glory of our legal system that acquitting a guilty man is less heinous than convicting an innocent one? At the time of the contest, I certainly had no proof of Sedgewick Bell's behavior.

Yet back in Woodmere, as I have intimated, I found myself with a great deal of time on my hands, and it was not long before the incident began to replay itself in my mind. Following the wooded trail toward the river or sitting in the breeze at dusk on the porch, I began to see that a different ending would have better served us all. Conviction had failed me again. I was well aware of the foolish consolation of my thoughts, yet I vividly imagined what I should have done. I heard myself speaking up; I saw my resolute steps to his chair on the stage, then the insidious, flesh-colored device in my palm, held up to the crowd; I heard him stammering.

As if to mock my inaction, however, stories of his electoral effort soon began to appear in the papers. It was a year of spite and rancor in our country's politics, and the race in West Virginia was less a campaign than a brawl between gladiators. The incumbent was as versed in treachery as Sedgewick Bell, and over my morning tea I followed their battles. Sedgewick Bell called him "a liar when he speaks and a crook when he acts," and he called Sedgewick Bell worse. A fistfight erupted when their campaigns crossed at an airport.

I was revolted by the spectacle, but of course I was also intrigued, and I cannot deny that although I was rooting for the incumbent, a part of me was also cheered at each bit of news chronicling Sedgewick Bell's assault on his lead. Oh, why was this so? Are we all, at base, creatures without virtue? Is fervor the only thing we follow?

Needless to say, that fall had been a difficult one in my life, especially those afternoons when the St. Benedict's bus roared by the guest house in Woodmere taking the boys to track meets, and perhaps the Senate race was nothing more than a healthy distraction for me. Indeed I needed distractions. To witness the turning of the leaves and to smell the apples in their barrels without hearing the sound of a hundred boys in the fields, after all, was almost more than I could bear. My walks had grown longer, and several times I had crossed the river and ventured to the far end of the marsh, from where in the distance I could make out the blurred figures of St. Benedict's. I knew this was not good for me, and perhaps that is why, in late October of that year when I read that Sedgewick Bell would be making a campaign stop at a coal-miners' union hall near the Virginia border, I decided to go hear him speak.

Perhaps by then the boy had become an obsession for me—I will admit this, for I am as aware as anyone that time is but the thinnest bandage for our wounds—but on the other hand, the race had grown quite close and would have been of natural interest to anyone. Sedgewick Bell had drawn himself up from an underdog to a challenger. Now it was clear that the election hinged on the votes of labor, and Sedgewick Bell, though he was the son of aristocrats and the chairman of a formidable corporation, began to cast himself as a champion of the working man. From newspaper reports I gleaned that he was helped along by the power of his voice and bearing, and I could easily imagine these men turning to him. I well knew the charisma of the boy.

The day arrived, and I packed a lunch and made the trip. As the bus wound west along the river valley, I envisioned the scene ahead and wondered whether Sedgewick Bell would at this point care to see me. Certainly I represented some sort of truth to him about himself, yet at the same time I also seemed to have become a part of the very delusion that he had foisted on those around him. How far my boys would always stride upon the world's stage, yet how dearly I would always hope to change them! The bus arrived early, and I went inside the union hall to wait.

Shortly before noon the miners began to come in. I don't know what I had expected, but I was surprised to see them looking as though they had indeed just come out of the mines. They wore hard hats, their faces were stained with dust, and their gloves and tool belts hung at their waists. For some reason I had worn my St. Benedict's blazer, which I now removed. Reporters began to filter in as well, and by the time the noon whistle blew, the crowd was overflowing from the hall.

As the whistle subsided I heard the thump-thump of his helicopter, and through the door in a moment I saw the twisters of dust as it hovered into view from above. How clever was the man I had known as a boy! The craft had been repainted the colors of military camouflage but he had left the sponsors the red-white-and-blue of their previous incarnation. He jumped from the side door when the craft was still a foot above the ground, entered the hall at a jog and was greeted with an explosion of applause. His aides lined the stairs to the high platform on which the microphone stood under a banner and a flag, and as he crossed the crowd toward them the miners jostled to be near him, knocking their knuckles against his hard hat, reaching for his hands and his shoulders, cheering like Romans at a chariot race.

I do not need to report on his eloquence, for I have dwelled enough upon it. When he reached the staircase and ascended to the podium, stopping first at the landing to wave and then at the top to salute the flag above him, jubilation swept among the throng. I knew then that he had succeeded in his efforts, that these miners counted him somehow as their own, so that when he actually spoke and they interrupted him with cheers it was no more expected than the promises he made then to carry their interests with him to the Senate. He was masterful. I found my own arm upraised.

Certainly there were five hundred men in that hall, but there was only one with a St. Benedict's blazer over his shoulder and no hard hat on his head, so of course I should not have been surprised when within a few minutes one of his aides appeared beside me and told me that the candidate had asked for me at the podium. At that moment I saw Sedgewick Bell's glance pause for a moment on my face. There was a flicker of a smile on his lips, but then he looked away.

Is there no battle other than the personal one? Was Sedgewick Bell at that point willing to risk the future of his political ideas for whatever childhood demon I still remained to him? The next time he turned toward me, he gestured down at the floor, and in a moment the aide had pulled my arm and was escorting me toward the platform. The crowd opened as we passed, and the miners in their ignorance and jubilation were reaching to shake my hand. This was indeed a heady feeling. I climbed the steps and stood beside Sedgewick Bell at the smaller microphone. How it was to stand above the mass of men like that! He raised his hand and they cheered; he lowered it and they fell silent.

"There is a man here today who has been immeasurably important in my life," he whispered into his microphone.

There was applause, and a few of the men whistled. "Thank you," I said into my own. I could see the blue underbrims of five hundred hard hats turned up toward me. My heart was nearly bursting.

"My history teacher," he said, as the crowd began to cheer again. Flashbulbs popped and I moved instinctively toward the front of the platform. "Mr. Hundert," he boomed, "from forty-five years ago at Richmond Central High School."

It took me a moment to realize what he had said. By then he too was clapping and at the same time lowering his head in what must have appeared to the men below to be respect for me. The blood engorged my veins. "Just a minute," I said, stepping back to my own microphone. "I taught you at St. Benedict's School in Tallywood, Virginia. Here is the blazer."

Of course, it makes no difference in the course of history that as I tried to hold up the coat, Sedgewick Bell moved swiftly across the podium, took it from my grip and raised my arm high in his own and that this pose, of all things, sent the miners into jubilation; it makes no difference that by the time I spoke, he had gestured with his hands so that one of his aides had already shut off my microphone. For one does not alter history without conviction. It is enough to know that I *did* speak, and certainly a consolation that Sedgewick Bell realized, finally, that I would.

He won the election not in small part because he managed to convince those miners that he was one of them. They were ignorant people, and I cannot blame them for taking to the shrewdly populist rhetoric of the man. I saved the picture that appeared the following morning in the *Gazette*: Senator Bell radiating all the populist magnetism of his father, holding high the arm of an old man who has on his face the remnants of a proud and foolish smile.

I still live in Woodmere, and I have found a route that I take now and then to the single high hill from which I can see the St. Benedict's steeple across the Passamic. I take two walks every day and have grown used to this life. I have even come to like it. I am reading of the ancient Japanese civilizations now, which I had somehow neglected before, and every so often one of my boys visits me.

One afternoon recently, Deepak Mehta did so, and we shared some brandy. This was in the fall of last year. He was still the quiet boy he had always been, and not long after he had taken a seat on my couch I had to turn on the television to ease for him the burden of conversation. As it happened, the Senate Judiciary Committee was holding its famous hearings then, and the two of us sat there watching, nodding our heads or chuckling whenever the camera showed Sedgewick Bell sitting alongside the chairman. I had poured the brandy liberally, and whenever Sedgewick Bell leaned into the microphone and asked a question of the witness, Deepak would mimic his affected southern drawl. Naturally, I could not exactly encourage this behavior, but I did nothing to stop it. When he finished his drink I poured him another. This, of course, is perhaps the greatest pleasure of a teacher's life, to have a drink one day with a man he had known as a boy.

Nonetheless, I only wish we could have talked more than we actually did. But I am afraid that there must always be a reticence between a teacher and his student. Deepak had had another small heart attack, he told me, but I felt it would have been improper of me to inquire more. I tried to bring myself to broach the subject of

Sedgewick Bell's history, but here again I was aware that a teacher does not discuss one boy with another. Certainly Deepak must have known about Sedgewick Bell as well, but probably out of his own set of St. Benedict's morals he did not bring it up with me. We watched Sedgewick Bell question the witness and then whisper into the ear of the chairman. Neither of us was surprised at his ascendance, I believe, because both of us were students of history. Yet we did not discuss this either. Still, I wanted desperately for him to ask me something more, and perhaps this was why I kept refilling his glass. I wanted him to ask, "How is it to be alone, sir, at this age," or perhaps to say, "You have made a difference in my life, Mr. Hundert." But of course these were not things Deepak Mehta would ever say. A man's character is his character. Nonetheless it was startling, every now and then when I looked over at the sunlight falling across his bowed head, to see that Deepak Mehta, the quietest of my boys, was now an old man.

Daniel Orozco

on

Steven Millhauser's *Flying Carpets*

> *When I was a child, I spake as a child, I understood as a child, I thought as a child: but when I became a man, I put away childish things.*
> —1 Corinthians 13:11

St. Paul's adage is the seed from which our dramas of nostalgia emerged. Stories of yearning for the irretrievable past are, I think, hard to write well, because they risk sentimentality—an excessive reaching for feeling that . . . well, feels contrived and false. The paradox is that stories of nostalgia are kind of *about* that excessive reaching, and so the writer is stymied by the Imitative Fallacy: how do you tell a story about sentimentality, while avoiding the excesses of sentimental prose?

"Flying Carpets" is told as memoir. The man doing the telling embodies the memory of the boy he was, and a childhood summer is evoked with sensory details as sharp as they are commonplace and quotidian—the flutter of sheets on clotheslines, the buzz of insects, the gleam of a bottle in the grass. It is sense memory that evokes the strongest emotions in us; that's *how* we remember. We experience the world through our senses, and in remembering we reach for sense memory in order to somehow feel what was, and is now gone.

I feel lost love not by thinking *I loved Amanda,* but by recalling her laugh, smell of her hair, the tiny scar on her chin. Nostalgia is evoked by the precision and accumulation of concrete sensory detail—in other words, by heeding that writerly chestnut: *Show, Don't Tell.*

However commonplace the thing remembered, it is this precision and accumulation that makes the thing—and the emotions associated with it—profoundly *remembered,* and felt, and true. That goes for sheets and Coke bottles. And, oh yes, flying carpets. And this is what elevates this drama of nostalgia from the masterly to the sublime. Flying carpets are the diversion of the summer—ridden by neighborhood boys, skimming rooftops, drifting over fences from backyard to backyard—until one day the novelty wears off. Summer wanes, the earth turns, and the toys are put away. The fantastic is rendered commonplace, and the magic of a boy's childhood is recalled with the melancholy of the man who can never experience such again.

Steven Millhauser

✸

Flying Carpets

In the long summers of my childhood, games flared up suddenly, burned to a brightness, and vanished forever. The summers were so long that they gradually grew longer than the whole year, they stretched out slowly beyond the edges of our lives, but at every moment of their vastness they were drawing to an end, for that's what summers mostly did: they taunted us with endings, marched always into the long shadow thrown backward by the end of vacation. And because our summers were always ending, and because they lasted forever, we grew impatient with our games, we sought new and more intense ones; and as the crickets of August grew louder, and a single red leaf appeared on branches green with summer, we threw ourselves as if desperately into new adventures, while the long days, never changing, grew heavy with boredom and longing.

I first saw the carpets in the back yards of other neighborhoods. Glimpses of them came to me from behind garages, flickers of color at the corners of two-family houses where clotheslines on pulleys stretched from upper porches to high gray poles, and old Italian men in straw hats stood hoeing between rows of tomatoes and waist-high corn. I saw one once at the far end of a narrow strip of grass between two stucco houses, skimming lightly over the ground at the level of the garbage cans. Although I took note of them, they were of no more interest to me than games of jump rope I idly watched on the school playground, or dangerous games with jackknives I saw the older boys playing at the back of the candy store. One morning I noticed one in a back yard in my neighborhood; four boys stood tensely watching. I was not surprised a few days later when my father came home from work with a long package under his arm, wrapped in heavy brown paper, tied with a straw-colored twine from which little prickly hairs stuck up.

The colors were duller than I had expected, less magical—only maroon and green: dark green curlings and loopings against a maroon that was nearly brown. At each end the fringes were thickish rough strings. I had imagined crimson, emerald, the orange of exotic birds. The underside of the carpet was covered with a coarse, scratchy material like burlap; in one corner I noticed a small black mark, circled in red, shaped like a capital *H* with a slanting middle line. In the back yard I practiced cautiously, close to the ground, following the blurred blue directions printed on a piece of paper so thin I could see my fingertips touching the other side. It was all a matter of artfully shifted weight: seated cross-legged just behind the center of the carpet, you leaned forward slightly to send the carpet forward, left to make it turn left; right, right. The carpet rose when you lifted both sides with fingers cupped beneath, lowered when you pushed lightly down. It slowed to a stop when the bottom felt the pressure of a surface.

At night I kept it rolled up in the narrow space at the foot of my bed, alongside old puzzle boxes at the bottom of my bookcase.

For days I was content to practice gliding back and forth about the yard, passing under the branches of the crab-apple trees, squeezing between the swing and ladder of the yellow swing set, flying into the bottoms of sheets on the clothesline, drifting above the row of zinnias at the edge of the garden to skim along the carrots and radishes and four rows of corn, passing back and forth over the wooden floor of the old chicken coop that was nothing but a roof and posts at the back of the garage, while my mother watched anxiously from the kitchen window. I was no more tempted to rise into the sky than I was tempted to plunge downhill on my bike with my arms crossed over my chest. Sometimes I liked to watch the shadow of my carpet moving on the ground, a little below me and to one side; and now and then, in a nearby yard, I would see an older boy rise on his carpet above the kitchen window, or pass over the sunlit shingles of a garage roof.

Sometimes my friend Joey came skimming over his low picket fence into my yard. Then I followed him around and around the crab-apple trees and through the open chicken coop. He went faster than I did, leaning far forward, tipping sharply left or right. He even swooped over my head, so that for a moment a shadow passed over me. One day he landed on the flat tar-papered roof of the chicken coop, where I soon joined him. Standing with my hands on my hips, the sun burning down on my face, I could see over the tall back-yard hedge into the weed-grown lot where in past summers I had hunted for frogs and garden snakes. Beyond the lot I saw houses and telephone wires rising on the hill beside the curving sun-sparkling road; and here and there, in back yards hung with clotheslines, against the white-shingled backs of houses, over porch rails and sloping cellar doors and the water arcs of lawn sprinklers shot through with faint rainbows, I could see the children on their red and green and blue carpets, riding through the sunny air.

One afternoon when my father was at work and my mother lay in her darkened bedroom, breathing damply with asthma, I pulled out the carpet at the foot of the bed, unrolled it, and sat down on it to wait. I wasn't supposed to ride my carpet unless my mother was watching from the kitchen window. Joey was in another town, visiting his cousin Marilyn, who lived near a department store with an escalator. The thought of riding up one escalator and down the next, up one and down the next, while the stairs flattened out or lifted up, filled me with irritation and boredom. Through the window screen I could hear the sharp, clear blows of a hammer, like the ticking of a gigantic clock. I could hear the clish-clish of the hedge clippers, which made me think of movie swordfights; the uneven hum of a rising and falling bee. I lifted the edges of the carpet and began to float about the room. After a while I passed through the door and down the stairs into the small living room and big yellow kitchen, but I kept bumping into pots and chair tops; and soon I came skimming up the stairs and landed on my bed and looked out the window into the back yard. The shadow of the swing frame showed sharp and black against the grass. I felt a tingling or tugging in my legs and arms. Dreamily I pushed the window higher and raised the screen.

For a while I glided about the room, then bent low as I approached the open window and began to squeeze the carpet through. The wooden bottom of the raised window scraped along my back, the sides of the frame pressed against me. It was like the dream where I tried to push myself through the small doorway, tried and tried, though my bones hurt, and my skin burned, till suddenly I pulled free. For a moment I seemed to sit suspended in the air beyond my window; below I saw the green hose looped on its hook, the handles and the handle shadows on the tops of the metal garbage cans, the mountain laurel bush pressed against the cellar window; then I was

floating out over the top of the swing and the crab-apple trees; below
me I saw the shadow of the carpet rippling over grass; and drifting
high over the hedge and out over the vacant lot, I looked down on
the sunny tall grass, the milkweed pods and pink thistles, a green
Coke bottle gleaming in the sun; beyond the lot the houses rose behind each other on the hill, the red chimneys clear against the blue
sky; and all was sunny, all was peaceful and still; the hum of insects;
the far sound of a hand mower, like distant scissors; soft shouts of
children in the warm, drowsy air; heavily my eyelids began to close,
but far below I saw a boy in brown shorts looking up at me, shading
his eyes, and seeing him there, I felt suddenly where I was, way up
in the dangerous air; and leaning fearfully to one side I steered the
carpet back to my yard, dropped past the swing, and landed on
the grass near the back steps. As I sat safe in my yard I glanced up
at the high, open window, and far above the window the red shingles of the roof glittered in the sun.

I dragged the heavy carpet up to my room, but the next day I
rose high above Joey as he passed over the top of the swing. In a
distant yard I saw someone skim over the top of a garage roof and
sink out of sight. At night I lay awake planning voyages, pressing
both hands against my heart to slow its violent beating.

One night I woke to a racket of crickets. Through the window
screen I could see the shadow of the swing frame in the moonlit
back yard. I could see the streetlamp across from the bakery down
by the field and the three streetlamps rising with the road as it curved
out of sight at the top of the hill. The night sky was the color of a
dark blue marble I liked to hold up to a bulb in the table lamp. I
dressed quickly, pulled out my carpet, and slowly, so as not to make
scraping noises, pushed up the window and the screen. From the
foot of the bed I lifted the rolled rug. It suddenly spilled open, like a

dark liquid rushing from a bottle. The wood of the window pressed against my back as I bent my way through.

In the blue night I sailed over the back yard, passing high over the hedge and into the lot, where I saw the shadow of the carpet rippling over the moonlit high grass. I turned back to the yard, swooped over the garage roof and circled the house at the level of the upper windows, watching myself pass in the glittery black glass; and rising a little higher, into the dark and dream-blue air, I looked down to see that I was passing over Joey's yard toward Ciccarelli's lot, where older boys had rock fights in the choked paths twisting among high weeds and thornbushes; and as when, standing up to my waist in water, I suddenly bent my legs and felt the cold wetness covering my shoulders, so now I plunged into the dark blue night, crossing Ciccarelli's lot, passing over a street, sailing over garage roofs, till rising higher I looked down on the telephone wires glistening as if wet with moonlight, on moon-greened treetops stuffed with blackness, on the slanting rafters and open spaces of a half-built house crisscrossed with shadows; in the distance I could see a glassy stream going under a road; spots of light showed the shapes of far streets; and passing over a roof close by a chimney, I saw each brick so sharp and clear in the moonlight that I could make out small bumps and holes in the red and ocher surfaces; and sweeping upward with the wind in my hair I flew over moon-flooded rooftops striped with chimney shadows, until I saw below me the steeple of a white church, the top of the firehouse, the big red letters of the five-and-dime, the movie marquee sticking out like a drawer, the shop windows dark-shining in the light of the streetlamps, the street with its sheen of red from the traffic light; then out over rows of rooftops on the far side of town, a black factory with lit-up windows and white smoke that glowed like light; a field stretching away; gleaming water; till I felt I'd strayed to the farthest edge of things; and turning back I flew high above the moonlit town, when suddenly I saw the hill with three streetlamps, the bakery, the swing frame, the chicken coop—and landing for a moment on the roof of the garage, sitting with my legs astride the peak, exultant, unafraid, I saw, high in the blue night sky, passing slowly across the white moon, another carpet with its rider.

With a feeling of exhilaration and weariness—a weariness like sadness—I rose slowly toward my window, and bending my way through, I plunged into sleep.

The next morning I woke sluggish and heavy-headed. Outside, Joey was waiting for me on his carpet. He wanted to race around the house. But I had no heart for carpets that day, stubbornly I swung on the old swing, threw a tennis ball onto the garage roof and caught it as it came rushing over the edge, squeezed through the hedge into the vacant lot where I'd once caught a frog in a jar. At night I lay remembering my journey in sharp detail—the moon-glistening telephone wires above their shadow stripes, the clear bricks in the chimney—while through the window screen I heard the chik-chik-chik of crickets. I sat up in bed and shut the window and turned the metal lock on top.

I had heard tales of other voyages, out beyond the ends of the town, high up into the clouds. Joey knew a boy who'd gone up so high you couldn't see him anymore, like a balloon that grows smaller and smaller and vanishes—as if suddenly—into blue regions beyond the reach of sight. There were towns up there, so they said; I didn't know; white cloud towns, with towers. Up there, in the blue beyond the blue, there were rivers you could go under the way you could walk under a bridge; birds with rainbow-colored tails; ice mountains and cities of snow; flattened shining masses of light like whirling discs; blue gardens; slow-moving creatures with leathery wings;

towns inhabited by the dead. My father had taught me not to believe stories about Martians and spaceships, and these tales were like those stories: even as you refused to believe them, you saw them, as if the sheer effort of not believing them made them glow in your mind. Beside such stories, my forbidden night journey over the rooftops seemed tame as a stroll. I could feel dark desires ripening within me; stubbornly I returned to my old games, as carpets moved in back yards, forming bars of red and green across white shingles.

Came a day when my mother let me stay home while she went shopping at the market at the top of the hill. I wanted to call out after her: Stop! Make me go with you! I saw her walking across the lawn toward the open garage. My father had taken the bus to work. In my room I raised the blinds and looked out at the brilliant blue sky. For a long time I looked at that sky before unlocking the window, pushing up the glass and screen.

I set forth high over the back yard and rose smoothly into the blue. I kept my eyes ahead and up, though now and then I let my gaze fall over the carpet's edge. Down below I saw little red and black roofs, the shadows of houses thrown all on one side, a sunny strip of road fringed with sharp-bent tree shadows, as if they had been blown sideways by a wind—and here and there, on neat squares of lawn, little carpets flying above their moving shadows. They sky was blue, pure blue. When I next glanced down I saw white puff-balls hanging motionless over factory smokestacks, oil tanks like white coins by a glittering brown river. Up above, in all that blue, I saw only a small white cloud, with a little rip at the bottom, as if someone had started to tear it in half. The empty sky was so blue, so richly and thickly blue, that it seemed a thing I ought to be able to feel, like lake water or snow. I had read a story once about a boy who walked into a lake and came to a town on the bottom, and now it seemed to me that I was plunging deep into a lake, even though I was climbing. Below me I saw a misty patch of cloud, rectangles of dark green and butterscotch and brown. The blue stretched above like fields of snow, like fire. I imagined myself standing in my yard, looking up at my carpet growing smaller and smaller until it vanished into the blue. I felt myself vanishing into blue. He was vanishing into blue. Below my carpet I saw only blue. In this blue beyond blue, all nothing everywhere, was I still I? I had passed out of sight, the string holding me to earth had snapped, and in these realms of blue I saw no rivers and white towns, no fabulous birds, but only shimmering distances of sky-blue heaven-blue blue. In that blaze of blue I tried to remember whether the boy in the lake had ever come back; and looking down at that ungraspable blue, which plunged away on both sides, I longed for the hardness under green grass, tree bark scraping my back, sidewalks, dark stones. Maybe it was the fear of never coming back, maybe it was the blue passing into me and soaking me through and through, but a dizziness came over me, I closed my eyes—and it seemed to me that I was falling through the sky, that my carpet had blown away, that the rush of my falling had knocked the wind out of me, that I had died, was about to die, as in a dream when I felt myself falling toward the sharp rocks, that I was running, tumbling, crawling, pursued by blue; and opening my eyes I saw that I had come down within sight of housetops, my hands clutching the edges of my carpet like claws. I swooped lower and soon recognized the rooftops of my neighborhood. There was Joey's yard, there was my garden, there was my chicken coop, my swing; and landing in the yard I felt the weight of the earth streaming up through me like a burst of joy.

At dinner I could scarcely keep my eyes open; by bedtime I had a temperature. There were no fits of coughing, no itchy eyes, or raw red lines under runny nostrils—only a steady burning, a heavy weariness, lasting three days. In my bed, under the covers, behind closed blinds, I lay reading a book that kept falling on my chest. On the fourth day I woke feeling alert and cool skinned. My mother, who for three days had been lowering her hand gently to my forehead and staring at me with grave, searching eyes, now walked briskly about the room, opening blinds with a sharp thin sound, drawing them up with a clatter. In the morning I was allowed to play quietly in the yard. In the afternoon I stood behind my mother on an escalator leading up to boys' pants. School was less than two weeks away; I had outgrown everything; Grandma was coming up for a visit; Joey's uncle had brought real horseshoes with him; there was no time, no time for anything at all; and as I walked to school along hot sidewalks shaded by maples, along the sandy roadside past Ciccarelli's lot, up Franklin Street and along Collins Street, I saw, in the warm and summery September air, like a gigantic birthmark, a brilliant patch of red leaves among the green.

One rainy day when I was in my room looking for a slipper, I found my rolled-up carpet under the bed. Fluffs of dust stuck to it like bees. Irritably I lugged it down into the cellar and laid it on top of an old trunk under the stairs. On a snowy afternoon in January I chased a Ping-Pong ball into the light-striped darkness under the cellar stairs. Long spiderwebs like delicate rigging had grown in the dark space, stretching from the rims of barrels to the undersides of the steps. My old carpet lay on the crumbly floor between the trunk and a wooden barrel. "I've got it!" I cried, seizing the white ball with its sticky little clump of spiderweb, rubbing it clean with my thumb, bending low as I ducked back into the yellow light of the cellar. The sheen on the dark green table made it look silky. Through a high window I could see the snow slanting down, falling steadily, piling up against the glass.

Issue 145, 1997

Norman Rush

on

Guy Davenport's *Dinner at the Bank of England*

The other day I realized that the contemporary American writer whose personal journals I most wished I could read before I die was Guy Davenport. In my scan, I included masters in every specialty—poetry, the essay, plays, short and long fictions. It still came out Davenport.

And it was Davenport because of his achievements in fiction. I mean his latter-day fictions. He tried, and then abandoned, the conventional narrative-driven change-of-consciousness short story early in his career while distinguishing himself in poetry, translation, and criticism. Twenty years elapsed, and then he emerged, utterly remade, as a creator of experimental prose works. His stories are unique constructs. They are put together with elegant skill and power and tend toward the unclassifiable. In fact, scrutinous readers may change their minds more than once in the matter of what exactly it is that they are reading: are these essentially armatures for Davenport's aphorisms and philosophical asides? Are they primarily demonstrations of the possibilities in the interpenetration of poetic and prose forms (and visual—he sometimes illustrated his pieces).

Are they freestanding baubles? In his "inhabiting," in his writing, of the minds of iconic figures in the history of Western art and thought, is he being obscurely didactic? Is he subtly deconstructing the inner lives of culture heroes like Picasso and Diogenes?—What?

Whether there is a larger subliminal architecture connecting Davenport's diverse works—something like the scaffolding of myth in Joyce's *Ulysses,* but subtler—is a question on which professional critics will disagree. (Interestingly, the first doctorate on James Joyce produced at Oxford University was by Guy Davenport.) Certainly there is a sexual subtheme that surfaces often enough in the stories (although not in "Dinner at the Bank of England") and most explicitly in his one novel, or suite of linked stories, *Apples and Pears.* His lyrical homoerotic and androgynic scenes have led to unease in some readers and doubtless played some role in the consistency with which mainstream literary honors eluded him.

I shouldn't emphasize the figuring-out or puzzle-solving processes involved in reading Davenport's works. That element is reflexive, and it takes place against the foremost and overwhelming experience in reading him, which is sheer literary pleasure—the pleasures of craft, surprise, indelible similes, and on. . . .

So, yes, Davenport is elusive, but the expedition to find him is its own reward.

Guy Davenport

⌖

Dinner at the Bank of England

—Bank of England, guvnor? Bank of England'll be closed this time
of day.

Jermyn Street, gaslit and foggy on this rainy evening in 1901,
pleased Mr. Santayana in its resemblance to a John Atkinson Grim-
shaw, correct and gratifyingly English, the redbrick church across
from his boardinghouse at No. 87 serenely *there,* like all of St.
James's, on civilization's firmest rock.

—Nevertheless, the Bank of England.

—Climb in then, the cabman said. Slipped his keeper, he said to his
horse. Threadneedle Street, old girl, and then what?

Quadrupedante sonitu they clopped through the rain until, with
a knowing sigh, the cabman reined up at the Bank of England. Mr.
Santayana, having emerged brolly first, popping it open, paid the
driver, tipping him with American generosity.

—I'll wait, guvnor. You'll never get in, you know.

But a bobby had already come forward, saluting.

—This way, sir.

—I'll be buggered, the cabman said.

The inner court, where light from open doors reflected from puddles, polished brass and sabres, was full of guards in scarlet coats with white belts, a livelier and more colorful *Night Watch* by a more Hellenistic Rembrandt.

The room where he had been invited to dinner by Captain Geoffrey Stewart was Dickensian, with a congenial coal fire in the grate under a walnut mantelpiece.

Captain Stewart, as fresh and youthful as he had been when they met the year before in Boston, was out of his scarlet coat, which hung by its shoulders on the back of a chair in which sat his bearskin helmet. A stately and superbly British butler took Santayana's brolly, derby and coat with the hint of an indulgent, approving smile. Whether he had been told that the guest was a professor from Harvard or whether he read his clothes, shoes and face as gentry of some species, he clearly accepted him as a gentleman proper enough to dine with the captain.

—You mean Victorian fug when you say *Dickensian,* the captain laughed. I have to do an inspection round at eleven, but as I believe I said, you're a lawful guest until then. The bylaws of the Bank of England allow the captain of the guard to have one guest, male. The fare is thought to be suitable for soldiers, and here's Horrocks with the soup, mock turtle, and boiled halibut with egg sauce will be along, mutton, gooseberry tart with cream, and anchovies on toast, to be washed down with these cold bottles, for you I'm afraid, I've been taken off wine. Not, I imagine your idea of a meal. Horrocks knows it's just right for his young gentlemen in scarlet.

—Philosophers, Santayana said, eat what's put before them.

—High table at Harvard will be amused. I'm awfully pleased you could come.

A handsome young barbarian out of Kipling, the captain's manners were derived from a nanny and from a public school and

modified by an officer's mess. The British are charming among
equals and superiors, fair to underlings, and pleasantly artificial to
all except family and closest friends.

—But you can't, you know, saddle yourself with being a foreigner, I
gather your family is Spanish but that you are a colonial, growing
up in Boston and all that. Most colonials are more English than the
English. You see that in Canadians. Your George Washington Irving,
we were told at school, is as pukka British as any of our authors.
Longfellow also. Same language, I mean to say.

—My native tongue is Spanish.

—Not a trace of accent. Of course you don't *look* English, I mean
American, but then you can't go by that, can you? Most of the Danes
I've seen look more English than we do, when they don't look like
Scots. You look South American. It's the moustache and the small
bones, what? I know a Spanish naval officer with absolutely the
frame of a girl. Probably cut my throat if I were to say so, devilish
touchy, your Spaniard. Doesn't Shakespeare say so somewhere?

—I'm various kinds of hybrid. Bostonians are a breed apart in the
United States. I can lay claim to being an artistocrat, but only through
intermarriages. As a Catholic I'm an outcast, and as a Catholic atheist I am a kind of unique pariah.

—That's jolly!

—I am, I think, the only materialist alive. But a Platonic materialist.

—I haven't a clue what that could mean. Sounds a bit mad.

—Doubtless it is. This wine is excellent.

—No offence, my dear fellow, you understand? Our fire needs a lump
or two of coal. Horrocks!

—The unexamined life is eminently worth living, were anyone so
fortunate. It would be the life of an animal, brave and alert, with instincts instead of opinions and decisions, loyalty to mate and cubs,
to the pack. It might, for all we know, be a life of richest interest and

happiness. Dogs dream. The quickened spirit of the eagle circling in high cold air is beyond our imagination. The placidity of cattle shames the Stoic, and what critic has the acumen of a cat? We have used the majesty of the lion as a symbol of royalty, the wide-eyed stare of owls for wisdom, the mild beauty of the dove for the spirit of God.

—You talk like a book, what? One second, here's somebody coming. Sorry to interrupt.

Horrocks opened the door to admit a seven-foot corporal, who saluted and stamped his feet.

—Sir, Collins's taken ill, sir. Come all over queasy like, sir, and shivering something pitiful, sir.

Captain Stewart stood, found a notecase in his jacket on the back of a chair, and ordered the corporal to pop Collins into a cab and take him to the dispensary.

—Here's a quid. Bring back a supernumerary. Watkins will sub for you.

—Sir, good as done, sir.

—Thank you, corporal.

And to Santayana, picking a walnut from the bowl and cracking it expertly:

—Hate chits. Rather pay from my own pocket than fill up a form. I suppose I have an education. Latin and Greek are cheerful little games, if you have the brains for them, and most boys do. Batty generals in Thucydides, Caesar in Gaul throwing up palisades and trenching fosses. Never figured out Horace at all.

—There are more books in the British Museum about Horace than any other writer.

—My God!

—Civilization is diverse. You can omit Horace without serious diminishment. I look on the world as a place we have made more or less hospitable, and at some few moments magnificent. When would you have liked to live, had you the choice, and where?

—Lord knows. Do drink up. Horrocks will think you don't appreciate the Bank of England's port. Eighteenth century? On the Plains of Abraham. The drums, the pipers, the Union Jack in the morning light. Wolfe reciting Gray's *Elegy* before the attack, to calm his nerves. Wouldn't have thought that there was a nerve in his body. Absolute surprise to the French, as if an army had appeared from nowhere. I would have liked to have been there.

—The plangent name, both biblical and Shakespearean, the Plains of Abraham. It was simply Farmer Abraham's cow pasture.

—Is it, now? Well, Bannockburn's a trout stream and Hastings a quiet village.

—And Lepanto the empty sea.

Horrocks permitted himself a brightened eye and sly smile. He was serving quality, after all.

—English mustard is one of the delights of your pleasant country. My friends the Russells would be appalled to know that one of my early discoveries here was cold meat pie with mustard and beer. I like to think that Chaucer and Ben Jonson wrote with them at their elbow.

—There's a half-batty Colonel Herbert-Kenny, in Madras I believe, who writes cookbooks under the name Wyvern. These address themselves to supplying a British mess with local vegetables, condiments and meat. Simplicity is his word. All the world's problems come from a lack of simplicity in anything you might think of, food, dress, manners. The bee in his bonnet is that food is character and that to eat Indian is to whore after strange gods. That's scripture, isn't it?

—He's right. Spinoza and Epicurus were spartan eaters.

—I thought Epicurus was a gourmet, or gourmand, banquets and puking?

—He has that reputation, a traditional misunderstanding. He ate simply. He did insist on exquisite taste, but the fare was basic and elementary.

—Herbert-Kenny must have read his books.

—Cheese and bread, olives and cold water. He and Thoreau would have got along.

—Not familiar with this Thoreau, a Frenchman?

—A New Englander, hermit and mystic. Americans run to originality.

—Examined his soul, did he? I heard a lot of that in America.

Horrocks poked up the fire, removed plates, replenished Santayana's glass, silently, almost invisibly.

The dormitory and the barracks had shaped his world. He was probably far more ignorant of sensual skills than an Italian ten-year-old, a virgin who would be awkward with his country wife, and would become a domestic tyrant and brute, but a good father to daughters and a just but not affecionate one to sons.

Their friendship was a sweet mystery. The British explain nothing, and do not like to have things explained. The captain had doubtless told his friends that he'd met this American who was dashedly friendly when he was in Boston, had even given him a book about Harvard College, where he was a professor wallah. Followed sports, the kind of rugger they call football in America. Keen on wrestling and track. Speaks real French and German to waiters, and once remarked, as a curiosity, that he always dreams in Spanish. Says we English are the Romans of our time, but Romans crossbred with Protestantism and an inch from being fanatics except that good Roman horse sense, which we take from the classics, and a native decency and a love of animals keep us from being Germans. Talks like a book, but no airs about him at all.

—I like this room, Santayana said. It is England. The butler, fireplace and mantel out of Cruikshank, the walnut chairs, the sporting prints, the polished brass candlesticks. You yourself, if a foreigner

who reads may make the observation, are someone to be encountered in Thackeray or Kipling.

—Oh, I say! That's altogether too fanciful. No butlers in America?

—Only Irish girls who drop the soup.

—Back to your being a materialist, Captain Stewart said. I'm interested.

—Your Samuel Butler was a materialist, the Englishman of En-
glishmen in our time. He was a sane Voltaire who was wholly disil-
lusioned intellectually while being in bondage to his comfort and
his heart, a character Dickens might have invented if he hadn't
his readers to consider. The nonconformist is an English type, a
paradox the English themselves fail to appreciate, for they have long
forgotten that exceptions might be a threat to the community. An
American Butler, even if he sounded like Emerson, would find himself too often in hot water.

—Don't know this Butler. Is *materialist* a technical term?

—The world is evident. Begin there.

The captain laughed.

—The substantiality and even the presence of the world has been
called into doubt by serious minds, by Hindus, by Chinese poets,
by Bishop Berkeley and German idealists.

—Extraordinary! Hindus! I daresay. And your being a materialist is
your firm belief that the world is, as you put it, evident? Does all this
have anything to do with anything?

Santayana laughed.

—No. What interests me is that all thought and therefore all action
stands on a quicksand of tacit assumptions. What we believe is what
we are and what we expect of others, and of fate.

—Here's my corporal again.

—Sir, Collins is taken care of, sir.

—Carry on, corporal.

—Sir! Yes, sir!

—Spirit lives in matter, which gives rise to it. We are integral with matter. We eat, we breathe, we generate, we ache. Existence is painful.

—Do try the walnuts. They're excellent. Do you think we live in good times or bad? I mean, do you want us all to be materialists?

—I am content to let every man and woman be themselves. I am not them. When man is at last defeated and his mind bound with ungiving chains, it will be through a cooperation of science and what now passes for liberalism. That is, through his intellect and his concept of the good, just and useful life. This is, of course, a cruel paradox, but it is real and inevitable. Science is interested only in cause and effect, in naked demonstrable truth. It will eventually tell us that consciousness is chemical and the self a congeries of responses to stimuli. Liberalism is on a course of analyzing culture into a system of political allegiances that can be explained by science, and controlled by sanctions, all with the best of intentions. All of life's surprises will be prevented, all spontaneity strangled by proscriptions, all variety canceled. White light conceals all its colors, which appear only through refractions, that is, through irregularity and pervasive differences. Liberalism in its triumphant maturity will be its opposite, an opaque tyranny and a repression through benevolence that no tyrant however violent has ever achieved.

—Here here! You're talking for effect, as at the Union.

—There is no fanaticism like sweet reason. You are as yet free, being wonderfully young, and having the advantage of the liberty of the army.

—Liberty, you say?

—The most freedom anyone can enjoy is in constraint that looks the other way from time to time. You know that from childhood and from school.

—The army is school right on. And one does and doesn't long to be out. I can't see myself as a major in India, parboiled by the climate and becoming more conservative and apoplectic by the hour.

—Youth does not have as much of childhood in it as early maturity has youth. There is an abrupt demarcation between child and adolescent, a true metamorphosis.

—Something like, yes.

—The English fireside is as congenial an institution as your culture has to offer. We Americans find your bedrooms arctic and your rain a trial, but the saloon of the King's Arms in Oxford, after freezing in the Bodleian or walking in the meadows, is my idea of comfort. As is this room, as well. And as a philosopher who speaks his mind, I delight in your receiving and feeding me in your picturesque undress, those terrible uncomfortable-looking galluses, do you call them? over your plain Spartan undyed shirt. I might be the guest of a young Viking in his house clothes.

—You should hear the major on the subject of gravy on a tunic. And you decline to convert me to materialism. What, then, to believe? Horrocks and I ought to have something to benefit us from a Harvard professor's coming to dine.

—We seem to need belief, don't we? Skepticism is more than likely unintelligent. It is certainly uncomfortable and lonely. Well, let's see. Believe that everything, including spirit and mind, is composed of earth, air, fire and water.

—That is probably what I have always believed. But, look here, my dear fellow, it's coming up eleven, when I must be on parade in the dead of night, with drums and fifes. All civilians must be home in their beds. Look, Horrocks will give you to the corporal, who will give you to the bobby outside, and you're on your own. This has been awfully jolly.

—It has, indeed, said Santayana, shaking hands.

—Good night, sir, Horrocks offered.

—Good night, and thank you, Santayana said, tendering him a shilling.

The rain had let up. He would walk to Jermyn Street, keeping the image of Captain Stewart in his martial undress lively in his imagination, as Socrates must have mused on Lysis's perfect body, or on Alcibiades whose face Plutarch wrote was the handsomest in all of Greece. The world is a spectacle, and a gift.

The perfect body is itself the soul.

If he was a guest at the Bank of England, he was equally a guest at his boardinghouse on Jermyn Street, the world his host. Emerson said that the joy of an occasion was in the beholder not in the occasion. He is wrong. Geoffrey Stewart is real, his beauty real, his spirit real. I have not imagined him, or his fireside, or his butler, or his wide shoulders or the tuft of ginger hair showing where the top button was left unbuttoned on his clean Spartan undervest.

Suppose that in a Spanish town I came upon an apparently blind old beggar sitting against a wall, thrumming his feeble guitar, and uttering an occasional hoarse wail by way of singing. It is a sight which I have passed a hundred times unnoticed; but now suddenly I am arrested and seized with a voluminous and unreasoning sentiment— call it pity for want of a better name. An analytical psychologist (I myself, perhaps in that capacity) might regard my absurd feeling as a compound of the sordid aspect of this beggar and of some obscure bodily sensation in myself, due to lassitude or bile, to a disturbing letter received in the morning, or to the general habit of expecting too little and remembering too much.

Mona Simpson

on

Norman Rush's *Lying Presences*

J ack liked his office and it was all right to like your office."

This is the first line of "Lying Presences." I worked at *The Paris Review,* when the manuscript arrived (atavistically, in a yellow manila envelope, by mail.) The then-managing editor uncharacteristically decided we should publish it after having read only this one opening sentence.

Editors, like curators, develop refined intuition.

"I know," she said, handing it to me to read.

Of course she was right.

There was something about the character's attitude, caught in the verb/object repetition—an obdurate defensiveness—that set in motion a conflict within the narrative voice itself.

Norman Rush was raised by a socialist and an amateur opera singer. His work bristles with zealous theory, political sophistication, and all the barbed sorts of knowledge that boys used to make girls feel bad about not having, the stories populated with cranks, rebels, ideologues, inventors, and their sarcastic cowed sons and lovers who have had enough of high-mindedness.

Everyone is always intelligent.

But that doesn't help them much.

Consider this rant in "Lying Presences," a story about two brothers.

"Everything about their grim father was coming back. It was okay to drink Benedictine because the Benedictines were okay, but no Chartreuse, ever, because there was something bad about the Carthusians. You were supposed to shun anyone who bought a Volkswagen, because of slave labor, and this was as late as the sixties. People who visited Spain before Casals went back were lepers. Their father had been a basement inventor. He had invented a dispenser cap, called Metercap, for toothpaste that would measure out a generous average dose and thus cut down waste. The company that bought it suppressed the invention. Waste was the enemy of mankind. The company was criminal. Property was theft and so on into the night. Roy was against waste."

That final sentence aligns Roy with their "grim" father.

Jack "liked one thing at his desk at a time. . . . The walls were not just a color but a "naïve yellow."" "At eight floors up, he was the right distance from sounds of the street."

In other words, the writer whispers, *a complete control freak.* "He might *concede* [italics mine] disappointment in the way his custom desk had worked out."

What is the product created in this carefully appointed office?

Commissions.

Jack is an agent, for illustrators of children's books. A logical consequence of growing up with a man who believed that "Everyone should buy *dented cans*."

Because Rush is essentially a comic writer, we know that something will disturb this fussy, modestly ambitious order.

The something turns out to be a brother.

"*Perfect. Just what he needed at this point*. He felt indescribable. *It was unfair*." The breathless third person narration manages to convey Jack's sensibility, without sympathizing with it. He blames his secretary, for leaving the door open when she went to lunch. "She was going to suffer."

While Jack is the epitome of modest ambition, modest success, a controlled scope of challenge, his brother Roy gave his entire twenty-nine thousand dollar inheritance from his father to a cult of UFO believers, which he joined wholehearted only to find himself embroiled in a theoretical battle. He came to believe that the enemy population that sent out space ships lived on human fear.

"This struck me about the same time it struck other people and it's an actual school by now, this part of it. But I do go beyond it. I do go beyond it. And I'm the only one," he explains to his brother, who replies "Anytime you want my reaction, say the word."

Neither character is wholly sympathetic. But with Rush's typical perversity, we find ourselves most empathic with the gullible, para-noid, fanatical Roy, who believes in UFOs, because in the action of the story, he's asking for the most simple favor; he wants room and board with his brother for a while, to get his life together.

And Jack, in the rationality that puts us in mind of meaningless philosophical puzzle, refuses this most basic hospitality and be-lieves himself justified.

Norman Rush

※

Lying Presences

J ack liked his office and it was all right to like your office. He
would say that basically it worked. It was nicely enigmatic. All
the tools of his trade, his papers and portfolios, were kept out of
sight in a block of chrome-plated file cabinets with unlabeled drawers. He liked one thing on his desk at a time. The only way somebody
uninitiated might guess he was an agent for illustrators of children's
books was through the painting on the wall behind him of a pig in
armor.

The walls were a naïve yellow. At eight floors up, he was the right
distance from the sounds of the street. His window looked across
onto the fluted blank raw cement wall of a telephone switching center, which in his opinion conveyed a faintly Romanesque feeling that
was congruent. He might concede some disappointment in the way
his custom desk had worked out. It was supposed to suggest an
obsidian cube, but the joins in the black plastic slabs could be de-
tected. The flooring, black rubber tile in a raised dot pattern, heavily underpadded, was a definite success. He bounced his heels on it
a little before attending to finishing his lunch.

What he wanted to know was why you had to be some kind of expert to unwrap these little foilbound wedges of Gruyère without getting cheese under your fingernails. Skinning garlic cloves was a similar thing.

Business had been good in this office. Maybe the subtle play-room associations made clients regress. It was an idea. He was scraping rusk crumbs into his palm with an index card when he heard something in the outer office. Afraid, he listened.

It was his brother.

Perfect. Just what he needed at this point. He felt indescribable. *It was unfair.* Showing up unannounced when he was supposed to be living happily ever after on the other side of the country was vintage Roy. All Jack wanted to know was who was to blame. Helen was, for leaving the office door open when she went to lunch. She was going to suffer. Jack made himself smile at Roy, credibly he thought. He got up. He held his palms up, showing a good-natured surrender to fate. Roy came over and they shook hands. They said each other's names.

Roy was about the same as three years ago. As usual and like their father he had something on his mind, as his expression was making abundantly clear. Roy was acting bloody but unbowed. Actually, that was Roy's main facial expression. Except that it was interesting that Roy was afraid of something. Roy had lost weight, some. But he was the same grim proletarian persona as always, with his cheap Coast Guard surplus raincoat, short haircut, foreman clothes, no tie, shirt buttoned to the throat. Roy was taking off his raincoat. Jack considered giving Roy the proletarian a tip. In Roy's shirt pocket the tops of four ballpoint pens showed, and more than one pen showing was like a full-page ad for insecurity. But why should he tell Roy anything?

Roy went to look for a chair in the outer office. Everything about their grim father was coming back. It was okay to drink Benedictine because the Benedictines were okay, but no Chartreuse, ever, because there was something bad about the Carthusians. You were supposed to shun anyone who bought a Volkswagen because of slave labor, and this was as late as the sixties. People who visited Spain before Casals went back were lepers. Their father had been a basement inventor. He had invented a dispenser cap, called Metercap, for toothpaste, that would measure out a generous average dose and thus cut down waste. The company that bought it suppressed the invention. Waste was the enemy of mankind. The company was criminal. Property was theft and so on into the night. Roy was against waste.

Roy was back, carrying a heavy pedestal chair that wasn't meant to be moved. He positioned it off the right corner of Jack's desk. He folded his raincoat scientifically into a pad and sat on it. Was the idea that sitting on it would somehow *press* it by body heat? Anything was possible.

Why was Roy here? Jack was trying to come up with a benign reason and getting nothing. Everything was settled between them, supposedly. Three years ago Roy had left for Phoenix taking his half of an inheritance that was not immense but not nothing, either. Roy had made his own bed, with a vengeance. Jack had argued the insanity of what Roy was doing, going out to be the executive secretary of some bizarre foundation having to do with flying saucer research. Roy was supposed to get perpetual room and board and subsistence, like an annuity, in exchange for his twenty-nine thousand. For a year newsletters from Roy's foundation had come, all of which Jack had returned unopened, marking them Of No Interest/ Return To Sender in black block letters that left nothing to the imagination vis-à-vis his contempt for the whole thing. Now this. And typically Roy had no reaction whatever to the office.

Naturally it developed that what Roy wanted from him was amazing.

Jack recapitulated, working to keep his tone unmocking, "Now see if I have this straight. What you say is I'm supposed to take you into the house, you live with us, for two or three months. And I do it without asking why or getting any reason for it from you that I can give to Judith. We just take you in. Like that. On my say so to Judith, just like that."

"That's what I'm asking." Roy was never apologetic. Probably that was admirable.

Jack said, "And just *nothing,* no personal history for my benefit on this? Whether you're in trouble or on the run or something like that? Well, look. A few years ago you did something I took exception to, would be putting it mildly. Now here you are. I mean, Roy, *there was money involved* if you recall. And what I pick up in all this is I'm out of line if I even speculate about what's happened. I take it the money is gone, somehow?"

Roy was a baritone. "Jack, I told you. I'm not asking for money. I need, and all I need, and for about two months maximum, is housing with you and Judy. I just need that. I don't plan to eat meals with you. What I wish is you'd accept it when I tell you I'm doing you a favor not telling you any details on this. And *please,* there is no legal angle on this! I guarantee if you just do this for me, just do it and don't question me, there's no disadvantage. Really."

"But Roy, why do I get the feeling . . . how can I put this . . . you're *doing me a favor* even asking me to do this for you, to put myself out, which is what it is? Why do I feel that?"

A silence resulted.

Jack said, "I don't think you grasp the position you put me in. Suppose we say this, though. First of all, you're my brother. Now suppose I say okay, you can stay with us, just so you give me *some* explanation of what's going on. Is that a lot to ask? I mean, considering I'm the one who has to carry this off with Judith? By the way, she wants to be called Judith instead of Judy. It's important. Professional thing."

Roy, still unreadable, said, "It sounds like what you're saying is to make something up."

"Roy, *hey,* don't do this. I'm telling you something that isn't so complicated. I need some explanation. I need something I can give Judith. If you knew anything about our relationship you'd know that at this point I can't just ask her to do something on faith or because she's my wife."

Roy looked thoughtful. "If I tell you something fairly fantastic, I wonder if you'll make a big judgment on it?"

"I'm trying to get through to you the position I'm in. It would really be smarter of you not to try and put me in a box. By the way, what about your bags? You must have more than that flight bag."

"In a locker at the station."

Roy rose, still thinking. Jack looked at his watch.

"Okay," Roy said.

Jack was unsure what that meant.

"I'll be back," Roy said.

"Could you make it around four, since I have to see a couple of people this afternoon? Four-thirty would be even better."

Roy nodded and left.

Jack was brilliantly spending the afternoon obsessing on causes. He knew it was pointless. It went back to their father and the feeling of being put down if you weren't sacrificing yourself for some reform or at the very least living on the exact amount of money and food it actually required to sustain you so that if you were doing nothing else in life you were avoiding waste. When he thought of the trial and anguish it had taken him just to get minimally free of that, it was pathetic. And, of course, no one ever raised the question of how much time anybody should devote to a cause aimed against a thing doomed to come to a natural end on its own whether you spent your life going to meetings over it or not. For example surely just the ratios of reproduction between eighteen million blacks and four million whites meant you could perfectly safely let apartheid lapse its way out of existence. Or people who belonged to the English Speaking Union, speaking of wasting your life promoting a sure thing. Who ever raised the question of how many people were actually doing cause work just for the opportunity it offers to display how much contempt they have for people who have to work for money, or actually want to work for money? Also why did Roy's flying saucer movement, if that was the right word for it, qualify as any kind of cause? So what if space civilizations were sending spaceships down. People seemed to accept flying saucers anyway, as a kind of strange fact of life, so what was the point in organizing around it?

Roy's luggage was going to be humiliating. It was almost a sufficient reason in itself for sending Helen home early. It was impossible.

How would he get Judith to be unsarcastic about Roy's ongoing one-man war on waste? Clothes would be an issue. If you spent money on clothes for anything with a little style you were decadent. I.e. you could find perfectly good secondhand clothes if you knew where to look. You could buy surplus or factory seconds or best of all make your own out of sacking. Probably Roy would show up with luggage that was somehow *handmade*. You should be examined for not buying day-old bread. Everyone should buy *dented cans*. Also there was a correct way to do all these things, which was just to do them and not be perceived as spending a lot of mental time on avoiding being duped. Water was the only thing to drink. Also it was free. The point of Roy's carrying around a change purse full of nuts and raisins was to avoid being duped into going into restaurants on impulse and wasting money, or if you did, you popped down some nuts and you'd order less. And by the way it was desirable to randomly skip meals because in the state of nature wasn't it obvious nobody was eating three meals a day? If you kept your belly full you were suppressing certain survival mechanisms, as he recalled it. Salt was a better dentifrice than toothpaste. Or was that their father? But then why invent a toothpaste cap? Salt had to be Roy.

Jack did some deep-breathing exercises to calm down. Of course Roy would never say anything about salt. You'd just have him wandering around the kitchen in the morning with a toothbrush, saying could he trouble you for some salt? And the salt would be in plain sight.

Jack heard the outer door open and close and bags being dropped. It was late enough that he could have assumed Roy wasn't coming. He could have gotten out ten minutes earlier, locking up and going. Roy was sensitive and might have decided to go away for good. Roy came in, rolling the pedestal chair on its base-rim this time. Suppose they'd met in the elevator? This was better. He was prepared.

He was not going to be intimidated. Or made to do something that was anything but in his interest and Judith's. That was his stance, period. Things cost money. He had the right to remind himself that things cost money, and, for example, nobody was going to chip in to pay Helen for the afternoon off Roy's arrival had forced him to give her.

It was getting dark out. The not altogether satisfactory ceiling lights were on. The office wasn't engineered for night work. He was not somebody who needed to work late. He thought of their mother standing at the head of the basement steps moaning down at their father to come to bed.

It was on Roy to begin.

Roy sat down, but was uncomfortable. He got up and went to lean against the wall beside the door, his hands in his pockets, his gaze directed upward at the wall behind Jack. Jack hoped Roy would curb his tendency to talk prolish—like a proletarian, Jack's private term for it—a tendency that manifested when Roy was discussing some subject he considered significant.

"Okay, I'll just start this the best I can.

"Something I never told anybody is important.

"You're too young to remember when Niles died. He was my favorite of all the uncles, somebody I really loved. Anyway, at the cemetery I was really upset and when they started lowering the coffin I just couldn't handle it. I walked away. Ran away down a path, just trying to get out of sight of what was happening. I was nine, about.

"I didn't go very far, not more than five minutes away through some trees and out to a place that overlooked a creek and two small hills with a gap between them. This was bright ten or eleven o'clock in the morning with absolutely clear skies.

"So I'm standing there all in turmoil when up in the sky I see something absolutely terrifying. It just floated across between the two hills. I'm telling you I can still feel the fear, just talking about it. What I saw was a metal thing that was painted, or rather colored black. What it looked most like was a clamshell or an open umbrella without the handle and made out of metal: you could see the rivets down along the ribs. It was about the size of a car. I saw it I'd say for about three full minutes. It was absolutely silent. I was terrified. The thing was real. I felt the thing had some ominous connection with Niles being dead. I saw every detail. It had no windows. I closed my eyes to see if it would still be there when I opened them. I looked at it with one eye closed. Looked at it through my fingers. It was real. I knew it was evil. My state of terror was just something inexpressible. Anyway, I got out of there, ran the hell back. That was all. I made myself forget about it. This was 1942. Of course I never told anybody. You know the atmosphere in the family. When I thought about it later, I mean as an adult, I wondered if there was some story or fairy tale or something about a box or device that comes to collect souls that maybe I knew of. But there was nothing I could associate it with. And the thing was real. Physical."

Roy closed his eyes briefly.

"So just let that incident stay in the background for a while."

Jack said, "This hallucination."

"Right. Just what I assumed it was myself, when I got older. Let it be in the background.

"Now as to me and the Society. I'm out of it. Actually, I was expelled. The money's gone.

"What happened is simple. I won't bore you with all the stages

and vicissitudes, but what happened is I reached a conclusion about
flying saucers that nobody in the Society could deal with, about
what they really are.

"One thing led to another and my position got untenable." Roy
shrugged.

Jack wondered when Roy's yes-yeah copula was going to show
up. Yes was what Roy felt comfortable saying, but yeah was what he
thought he really ought to be saying, being a man of the people. So
he would say yes (yeah), with a slight diminuendo on the yeah. Stress
would do it. Jack wondered whether the fact that nobody really
changes was encouraging or tragic.

Roy was ready to go on. "First you have to know the Society's
line, which used to be my line, no question, which is that saucers are
real and they're extraterrestrial. The term for it is ETH, extraterrestrial hypothesis, in case you care. The Society is the Vatican of
ETHism. Anyway, the saucers are pieces of advanced technology
from some other planetary system, you can prove their existence by
radar returns and so on and there's other physical evidence we won't
go into, blah blah blah. So okay."

Roy tucked his shirt in more neatly all around. "But here and
there a few people began to wonder. For instance, you start studying
the close encounter cases where witnesses report occupants in and
around a landed saucer. It makes no sense. You never get two encounters with beings who look like they come from the same planet.
Your occupant reports run all the way from giants to midgets, no
eyes, no mouths, Greek god types, robots, spacesuits, tunics, cat
eyes, triangular faces, no ears, pointed ears, flippers instead of hands,
webbed hands, you name it. Now take a look at craft descriptions.
Another circus! Large, small, transparent, globular, cigar-shaped,
mother ships, baby ships, cylindrical, lenticular, they divide in two,
they turn into clouds . . . and on and on and on.

"So the ETHists have a slight problem. You have to start reject-
ing reports that don't fit. You have to start calling certain people liars while other people whose stories are just as good are not liars.

"Now take a look at something else interesting: the phenomenon
appears to be getting more vigorous and exotic over time. Saucer
sightings started out as primarily visual arm's length kinds of things.
Then you start getting some fairly trivial side effects like broken tree
branches and holes in the ground. Then it turns out the saucers can
blank out electrical systems in cars. Then in about the sixties you
start getting abduction reports, usually with some gruesome physical examination by the aliens thrown in. Or there may be some suggestion the aliens are into collecting sperm or ova or something
similarly menacing. They induce amnesia and it sometimes takes
hypnosis to even get at what happened. Then beginning in the seventies you get farmers finding their cattle mutilated, dead, all their
blood drained out and various body parts excised by laser, it looks
like. And the cattle are lying in fields with no tracks on the ground.
And people are reporting seeing lights in the sky. So what is *this* all
about?"

Jack said, knowing it was the wrong thing to say, "The first
thing I'd do if I decided to go into this would be invest in a good lie
detector."

"Jack, let's try and proceed straight through this. One problem
is, you don't know the literature. I guess what I'm saying is take my
word for it that once you screen out all the liars you still have something vast going on. For the sake of argument can we assume some
real things are happening to people who are for the most part reporting them in good faith, or not? I mean, I'm a case in point. I had
an experience of a real thing and I can swear to God to you it was
absolutely real, real in the same exact sense as brushing your teeth."

"Be my guest," Jack said.

Roy began walking back and forth.

"Okay, just about this point an historical element comes into it. Somebody going through old newspapers finds something interesting. It seems in the eighteen-nineties there was a wave of sightings of things called mystery airships. These were weird items, aerodynamically impossible naturally, with vanes and propellers and sometimes even paddle wheels. They were reported coast to coast in the U.S. Then slightly later, in England, a similar thing, except these were cigar-shaped. There was a threat element, too. There were some petty disappearances of animals. And there was the suggestion that these things were going to drop explosives in some connection. Then the whole thing stops. The airships did the usual meaningless repertory, mainly startling people with beams of blinding light.

"*What is going on here?* And of course the Society has to take the position that all these old reports must have been a newspaper hoax, blah blah blah.

"What I was coming around to, or being *driven* around to, was an idea some other people were getting. The idea is that the whole flying saucer phenomenon is basically part of the spectrum of other psychic phenomenon. That is, a flying saucer behaves more like a ghost in almost every respect than it does like a piece of machinery. It belongs right in there with apparitions, materializations, poltergeists. The difference is in magnitude only. Period.

"Now it's important to understand I'm not claiming any originality about this part of it. This struck me about the same time it struck other people and it's an actual school by now, this part of it. But I do go beyond it. I do go beyond it. And I'm the only one."

Roy sat down again.

"Anytime you want my reaction, say the word," Jack said.

"Not quite yet.

"So.

"So I was keeping pretty much undercover with this at the Society. It amounted to a conversion and I had to consider how hard I was going to fight for it, when to come out with it, all that sort of petty thing, when I figured out the next part of it."

Jack reminded himself to be patient, be wary.

"The Society rents computer time," Roy said. "One thing they do is keep building the data base. There is an immense amount of stuff to work with, all kinds of data.

"I was looking at the distribution of sightings by hour of the night (almost all of them are at night), by month, and by location. There's a wave pattern which is pretty marked and suddenly I knew what it was. Or rather . . . I got a theory of the answer to what it was. I was looking at these patterns and what I was seeing was a *feeding pattern*.

"I was looking at predation curves, which I know something about. Think about it."

"I don't think I'm following. You mean the flying saucers are out trying to *eat* people . . . ? I'm not following, Roy."

"Okay, take a step back. First let's say we provisionally assimilate flying saucers to other psychic phenomena. Okay then. Now.

"What would you say is the single most salient common feature of psychic events, broadly speaking?

"Let me tell you. The single most important common feature of psychic phenomena is their absolute pointlessness. Psychic research is the study of pointless events. You can see what I mean. Hauntings and apparitions are pointless, the Loch Ness monster is pointless, the abominable snowman, poltergeists are supremely pointless. Strange and fearful events that never, ever, lead anywhere or cumulate in anything. Of course, you have your inescapable specialists who specialize in manufacturing explanations of what these strange things purport. The Society is one. Or some fraud of a psychic sits down in a haunted house and comes up with some song and dance about an earthbound spirit. Exorcists. And so on.

"Wait, before you object let me lay out the whole thing so you can object to the whole thing. A strange thing happens. I started asking myself why are all these manifestations so pointless? Of course a lot of things you never get an explanation for, not even a lying one. In England in the eighteenth century there was a character called Springheel Jack, who was a figure that knocked on your door, had some kind of lantern box on his chest, made a terrifying face and then shot up into the air and disappeared. This happened all over London. What was the point? Take something else: animal reports—escaped lions and tigers reported seen roaming around in the suburbs someplace. You see it in the papers periodically. People see them but the local circus zoo says no animals are missing. They never catch them. Of course, you can fall back on everybody being a liar if you want. But take just the one case from my own life. It happened. Would you say I'm a liar?"

"No, the reverse," Jack said.

"The Loch Ness monster is a good example. Bigfoot: some terrifying yells in your backyard and chickens with their heads torn off and maybe some dung. The Black Dogs of Kent. Poltergeists. Light bulbs explode, fires start, scissors follow you around . . . what for?

"Okay, so there's no point in terms of purpose. But there is something else. What's *produced* in all these displays? Ask yourself that question and you get one answer. The product is fear. The product is extreme human fear, mostly fear to the exquisite point of fear of death, or capture, or alteration, or injury, or abduction, what have you. Big, rich blooms of fear. And when do these strange events tend to take place? *Almost always* when people are by themselves, alone, unsupported by other people, in lonely places, often or mostly at night. I can show you a graph of UFO sightings and the number involving more than one person is too low, not normal.

"So you can see what this turns into is a general theory of apparitions, of which the saucer part is just one branch."

Their father would be in ecstasy. Here was Roy the champion of an idea so hopeless of adoption that everyone is supposed to marvel. Yet how could you not devote your life to it? If you did and no one believed you and then you died and were proved right, so much the better. Genius!

Roy continued. "The short of it is that there's something . . . I'm willing to call it a life-form, a population . . . a thing that, one, targets on individual vulnerable people . . . two, somehow activates some negative belief pattern of the individual . . . three, converts that into a somehow material quick display. Then it eats the fear.

"Now I know there are a lot of somehows in there but I'm giving this to you very quick and rough. I have ideas about all the mechanisms involved. Don't say anything yet.

"Just a couple of things I need to add. The thing is ancient and vast and permanent and basically evil. Also, it *adapts*! It has to. You could even develop some sympathy for it if you let yourself. It has two serious enemies, scientific progress and stupid human optimism. Show you what I mean.

"It relies on people having a stock of things to be afraid of. You can see it easily in the case of ghosts. In order for a ghost to appear there has to be a prior notion that a ghost is likely to be attached to a certain place or a certain kind of place. But science marches on and fewer and fewer people are disposed to believe in ghosts. The threshold gets higher. Everything is squeezing the thing, really, if you look at it. Secularization, science, urbanization, pushing people into mutual supportive crowds, streetlighting. And another thing. As a species we seem determined to give the most optimistic interpretation to a thing that we can. You no sooner get spiritualism off to a roaring start with the dead coming back being nasty and vengeful than people start churchifying the movement into modern spiritualism with its happy summerland view of death. The optimists are already at work on the saucers, saying Oh they're only here to make us respect nature and they're going to give us some damned wisdom scroll pretty soon or a cure for cancer: don't be afraid. Poor entities. It's hard. Did you see *Close Encounters?* The saucer people live in a giant thing like a wedding cake and they are so gentle . . .

"Look, the whole psychic plenum is lies! *Lying presences command it.* The saucers have nothing to do with space, lake monsters have nothing to do with plesiosaurs, ghosts have nothing to do with the dead. I'm getting excited."

Roy stopped. And Jack had the sense that Roy was afraid. What could be done with that?

Roy briefly pressed his knuckles into the crown of his head, a headache treatment.

Roy resumed before Jack felt fully ready.

"Now we need to focus on the saucers. Maybe as I was saying we should have a certain amount of sympathy for the phenomenon. It gets hungry. And here we have the situation of the host population getting harder and harder to terrify. Think how easy it must have been to go out and feed in pagan times, for example, when everybody was doing human sacrifices. Pens full of people knowing they were going to be put to death, a whole spectrum of fears, animism, every tree or rock with some guardian entity associated with it you had to be careful not to offend. You might not even need to manifest at all.

"Okay. Then come the more refined religions, but you still have an evil adversary element in the religion that people really believe in. So you can still operate. Then religion moderates even further and the evil forces get to be merely symbolic. The whole backdrop of folklore about witches and vampires and ghosts gets removed by science and the new sanitized religions. You can imagine the thing getting desperate. What it needs is some kind of fear coming out of technology and science itself, since they're not going to go away. Themselves, I meant to say.

"It's interesting. Did you ever hear about the ghost rockets they had in Sweden in the late thirties, just before the war? A whole wave of reports of frightening huge rockets going over and never hitting anything. Clearly an abortive try.

"Okay, I'm giving you too much detail.

"So the thing needs something coming out of science itself, something that's going to be a plausible occasion for fear it can manipulate. So of course this is what we get. How it starts is beside the point, in a way. It starts. Flying discs from somewhere seen in the sky. It gets on the radio. We're being visited by craft from other planets. They have an awesome technology. They threaten our aircraft (famous early case on this, the Mantell case). They're invulnerable to our technology and their intentions are unknown. They become terrifying.

"Everything is working! The thing gets quickly associated with disappearances like the Mantell case or those six seaplanes that disappeared off Florida, right or wrong. They pick you up and do things to you that you can't remember. They make electrical systems fail. What's more terrifying than something that makes your *car* not work, for an American? Nothing. It multiplies: lonely roads, night, isolated people . . ."

Jack wanted to change the subject. He knew he was being irrational. There was too much green in the wall color, at least by artificial light. The situation was bad, too theatrical because of the silence of the empty building, which was becoming intrusive. Roy was talking.

". . . and the structure of the thing is fascinating. You have your garden variety type-one encounters which means close approaches of lights that scare you but they may not even come that close. Just some anomalous light is all it takes to get a fear-rush going. Then you have a scale of manifestations all the way up to full-dress abductions, time-loss, where you get your genitals toyed with and needles inserted. There's a parsimony in the way the thing works that's really admirable. The big events keep the fear game going. The little lights cruise around and do okay during the interims, although all the entrepreneurial propaganda about our friends the space brothers is unhelpful. Fear is the key.

"The thing of actual physical effects is fascinating. I mean, they can do it, no question about it. But you have to remember that the pattern of token physical effects going along with psychic events is absolutely traditional. Take poltergeists: okay, they can start fires and displace crockery in your house. The pattern of injury to small animals that you have with bigfoot and these other swamp fakes, I don't know how that works. Maybe the thing initially capitalizes on regular kinds of predation and just manifests in the vicinity. Then it develops the means to duplicate the effect. But once the circuit is formed with a really strong fear template, they really are able to have physical effects, aside from just the visual. What the limit is I don't know.

"Now just one other sinister thing. The number of reports from couples and groups larger than three is going up. Which suggests the thing is getting stronger and learning to tap groups. Has to be looked at more but it seems to be definite.

"This is like giving birth, doing this. I feel better."

Jack could wait. It was crucial to make Roy wait. After all, whether he knew it or not what Roy had was the theory of what's wrong with everything in the world. What vistas etcetera of peace and harmony would be opened up if only this force could be slain or confined and so on. Genius! Jack hated to be in the building after business hours. It was a deep thing with him. This had to be finished.

Jack had to trust himself. He began blindly, not knowing what he was going to say.

"You're saying we're slaves or something."

It got Roy immediately. "No, man, you don't listen! *Don't improve on me!*"

Jack pressed on. "Also, and tell me if this is wrong, you and you alone are the one human being who's figured this vast thing out."

"Probably I'm not. I'm the only one I know, is all. Look. It's a hypothesis. Look, nobody can figure out what Gurdjieff meant when he said we were food for the moon, maybe he knew something. Anyway, it isn't important."

"On the contrary," Jack said. A point occurred to him. He knew it was petty. "Also, Roy, what about children? You'd think children would naturally be the ones involved in these experiences all the time, because of being credulous. . . ."

"They are, a lot," Roy said. "But it's interesting they aren't more. One answer is that you get kids less and less disciplined via the bogeyman and fear-objects than they used to be. Also, and this is just guessing, but I think they're probably not ripe yet: what you'd want, I would guess, is the fear product of a mature nervous system, not the little squib you might get from a child."

Jack could project a demand for money materializing out of this. He had to focus.

The phone on his desk began to ring. He indicated to Roy that it was to be ignored. This was good. He concentrated. He needed to consolidate.

Jack said, "So, obviously, with these views you become persona non grata around the Society. That figures.

"Anyway, we can summarize. What you're saying is there's this widespread invisible force or parasite that lives on human fear. It preys mainly on isolated individuals but now you say couples. And it changes as the culture changes. It works by energizing certain mental patterns of belief and turning them into real scenes of varying degrees of materiality, depending. The saucer phase is part of a thing stretching back into the past as far as werewolves. The population of this enemy, it looks like, is growing. Or maybe keeping pace with human population. Is that fair?"

Roy looked unhappy. "Yes (yeah). Keeping in mind that what I'm giving you is the Olive Pell Bible, so to speak. There's so much detail on each step that I'm not giving . . ."

"I'm curious about what ever happened to boring from within, Roy. Why you couldn't just keep your head down and slowly . . ."

"That's what I thought I was doing. Somebody talked."

"So now the reason you need to stay with somebody is . . . say it again?"

Roy was tiring. "I don't know. I really need to. Not for long. I need to be around people. It would be short term."

"I think you're being evasive. You think you're in danger, possibly, am I right? Don't want to be alone? Come on."

He had Roy really wary now. An approach was coming to him.

"And about this thing getting stronger," Jack said. "Something about that interests me. Say more about that."

"I can't say much except that it is. I'm not competent. It may be the difference between being able to exploit just individual biological electromagnetic fields, which are relatively weak, and modern artificial ones, which are incredibly strong. Or that could be all wrong."

"Can I ask you what's the macro side of this thing as you see it? You must've thought about it, such as, what about wars? I mean, you'd think the thing would flourish during wars with so many people in fear of death over whole areas. So is the thing, say, implicated in wars, possibly?"

Jack felt safe. He knew what to do.

"I don't speculate about it," Roy said.

"But why not? Would you say the incidence goes up in the periods between wars, offhand?"

"All I know is it does go up between wars. But there could be all kinds of reasons for that. I don't speculate about it."

"And the thing is getting stronger."

"I already said that. Yes (yeah)."

Roy's voice was up in the top of his throat. He looked damp.

Now Jack could do it. There was enough. It was only a question of which accusations to use. Roy could be part of the thing, spreading it. Or attracting it. It was a position. He had to drive Roy out, this time for good. In no way was he going to subject Judith to this. He had obligations. Everything was involved. He had figured things out. You struggled to escape a stupid artisan mentality and you did and here was your brother, a pauper but somehow so interesting. Never. It was not going to happen.

He would use rage.

Ali Smith

on

Lydia Davis's *Ten Stories from Flaubert*

Even in a form where economy, wit, and distillation are the norm, the stories of Lydia Davis stand out for their precision. Their effect is homeopathic. A two-line or paragraph-sized story by Davis can deliver a whole thinking universe.

"Ten Stories" came about when Davis (who is also a translator) was working on a new translation of *Madame Bovary* and reading through Flaubert's letters to his friend and lover Louise Colet. "Every now and then," Davis explained in an interview, "he would tell Louise a little story about something he had recently experienced or heard, and it began to strike me that these were nicely formed, discrete tales that with some revision would make good individual stories."

Are they translations? Are they by Flaubert? Are they by Davis? "Ten Stories" gives no clear indication of where Flaubert ends and Davis begins, or of how each story connects to the others, or is meant to. The cycle is both intimate and distanced. It deals in oppositions, cold and warm, black and white, tame and wild. It demonstrates compassion by an unfussed analysis of brutality. It examines several kinds of leave-taking: from the everyday journeying we do away from the beloved, all the way to the final separation of the grave.

Random juxtapositions resonate: connections appear as if by themselves. The beginning of "Ten Stories" announces a reversal of expectations, class, history. By the ending, love and loss have bloomed at the center of desolation. The sureness of arrangement (especially the placement of the next-to-last piece, "The Exhibition") shows a deep editorial instinct at work.

"I wonder if thoughts are fluid, and flow downward, from one person to another." In this story of stories told by someone else, no journey is solo, because telling itself is revealed as a communal form, a communal act.

Lydia Davis

✠

Ten Stories from Flaubert

THE COOK'S LESSON

Today I have learned a great lesson; our cook was my teacher. She is twenty-five years old and she's French. I discovered that she *does not know* that Louis-Philippe is no longer king of France and we now have a republic. And yet it has been five years since he left the throne. She said the fact that he is no longer king simply does not interest her in the least—those were her words.

And I think of myself as an intelligent man! But compared to her I'm an imbecile.

AFTER YOU LEFT

You wanted me to tell you everything I did after we left each other.

Well, I was very sad; it had been so lovely. When I saw your back disappear into the train compartment, I went up on the bridge to watch your train pass under me. That was all I saw; you were inside it! I looked after it as long as I could, and I listened to it. In the other

direction, toward Rouen, the sky was red and striped with broad
bands of purple. The sky would be long dark by the time I reached
Rouen and you reached Paris. I lit another cigar. For a while I
paced back and forth. Then, because I felt so numb and tired, I went
into a café across the street and drank a glass of kirsch.

My train came into the station, heading in the opposite direction
from yours. In the compartment, I met a man I knew from my school-
days. We talked for a long time, almost all the way back to Rouen.

When I arrived, Louis was there to meet me, as we had planned,
but my mother hadn't sent the carriage to take us home. We waited
for a while, and then, by moonlight, we walked across the bridge and
through the port. In that part of town there are two places where we
could hire a hackney cab.

At the second place, the people live in an old church. It was dark.
We knocked and woke the woman, who came to the door in her night-
cap. Imagine the scene, in the middle of the night, with the interior of
that old church behind her—her jaws gaping in a yawn; a candle
burning; the lace shawl she wore hanging down below her hips. The
horse had to be harnessed, of course. The breeching band had broken, and we waited while they mended it with a piece of rope.

On the way home, I told Louis about my old school friend, who
is his old school friend too. I told him how you and I had spent our
time together. Out the window, the moon was shining on the river. I
remembered another journey home late at night by moonlight. I described it to Louis: There was deep snow on the ground. I was in a
sleigh, wearing my red wool hat and wrapped in my fur cloak. I had
lost my boots that day, on my way to see an exhibition of savages
from Africa. All the windows were open, and I was smoking my
pipe. The river was dark. The trees were dark. The moon shone on
the fields of snow: they looked as smooth as satin. The snow-covered
houses looked like little while bears curled up asleep. I imagined

that I was in the Russian steppe. I thought I could hear reindeer snorting in the mist, I thought I could see a pack of wolves leaping up at the back of the sleigh. The eyes of the wolves were shining like coals on both sides of the road.

When at last we reached home, it was one in the morning. I wanted to organize my work table before I went to bed. Out my study window, the moon was still shining—on the water, on the tow path, and, close to the house, on the tulip tree by my window. When I was done, Louis went off to his room and I went off to mine.

THE VISIT TO THE DENTIST

Last week I went to the dentist, thinking he was going to pull my tooth. He said it would be better to wait and see if the pain subsided.

Well, the pain did not subside—I was in agony and running a fever. So yesterday I went to have it pulled. On my way to see him, I had to cross the old market-place where they used to execute people, not so long ago. I remembered that when I was only six or seven years old, returning home from school one day, I crossed the square after an execution had taken place. The guillotine was there. I saw fresh blood on the paving stones. They were carrying away the basket.

Last night I thought about how I had entered the square on my way to the dentist dreading what was about to happen to me, and how, in the same way, those people condemned to death also used to enter that square dreading what was about to happen to them— though it was worse for them.

When I fell asleep I dreamed about the guillotine; the strange thing was that my little niece, who sleeps downstairs, also dreamed about a guillotine, though I hadn't said anything to her about it. I wonder if thoughts are fluid, and flow downward, from one person to another, within the same house.

POUCHET'S WIFE

Tomorrow I will be going into Rouen for a funeral. Madame Pouchet, the wife of a doctor, died the day before in the street. She was on horseback, riding with her husband; she had a stroke and fell from the horse. I've been told I don't have much compassion for other people, but in this case, I am very sad. Pouchet is a good man, though completely deaf and by nature not very cheerful. He doesn't see patients, but works in zoology. His wife was a pretty Englishwoman with a pleasant manner, who helped him a good deal in his work. She made drawings for him and read his proofs; they went on trips together; she was a real *companion*. He loved her very much and will be devastated by his loss. Louis lives across the street from them. He happened to see the carriage that brought her home, and her son lifting her out; there was a handkerchief over her face. Just as she was being carried like that into the house, feet first, an errand boy came up. He was delivering a large bouquet of flowers she had ordered that morning. O Shakespeare!

THE FUNERAL

I went to Pouchet's wife's funeral yesterday. As I watched poor Pouchet, who stood there bending and swaying with grief like a stalk of grass in the wind, some fellows near me began talking about their orchards: they were comparing the girths of the young fruit trees. Then a man next to me asked me about the Middle East. He wanted to know whether there were any museums in Egypt. He asked me:

"What is the condition of their public libraries?" The priest standing over the hole was speaking French, not Latin, because the service
was a Protestant one. The gentleman beside me approved, then made
some slighting remarks about Catholicism. Meanwhile, there was
poor Pouchet standing forlornly in front of us.

We writers may think we invent too much—but reality is worse
every time!

THE COACHMAN AND THE WORM

A former servant of ours, a pathetic fellow, is now the driver of a
hackney cab—you'll probably remember how he married the daughter of that porter who was awarded a prestigious prize at the same
time that his wife was being sentenced to penal servitude for theft,
whereas he, the porter, was actually the thief. In any case, this unfortunate man Tolet, our former servant, has, or thinks he has, a
tapeworm inside him. He talks about it as though it were a living
person who communicates with him and tells him what it wants,
and when Tolet is talking to you, the word *he* always refers to this
creature inside him. Sometimes Tolet has a sudden urge and attributes it to the tapeworm: "*He* wants it," he says—and right away
Tolet obeys. Lately *he* wanted to eat some fresh white rolls; another
time *he* had to have some white wine, but the next day *he* was out-
raged because he wasn't given red.

The poor man has by now lowered himself, in his own eyes, to
the same level as the tapeworm; they are equals waging a fierce battle
for dominance. He said to my sister-in-law lately, "That creature has
it in for me; it's a battle of wills, you see; he's forcing me to do what
he likes. But I'll have my revenge. Only one of us will be left alive."
Well, the man is the one who will be left alive, or, rather, not for long,
because, *in order to kill the worm and be rid of it,* he recently swal-

lowed a *bottle of vitriol* and is at this very moment dying. I wonder if you can see the true depths of this story.

What a strange thing it is—the human brain!

THE EXECUTION

Here is another story about our compassion. In a village not far from here, a young man murdered a banker and his wife, then raped the servant girl and drank all the wine in the cellar. He was tried, found guilty, sentenced to death, and executed. Well, there was such interest in seeing this peculiar fellow die on the guillotine that people came from all over the countryside the night before—more than *ten thousand* of them. There were such crowds that the bakeries ran out of bread. And because the inns were full, people spent the night outside: to see this man die, *they slept in the snow.*

And we shake our heads over the Roman gladiators. Oh charlatans!

THE CHAIRS

Louis has been in the church in Mantes looking at the chairs. He has been looking at them very closely. He wants to learn as much as he can about the people from looking at their chairs, he says. He started with the chair of a woman he calls Madame Fricotte. Maybe her name was written on the back of the chair. She must be very stout he says—the seat of the chair has a deep hollow in it, and the prayer stool has been reinforced in a couple of places. Her husband may be a notary, because the prayer stool is upholstered in red velvet with brass tacks. Or, he thinks, the woman may be a widow, because there is no chair belonging to Monsieur Fricotte—unless he's an atheist. In fact, perhaps Madame Fricotte, if she is a widow, is looking for another husband, since the back of her chair is heavily stained with hair dye.

THE EXHIBITION

Yesterday, in the deep snow, I went to an exhibition of savages that had come here from La Havre. They were Kaffirs. The poor negroes, and their manager too, looked as if they were dying of hunger.

You paid a few pennies to get into the exhibition. It was in a miserable smoke-filled room up several flights of stairs. It was not well attended—seven or eight fellows in work clothes sat here and there in the rows of chairs. We waited for some time. Then a sort of wild beast appeared wearing a tiger skin on his back and uttering harsh cries. A few more followed him into the room—there were four altogether. They got up on a platform and crouched around a stew pot. Hideous and splendid at the same time, they were covered with amulets and tattoos, as thin as skeletons, their skin the color of my well-seasoned old pipe; their faces were flat, their teeth white, their eyes large, their expressions desperately sad, astonished, and brutalized. The twilight outside the windows, and the snow whitening the rooftops across the street, cast a gray pall over them. I felt as though I were seeing the first men on earth—as though they had just come into existence and were creeping about with the toads and the crocodiles.

Then one of them, an old woman, noticed me and came into the audience where I was sitting—she had, it seems, taken a sudden liking to me. She said some things to me—affectionate things, as far as I could tell. Then she tried to kiss me. The audience watched in surprise. For a quarter of an hour I stayed there in my seat listening to her long declaration of love. I asked their manager several times what she was saying, but he couldn't translate any of it.

Though he claimed they knew a little English, they didn't seem to understand a word, because after the show came to an end, at last—to my relief—I asked them a few questions and they couldn't answer. I was glad to leave that dismal place and go back out into the snow, though I had lost my boots somewhere.

What is it that makes me so attractive to cretins, madmen, idiots, and savages? Do those poor creatures sense a kind of sympathy in me? Do they feel some sort of bond between us? It is *infallible*. It happened with the cretins of Valais, the madmen of Cairo, the monks of upper Egypt—they all persecuted me with their declarations of love!

Later, I heard that after this exhibition of savages, their manager abandoned them. They had been in Rouen for nearly two months by then, first on the boulevard Beauvoisin, then in the Grande Rue, where I saw them. When he left, they were living in a shabby little hotel in the Rue de la Vicomté. Their only recourse was to take their case to the English consul—I don't know how they made themselves understood. But the consul paid their debts—four hundred francs to the hotel—and then put them on the train for Paris. They had an engagement there—it was to be their Paris debut.

MY SCHOOL FRIEND

Last Sunday I went to the Botanical Gardens. There, in the Trianon Park, is where that strange Englishman Calvert used to live. He grew roses and shipped them to England. He had a collection of rare dahlias. He also had a daughter who used to fool around with an old schoolmate of mine named Barbelet. Because of her, Barbelet killed himself. He was seventeen. He shot himself with a pistol. I walked across a sandy stretch of ground in the high wind, and I saw Calvert's house, where the daughter used to live. Where is she now?

They've put up a greenhouse near it, with palm trees, and a lecture hall where gardeners can learn about budding, grafting, pruning, and training—everything they need to know to maintain a fruit tree! Who thinks about Barbelet anymore—so in love with that English girl? Who remembers my passionate friend?

Wells Tower

on

Evan S. Connell's *The Beau Monde* *of Mrs. Bridge*

How does this little story of India Bridge, marooned in her mannerly universe where not much happens, inflict a vaster hurt than the cirrhotic, erotic mayhem you find in nearly every other fictional study of Fedora Age malaise? Cheever's people were at liberty to vent generational anguish with smashed crockery and marriages. Not so in Mrs. Bridge's world, where the wisdom of Emily Post seems to operate as Newtonian law. Glassware is unshatterable on country club row. Conventional narrative physics—dramatic momentum, conflict, arc—slow, shrink, fizzle under the atmospherics that pressurize the habitat of Mrs. Bridge. In the vacuum of Kansas City, no one can hear you scream.

Its fragmentary structure is the story's lonely soul. Extended through the pair of brilliant novels (*Mrs. Bridge* and *Mr. Bridge*) prefigured here, Connell's mosaic tile vignettes are the fuel cells of the portrait's desolating power. The transformative incident, the life-altering epiphany can't happen on Mrs. Bridge's diffident planet, where existence is confined to minor moments. In aggregate, these miniatures demand from the reader a unique sort of sympathy. It's a wholly original sorrow we feel for a woman who, when gunmen raid a cocktail party, reflects not at all on her brush with death; only that one of the bandits lacked a necktie, and the diamond ring stolen from Mrs. Noel Johnson was, embarrassingly, false.

Evan S. Connell

The Beau Monde of Mrs. Bridge

PARKING

The black Lincoln that Mr. Bridge gave her on her 47th birthday was a size too long and she drove it as cautiously as she might have driven a locomotive. People were always blowing their horns at her or turning their heads to stare when they went by. The Lincoln was set to idle too slowly and in consequence the engine sometimes died when she pulled up at an intersection, but as her husband never used the Lincoln and she herself assumed it was just one of those things about automobiles, the idling speed was never adjusted. Often she would delay a line of cars while she pressed the starter button either too long or not long enough. Knowing she was not expert she was always quite apologetic when something unfortunate happened, and did her best to keep out of everyone's way. She changed into second gear at the beginning of any hill and let herself down the far side much more slowly than necessary.

Usually she parked in a downtown garage where Mr. Bridge rented a stall for her. She had only to honk at the enormous doors, which would then trundle open, and coast on inside where an attendant would greet her by name, help her out, and then park the formidable machine. But in the country club district she parked on the street, and if there were diagonal stripes she did very well, but if parking was parallel she had trouble judging her distance from the curb and would have to get out and walk around to look, then get back in and try again. The Lincoln's seat was so soft and Mrs. Bridge so short that she had to sit very erect in order to see what was happening ahead of her. She drove with arms thrust forward and gloved hands tightly on the large wheel, her feet just able to depress the pedals all the way. She never had serious accidents but was often seen here and there being talked to by patrolmen. These patrolmen never did anything partly because they saw immediately that it would not do to arrest her, and partly because they could tell she was trying to do everything the way it should be done.

When parking on the street it embarrassed her to have people watch, yet there always seemed to be someone at the bus stop or lounging in a doorway with nothing to do but stare while she struggled with the wheel and started jerkily backward. Sometimes, however, there would be a nice man who, seeing her difficulty, would come around and tip his hat and ask if he might help.

"Would you, please?" she would ask in relief, and after he opened the door she would get out and stand on the curb while he put the car in place. It was a problem to know whether he expected a tip or not. She knew that people who stood around on the streets were in need of money, still she did not want to offend anyone. Sometimes she would hesitantly ask, sometimes not, and whether the man would accept a twenty-five-cent piece or no, she would smile brightly up at him, saying, "Thank you so much," and having locked the Lincoln's doors she would be off to the shops.

MINISTER'S BOOK

If Mrs. Bridge bought a book it was almost always one of three things: a best seller she had heard of or seen advertised in all the stores, a self-improvement book, or a book by a Kansas City author no matter what it was about. These latter were infrequent, but now and again someone would explode on the midst of Kansas City with a Civil War history or something about old Westport Landing. Then, too, there were slender volumes of verse and essays usually printed by local publishing houses, and it was one of these that lay about the living room longer than any other book with the exception of an extremely old two-volume set of *The Brothers Karamazov* in goldpainted leather which nobody in the house had ever read and which had been purchased from an antique dealer by Mr. Bridge's brother. This set rested gravely on the mantelpiece between a pair of bronze Indian chief heads—the only gift from cousin Lulubelle Watts that Mrs. Bridge had ever been able to use—and was dusted once a week by Hazel with a peacock feather duster.

The volume that ran second to *The Brothers Karamazov* was a collection of thoughts by the local minister, Dr. Foster, a short and congenial and even jovial man with a big, handsome head capped with soft golden white hair that he allowed to grow long and which he brushed toward the top of his head to give himself another inch or so. He had written these essays over a period of several years with the idea of putting them into book form, and from time to time would allude to them, laughingly, as his memoirs. Then people would exclaim that he surely mustn't keep them to himself until he died, at which Dr. Foster, touching the speaker's arm, would laugh heartily and say, "We'll think it over, we'll think it over," and clear his throat.

At last, when he had been preaching in Kansas City for seventeen years and his name was recognized, and he was always mentioned in *The Tattler* and sometimes in the city paper, a small publishing firm took these essays which he had quietly submitted to them several times before. The book came out in a black cover with a dignified grey-and-purple dust jacket which showed him smiling pensively out of his study window at dusk, hands clasped behind his back and one foot slightly forward.

The first essay began: "I am now seated at my desk, the desk that has been a source of comfort and inspiration to me these many years. I see that night is falling, the shadows creeping gently across my small but (to my eyes) lovely garden, and at such times as this I often reflect on the state of Mankind."

Mrs. Bridge read Dr. Foster's book, which he had autographed for her, and was amazed to find that he was such a reflective man, and so sensitive to the sunrise which she discovered he often got up to watch. She underlined several passages in the book that seemed to have particular meaning for her, and when it was done she was able to discuss it with her friends, who were all reading it, and she recommended it strongly to Grace Barron who at last consented to read a few pages.

With ugly, negative books about war and communists and perversion and everything else constantly flooding the counters this book came to her like an olive branch. It assured her that life was worth living after all, that she had not and was not doing anything wrong, and that people needed her. So, in the shadow of Dostoievsky, the pleasant meditations of Dr. Foster lay in various positions about the living room.

MAID FROM MADRAS

The Bridges gave a cocktail party not because they wanted to have cocktails with a mob of people, but because it was about time for them to be giving a party. Altogether more than eighty people stood and wandered about the home which stood on a hillside and was in the style of a Loire valley château. Grace and Virgil Barron were there, Madge and Russ Arlen, the Heywood Duncans, Wilhelm and Susan Van Metre looking out of place, Lois and Stuart Montgomery, the Beckerle sisters in ancient beaded gowns and looking as though they had not an instant forgotten the day when Mrs. Bridge had entertained them in anklets, Noel Johnson huge and by himself because she was in bed suffering from exhaustion, Mabel Ehe trying to start serious discussions, Dr. and Mrs. Batchelor whose Austrian refugee guests were now domestics in Los Angeles, and even Dr. Foster, smiling tolerantly, appeared for a whisky sour and a cigarette while gently chiding several of the men about Sunday golf. There was also an auto salesman named Beachy Marsh who had arrived early in a double-breasted pin-stripe business suit instead of a tuxedo, and being embarrassed about his mistake did everything he could think of to be amusing. He was not a close friend but it had been necessary to invite him along with several others.

Mrs. Bridge rustled about the brilliantly lighted home checking steadily to see that everything was as it should be. She glanced into the bathrooms every few minutes and found that the guest towels, which resembled pastel handkerchiefs, were still immaculately overlapping one another on the rack—at evening's end only three had been disturbed—and she entered the kitchen once to recommend that the extra servant girl, hired to assist Hazel, pin shut the gap in the breast of her starched uniform.

Through the silver candelabra and miniature turkey sandwiches

Mrs. Bridge went graciously smiling and chatting a moment with everyone, quietly opening windows to let out the smoke, removing wet glasses from mahogany table tops, slipping away now and then to empty the onyx ashtrays she had bought and distributed throughout the house.

Beachy Marsh got drunk. He slapped people on the shoulder, told jokes, laughed loudly, and also went around emptying the ashtrays of their magenta-colored stubs, all the while attempting to control the tips of his shirt collar which had become damp from perspiration and were rolling up into the air like horns. Following Mrs. Bridge halfway up the carpeted stairs he said hopefully, "There was a young maid from Madras, who had a magnificent ass; not rounded and pink, as you probably think—it was grey, had long ears, and ate grass."

"Oh, my word!" replied Mrs. Bridge, looking over her shoulder with a polite smile but continuing up the stairs, while the auto salesman, plucked miserably at his collar.

LAUNDRESS IN THE REAR

Every Wednesday the laundress came, and as the bus line was several blocks distant from the Bridge home someone would almost always meet her bus in the morning. For years the laundress had been an affable old negress named Beulah Mae who was full of nutshell wisdom and who wore a red bandanna and a dress that resembled a dyed hospital gown. Mrs. Bridge was very fond of Beulah Mae, speaking of her as "a nice old soul" and frequently giving her a little extra money or an evening dress that had begun to look dated, or perhaps some raffle tickets that she was always obliged to buy from girl scouts and various charities. But there came a day when Beulah Mae had had enough of laundering, extra gifts or no, and without saying a word to any of her clients she boarded a bus for California to live out her life on the seashore. For several weeks Mrs. Bridge was without a laundress and was obliged to take the work to an establishment, but at last she got someone else, an extremely large and doleful Swedish woman who said during the interview in the kitchen that her name was Ingrid and that for eighteen years she had been a masseuse and liked it much better.

When Mrs. Bridge arrived at the bus line the first morning Ingrid saluted her mournfully and got laboriously into the front seat. This was not the custom, but such a thing was difficult to explain because Mrs. Bridge did not like to hurt anyone's feelings by making them feel inferior, so she said nothing about it and hoped that by next week some other laundress in the neighborhood would have told Ingrid.

But the next week she again got in front, and again Mrs. Bridge pretended everything was all right. However on the third morning while they were riding up Ward Parkway toward the house Mrs. Bridge said, "I was so attached to Beulah Mae. She used to have the biggest old time riding in the back seat."

Ingrid turned a massive yellow head to look stonily at Mrs. Bridge. As they were easing into the driveway she spoke: "So you want I should sit in the back."

"Oh, Gracious! I didn't mean that," Mrs. Bridge answered, smiling up at Ingrid. "You're perfectly welcome to sit right here if you like."

Ingrid said no more about the matter and next week with the same majestic melancholy rode in the rear.

FRAYED CUFFS

Ordinarily Mrs. Bridge examined the laundry but when she had shopping to do, or a meeting, the job fell to Hazel who never paid much attention to such things as missing buttons or loose elastic. Thus it was that Mrs. Bridge discovered Douglas wearing a shirt with cuffs that were noticeably frayed.

"For Heaven's sake!" she exclaimed, taking hold of his sleeve. "Has a dog been chewing on it?"

He looked down at the threads as though he had never before seen them.

"Surely you don't intend to *wear* that shirt?"

"It looks perfectly okay to me," said Douglas.

"Just look at those cuffs! Anyone would think we're on our way to the poorhouse."

"So is it a disgrace to be poor?"

"*No!*" she cried. "But we're *not* poor!"

EQUALITY

Mrs. Bridge approved of equality. On certain occasions when she saw in the newspapers or heard over the radio that labor unions had won another victory she would think: "Good for them!" And, as the segregational policies of the various states became more and more subject to criticism by civic groups as well as by the federal government, she would feel that it was about time, and she would try to understand how discrimination could persist. However strongly she felt about this she was careful about what she said because she was aware that everything she had was hers through the efforts of one person: her husband. Mr. Bridge was of the opinion that people were not equal. In his decisive manner of speaking, annoyed that she should even puzzle over such a thing, he said, "You take all the people on earth and divide up everything, and in six months everybody would have just about what they have now. What Abraham Lincoln meant was equal rights, not equal capacity."

This always seemed exactly what she was trying to point out to him, that many people did not have equal rights, but after a few minutes of discussion she would be overwhelmed by a sense of inadequacy and would begin to get confused, at which he would stare at her for a moment as though she were something in a glass box and then resume whatever he had been doing.

She invariably introduced herself to members of minority groups at whatever gathering she found herself associating with them.

"I'm India Bridge," she would say in a friendly manner, and would wish it were possible to invite the people into her home. And when, among neighborhood friends she had known for a long time and who offered no unusual ideas, the increased means of certain classes were discussed, she would say, "Isn't it nice that they can have television and automobiles and everything."

In a northern town a negro couple opened a grocery store in a white neighborhood; that night the windows were smashed and the store set afire. Newspapers published photographs of the ruined property, of two smirking policemen, and of the negro couple who had lost their entire savings. Mrs. Bridge read this story while having breakfast by herself several hours after her husband had left for work. She studied the miserable faces of the young negro and his wife. Across the newspaper the morning sun slanted warm and cheerful, in the kitchen Hazel sang hymns while peeling apples for a pie, all the earth as seen from her window seemed content, yet such things still came to pass. In her breakfast nook, a slice of buttered toast in hand, Mrs. Bridge felt a terrible desire. She would press these unfortunate people to her breast and tell them that she, too, knew what it meant to be hurt but that everything would turn out all right.

GLOVES

She had always done a reasonable amount of charity work along with her friends, particularly at a little store on 9th street where second-hand clothing that had been collected in drives was distributed. In this store were two rooms, in the front one a row of card tables placed together, behind which stood the charity workers who were to assist people seeking something to wear, and in the back room were several more card tables and collapsible wooden chairs where Mrs. Bridge and her fellow workers ate their lunch or relaxed when not on duty in front.

She often went down with Madge Arlen. One week they would drive to their work in the Arlen's Chrysler, the next week in Mrs. Bridge's Lincoln, and when this was the case Mrs. Bridge always drew up before the garage where her parking stall was rented. She honked, or beckoned if someone happened to be in sight, and shortly one of the attendants whose name was George would come out buttoning up his jacket and he would ride in the rear seat to the clothing store. There he would jump out and open the door for Mrs. Bridge and after that drive the Lincoln back to the garage because she did not like it left on the street in such a neighborhood.

"Can you come by for us around six, or six-fifteen-ish, George?" she would ask.

He always answered that he would be glad to, touched the visor of his cap, and drove away.

"He seems so nice," said Mrs. Arlen as the two of them walked into their store.

"Oh, he is!" Mrs. Bridge agreed. "He's one of the nicest garage men I've ever had."

"How long have you been parking there?"

"Quite some time. We used to park at that awful place on Walnut."

"The one with the popcorn machine? Lord, isn't that the limit?"

"No, not that place. The one with the Italians. You know how my husband is about Italians. Well, that just seemed to be headquarters for them. They came in there to eat their sandwiches and listen to some opera broadcast from New York. It was just impossible. So finally Walter said, 'I'm going to change garages.' So we did."

They walked past the row of card tables piled high with soiled and sour unwashed clothing and continued into the back room where they found some early arrivals having coffee and eclairs. Mrs. Bridge and Mrs. Arlen hung up their coats and also had coffee, and then prepared for work. The reform school had sent down some boys to assist and they were put to work untying the latest sacks of used clothing and dumping them out.

By two o'clock everything was ready for the day's distribution. The doors were unlocked and the first of the poor entered and approached the counter behind which stood Mrs. Bridge and two others with encouraging smiles, all three of them wearing gloves.

ROBBERY AT HEYWOOD DUNCANS

The Bridges were almost robbed while attending a cocktail party at the Heywood Duncans'. Shortly after ten o'clock, just as she was taking an anchovy cracker from the buffet table, four men appeared in the doorway with revolvers and wearing plastic noses attached to horn-rimmed glasses for disguise. One of them said, "All right, everybody. This is a stick-up!" Another of the men—Mrs. Bridge afterwards described him to the police as not having worn a necktie—got up on the piano bench and from there stepped up on top of the piano itself where he pointed his gun at different people. At first everybody thought it was a joke, but it wasn't because the robbers made them all line up facing the wall with their hands above their heads. One of them ran upstairs and came down with his arms full of fur coats and purses while two others started around the room pulling billfolds out of the men's pockets and drawing rings from the ladies' fingers. Before they had gotten to either Mr. or Mrs. Bridge, who were lined up between Dr. Foster and the Arlens, something frightened them and the one standing on the piano called out in an ugly voice, "Who's got the keys to that blue Cadillac out front?"

At this Mrs. Ralph Porter screamed, "Don't you tell him, Ralph!"

But the bandits took Mr. Porter's keys anyway and after telling them all not to move for thirty minutes they ran out the porch door.

It was written up on the front page of the newspaper, with pictures on page eight, including a close-up of the scratched piano. Mrs. Bridge, reading the story in the breakfast room next morning after her husband had gone to work, was surprised to learn that Stuart Montgomery had been carrying just $2.14 and that Mrs. Noel Johnson's ring had been zircon.

FOLLOW ME HOME

How the scare actually started no one knew, although several women, one of whom was a fairly close friend of Madge Arlen, claimed they knew the name of someone who had been assaulted not far from Ward Parkway. Some thought it had happened near the Plaza, others thought farther south, but they were generally agreed that it had happened late at night. The story was that a certain lady of a well-known family had been driving home alone and when she had slowed down for an intersection a man had leaped up from behind some shrubbery and had wrenched open the door. Whether the attack had been consummated or not the story did not say, the important part was that there had been a man and he had leaped up and wrenched open the door. There was nothing in the paper about it, nor in *The Tattler* which did not print anything unpleasant, and the date of the assault could not be determined for some reason, only that it had been on a dark night not too long ago.

When this story had gotten about none of the matrons wished to drive anywhere alone after sundown. As it so happened they were often obliged to go to a cocktail party or a dinner by themselves because their husbands were working late at the office, but they went full of anxiety, with the car doors locked. It also became customary for the husband-host to get his automobile out of the garage at the end of an evening and then to follow the unescorted matrons back to their homes. Thus there could be seen processions of cars driving cautiously and rather like funerals across the boulevards of the country club residential district.

So Mrs. Bridge came home on those evenings when her husband did not get back from the office in time, or when he was too tired and preferred to lie in bed reading vacation advertisements. At her driveway the procession would halt, engines idling, while she drove into the garage and came back out along the driveway so as to be constantly visible, and entered by the front door. Having unlocked it she would step inside, switch on the hall lights, and call to her husband, "I'm home!" Then, after he had made a noise of some kind in reply, she would flicker the lights a few times to show the friends waiting outside that she was safe, after which they would all drive off into the night.

NEVER SPEAK TO STRANGE MEN

On a downtown street just outside a department store a man said something to her. She ignored him. But at that moment the crowd closed them in together.

"How do you do?" he said, smiling and touching his hat.

She saw that he was a man of about fifty with silvery hair and rather satanic ears.

His face became red and he laughed awkwardly. "I'm Gladys Schmidt's husband."

"Oh, for Heaven's sake!" Mrs. Bridge exclaimed. "I didn't recognize you."

CONRAD

While idly dusting the bookcase one morning she paused to read the titles and saw an old red-gold volume of Conrad that had stood untouched for years. She could not think how it happened to be there. Taking it down she looked at the flyleaf and found: *Ex Libris* Thomas Bridge.

She remembered then that they had inherited some books and charts upon the death of her husband's brother, an odd man who had married a night club entertainer and later died of a heart attack in Mexico.

Having nothing to do that morning she began to turn the brittle, yellowed pages and slowly became fascinated. After standing beside the bookcase for about ten minutes she wandered, still reading, into the living room where she sat down and did not look up from the book until Hazel came in to announce lunch. In the midst of one of the stories she came upon a passage that had once been underlined, apparently by Tom Bridge, which remarked that some people go skimming over the years of existence to sink gently into a placid grave, ignorant of life to the last, without ever having been made to see all it may contain. She brooded over this fragment even while reading further, and finally turned back to it again, and was staring at the carpet with a bemused expression when Hazel entered.

Mrs. Bridge put the book on the mantel for she intended to read more of this perceptive man, but during the afternoon Hazel automatically put Conrad back on the shelf and Mrs. Bridge did not think of him again.

VOTING

She had never gone into politics the way some women did who were able to speak with masculine inflections about such affairs as farm surplus and foreign subsidies. She always listened attentively when these things came up at luncheons or circle meetings; she felt her lack of knowledge and wanted to know more, and did intend to buckle down to some serious studying. But so many things kept popping up that it was difficult to get started, and then too she did not know exactly how one began to learn. At times she would start to question her husband but he refused to say much to her, and so she would not press the matter because after all there was not much she herself could accomplish.

This was how she defended herself to Mabel Ehe after having incautiously let slip the information that her husband told her what to vote for.

Mabel Ehe was flat as an adolescent but much more sinewy. Her figure was like a bud that had never managed to open. She wore tweed coats and cropped hair and frequently stood with hands thrust deep into her side pockets as if she were a man. She spoke short positive sentences, sometimes throwing back her head to laugh with a sound that reminded people of a dry reed splintering. She had many bitter observations in regard to capitalism, relating stories she had heard from unquestionable sources about women dying in childbirth because they could not afford the high cost of proper hospitalization or even the cost of insurance plans.

"If I ever have a child—" she was fond of beginning, and would then tear into medical fees.

She demanded of Mrs. Bridge: "Don't you have a mind of your own? Great Scott, woman, you're an adult. Speak out! We've been emancipated." Ominously she began rocking back and forth from her heels to her toes, hands clasped behind her back while she frowned at the carpet of the Auxiliary clubhouse.

"You're right," Mrs. Bridge apologized, discreetly avoiding the smoke Mabel Ehe blew into the space between them. "It's just so hard to know *what* to think. There's so much scandal and fraud, and I suppose the papers only print what they want us to know." She hesitated, then, "How do you make up *your* mind?"

Mabel Ehe removed the cigarette holder from her small cool lips. She considered the ceiling and then the carpet, as though debating on how to answer such a naïve question, and finally suggested that Mrs. Bridge might begin to grasp the fundamentals by a deliberate reading of certain books, which she jotted down on the margin of a tally card. Mrs. Bridge had not heard of any of these books except one and this was because its author was being investigated, but she decided to read it anyway.

There was a waiting list for it at the public library but she got it at a rental library and settled down to go through it with the deliberation that Mabel Ehe had advised. The author's name was Zokoloff, which certainly sounded threatening, and to be sure the first chapter was about bribery in the circuit courts. When Mrs. Bridge had gotten far enough along that she felt capable of speaking about it she left it quite boldly on the hall table, however Mr. Bridge did not even notice it until the third evening. He thinned his nostrils, read the first paragraph, grunted once, and dropped it back onto the hall table. This was disappointing. In fact, now that there was no danger involved, she had trouble finishing the book. She thought it would be better in a magazine digest, but at last she did get through and returned it to the rental library, saying to the owner, "I can't honestly say I agree with it all but he's certainly well informed."

Certain arguments of Zokoloff remained with her and she found that the longer she thought about them the more penetrating and logical they became; surely it *was* time, as he insisted, for a change in government. She decided to vote liberal at the next election, and as time for it approached she became filled with such enthusiasm and anxiety that she wanted very much to discuss government with her husband. She began to feel confident that she could persuade him to change his vote also. It was all so clear to her, there was really no mystery to politics. However when she challenged him to discussion he did not seem especially interested, in fact he did not answer. He was watching a television acrobat stand on his thumb in a bottle and only glanced across at her for an instant with an annoyed expression. She let it go until the following evening when television was over, and this time, he looked at her curiously, quite intently, as if probing her mind, and then all at once he snorted.

She really intended to force a discussion on election eve. She was going to quote from the book of Zokoloff. But he came home so late, so tired, that she had not the heart to upset him. She concluded it would be best to let him vote as he always had, and she would do as she herself wished, still upon getting to the polls, which were conveniently located in the country club shopping district, she became doubtful and a little uneasy. And when the moment finally came she pulled the lever recording her wish for the world to remain as it was.

Joy Williams

on

Dallas Wiebe's *Night Flight*
to Stockholm

N ight Flight to Stockholm" appeared in Issue #73 of *The Paris Review* in the spring of 1978. What a frolic! It really is one of the funniest, most grotesque pieces ever written and this *in the day* when all manner of crazy things were going on. More than thirty years later I still remember the terms exacted for each publication and publishing honor the unnamed narrator achieved. After being hooted off the stage at an MLA convention when he attempts to present his paper "Metaphorical Thinking as the Cause of the Collapse of British and American Literature," he makes the fateful call to one Gabriel Ratchet, "an expert on contracts."

"Gabe," he says, "I'm going to be sixty-six tomorrow . . . and I've been writing fiction all my life and no one's ever published a word of it and I'd give my left pinkie to get into *The Paris Review.*"

Well. Done. Ratchet, as agent, has many contacts, many of whom desire body parts for any number of frivolous reasons and who have uncanny influence in the world of publishing. It's all who you know, after all. Thus a pinkie for *The Paris Review,* two testicles for *Tri-*

Quarterly (surely it would be *Harper's* now), a left hand for *Esquire,* and a pair of ears for *The New Yorker,* after which success is assured.

"The stumps on the sides of my head tingled in the cold air as I walked out into a new reputation as one of the finest short story writers in America."

A left arm is exacted for a collection published by Doubleday, a left foot is taken when Knopf acquires his novel. By the time the National Book Award and the Pulitzer are won there's very little left of our author, though canny super-agent Ratchet manages to parlay his eyes into a Nobel Prize. Thus this suppurating wad, this package in a basket, one of the Immortals, is flown to Stockholm for the biggest literary award of them all.

"I can imagine," the package thinks, "the attendants in black knickers with the little black bows by the knees who will carry me onto the clapping stage. I can imagine the old black king squinting through his thick glasses down into the wicker basket with the two handles and the white Cannon sheets. As my snot begins to leak out over my upper lip, I can hear myself asking him to clear the ear wax out of my shallow ears so that I can hear him clearly when he extols the virtues of long-suffering, when he prattles about how some people overcome severe handicaps to go on to greatness, when he maunders about the indomitable will of the human spirit, while the old black queen gurgles and snickers down at the heady, winning lump."

Wiebe is not content to be so cut and dried, as it were, about the Faustian arrangement, however. With each success the writer has to submit to editorial advice, all part of the contract. *Erase the tear stains from the margin . . . no openings with dialogue . . . no rhetorical questions in narrative . . . no flashbacks . . . create emphasis by syntax . . .* and so on, the very craft demands all the university writing programs were offering as they ladled out the talent. *Complicate*

*the emotional and psychological dimensions of the action . . . vary
sentence rhythms . . . stop misusing "momentarily."*

Another aspect of this brilliant little tale are the preposterous
names, everybody's name save for the heady winning lump. Wiebe
admits lifting them from a K. M. Briggs book, *The Anatomy of Puck.*
For me, it's too much sky-blue frosting on a wacky cake, but with a
name like Dallas Wiebe, one might be predisposed to such playful-
ness in a way that Richard Ford, say, would not.

"Night Flight to Stockholm" is one of my favorite *Paris Review*
stories ever. Wiebe also wrote a great story about mucus, about Mr.
and Mrs. Mucus to be exact. But I don't think *The Paris Review*
published that one.

Dallas Wiebe

⌘

Night Flight to Stockholm

I owe all this to Gabriel Ratchet. It was he who arranged for the round-trip ticket, two seats side by side, on Scandinavian Airlines, got me my reservation in the King Gustaf Holiday Inn, deodorized my basket, put in the new sheets, put on my new, formal black sack with the white ribbon drawstring around the top and bathed my suppurating stumps for the journey. He even carried one end of my wicker laundry basket when I went aboard. In the darkness, I heard him instructing the stewardesses as to how to clean me, how to feed and water me and when to turn me. I heard money changing hands. I heard his stomachy laugh and the ladies' bovine grunts. I think I heard a stewardess pat his little bald head. Then came my first lift-off. The great surge of the old Boeing 747 sliding my butt and stumps against one end of the basket and then the floating and my ears popping. Into glorious, golden dreams in my black chute. Into non-stop gliding through images of published books, careful emendations, green surgical gowns, and the rustle of paper money, the clink of prizes and the odor of immortality. It was Gabriel Ratchet who gave me this slow drifting in the darkness 50,000 feet over Iceland, the North Atlantic, Ireland, England, the North Sea and Norway as we, as I hear from the pilot, descend into our landing pattern for Stockholm and me about to meet the king of Sweden and, I assume, his wife and all the little royalties. I wonder what they'll sound like; I wonder how they'll smell.

I owe all this to Gabriel because he is an expert in contracts. He's made contracts for musicians, painters, sculptors, quarterbacks, pole vaulters, jugglers, born-again Christians and presidents. He's negotiated the careers of farmers, professors, poets, priests, baseball pitchers, terrorists and airline pilots. For the past thirty years he's had his hand in more success than you can shake a scalpel at because of his immense number of contacts. He says he brought it with him from the womb. I can believe it.

Gabriel—his clients call him Gabe or Gabby—was born on the western slope of Muckish Mountain in Donegal in 1935, exact day unknown he says, when his mother saw some white horses hung with silver bells. He came to Chigcao, IL., he says, when the potato crop failed around Bloody Foreland in 1951. I don't remember any potato famines in Ireland since the nineteenth century, but I'm always willing to lend him an ear and listen to his stories. He came to Chicago, he says, because he is a creature of our own flesh and blood and likes a city where every man has his price. He says his contracting business didn't go well at first. In fact, he was on his last leg when he met Isobel Gowdie in October, 1956, in the Chicago Art Institute while he and she were standing and staring at some water lilies by Monet. According to his own account, Gabriel sighed and said, "Hell, Peg Powler can paint better than that." Isobel, having an eye to the main chance, immediately answered, "Richard Tarlton has one foot in the grave. Can you give him a hand?" Gabe's life as a public servant and a successful entrepreneur began with that moment because he negotiated a contract whereby for a shake and a cut Ambroise Paré became the first wealthy one-armed undertaker in Hellwaine, ME.

I first met Gabe in the lobby of the Palmer House in December of 1977 when I was there for an MLA convention. He was loitering around the packed lobby, looking, I later found out, for failures with whom he could do some business. He was sidling about, handing out, quietly and covertly, little business cards, red letters on green, that gave his name, Gabriel "Ballybofey" Ratchet, his office, 1313 Spoorne Ave., Chicago, his telephone number, 393-6996, his office hours, "At Your Convenience," his profession, "Contractor," and his motto, "Don't limp in obscurity, get a leg up on this world." He gave me his last card and said he'd never seen so many potential clients. He said he'd had his eye on me for some time and I was cut to the quick. We chatted, there in that mob, for a while and I asked him about himself. He told me that he was short because of that potato famine in his youth. His nose and ears were gnarled because his mother had been frightened by Peg O'Nell when she, his dear mother, was nursing him and her left teat had immediately dried up while in his mouth. His teeth were rotted out and his head was bald because his wife of two years, Joan Tyrrie of Creke Abbey, MT., had tried to poison him with bat slobber. He managed, he said, to overcome the poison by eating stuffed grasshoppers, roasted ants and mice roasted whole and threw her into the Chicago River. He said she'd been bad from the start and he was surprised his marriage in the year of 1955 lasted the two years that it did. Gabe said that her stepmother had given her a bottle of flat beer and some sour bread for a dowry and that after their marriage in Calkett Hall all she wanted to do was to be friendly with the goats and comb their beards. He said there was saltpeter in her heaven and gold in her hell and that her angels were sufficiently embodied to be impeded by their armor and damaged by gunpowder. I told him my problems and he said that I was too old to fool around any longer, that I would have to fight tooth and nail to make it. I said I'd call him if I needed his service.

I needed his help a lot sooner than I thought then because my paper which I presented at that MLA convention was laughed at. When I began my opening remarks I heard tittering. When I asked for silence, they guffawed. When I introduced my paper—"Metaphorical Thinking as the Cause of the Collapse of British and American Literature" by Professor Meyric Casaubon, Department of English, University of Tylwyth Teg, Wales, OR.—they hooted and snarled and shot out their lips. They waggled their beards and gnashed their teeth on their pipe stems. Even my old friend, Bock Urisk, who claimed he could hear grass growing, could run so fast when he was young that he had to keep one leg over his shoulder to stay in sight, could break stones on his thighs they were so hard and could spin a windmill by blowing through one nostril, waved his open palms past his ears and held his nose. I got the message when Richard Tynney of Gorleston, DE., the chairman of the panel, and Sir John Shepe of Wanstrowe, IA., the moderator, got up, dropped their pants and showed me their bare asses. I was mooned for metaphors and that was the end, I thought. I walked off the stage, my green suit striking among the black turtle necks, my thick black hair bobbing over the seated howlers, my hooked nose, my protuberant chin and my green eyes lifted high in disdain, even though I was without socks and my huge belly bounced and rumbled. I walked out of the room, my white Converse All-Stars squeaking on the waxed floors, my white tie and my blue shirt spotted with my sweat. I decided then to go back to what I'd always been doing anyway, writing fiction. I took out the green card with the red letters.

It was a Thursday when I lifted the phone and called him. I said, "Gabe, I'm going to be sixty-six tomorrow, Friday, January 13, 1978, and I've been writing fiction all my life and no one's ever published a word of it and I'd give my left pinkie to get into *The Paris Review.*" And I did because Gabriel was interested at once and told me he'd get in touch with me the next day because he thought he might find a buyer. He did. The next day Gabe came around and said he had a friend, Tom Reid, whose ancestor was killed at the battle of Pinkie in 1547 and who needed to get his self-respect back. According to Gabriel, Tom had agreed to see to it that my story, "Livid With Age," would be published in *The Paris Review* for my left pinkie. And he did. He told me to type my story, double-spaced, on clean white paper. Not to use eraseable paper. He said I should make my setting exact in place and time, not to moralize at the end of my story and to get rid of the false intensifiers like "literally," "really," "utterly," "just," "veritable," "absolutely," "very" and "basically." Create emphasis by syntax, he said. He also told me to clean the sweat stains off. I did all that and when my story came out, I went to Dr. Dodypol and had the finger removed surgically and under anesthesia. His head nurse, Kate Crackernuts, wrapped the finger in cotton bandages and in red tissue paper with a yellow ribbon around it and I walked out a published author and weighing three ounces less than when I walked in. And made money on it too, because the operation cost fifty dollars and I was paid sixty for my story.

A month after the appearance of "Livid With Age," I sent another story out, "Liam Sexob Lives in Loveland," to *TriQuarterly.* It seemed like it came back the same day, although of course it didn't, and I knew that I needed Gabriel Ratchet again and his influence. I found him sitting in the Trywtyn Tratyn Pub, drinking Habitrot and flirting with Jenny Greenteeth. "Look, Gabe," I said, "I need help. I'd give my left testicle to my story in *TriQuarterly.*" Gabe didn't even look at me when he said, "Make it two and I think I can get you a deal." I allowed as how I'd probably go along with it and he said he'd talk to Marmaduke Langdale, who needed them for his Whitsun Rejoicings. Gabe did and I did. Dr. Nepier from Lydford in Bercks and his head nurse, Sarah Skelbourn, removed them on a cold Friday in December of 1978. Sarah wrapped them in white bandages, green tissue paper and red ribbons. I took them to Gabriel, who was satisfied with the merchandise and told me that Marmaduke Langdale said I should change the title of the story to "Silence on the Rive Gauche," change the name of the main character Liam Sexob to Burd Isobel, eliminate the doublings, get rid of the colloquial style, erase the tear stains from the margins of pages 4, 14 and 22, and stop using exclamation points, dashes, underlinings for emphasis and the series of periods that indicate ellipses. I did all that. Retyped the story on good, twenty pound linen bound and sent it off to *TriQuarterly*. They accepted it within a week and I was on my way to my second story in print.

When "Silence on the Rive Gauche" came out, I asked Gabriel Ratchet to be my permanent agent. He agreed and in July of 1979 Dr. Louis Marie Sinistrari and his colleague, Isidore Liseaux, removed my left hand which I figured I didn't need anyway because I can only type with my right hand and right arm, wrapped it in blue and red striped gift paper, tied it with black ribbon, and sent it to Mr. Greatorex, the Irish Stroker, who wrote back from the Island of Hy Brasil, MD., that I should stop using participial phrases, get the inactive detail out of my descriptions, stop using literary language with its euphemisms and circumlocutions and not to use exclamations such as "needless to say," "to my amazement" and "I don't have to tell you." He also suggested that I not send in pages with blood stains on them. I did everything he said and *Esquire* accepted my story, "Moles' Brains and the Right to Life."

Even though I was still anemic from my last publication, I decided in January of 1980 to bid for the *New Yorker*. Gabe sent out

the message and Durant Hotham wrote from Yatton Keynel, ME.,
that he would do it for a pair of ears if I would promise to stop using
abnormal word order, get rid of the *faux-naif* narrator, eliminate all
cliches from my narrative, would isolate point of view in one character or one narrator and would clean my snot off the manuscript. I
did what he said and sent in the manuscript of "Muckelawee." Durant wrote back his thanks for the contract and told me to visit Peg
Powler at 1369 Kelpie Street and she would have some directions
for me. I went. She had directions and told me to go to Dr. Arvira-
gus at the Abbey Lubbers Clinic. I went. When I walked out of the
Clinic, I had my ears in a red and gold bag tied at the top with green
ribbon. The stumps on the sides of my head tingled in the cold air as
I walked out into a new reputation as one of the finest short story writers in America.

When I suggested a book of short stories to Gabriel, he shivered.
He suggested that I rest for a while and get myself together before I
made any more deals. I told him he'd made a lot of money off my
publications and that he would make a lot more. Just to do his work
as my agent and let me worry about the parts. He did admit that he
had an offer. That he needed a left arm, even if there was no hand
attached to it. A Dr. William Drage of Hitchin, AR., needed it to fit
out Margaret Barrance so that she could attend a ball because not
having a left arm there was nothing for her to lay across the shoulder
of her male partner while she danced. Gabriel told me that I would
have to go to Hitchin for the transplant. I agreed and I did in March
of 1981. But before he removed the left arm, he told me that the deal
was contingent on my editing my manuscript carefully, to carefully
control the secondary patterns, to make the deuteragonist more important in all the stories, to research materials for the stories, to make
the stories more weird, more strange, more uncomfortable for the
reader. Clean the ear wax off my pages. I promised I'd do all he told

me to do and he took my arm and sewed it onto Margaret, who six months later danced in her first ball at the age of thirty-three, wearing a blue and gold dress with a red sash around her waist, while Doubleday published my collection of short stories, *The Cry of Horse and Hattock* (September, 1981).

Because my recovery times were lengthening, I decided that a novel should be my next reduction and when I mentioned it to Gabriel Ratchet he fell on the floor and chortled. I told him to get his little carcass off the floor and get to work. He did. He got bids for my nose, my feet, my legs, my eyes, my penis and my kidneys. I bid one left foot. The law firm of Morgue, Arsile and Maglore handled the negotiations and in February of 1982 Ratchet finalized the contract with Ms. Ruth Tongue of Somorset, KS., by which I agreed to furnish her with one left foot in return for the publication of my novel, *Flibberty Gibbet,* by Knopf. My part of the contract was that I had to stop misusing "transpire," "problematical," "livid," "momentarily," "presently," and "loin." My sentences were to be made more simple. I was to use more active verbs with agents doing actions. I was to get out the melodrama. I also agreed not to use any anthropomorphizing metaphors, not to personify anything not human, to make only direct descriptions of characters, objects and actions and not to leak urine on my manuscript. Gabriel also negotiated an interesting addendum to the contract and that was that if the book could be made to win a national prize then my part of the bargain was the left foot and the whole left leg. Wouldn't you know; Ms. Tongue got the whole leg when *Flibberty Gibbet,* clad in a dust jacket of red, black and orange, won the National Book Award for 1982. They carried me up to the podium in a rocking chair and I shook hands for the last time when I accepted the award.

Rachet's account books, which he read to me before I left O'Hare, read as follows after that:

April 4, 1983: Right foot. To Tommy Rawhead of Asmoday, ND.
Complicate the emotional and psychological dimensions of the action. Careful selection of names. Vary sentence rhythms. Tonal varia-
tion. Shit off pages. Novel: *Brachiano's Ghost.* Macmillian. Black and
grey cover. Red chapter headings. Plus right leg: Pulitzer Prize. Done.
July 16, 1984: Right hand. To Elaby Gathen of Hackpen, MI. Correct spelling of "existence," "separate" and "pursue." No redundancy
in nouns and verbs in their modifiers. Play games with readers. No
slobbering on pages. Book of short stories: *The Blue Hag of Winter.*
Random House. Gold on black cover. Red title page. Right arm also:
O'Henry Award, St. Lawrence Award for Fiction and Chair at Columbia. Done.
February 10, 1985: Two eyes. To Billy Blind of Systern, DE. No use
of "etc.," the suffix "-wise," correct use of "as." No rhetorical questions in narrative. No openings with dialogue. No flashbacks. Include
all senses in descriptions. No pus on pages. Two volume novel: *Sam-
mael.* Little, Brown. Red, green and blue cover. Nobel Prize. Done.

   As I float over the shadowed northern world, I think now that we
all go off into darknesses, bit by bit, piece by piece, part by part. We
all disintegrate into our words, our sentences, our paragraphs, our
narratives. We scatter our lives into photographs, letters, certificates,
books, prizes, lies. We ride out the light until the records break one
by one. We sit out the days until the sun gets dimmer and dimmer.
We lie about in the gathering shadows until North America, South
America, Australia, Antarctica, Asia, Africa and Europe lie about
on the dark waters of our globe. It is crack time in the world of flesh.
It is shatter time in the world of limbs. It is splatter time in the world
of bones. It is the last splinter of the word. I have tasted the double-
deal. I have smelled the sleight-of-hand. I have heard the cryptic
whisper. I have felt the cold riddle. Because no one stands apart

from his stone. No one laughs apart from his crust. No one breathes apart from his shriveling. No one speaks apart from his silence. To lie down in a wicker basket is not to lie apart. To be turned on soft, pus-soaked sheets is not to be turned alone. To be fed through tubes is not to eat alone. To drink and choke is to spit up for all. To float through the night is the journey we all take sooner or later until the bright and shining morning star breaks and there is no more.

I can feel the huge plane starting to descend. My seventy-four year old ears are popping. The stewardess who smells like a dead dog has already rolled me over so that I won't aspirate if I vomit. She's strapped me tightly in place on my two seats. I can feel the safety belts across my rump and ribs. I feel the descent into darkness and I know that I have not given up anything that I could not do without. I know that you can live with less than you came in with. I know that wholeness is not everything and that if you will give an eye for a prize you'll be a sure winner. I can feel my long, white hair sliding and shaking over my stumpy ears as the plane bucks and banks for the landing. I can imagine the attendants in black knickers with the little black bows by the knees who will carry me onto the clapping stage. I can imagine the old black king squinting through his thick glasses down into the wicker basket with the two handles and the white Cannon sheets. As my snot begins to leak out over my upper lip, I can hear myself asking him to clean the ear wax out of my shallow ears so that I can hear him clearly when he extols the virtues of long-suffering, when he prattles about how some people overcome severe handicaps and go on to greatness, when he maunders about the indomitable will of the human spirit, while the old black queen gurgles and snickers down at the heady, winning lump. And I hope it's a prince, princess or princeling who will hold the microphone down into the basket so that while pus oozes from my eye sockets I can whisper my acceptance speech. I hope I can control my saliva.

I hope I don't shed tears. I wonder if there will be flowers to add their smells to the noises, the tastes and the temperatures. I wonder if anyone will manage to get a sip of Champagne to me. That thumping, bumping and bouncing must be the runway.

Contributors

⁂

DANIEL ALARCÓN hails from Peru, but now lives in Oakland, California. He is the author of the story collection *War by Candlelight*, winner of 2006 PEN/Hemingway Award, and the internationally acclaimed novel *Lost City Radio*.

DONALD BARTHELME was the author of over one hundred short stories, and four novels, including *The King*. A cofounder of *Fiction*, he served as the director of PEN, as well as the Authors Guild. He died in 1989.

ANN BEATTIE is the award-winning author of numerous novels, short story collections, and a novella, *Walks with Men*.

DAVID BEZMOZGIS is a filmmaker and fiction writer. In 2010, he was named to *The New Yorker*'s "20 Under 40" list. He is the author of the award-winning collection *Natasha: And Other Stories*, and a novel, *The Free World*.

JORGE LUIS BORGES was an Argentinean writer, translator, and poet. He is the author of several short story collections, including *Ficciones* and *The Aleph and Other Stories*. He died in 1986.

JANE BOWLES was the author of *Two Serious Ladies* and a play, *In the Summer House*. She died in 1973.

ETHAN CANIN is a writer and physician. He is the author of four novels and two short story collections, including *The Palace Thief,* and teaches at the Iowa Writers' Workshop.

RAYMOND CARVER was the author of numerous poems and short story collections, including *Cathedral*. He died in 1988.

EVAN S. CONNELL is the author of several poems, short stories, and novels, including *A Long Desire*. His bestselling biography of George Custer, *Son of the Morning Star,* was adapted into an Emmy-winning miniseries, and in 2009 he was a finalist for The Man Booker International Prize for lifetime achievement.

BERNARD COOPER is the author of a collection of essays, *Maps to Anywhere;* a memoir, *Truth Serum;* an autobiographical novel, *A Year of Rhymes;* and the short story collection *Guess Again*. The recipient of numerous awards and fellowships, he currently teaches writing at Bennington College.

GUY DAVENPORT was a writer of fictional miniatures and essays, as well as a translator, a teacher, and an artist. He died in 2005.

LYDIA DAVIS is a critically acclaimed translator and fiction writer. Her short story collection *Varieties of Disturbance* was a finalist for the 2007 National Book Award, and in 2005, she was named a Fellow of the American Academy of Arts and Sciences.

DAVE EGGERS is the bestselling author of *Zeitoun* and *A Heartbreaking Work of Staggering Genius.* His novel *What Is the What: The Autobiography of Valentino Achak Deng* was a 2006 finalist for the National Book Critics Circle Award, and he is the founder of *McSweeney's* and *The Believer.*

JEFFREY EUGENIDES is the author of several short stories and novels, including *Middlesex,* winner the Pulitzer Prize in 2003, and *The Marriage Plot.*

MARY GAITSKILL is the author of five works of fiction, including *Veronica* (a 2005 finalist for the National Book Award), *Two Girls Fat and Thin,* and the short story collection *Bad Behavior.* She is the recipient of a Guggenheim Fellowship, and teaches creative writing at Syracuse University.

THOMAS GLYNN is the author of several novels, including *Watching the Body Burn.* His most recent work is *Hammer. Nail. Wood.*

ALEKSANDAR HEMON is the author of three short story collections and *The Lazarus Project,* a finalist for the National Book Critics Circle Award in 2008. He is the recipient of a Guggenheim Fellowship and a MacArthur Foundation grant.

AMY HEMPEL is a journalist and the author of several short story collections, including *Reason to Live.* Her most recent work is *The Collected Stories,* a compilation of her stories from 1985 to 2005.

MARY-BETH HUGHES is the author of a novel, *Wavemaker II,* and a short story collection, *Double Happiness.*

DENIS JOHNSON is the author of six novels, three collections of poetry, and one book of reportage. His novel *Tree of Smoke* was the 2007 winner of the National Book Award.

JONATHAN LETHEM is the author of seven novels and two volumes of essays, including *The Ecstasy of Influence: Nonfictions, Etc.*

SAM LIPSYTE, a Guggenheim Fellow, is the author of several novels and a short story collection, *Venus Drive: Stories.* His most recent novel is *The Ask.*

BEN MARCUS is a novelist, short story writer, and critic. He is the former fiction editor of *Fence,* and the author of the novel *The Flame Alphabet.*

DAVID MEANS is the author of the short story collection *The Spot,* a *New York Times Book Review* Notable Book for 2010. In addition to *The Paris Review,* his work has appeared in *Esquire, The New Yorker,* and *Harper's.*

LEONARD MICHAELS was the author of the short story collection, *Going Places,* and the novel *The Men's Club,* among others. He died in 2003.

STEVEN MILLHAUSER is the author of several short story collections and novels, including *Martin Dressler,* winner of the Pulitzer Prize in 1997.

LORRIE MOORE is the bestselling author of several short story collections, including *Birds of America,* and three novels. She is the recipient of several awards and fellowships, and her work has been anthologized in *The Best American Short Stories of the Century,* edited by John Updike and Katrina Kenison.

CRAIG NOVA is the author of one autobiography and twelve novels, including *The Good Son, Cruisers,* and *The Informer.* The winner of an Award in Literature from the American Academy and Institute of Arts and Letters in 1984, he is also the recipient of a Guggenheim Fellowship.

DANIEL OROZCO is the award-winning author of *Orientation and Other Stories.* His stories have been widely anthologized, and he is currently at work on a novel.

MARY ROBISON is the author of several novels and short story collections, including *Tell Me: 30 Stories.* She won the Los Angeles Times Book Prize in 2001 for her novel *Why Did I Ever.* A recipient of a Guggenheim Fellowship, she currently teaches at the University of Florida.

NORMAN RUSH is the author of three novels, including *Mortals,* winner of the National Book Award in 1991. His debut, *Whites,* was a finalist for the Pulitzer Prize in 1987.

JAMES SALTER is the author of numerous screenplays, essays, novels, and short stories, including *Dusk and Other Stories,* winner of the PEN/Faulkner Award in 1989. In 2000, he was elected to The American Academy of Arts and Letters.

Mona Simpson is the award-winning author of five novels, including *Anywhere But Here* and, most recently, *My Hollywood*. She is
a former editor of *The Paris Review*.

Ali Smith is the author of numerous plays, novels, and short story
collections, including *The First Person and Other Stories* and,
most recently, the novel *There But For The*. Her work has been
twice nominated for The Man Booker Prize and The Orange
Prize for Fiction.

Wells Tower's short fiction and journalism have appeared in *The
New Yorker, Harper's, McSweeney's,* and *The Paris Review*. He
is the author of the short story collection *Everything Ravaged,
Everything Burned,* and was named one of *The New Yorker*'s "20
Under 40" fiction writers.

Dallas Wiebe was the author of several volumes of stories, essays,
and poems, as well as the founder of the creative writing program
at the University of Cincinnati. He died in 2010.

Joy Williams is the author of four novels, three story collections, a
book of nonfiction, and a travel guide. Her most recent novel,
The Quick and the Dead, was a finalist for the Pulitzer Prize in
2001.

Acknowledgments

The editors wish to thank Josh Anderson, Allison Bulger, Jessica Calderon, Julian Delacruz, Emma Gallwey, Elizabeth Nelson, Artemis Niederhoffer, and Emma del Valle and all of the writers, past and present, who contributed their work to this anthology.